'I'm going to g**s to think about the engagemen misplace it.'**

'I may not agree to anything.'

'Your call.' Leo shrugged. 'I anticipate six weeks of inconvenience. Think about the trade-off.' He stood up and glanced at his watch to find that far more time had gone by than he'd expected. 'Just one more thing to consider…'

Sammy had scrambled to her feet, but she was still keeping her distance. She wasn't going to touch this offer with a bargepole. Was she…? It smacked of blackmail, and surely any form of deceit, however well intended, was a bad thing…

'What's that?' She eyed him warily.

'You asked why you're perfect for this…arrangement.' He kept his eyes fixed on her face as he began putting on his coat. 'You understand the rules. I don't mean the rules that involve pretending…I mean the rules that dictate that this isn't for real. You're not one of my women who might get it into their heads that a fake engagement will turn into a real engagement.'

'No. I'm not.' Because there was no way he would ever consider getting engaged for real to someone like her. She'd never wanted to slap someone as much as she wanted to slap him.

'So we're on the same page,' Leo drawled, tilting his head at her. 'Always a good thing. I'll be in touch tomorrow evening for your decision…my wife-to-be.'

Cathy Williams can remember reading Mills & Boon books as a teenager, and now that she is writing them she remains an avid fan. For her, there is nothing like creating romantic stories and engaging plots, and each and every book is a new adventure. Cathy lives in London, and her three daughters—Charlotte, Olivia and Emma—have always been, and continue to be, the greatest inspirations in her life.

Books by Cathy Williams

Mills & Boon Modern Romance

Snowbound with His Innocent Temptation
A Virgin for Vasquez
Seduced into Her Boss's Service
The Wedding Night Debt
A Pawn in the Playboy's Game
At Her Boss's Pleasure
The Real Romero
The Uncompromising Italian
The Argentinian's Demand
Secrets of a Ruthless Tycoon
Enthralled by Moretti
His Temporary Mistress

The Italian Titans

Wearing the De Angelis Ring
The Surprise De Angelis Baby

One Night With Consequences

Bound by the Billionaire's Baby

Seven Sexy Sins

To Sin with the Tycoon

Visit the Author Profile page at millsandboon.co.uk for more titles.

BOUGHT TO WEAR THE BILLIONAIRE'S RING

BY
CATHY WILLIAMS

First Published in Great Britain 2017
By Mills & Boon, an imprint of HarperCollins*Publishers*
1 London Bridge Street, London, SE1 9GF

© 2017 Cathy Williams

ISBN: 978-0-263-92509-8

Printed and bound in Spain
by CPI, Barcelona

BOUGHT TO WEAR THE BILLIONAIRE'S RING

CHAPTER ONE

'So…' LEO MORGAN-WHITE handed his father a glass of claret and sat down opposite him.

Harold had travelled all the way from Devon and had been delivered only half an hour previously by his chauffeur. It had been a surprise visit, which he had been told by his agitated father the evening before couldn't wait.

Despite this, they had yet to get down to business and, although Leo knew what it concerned, he was still puzzled as to why it couldn't have waited until the weekend when he would gladly have travelled to Devon.

But his father was emotional and impulsive and so it was nigh on impossible to gauge just how important his news actually was. Leo couldn't think that it would be important enough to have him rushing up to London, a city he tried to avoid at all costs.

'Too noisy,' he was fond of complaining. 'Too crowded. Too polluted. Too many expensive shops selling nonsense. A man can't hear himself think there! You know what I say, Leo—if you can't hear the grass growing, you're in the wrong place!'

'What's going on?' Leo now asked, reclining back and stretching out his long legs. He carefully placed his glass on the table next to him and linked his fingers loosely on his stomach.

His father's eyes were glistening and he looked on the verge of bursting into tears. His chin was wobbling and his breathing was suspiciously uneven. Leo knew from experience that it was always better to ignore these signs of an imminent breakdown and focus on what needed to be discussed. His father needed very little encouragement when it came to shedding tears.

It was a trait Leo had thankfully not inherited. Indeed, anyone would have been forgiven for thinking that the two were not related at all as, both temperamentally and physically, they couldn't have been more different.

Where Leo was long, lean and darkly handsome, a legacy from his Spanish-born mother, his father was of an average height and rotund.

And where Leo was cool, composed and cut-throat, his father was unapologetically emotional and fond of dramatic outbursts. Leo's mother had died a little over a decade ago, when Leo had been twenty-two, and he remembered her as a tall, ridiculously good-looking woman who, having inherited her family's business at the tender age of nineteen, had been very clever, very shrewd and who had a natural flair for running a company. On paper, she and his father should have had nothing in common and yet theirs had been a match made in heaven.

In an age where men went out to work and women kept the home fires burning, his home life had been the opposite. His mother had run the family business, which she had brought from Spain with her, while his father, a hugely successful author, had stayed at home and written.

In a weird and wonderful way, opposite poles had attracted.

Leo loved his father deeply and his eyes narrowed as Harold carefully took a sheet of paper from his pocket and pushed it across the table to his son.

He fluttered one hand and looked away, before saying in a shaky voice, '*That* woman has emailed me this...'

Leo eyed the sheet of paper but didn't reach for it. 'I've told you that you need to stop getting yourself worked up about this, Dad. I have my lawyers working on it. It's all going to be all right. You just have to be patient. The woman can fight all she likes but she won't be getting anywhere.'

'Just you read what she has to say, Leo. I...I can't bring myself to read it out loud.'

Leo sighed. 'How is the book coming along?'

'Don't try and distract me,' his father responded mournfully. 'I haven't been able to write a word. I've been too worried about this business to spare a thought for how DI Tracey is going to solve the case. In fact, I don't care! At this rate, I may never put pen to paper again. It's all very well for you business types...adding up numbers and sitting round conference tables...'

Leo stifled a smile. He was worth billions and did a lot more than just add up numbers and sit round conference tables.

'She's made threats,' Harold said, sucking in a shaky breath. 'You read the email, Leo. The woman says she's going to fight for custody and she's going to win. She says she's spoken to her lawyer and although Sean stated in his will that Adele was to come to you if anything happened to him, Louise never agreed and now they're both gone. All that matters is that Adele's well-being would be put in jeopardy if she stays with that woman.'

'Heard it all before.' Leo drained his claret and stood up, massaging the back of his neck as he strolled towards the expanse of glass that separated him from the busyness of London which never stopped, even in the most prestigious of postcodes.

His apartment occupied the top two floors of an impressive Georgian building. He had hired the most prestigious architect in the city who had cleverly used the vast space to create an elegant blend of old and new, leaving the coving and fireplaces and ceiling details intact while changing pretty much everything else. The result was an airy, four-bedroomed testament to what could be done when money was no object.

The walls were adorned with priceless modern art. The decor was muted—shades of grey and cream. People's mouths fell open the second they walked through the door but Leo was barely aware of his surroundings. They didn't intrude and that was the main thing.

'This is different, Leo.'

'Dad,' he said patiently, 'it's not. Gail Jamieson wants to hang on to her granddaughter for dear life because she thinks it's a conduit to my money but she's utterly ill-equipped to look after a five-year-old child. She'll be especially ill-equipped when my money stops and she has to fend for herself. The fact is…this is a case I will win. I don't want to throw money at the woman but if I have to, I will. She'll take it and head for the hills because, like her daughter before her, Gail is a money-grabbing gold-digger who's not above manipulating a situation for her own advantage. Need I remind you of the train of events that led Sean to Australia?'

His father grunted and Leo didn't push it. They both knew Sean for the man he had been.

Seven years younger than Leo, Sean had arrived on their doorstep at the age of sixteen, along with his mother, Georgia Ryder, with whom Leo's father had fallen head over heels in love less than a year after Leo's mother had died.

From the very beginning Sean, an incredibly pretty boy with overlong blond hair and light blue eyes, had been lazy and spoiled. Once his mother had a ring on her finger and free access to the Morgan-White millions, he had quickly become even more demanding and petulant. His studies had fallen by the wayside and, cosseted by his mother, he had spent his time hanging around with a gang of like-minded teenagers who had gravitated towards him like bees round a honeypot. It hadn't been long before drugs had crept into the scene.

Leo's father, with the ink on the marriage certificate barely dry, had woken up from his grief-induced daze and realised the size of the mistake he had made. He didn't want a blonde bombshell twenty years his junior pretending to love him when the only thing she loved was his money. He wanted to mourn the passing of the woman he had loved. He wanted uninterrupted misery.

Leo had taken Sean to one side and had given him the talking-to of his life, which had done no good at all. The opposite. Within two years Sean had dropped out of school. Within four, he had become heavily involved with Louise Jamieson, an enthusiastic member of the club for losers to which he belonged, and by the time his mother, after a series of unabashed flings with men her own age, had quit her marriage to Harold and begun her bid for as much alimony as she could get, Sean had moved to Australia with a heavily pregnant wife.

By this time Leo's father had all but given up. His writing had stopped completely and his editor's frantic communications had remained unanswered. He had become a virtual recluse and Leo had been left to pick up the pieces.

Unchecked, Georgia had spent vast sums of money on everything under the sun, from diamonds and tiaras to horses, cars and exotic holidays abroad, while she still had access to her soon-to-be ex-husband's bank accounts. She had lavished money on her son. Leo, building his own career, had not had his eye sufficiently on the ball to have stopped the momentum.

By the time the nuts and bolts of the messy divorce had been ironed out, his father had been left with a bank account that had been severely dented. The fact that he hadn't put pen to paper for years hadn't helped.

Then Georgia was catapulted to her death off a hairpin bend on a road while vacationing in Italy with the money she had squeezed out of Harold. Left to make the decision, Leo would have thrown Sean to the wolves but his father, much softer and with a conscience that could be pricked by almost anything, had continued to send money to his former stepson. He had dug deep to make sure Sean's daughter had all the things he would have given her, had she lived in the same country. He had begged for photos and had been thrilled with the handful of pictures Sean had emailed over.

He had tried to make plans to visit but Sean had always had an excuse.

Georgia had been a disaster and her son had been no less of a catastrophe and, unlike his sentimental father,

Leo wasn't going to allow emotions to hold sway over the outcome of this bizarre custody battle.

He would win because he always won. Louise's mother, whom he had met once when he went to Australia, had confirmed all his suspicions that the last thing she was concerned about was the welfare of her grandchild. She was an appalling woman and no appalling woman was going to get the better of him.

'She says that it doesn't matter how much money you have to fight this, Leo. She's going to win because you're not fit to be a father to Adele.'

Leo stilled. His father's eyes had welled up. Reluctantly, he retrieved the paper from where his father had earlier shoved it to him and carefully read the email that had been sent by Ms Jamieson.

'Now you see what I mean, Leo.' His father's voice shook. 'And the woman has a point. You have to see that.'

'I see nothing of the sort.'

'You don't lead a responsible life.' Harold's voice firmed. 'Not as far as bringing up a young child is concerned. You spend half your life out of the country...'

'How else am I supposed to run my companies?' Leo interjected, enraged that a woman who appeared to have the morals of a sewer rat should dare to criticise him. 'From an armchair at home?'

'That's not the point. The point is that you *do* spend a great part of the year out of the country. How is that supposed to be good for the well-being of a five-year-old child? Furthermore, she's not wrong when she says that you...' His hands fluttered in a gesture of resignation and disappointment.

Leo's mouth thinned. He knew that the choices he

made when it came to women did not fill his father's heart with glee. He knew that Harold would have done anything to have seen him happily settled down with a nice, respectable girl who would have those home fires burning for him when he returned home after a long day toiling in the fields.

It wasn't going to happen. Leo had too much first-hand experience of how life could be derailed when emotions got in the way of common sense and good judgement. No matter that his father had adored his wife—when Mariela Morgan-White had died, he had been left a broken man. Yes, some idiots might fall for that hoary old chestnut about it being better to have loved and lost than never to have loved at all, but Leo had never signed up to that.

His father might not have agreed with Leo's choices but he had stopped trying to take him to task about them, and this was the first time in years that he had voiced his disappointment.

'Your face is never out of the papers,' Harold admonished, dabbing his eyes and then looking sternly at his son. 'There's always some…some silly little thing hanging on to your arm, batting her eyelashes at you.'

Leo flushed with irritation. 'We've covered this ground already.'

'And we'll cover it again, son.' Harold sniffed and, just like that, Leo realised it was as though the energy and life force had been sucked out of him, leaving behind a shell. He was an aging man and it seemed as though he had suddenly lost the will to live.

'You choose to do what you like when it comes to… women,' his father said quietly. 'And I know better now than to try and point you in the right direction. But this is more than being *just about you*. The woman claims that you're morally unfit to take guardianship of the child.'

Leo pushed his hands through his hair and shook his head. 'I'll take care of it,' he said grimly.

Theoretically, he and his father could simply reach an agreement to pull the plug on the money. Sean, after all, hadn't been in any way related to either of them, but he knew and personally agreed that the child should not be allowed to suffer because of the mistakes of her parents. Like it or not, she was a moral responsibility.

'It's a worst-case scenario.' His father shook his head and pressed his fingers to his eyes.

'You're upsetting yourself, Dad.'

'Wouldn't you if you were in my shoes?' He looked up. 'Adele is important to me and I cannot lose.'

'If the law refuses to budge—' Leo spread his hands in a gesture of frustration '—then there's only so much I can do. I can't kidnap the child and then hide her until she turns eighteen.'

'No, but there *is* something you can do…'

'I'm struggling to think what.'

'You could get engaged. I'm not saying married, but engaged. You could present the court with the sort of responsible image that might persuade them into thinking that you're a good bet as a father figure for Adele.'

Leo stared at his father in silence. He wondered whether the events of the past few weeks had finally pushed the man over the edge. Either that or he had misheard every single word in that sweeping, unbelievable statement.

'*I could get engaged…?*' Leo shook his head with rampant incredulity. 'Do you suggest I purchase a suitable candidate online?'

'Don't be stupid, son!'

'Then I'm not following you.'

'If you need to present the image of a solid, dependable, *normal* human being with a *serious* and *suitable* woman by your side, then I don't know why you wouldn't do that. For me. For Adele.'

'Serious and suitable woman?' Leo spluttered. He didn't do either serious *or* suitable when it came to women. He did frivolous and highly unsuitable. He liked it that way. No involvement, easy to dispatch. If they enjoyed his money, then that was fine because he wasn't going to marry any of them. When it came to women, the revolving door that brought them in and took them out was efficient and worked for him.

'Samantha.' His father dropped the name with the flair of a magician pulling a rabbit out of a hat.

'Samantha…' Leo repeated slowly.

'Little Sammy Wilson,' Harold expanded. 'You know who I'm talking about. She would be perfect for the part!'

'You want me to involve *Samantha Wilson* in a far-fetched charade to win custody of Adele?'

'It makes perfect sense.'

'In whose world?'

'Don't be rude, son!' Harold reprimanded with an unusual amount of authority.

'Does she know about this? Have you two been plotting this crazy scheme behind my back?' Leo was aghast. His father had clearly taken leave of his senses.

'I haven't mentioned a word of this to her,' Harold admitted. 'Well, you know that she only manages to get to Salcombe on weekends…'

'No, I didn't. Why would I?'

'You will have to broach the subject with her. You can be very persuasive and I don't see why you wouldn't bring those considerable skills to bear on this. It's not as though I ask favours of you as a general rule. I think it's the very least you can do, son. I would so love to know Adele is safe and cared for and we both know that Gail would make as bad a grandparent as her daughter made a parent. I would spend the remainder of my days fearing for what might happen to the girl…'

'Gail might be many things,' Leo returned drily, 'but aren't you over-egging the pudding here?'

His father breezed over the interruption. 'And you would condemn a child to a future with a woman of that calibre? *We both know the rumours about her*…' His eyes, when they met Leo's, were filled with sadness. 'I can't force you but I'm very much afraid that I… Well, what would be the point of my living…?'

Samantha hadn't been in her tiny rented flat for more than half an hour before she heard the insistent buzz of her doorbell and she grimaced with annoyance.

She had too much to do to waste time on a cold-caller. Or, worse, her neighbour from the flat upstairs, who had a habit of randomly showing up around this hour, a little after six in the evening, for wine with someone too polite and too soft-hearted to turn her away.

Samantha had spent many hours listening to her neighbour discuss her latest boyfriend or weep over a broken heart that would never be mended.

Right now, she simply had too much to do.

Too much homework from her eight-year-old charges to mark. Too many lessons to prepare. Too much red tape with Ofsted to get through. Not to mention the bank, who had been politely reminding her mother for the past three months that the mortgage hadn't been paid.

But whoever was at the door wasn't about to go away, not if the insistent finger on the button was anything to go by.

Sweeping the stack of exercise books off her lap and onto the little coffee table by the side of her chair and plunging her feet into her cosy bedroom slippers, she was working out which negative response, depending on who was at the door, she would be delivering so that her evening remained uninterrupted.

She yanked open the door and her mouth fell open. Literally. She stood there like a stranded goldfish, eyes like saucers, because the last person she ever, in a million years, had expected to see was standing in front of her.

Or rather lounging, his long, muscular body indolently leaning against the door frame, his hands thrust into the pockets of his black cashmere coat.

It had been several weeks since she had seen Leo Morgan-White.

He had nodded to her from across the width of his father's massive drawing room, which had been crowded with at least three dozen locals, all friends from the village where his father and her mother lived. Harold was a popular member of the community and his annual Christmas party was something of an event on the local calendar.

She hadn't even spoken to Leo that night. He'd been there with a leggy brunette who, in the depths of winter, had been wearing something very bright and very short, garnering attention from every single male in the room.

'Have I come at a bad time?'

He'd taken the bait. Sly old fox that his father was, Leo had been persuaded into doing the unthinkable by the threat of ill health and a return of the depression that had dogged his father for years and from which he was only recently surfacing.

Of course, Harold genuinely and truly wanted Adele close to him and safe and, of course, he truly believed, and was probably spot on, that Gail would turn out to be a horrendous influence on her five-year-old grand-daughter, but when he had pulled the ill-health-so-what's-the-point-of-carrying-on? threat from the hat Leo had confessed himself to be beaten.

So here he was, two days later, with the soon-to-be object of his desire standing in front of him in some dull grey outfit and a pair of ridiculous, brightly coloured bedroom slippers.

'Leo?' Sammy blinked and wondered whether it was possible for stress to induce very realistic hallucinations. 'What do you want? How did you find out where I live? What on earth are you doing here?'

'Lots of questions, and I'll answer them just as soon as you invite me in.'

Struck by a sudden thought, Sammy paled and stared up at him. 'Has something happened? Is your dad all right?' She was finding it very difficult to think but then the wretched man had always had that effect on her. Something about his devastatingly good looks. He was just so…*so much larger than life.*

Taller, more striking, with the rakish, swarthy sexiness of a pirate. Next to him, the rest of the male population always seemed to pale in comparison and, considering the long, long line of women he had run through over the years, she wasn't the only one who thought so.

Unlike that long, long line of women, though, she knew better than to let all that drop-dead male sexiness get to her.

She still cringed in shame when she thought back to that awful incident years ago. She'd had gone along to a party at *the big house*, as everyone in the village called the Morgan-White mansion up on the hill.

The place had been teeming with people. It had been a birthday bash for Leo and half the world seemed to be there. Heaven only knew why she'd been invited but she imagined that it had been something of a pity invite and, whilst she had cringed at the thought of going, she had been encouraged by the fact that several of the locals had also been on the guest list so she wouldn't be a complete fish out of water. She'd spent ages choosing just the right dress. She'd only spotted him from a distance later, when she had been standing in the garden and, miracle of miracles, he had shown up right next to her and they had chatted for what had seemed like ages. He'd torn himself away from his gilded crowd and Sammy had been on cloud nine until, late in the evening, a very tall, very blonde girl had broken free from the group and confronted her just outside the marquee which had been erected in the garden.

'You're making a bloody fool of yourself,' she'd hissed, words slurring from too much free champagne. 'Can't you see that Leo is never, and I mean *never*, going to give you the time of day? You may have grown up next to him but you're poor, you're fat and you're boring. You're making a laughing stock of yourself.'

Her infatuation had died fast. Since then, watching off and on from the sidelines, she had come to see just how repulsive his approach to women was. He picked them up and then, when he'd got what he wanted and boredom began setting in, he dumped them without a backward glance and moved on.

Romantic at heart, with a core of firmly held family values, Sammy marvelled that she could ever have looked twice at someone like Leo. But, then again, she'd been young and he'd been crazily good-looking.

'He's been better. Are you going to invite me in or are we going to have this conversation here?'

'I suppose you can come in.'

Great start, Leo thought wryly. *A very auspicious beginning to what's intended to be the relationship of a lifetime.*

He hadn't thought about how she was going to react to his proposition but he didn't expect too much protesting. He was, after all, bringing a great deal of money to the table and, as everyone knew, money talked a lot louder than words.

Anne Wilson, Samantha's mother, was a close friend of his father's and had been since Leo's mother had fallen ill and Anne, a nurse at the local hospital, had gone beyond the call of duty to help out. Their bond had strengthened over the years as she had proved to be a solid rock upon whom his father had often leaned, particularly after his acrimonious divorce from Georgia.

It was no surprise then that Anne had confided in Harold about her ill health and the money problems she

was having with the bank because she had been forced
to quit her job. Though Harold had offered to give her
the money, and, when that hadn't worked, to lend it to
her, she had refused.

'So…' Sammy folded her arms and stared at him almost
before he had shut the door behind him. 'What have you
come here for?' He was so good-looking that she could
barely look at him without blushing.

Leo's fabulous looks had to do with far more than just
the arrangement of his features. Yes, he was indecently
perfect, from the long, dark, thick lashes that shielded
equally dark eyes and the straight, arrogant nose to the
sensuous curve of his mouth. Yes, he had the toned,
lean, six-foot-two-inch frame of an athlete and the lazy
grace of some kind of predatory jungle animal, but he
also generated an impression of power that was frankly
mesmerising.

'Are you always so welcoming to visitors?' Leo
drawled, ignoring her bristling hostility to shrug off
his coat, which he proceeded to dump on the coat hook
by the front door.

The house had clearly been made into flats, each
with a separate entrance and, from the looks of it, on the
cheap. Too much door-slamming and the whole struc-
ture would collapse like a house of cards.

'I happen to be very busy at the moment,' Sammy
said shortly. She led the way into the sitting room and
gestured to the mound of exercise books which she had
been about to look at.

He sat himself in a chair. He had come to visit for
reasons she couldn't begin to understand and she was
furious with herself for the silly heat that was pouring
through her.

* * *

She was as awkward as he recalled. He'd never spoken to her without getting the feeling that she would much rather have been somewhere else. He'd never really paid a huge amount of attention to her appearance in the past, simply absorbing the impression that she didn't dress to impress, but now that she was going to be the love of his life he couldn't help but notice that she *really* had mastered the art of not making an effort.

Accustomed to women who bent over backwards to show off flawless bodies, who devoted unreasonable amounts of time to their appearance, he was weirdly disconcerted by someone who didn't seem to give a hoot. He stared at her narrowly, recognising that, despite the appalling dress sense and the mop of blond hair that had been piled on top of her head and secured with a fluorescent elastic band, there was a certain pretty appeal to her heart-shaped face. Plus she had amazing eyes. Huge, cornflower blue with long lashes.

'I take it you're not interested in pleasantries, so shall I skip past the bit where I ask you how you are and what you've been up to recently?'

'Do you care how I am and what I've been up to recently?'

'You should sit down, Sammy. The reason I'm here is because I have something of a complicated favour to ask. If you insist on hearing me out on your feet, then you're going to have aching calves by the time I'm through.'

'A favour? What are you talking about? I don't see how I could possibly help you out with anything.'

'Sit down. No, better still…why don't you offer me a glass of wine? Or a cup of coffee?'

* * *

Sammy resisted scowling. By nature, she was a kind-hearted woman who would never have dreamed of being downright rude to anyone she knew, but something about Leo always got her back up. She'd long ago written him off as too rich, too good-looking and too arrogant, and the way he had settled into her flat and was proceeding to order her about was only hardening her attitude.

She would quite have liked to have asked him politely to clear off.

As though reading her mind, Leo raised his eyebrows and subjected her to a long, appraising look that made her go red.

'Okay,' he drawled, 'I'll cut to the chase, shall I?' He shifted slightly, reached inside his trouser pocket and withdrew a small box which he dumped on the table in front of him. 'I'm here to ask you to marry me.'

CHAPTER TWO

SAMMY BLINKED AND then folded her arms, body as rigid as a plank of wood. Anger was bubbling up inside her. After one glance at the navy blue box he had dumped on the table, she hadn't deigned to give it a second look.

'Is this some kind of joke?' she asked coldly.

'Do I look like the kind of man who would show up on a woman's doorstep and propose marriage as a joke?'

'I have no idea, Leo. I don't know what kind of person you are.' Aside, she thought furiously, from the obvious.

'Open the box.'

Sammy eyed it with a guarded expression and did nothing of the sort. But her fingers were twitching and, uttering a soft, impatient curse under her breath, she reached down and flipped open the lid.

An engagement ring nestled on a deep blue velvet cushion. The exquisite solitaire diamond blinked at her and she blinked back at it, utterly dumbfounded. Her hand was shaking as she placed the box, still open, back on the table and moved to sit down on the chair facing him.

'What the heck is going on here, Leo? You can't possibly be serious. You show up here with an engagement ring, asking me to marry you. Something's wrong. What is it? Is that ring even real?'

'Oh, it's a hundred per cent real. And guess what? You get to keep it when this is all over.'

Sammy's head was swimming. Less than an hour ago, she was a stressed out primary school teacher with a stack of exercise books to mark. Now, she was the main character in some weird parallel universe story with a sexy billionaire sitting on one of her chairs and an engagement ring in front of her.

Nothing about this scenario was making any sense.

'When *what's* all over?' she asked as she tried to make sense of the situation and came up blank.

Leo sighed. Maybe he should have forewarned her but what would have been the point? She would still have been utterly bewildered. Much better that he was sitting in front of her so that he could explain the situation face-to-face.

If she couldn't believe that this was happening then they were roughly on the same page.

Beyond the fact that the words *will you marry me* had never featured in any scenario he had ever envisaged for his future, he certainly would never have chosen Samantha Wilson as the recipient of his proposal.

He had met the woman over the years in countless different situations and he had been left with the impression of someone so background as to be practically invisible. She'd never been rude to him. She had always answered his questions politely, barely meeting his eyes before scuttling away as soon as she could. Aside from one conversation years ago. A conversation lodged at the back of his brain… But, after that, he had met her again—had tried to engage her attention—and nothing. He had no idea whether she had a boyfriend or not, whether she had a social life or not, whether she had hobbies or not.

In his world, where women strutted around like flamboyant peacocks, she was the equivalent of a sparrow. Perfect, of course, for the job at hand but hardly the sort of woman he would ever have looked at twice in *that* way.

'I suppose you know about Sean and his wife,' Leo began.

She nodded slowly. 'I'm sorry. You have my condolences. It was a horrible end for both of them. What on earth would have persuaded Sean to take *flying lessons,* of all things? And to have flown solo in bad weather with Louise, without his instructor... It beggars belief. But I'm so sorry.'

'No need for the sorrow or the condolences—' he waved aside '—I wasn't close to Sean so I can't say his absence is going to leave a big hole in my life.'

'That's very honest of you.'

She was looking at him with those huge, surprisingly riveting blue, blue eyes and, while her voice was perfectly serious, Leo couldn't help but suspect a thread of sarcasm underlying her remark. She'd never struck him as the sarcastic type.

'I suppose you're also aware that my father has been extremely upset that Sean's daughter, whom he considers his granddaughter, remains in Australia as a ward of her maternal grandmother.'

'It's a shame, but I'm sure she'll be allowed over to visit your dad in time, once she's a bit older. Look, Leo, I still don't see what this has to do with me or—' her eyes flicked down to the box burning a hole on the table in front of her '—or that engagement ring.'

'When Sean and Louise died, it was presumed that the child would be sent over here to live with me. Louise was an only child from a difficult background, without any extended family who could take Adele under their wing and Louise's mother also had a somewhat… colourful history.'

'I know there have been rumours…'

'My father receives monthly requests from her for handouts and that is in addition to the money he continued to send to Sean over the years, well after his divorce from Sean's mother was finalised.'

'Your dad has a soft heart,' Sammy said warmly.

'A soft heart is only a small step away from being a soft touch,' Leo muttered and she frowned disapprovingly at him.

'I'm sure the money he sent over was really useful…'

'I'm sure it was,' Leo responded drily. 'The question is, useful to whom? But no matter. That's history. What we're dealing with is the present, which brings me to the subject of the engagement ring…' Admittedly, he had sprung this on her and had expected nothing but shock. Horror, however, hadn't entered the equation because, whether the engagement was fake or not, he couldn't think of a single woman who wouldn't have been thrilled to see a diamond like that and to know that it was destined for *her* finger.

Right now, the woman sitting in front of him was glancing down at the box with a moue of distaste, as though looking at something that could prove infectious in a nasty way.

'My father has recently received an unpleasant email

suggesting that Adele, against all common sense and
certainly not in her best interests, may end up remaining in Australia with Sean's mother-in-law. The woman
has clearly decided that it makes sense financially for
her to hang on to Adele because, as long as she has the
child in her custody, she will continue to receive money
from my father, which, incidentally, is actually money
from me. You may or may not know that his writing
has been off the boil for a long time. The family company is doing well but I would rather not be financially
embroiled with this woman forever.'

'I'm just wondering what all of this has to do with
me,' Sammy confessed.

This had to be the longest conversation in recent
years that she had ever had with the man and she was
mortified because the cool composure she was at pains
to display was at vibrant odds with what she was feeling. She certainly wasn't cool and composed inside. In
fact, she was all over the place.

Her senses were on full alert and she didn't fully
understand *why*.

Surely she was mature enough not to turn into a dith-
ering wreck simply because she happened to be in the
company of a man who was too attractive for his own
good? She was a working woman, a teacher, with heaps
of responsibility, someone with enough life experience
behind her to recognise Leo for the man he really was
as opposed to the one-dimensional, gorgeous cardboard
cut-out who had once turned her silly teenage head…

Except…

Maybe her life experience was sorely lacking in a
certain vital area. Maybe that was why just looking at
him was making her skin tingle.

She had plenty of experience in caring for her mother, as she had been doing for the past year and a half. She knew all about communicating with doctors and hospitals and nurses and making her voice heard because her mother, although she had been a nurse herself, had been swallowed up with fear and confusion. She had needed someone strong to lean on and that person had been her, Sammy. And she had plenty of experience under her belt of taking charge, of controlling unruly primary school children until they were as meek as little lambs.

She had argued with bank managers and spent hours trying to balance the books and had exhausted herself with pep talks to her mother, convincing her that the cottage was safe even though the mortgage payments had fallen behind.

And, through it all, she had done her best to hang on to her sense of humour and her sense of perspective.

But there was that whole other area where she had no experience at all.

A vast, blurry, opaque space where she was a stranger because, despite having had two serious boyfriends, she had yet to test the sexual waters.

They had both been attractive and she'd liked them very much. In fact, they'd ticked all the boxes in her head in terms of suitability and yet…she just hadn't *fancied* them enough to go the whole way.

She and Pete had broken up over a year and a half ago, and since then she had resigned herself to the fact that there was probably something wrong with her. Some faulty gene in her make-up. Maybe it was because there had been no father figure in her life since she had been a kid, yet, even to her, that argument made no sense.

So she'd long stopped analysing the whys and maybes.

She hadn't taken into account that her lack of experience in that small, stupid area, *insignificant in the big scheme of things*, might have left her vulnerable to a man like Leo, with his sexy, spectacular good looks and that lazy, assessing charm that oozed from every pore.

'Sean had the foresight, strangely, to leave something of a will,' he was saying now, 'a scrap of paper signed by a friend. In it, he indicated that, should anything happen to him, I should take guardianship of the child. I'm sure,' Leo elaborated with scrupulous honesty, 'that that particular light bulb idea had something to do with my financial worth.'

'That's very cynical of you.' Sammy was still smarting from the realisation that while two perfectly good boyfriends hadn't been able to get to her, this utterly inappropriate man seemingly could. At least if the crazy somersaulting in her stomach was anything to go by.

'So I'm cynical.' He shrugged and stared at her. 'It's a trait that's always stood me in good stead.'

'If Sean meant for you to have Adele, then what's the problem?'

'The problem is the harridan of a grandmother who's decided to hire a lawyer to argue the case that I'm unfit to be the child's guardian. A scrap of paper, she maintains, counts for nothing, especially considering my former stepbrother lived with a stash of alcohol and drugs within easy reach.'

Sammy didn't say anything and Leo frowned because he could read what she was thinking as clearly as if her thoughts had been transcribed in neon lettering across her forehead.

'The woman isn't equipped to raise Adele,' he grated. 'Even if she had been an angel in human form, it would still be a big ask for her to take over the role of looking after an energetic five-year-old child. Had I felt that she might conceivably be mentally fit for the job then I'd back off, but she isn't. At any rate, my father is distraught at this turn of events.'

'He's always mourned the fact that he never got to see her. He talked about that a lot to me and Mum.'

'Yes, well…' Somehow that simple statement of fact, which came as no shock at all to Leo, indicated a familiarity that was a little unsettling. 'Here's where we're nearing the crux of the matter. I've been accused of having too many women and spending too much time out of the country.' He raked his fingers through his hair and gestured in a manner that was redolent with frustration and impatience.

Sammy remained silent because, from all accounts, those were some pretty accurate accusations.

'Well…' she finally said. 'I suppose there might be some truth in that. From everything I've heard, I mean, that's to say…'

'Please—' Leo scowled darkly '—don't let good manners stand in the way of saying what's on your mind. I take it the rumours about me have come from my father?'

'No!'

'Do you three just sit around gossiping about my love life?'

'No! You've got the wrong end of the stick.'

'Have I? From the sounds of it, once my father has

finished lamenting the fact that he's been denied access to his "granddaughter," he brings out the tea and biscuits and gets down to the gritty business of discussing my personal life!'

'It's not like that at all!' Sammy was mortified at the picture he was painting. 'Your dad mentioned ages ago that he wished he saw more of you and that you worked too hard. He worries about your health, that's all.'

'I've never had a day's illness in my life.'

'Working too hard can bring on all sorts of problems,' Sammy said, fidgeting, her colour high. 'Stress can be a killer. That's what worries your dad.'

'That being the case,' Leo drawled, 'he must know that I'm in no danger of collapsing from working too hard or being too stressed because I have my safety valves in the form of my very diverting playmates.'

Sammy's breath caught in her throat, which was suddenly so dry that she could barely get her words out.

It struck Leo that those very diverting playmates were going to have to take a back seat, at least for the time being, and he was a little surprised that he didn't feel more gutted at the prospect. He was a highly sexual man with a very energetic libido, but recently, beautiful and obliging women who were always willing to go the extra mile for him had left him dissatisfied.

His palate was jaded.

Perhaps now was a very good time to indulge in a fake engagement with a woman he had precisely nothing in common with. A couple of months pretending to be in love with someone who didn't stand a chance of rousing his interest might be just the ticket. He would resume life with renewed vigour and things would be back to normal. And a bout of celibacy never killed anyone.

'Which—' he brought the conversation neatly back to the point at hand '—brings us back to the problem. I don't, according to my father, make a credible guardian with my reputation, and I will be under scrutiny because I will be travelling to Melbourne to sort this situation out. Eyes will be on me. I need credibility—and here is where you come in. I need a fiancée to show my stability to the Melbourne courts and he's suggested that you would be perfect for the part.'

Sammy stared at him. So that was what all of this was about. The ring. The proposal. It was so preposterous that she was torn between bursting into manic laughter and propelling him out of her flat.

She did neither. Instead, she said, 'You've got to be kidding, right?'

'As I've already told you, I have better things to do than show up here for a laugh. This is no joke, Samantha.' He leaned forward and looked at her with utter seriousness. 'My father refuses to accept that he may never see Adele. The fact that Sean was his stepson for a short period of time rather than his own flesh and blood and that any tenuous family connection they might have once had ended when he and Georgia divorced makes not a scrap of difference to him, but then he's that kind of man, as I expect you already know. He sees this as his last chance to do something about the situation and he can't understand any hesitancy on my part to leap aboard the plan.'

'I'm not going to go with you to the other side of the world so that I can pretend to be your fiancée, Leo!' Agitated, Sammy leapt to her feet and began pacing the room. Her thoughts were all over the place and her body was burning.

'Why would you want me to be your *fake fiancée*, anyway?' She spun round to look at him, hands on hips. 'Why don't you just pick one of those women from your little black book? You have enough to choose from! Every time I open a tabloid I seem to see you some-where in the gossip columns with a glamour model hanging on to you for dear life.'

Leo's eyebrows shot up and he gave her a slow, curl-ing smile. 'Follow me in the tabloids, do you?'

'Trust you to put that spin on it,' Sammy muttered under her breath, which seemed to amuse him further. 'I won't do it,' she said flatly. 'You can have your pick of any woman you want so go ahead and pick one of them.'

'But none of them will do,' Leo said smoothly and Sammy paused to frown.

'Why not?'

He looked at her for a long while in perfect silence and it didn't take her long to get the message.

'Too glamorous,' Sammy said slowly, while she pointlessly wished the ground would open and swal-low her, disgorging her somewhere on the other side of the world. 'You need someone plain and average, some-one who would give the right image of a responsible other half, able to take on a young child.'

Accustomed to telling it like it was, Leo had the grace to flush. 'The women I date would be inappro-priate—' he smoothed over the unvarnished bluntness of her statement '—it has nothing to do with looks.'

'It has *everything* to do with looks,' Sammy retorted, her voice shaking. 'I want you to leave. Right now. I'd love to be able to help your father but I draw the line at being manipulated into playing the part of your dreary fiancée so that you can try and fool the authorities in Australia into believing that you're a halfway decent guy with a few responsible bones in his body!'

Leo was outraged at the barrage of insults contained in that outburst. *Halfway decent guy? A few responsible bones?*

He stayed right where he was, a solid mass of sheer physical strength. He wasn't going anywhere and she would be more than welcome to try and budge him if she wanted. She wouldn't get far.

'Leave!' she snapped.

'Sit,' he returned.

'How dare you come into my house and…and…?'

'I'm not done with this conversation.' Leo looked at her steadily and she gritted her teeth in impotent fury.

There was no way she could force him out. He was way too big and far too strong. *And he knew it.*

'There's nothing else to say,' she told him in a frozen voice. 'There's no way you could persuade me to go along with your scheme.' Those cruelly delivered words from when she was a teenager had rushed back towards her with the force of a freight train. As an awkward, self-conscious adolescent she hadn't been his type and as a twenty-six-year-old woman she *still* wasn't his type…

She didn't care because, as it happened, he was no more her type than she was his, but it still hurt to have it shoved down her throat.

'Sure about that?'

Sammy didn't bother to answer. Her arms were still folded, her face was still a mask of resentment, her legs were still squarely apart as she continued to stare down at him.

He couldn't have looked more relaxed.

She marvelled how someone who adored his father so much could actually be so odious, but then he was a high-flying businessman with no morals to speak of when it came to women so why was she surprised?

'One hundred per cent sure,' she threw at him.

'Because I haven't just popped along here to ask a favour without bringing something to the table...'

'I don't see what you could possibly *bring to the table* that could be of any interest to me.'

'I like the moral high ground,' he murmured in a voice that left her in no doubt that the moral high ground was the very last thing he liked. 'But, in my experience, moral high grounds usually have their foundations built on sand. Why don't you sit down and finish hearing me out? If, at the end of what I have to say, you're still adamant that you want no part of this arrangement, then so be it. My father will be bitterly disappointed, but that's life. He won't be able to accuse me of not trying.'

Sammy hesitated. He wasn't going anywhere. The wretched man was going to stay put until he had said what he had come to say—the whole speech and nothing but the whole speech.

Why waste time arguing?

She perched on the edge of the chair and waited for him to continue.

He was truly a beautiful human being, she thought. All raven-black hair and piercing black eyes and fantastically chiselled features. It was hardly the time to be thinking this, but she just couldn't help herself.

Was it any wonder that there weren't many women between the ages of twenty-one and ninety-one who wouldn't have crashed into a lamp post to grab a second look?

She tried to imagine one of those women he dated trying to pass herself off as a suitable bride-to-be and, whilst it certainly worked from the gorgeous couple aspect, the whole thing fell apart the second a little girl was put in the equation.

'Your mother hasn't been well,' Leo said quietly. 'I'm sorry that this is the first time I've…commiserated.'

'She's going to be fine.' Sammy tilted her chin at an angle but, as always when she thought about her mother, the tears were never very far away.

'Yes. I've been told the chemotherapy has been successful and that the tumour has shrunk considerably. You must be relieved.'

'I don't understand what my mother has to do with any of this.'

'Then I'll come straight to the point.' He hadn't felt a single qualm when he had considered using money as leverage in this bartering process. This was the world he occupied. It was always a quid pro quo system.

Now, however, he was assailed by a sudden attack of conscience. Something about the way her eyes were glistening and the slight wobble of her full pink lips.

No wonder she and his father got on like a house on fire, he thought. They were equally sentimental.

It was yet another reason why the arrangement would work for them because her emotionalism was guaranteed to get on his nerves. There would be no chance of any lines between them getting blurred.

'It would appear,' he said heavily, 'that there's a problem with the mortgage repayments on the house your mother's in.'

'How do you know that?'

'The same way you seem to have great insight into *my* personal life,' he returned coolly. 'Our respective parents seem to do an awful lot of confidence sharing. At any rate, the fact is that there is a real threat of the bank closing on the house if the late payments aren't made soon.'

'I've been to see the bank.' Sammy's skin burnt because she hated this sliver of her life being exposed. It was none of his business. 'Mum's had to give up her job, with all the treatment, and I've had to move to a different, more expensive place here because the landlord in my last place wanted to sell. Plus there've been all the additional costs of travelling back and forth every weekend, sometimes during the week, as well. I haven't been able to contribute as much as I would have liked to the finances but they said they understood at the bank.'

'Banks,' Leo informed her kindly, 'have never been noted for their understanding policies. They're not charitable organisations. The most sympathetic bank manager, under instruction, will foreclose on a house with very little prior warning. I also appreciate that it costs you dearly to be working so far from your mother at a time when she needs you to be on hand.'

'Your dad had no right to tell you all that stuff…'

'Was any of it confidential information?'

Sammy didn't reply. No, none of it was confidential, although sitting here right now and listening to him explain her life to her made her think that perhaps it ought to have been.

Naturally, he would never understand what it might be like to really have to count pennies and to struggle against all odds to meet the bills. He had been born into money and, even in the village, his name was legend as the guy who had built his own empire and turned it into a gold mine.

'Didn't think so. I know he offered to give your mother money to help her out of this little sticky patch but she refused.'

'And I don't blame her,' Sammy said, her cheeks dully flushed. 'There's such a thing as pride.'

'Yes. It usually comes before a fall. No matter. I get it. But the fact remains that you are both facing considerable financial challenges, so here is my proposal.' He allowed anticipation to settle before continuing. 'In return for your services, so to speak, I will settle all outstanding money owing on your mother's house.' He raised one hand as though she had interrupted although, in fact, she couldn't have uttered a word if she'd wanted to. She was mesmerised by him. By the movement of his mouth as he spoke, by the steady flex of muscle discernible under his clothing, by the elegance of his gestures and the commanding timbre of his voice.

'Furthermore,' he continued, 'I understand that your dream is to work freelance. Your degree was in graphic art and, whilst you do as much freelance work as you can get your hands on, it's impossible to make the jump because you need to have a steady income.'

Sammy paled. 'Now *that*,' she burst out, 'definitely *was* confidential!'

'Is that some of your work over there?' Leo nodded to a desk by the window and the layers of stiff board piled to one side. Without giving her time to answer, far less swoop to the rescue of the job she was currently trying to find the time to work on, he began rifling through the illustrations she had so far completed while she remained frozen to the spot, mouth open.

'They're good.' Leo turned to face her. He was genuinely impressed. 'Don't glare at me as though I've exposed state secrets,' he said drily. 'This is the second part of my proposition. Not only am I willing to settle the debt on your mother's house but I will also get builders in to construct a suitable extension at the back of the property.'

'A suitable extension?' Sammy said faintly.

'To accommodate this—' he gestured to the desk and the artwork he had just been rifling through '—you setting up your own business where your mother is. No more commuting. No more wasting money on rent you can barely afford. And not only that, Sammy, but I will immediately instigate a steady income that will cover the transition period between you giving up your teaching post here and establishing yourself in your field.'

Sammy was beginning to sympathise with anyone unfortunate enough to have been run over by a steamroller. 'It's a ridiculous suggestion...' she protested, but she could hear telltale signs of weakness in her voice. 'Go to Melbourne...? Pretend to be engaged to you...? It's crazy.'

'Perhaps if you just had yourself to consider,' Leo pointed out with inexorable, irrefutable logic, 'you could spend the next hour talking about your pride or maybe just chuck me out of here immediately, but this isn't just about you. Your mother's future is involved here, as well.'

'And it's not fair of you to drag her into this.'

'Who said that life was fair? If life was fair, that harridan wouldn't be trying to hang on to a granddaughter she probably doesn't even want for the sake of what she thinks she might be able to coerce out of me. Agree to my proposal and I could have builders at the house first thing in the morning to ascertain what needs to be done. All you would have to do is hand your notice in and look forward to a life of no stress, close to your mother.'

Sammy thought of the amount of time she had spent trying to get the books to balance and trying to work out how many more hours she could put into her illustrations so that more income could be generated.

'What happens if you get custody of the little girl?' she questioned eventually, forcibly tearing herself away from that stress-free vision he had been dangling in front of her.

'I'll cross that bridge when I get to it. I can afford the very best day care, the very best schools and during the holidays there will be the option of spending time by the sea with my father.'

Sammy's brow pleated and Leo felt he should jump in before she began testing the moral high ground once again.

'I'm going to give you forty-eight hours to think about my proposition. Time for you to work out the nitty-gritty details and break the glad tidings to your mother, although there's a fair to middling chance that she already knows that I'm here with you right now, thanks to my father. I'll leave the engagement ring here. Try not to misplace it.' He told her how much it had cost and her mouth fell open. 'No point getting something cheap and nasty. You'd be surprised what a nosy reporter can spot through a telephoto lens. If you agree to this, no one must think that it's anything but genuine.'

'I may not agree to anything.'

'Your call.' He shrugged. 'Just think about the trade-off.' He stood up and glanced at his watch to find that far more time had gone by than he'd expected. 'One more thing to consider...'

Sammy had scrambled to her feet but she was still keeping her distance. She wasn't going to touch this offer with a bargepole. Was she? It smacked of blackmail and surely any form of deceit, however well intended, was a bad thing...

'What's that?' She eyed him warily.

'You asked why you're perfect for this...arrangement.' He kept his eyes fixed on her face as he began putting on his coat. 'You understand the rules. I don't mean the rules that involve pretending—I mean the rules that dictate that this isn't for real. You're not one of my women who might get it into their heads that a fake engagement might turn into a real engagement.'

'No. I'm not.' *Because there was no way he would ever consider getting engaged for real to someone like her.* She'd never wanted to slap someone as much as she had spent the past couple of hours wanting to slap him.

'So we're on the same page,' Leo drawled, tilting his head at her. 'Always a good thing. I'll be in touch for your decision.'

'You're going to traipse all the way back here...?'

'Oh, no. I'll call you. And no need to give me your mobile number. I already have it.' He allowed himself a mocking half smile. 'I look forward to talking to you soon...my wife-to-be.'

CHAPTER THREE

HE WAS SO damned sure of himself!

Sammy had spent the next forty-eight hours fuming. Her ability for recall was obviously world-class because she could remember every detail of Leo's visit and every fleeting expression on his face as he had laid out his proposal.

The fact that he had waltzed in with an engagement ring said it all. He hadn't expected to leave her flat without a satisfactory conclusion to his offer.

He hadn't arrived on her doorstep to ask a favour of her. He had arrived on her doorstep to blackmail her into helping him out. He'd held all the trump cards and he'd known that she would have been unable to refuse him.

As he had cleverly pointed out, her agreement to go along with him would make a world of difference to her mother and would relieve her of the constant low-level stress of worrying about the house and the unpaid remainder of mortgage. The fact that she would also have her daughter around and at hand for as long as was necessary had been just another bonus factor.

The deal was done before he'd issued her a time limit in which to make her mind up. He'd even correctly predicted that her mother had been well aware of his proposition so there had been no shock or surprise when Sammy had called to discuss it with her.

And now here she was, waiting for him to show up like a sixteen-year-old nervously counting the minutes until her date showed up to take her to the prom.

Except Leo was no normal date and her nerves did not stem from eager excitement.

She saw his car when it had almost come to a stop outside the house and she hurriedly flew back from the window and then waited until she heard the buzz of the doorbell.

She had dressed in defiant combat mode—literally. A pair of combat trousers, a green long-sleeved thermal vest, over which she had on her warmest army-green jumper, trainers and her waterproof coat with its very sensible furry hood.

She pulled open the door and, for a second, the breath caught in her throat as she stared up at him.

It was freezing. Sleet was falling, the skies the colour of lead. Yet, for all the discomfort of the weather, Leo still managed to look expensive, elegant and sexy in black jeans, a black jumper and a tan trench coat.

'You're not wearing the engagement ring' was the first thing he said.

'I didn't think there was any need to stick it on just yet.'

'Every need. The loving couple wants to advertise their love, not hide it away like a shameful secret. Where is it?'

'It's in my bag.'

'Then I suggest you fetch it out and put it on. And there's something else.' He eyed her outfit. 'I'm under strict orders not to tell you this, but there's a little surprise reception waiting for us when we get to my father's house.'

Sammy, in the act of rustling through her backpack to locate the box with the engagement ring, froze. *'Surprise reception?'*

'My father's idea. You know he's inclined towards sentimentality.'

'This is a *fake* engagement, Leo! It's going to last until Adele is over here and then there's going to be a *fake* break-up!'

'Believe me, I told him that, but he said the whole thing wouldn't sit right without some kind of celebration marking the big event. He's got a point. Over the years, he hasn't exactly been reticent when it's come to voicing his desire to see me married off. After our last conversation, he confessed that he's done a bit of complaining to his cronies at the bowling club and the gardening club and all those other clubs he's joined, that he'd like nothing more than to have a wonderful daughter-in-law. Apparently, it's what my mother would have wanted. It seems he had chatty conversations with her every so often and she told him that she was keen to see me settle down. I have no doubt that that little titbit has also been discussed over fertiliser tips for the roses. It would seem odd if his dearest wish were to come to pass and he kept it to himself,' Leo told her flatly. 'His friends would be mortally offended and, worse, some might suspect that he was making the whole thing up.' He glanced across at her. 'And, like I said, there can be no room for speculation about this.'

'It just doesn't seem right, Leo.'

Leo clicked his tongue impatiently. 'We wouldn't

be doing this if Gail weren't so patently unfit to be in charge of the child.'

'You should stop calling her *the child*. It makes you seem cold and unfeeling.'

'We're getting off-topic,' Leo drawled. He held up a bag, which she hadn't noticed him holding, and dangled it in front of her. 'Little present here for you.'

'Huh?'

'Outfit for the engagement party you don't know about. I thought a dress might suit the occasion a little more than jeans and a jumper, which I somehow knew you'd greet me in. Little did I know that you would go one step further and dress for all-out war. And don't argue with me on this one, Sammy. Put it on and let's get going.'

Sammy bristled but he wasn't going to budge and she snatched the bag from him. Pink, with fancy black lettering, clearly designer. Clearly the sort of thing he liked seeing women in, which would be just the sort of thing she wouldn't want to wear. 'Bossy,' she muttered, heading inside.

'And another small point.' He stayed her. 'We're supposed to be engaged. People who are engaged are generally happy and pleased to be in one another's company. Sniping and snarling is going to have to stop. Do I make myself clear?'

Sammy went beetroot-red. 'I feel as though I've been forced into doing this,' she admitted truthfully. 'And now I'm being ordered to get dolled up.'

'I'm no more a fan of deception than you are, believe it or not. I've had to rearrange vast swathes of my working life to accommodate the joy of being engaged and getting out to Australia to sort out a woman who has been a thorn in my side since Sean died. Throw into the mix that I find myself coping with someone who seems to have perfected the art of moaning, and you get the picture that I'm not exactly a willing participant in this situation! And, just for the record, you should try thinking about all the upsides of being *forced into doing this*. Life is going to be very sweet for you from here on in. If stress causes ill health then you should be fighting fit for a hundred years! And you might just like the dress I brought for you. I'll wait here while you put it on.' He glanced at his watch pointedly and lounged against the wall in we're-on-a-deadline-here mode.

She had expected small, tight and borderline tarty. It was what the women he went out with wore. That was his preferred style of dress for a woman. So she was startled to find herself stepping into the most beautiful soft, dusky pink woollen dress imaginable. Long-sleeved, knee-length, simple cowl neck, it was soft and demure and fitted her like a glove and she hated to admit it but she loved it.

She also hated to admit that it challenged her view of him as a womanising playboy who had got his own way on this, secured his deal with her and now wanted to dress her up like the sort of doll he imagined would pass muster on his arm in the role of fiancée. This dress was classy and it had been, she was forced to concede, a thoughtful purchase. He had actually considered how she would react in her scruffy clothes at a surprise gathering and had pre-empted her embarrassment by providing her with the perfect outfit.

She was much subdued when she joined him back in the hallway, where he was still lounging against the wall, scrolling through his cell phone.

Brilliant eyes shielded as he looked at her, Leo straightened and briskly congratulated her on the quick change of clothes.

Not a word about how she looked, she thought with a flare of disappointment, which she immediately quelled because *none of this was real*.

'Do I look a little more presentable?' Had she actually meant to ask that?

'Definite step up from the war zone look,' he murmured. He opened the car door for her and she stepped inside. 'Now all we need is a smile now and again and some lingering, tender glances and you'll be the complete package.'

'You're very cold, aren't you?' She absently thought that he was truly breathtakingly handsome. 'And your dad is such a warm person.'

'And look where it got him,' Leo responded without skipping a beat. 'After my mother died, he couldn't cope with solitude so he allowed his emotions to carry him away and he ended up with Georgia. Need I say more?'

'He was vulnerable,' Sammy admitted, startled out of her idle gazing at his profile.

'He was vulnerable because he allowed himself to get swept away by his emotions. If that doesn't convince you that emotions are best left at the front door, think about Sean. I admit he was never the most focused guy in the world but who knows. He might have achieved something if he hadn't been taken in by Louise.'

'So your answer is to just…lock your emotions in a box and throw away the key?'

'It's stood me in excellent stead over the years.'

Sammy could now understand why his father was so desperate to have contact with Adele. He would have wanted to anyway because that was simply the kind of man he was, gentle and effusive and warm, but, with no prospect of his own son rushing down the aisle in a hurry to start the next generation of little Morgan-Whites, he probably saw Adele as his one and only chance of having what amounted to a grandchild.

'Don't you plan on marrying…for real?'

'Depends what you call *for real*,' Leo replied drily. 'If by *for real* you're asking whether I'll ever throw caution to the winds and nurture unrealistic expectations about fairy-tale romances lasting a lifetime, then no. Not a chance. If, on the other hand, you're asking whether I may one day seal a union with a woman with whom I can enjoy some intellectual banter, a woman who is financially self-sufficient in her own right and who has enough of a life of her own to not need constant attention, then who knows? It's a possibility, although it has to be said that it's nowhere near being on the horizon at this moment in time.'

'That sounds like a lot of fun,' Sammy couldn't resist saying and he burst out laughing, a rich, sexy laugh that made her bloom with confusing, forbidden pleasure inside.

'Of course,' he murmured, 'there would also have to be certain things in place for the equation to work.'

'Like what?'

He briefly took his eyes off the road to look at her and Sammy felt bright colour crawl up from the tips of her toes to her hairline because she realised immediately what those *certain things* were.

Flustered, she looked away and stared straight out through the window, out into an unlit blackness, and heard him burst out laughing again.

'So you see,' he murmured when his laughter had trailed off, 'this little rescue package is as much of a hardship for me as it is for you. Not only will my working habits have to be constrained but so will my—'

'I get it,' she interrupted hastily.

He laughed again and then asked conversationally, 'Not the same for you?'

'I don't change boyfriends,' Sammy retorted coldly, 'the way I change outfits.'

'Now, now, are you implying that I do?'

'Don't you?'

'I'm not looking for love ever after,' he told her. 'But I enjoy having fun and I enjoy being in the company of women who like having fun with me.'

'It's just as well this is a fake engagement,' Sammy told him airily, while her mind toyed feverishly with images of him *having fun with his fun women*.

'Because you're looking for your soulmate?'

'That's right. There's nothing wrong with that.' She thought of her ex-boyfriends and marvelled that the theory of the perfect soulmate could be so different from the reality. It didn't mean that the guy for her wasn't out there. It just meant that she had to kiss one or two frogs before she got to him.

'Well, to each their own.' Leo shrugged indifferently. 'And that, as I said before, is just one of the reasons why this is such a good fake engagement. We're not even beginning to sing from the same song sheet when it comes to relationships. Now, let's talk about how we met and how long we've been seeing one another.'

The sleet had turned to snow by the time they made it to Happenden Court, which crested a hill and was reached via a long tree-bordered avenue. In summer, it was a glorious approach to the magnificent country estate but now, in the bitter, biting wind, it was no less impressive but rather a bleak and haunting view, especially with nightfall fast approaching.

The house ahead, however, was bathed in light.

Sammy absolutely loved the house. Admittedly, it was way too big for one man on his own, but Harold had lived in a small group of rooms in the massive property, only opening up the rest of the house on special occasions. In summer, people actually paid to visit the gardens and the part of the historic house which was largely unused.

He claimed he couldn't part with it even though it was huge and expensive to maintain. Too many memories, he had told Sammy once.

'He needs to downsize.' Leo read her mind as he swung the car into the courtyard. 'He might be emotional, but he's as stubborn as a mule. Remember to look surprised when you walk through the door.'

'The entire village won't be there, will they? Hiding in the living room with the lights off?'

'That could be a dangerous approach to take, considering most of the assembled crowd are in their seventies and eighties. And remember to look as though you've found true love with me.'

'Why? Do you think they've got a hotline to the paparazzi?'

She knew how she sounded. Petulant and sulky and childish. And yes, she'd signed up for a deal with the devil and she knew that she should be taking it on the chin instead of moaning and groaning. And yes, he was right. Whether she liked to admit it or not, the financial pressures that had been keeping her awake for over a year would be erased. Like a teacher sweeping into the classroom, he would wipe the whiteboard clean and she would be able to start afresh.

How many times had she fantasised about this very thing?

But every time she looked at him, it hit home just how steep the price she would be paying was. He did something to her. He unsettled her. Between that and her conscience, the next few weeks were not going to be a walk in the park.

How could she pretend to be in love with someone who unsettled her? When she fundamentally disliked what he stood for? When his approach to life was so different from hers? Surely one glance and anyone would see through the sham. Especially Gail Jamieson, who had a lot to lose if she didn't gain custody of her grand-daughter. They would be going to Australia and she would be playing out this charade in front of people who wouldn't be as forgiving and thrilled to see him engaged as the people waiting inside the house. Plus, deceiving people she had known since childhood didn't sit right and that, in itself, filled her with anxiety.

Thrilled they might be, but wouldn't they be able to see through her phoney smiles in a second? She could only hope that they would take their cue from her mother, who, after a long phone call with Sammy, knew the lie of the land.

'That's exactly what I'm talking about,' Leo grated, grinding the powerful car to a stop and turning to look at her as he killed the engine.

Sammy's thoughts were on her mother. She had been surprisingly upbeat about the situation, given the fact that it had been relayed by her daughter in a tone of voice that had been thick with resignation, doom and gloom.

But then her mother, Sammy reasoned, would have spent many more long hours as witness to Harold's despondency at not having his granddaughter in the same country. She would have lived through the nightmare of Gail's interference and demands and the horrible prospect of those demands continuing while any supportive role to Adele was shoved aside.

Plus she would have never argued that Sammy had made the wrong decision. If she *had* disagreed with her daughter, she would have kept her opinions to herself because the habit of being supportive of the decisions Sammy made was just too ingrained.

They had operated as a unit for a very long time.

'Sammy!'

'Huh?' Sammy blinked and surfaced out of her thoughts to focus on the man frowning at her.

Leo raked frustrated fingers through his hair and continued to frown at her because she'd been a million miles away just then. He'd been talking to her and, instead of paying attention to what he'd been saying, she'd blanked him out.

'I was *talking to you*,' he said grittily.

The surly edge to his voice suddenly lightened her mood and snapped her out of her thoughts. She looked at him, amused, because he had sounded, just then, like a sulky child.

'Care to share the joke?' He scowled and she grinned.

'You're angry because I wasn't giving you one hundred per cent of my attention? I guess,' she said shrewdly, 'you're not accustomed to women who don't give you *one hundred per cent* of their attention.'

'Don't be ridiculous,' Leo growled.

'I'm not! But just because you're *my fiancé* doesn't mean that I have to agree with everything you say and snap to attention the second you give a command.'

'Rebelling and being argumentative isn't going to persuade anyone that we're an item. Now, out we go. They're waiting for us and don't forget to look shocked. There's nothing worse than someone who isn't suitably flabbergasted at a surprise party thrown for them.'

Almost at the door, she paused to rest her hand on his arm.

Leo looked down at her, expecting defiance and that mulish stubbornness he was fast becoming accustomed to. Instead, she looked suddenly vulnerable and defensive.

Her complexion was so satiny smooth that he found himself staring. She had carved a niche for herself in the background and she had done that by deliberately making sure to downplay every single asset she had.

But the more he looked at her, the more appealing her attraction seemed to be.

He shook himself out of this strange line of thought, inserted his key into the lock and turned it, pushing open the front door and stepping back to allow her past him.

It had been several weeks since Sammy had visited the house but, as always, she stood for a few minutes breathing in its spectacular, unique magnificence.

Despite the historic interest of the building, it still managed to look lived-in, probably because of the eclectic mix of period furniture and the scattering of beautiful objects which Leo's parents had gathered over the years.

Mariela, having come from some wealth herself, had brought with her paintings and art pieces that were wonderfully exotic and there were unique touches everywhere that gave the house a very special feel. On the highly polished circular table in the hallway there was a massive arrangement of fresh flowers and Sammy breathed in the wonderful floral scent, as powerful as incense, temporarily forgetting why she was here.

Blissful oblivion didn't last long. She heard the babble of voices from behind one of the doors and quailed.

'Chin up,' Leo commanded. 'We're in love. Don't look as though you have a hot date with the hangman.'

He was walking briskly towards the sitting room and she hustled in his wake, horribly self-conscious and frantically wondering how she was going to pull this all off whilst looking suitably surprised. And, of course, delighted. She hoped that she might discover award-winning talents she had hitherto never suspected.

Leo knocked on the sitting room door then pushed it open and stood aside and, as she took a deep breath and hesitated, he pulled her into him and swung her round to face him.

He was smiling.

For a second, everything flew out of her head. This was a smile meant for her and, as she looked at him, she felt the whole room in front of her disappear—the voices, the people, the clinking of glasses, the laughter.

Her breath caught. Could she have forgotten how to breathe? Was that possible?

Her body was burning, her breasts aching and a strange sensation pooling between her thighs.

'Darling—' Leo laughed '—a little surprise party for us. I wanted to tell you but I was sworn to secrecy...'

This in a voice just loud enough to generate a round of delighted applause from, as she'd feared, at least forty of the great and the good from the village, all people she had known since forever.

And now she was going to have to look rapturous.

She began to turn and then he caught her face in his hands and lowered his head...

And kissed her. The tip of his tongue teased her full lower lip and Sammy instinctively opened her mouth, her whole body leaning into him, wanting the feel of his hard masculine body against hers. The taste of his tongue against hers sent desire ripping through her with the force of a raging inferno.

She didn't understand her powerful, immediate response to his caress. She just knew that it owned her.

And then he drew back, leaving her trembling and dazed, mouth swollen from his kiss, eyes over-bright and glittering.

'Excellent,' he murmured into her ear. 'I think it's safe to say that you don't have to worry about stage fright any more. We couldn't have been more convincing.'

CHAPTER FOUR

THE WHOLE VILLAGE now knew that Harold Morgan-White's son was engaged to lovely little Sammy Wilson. And wasn't it just fantastic because hadn't Harold been complaining for *years* about his overworked, stressed out son who was never going to settle down?

'If we don't escape soon,' he had told her as the last of the guests was being shown to the door, 'the next surprise occasion will include the vicar, the organist and a marriage service.'

'Our parents would never allow that,' Sammy had been quick to refute. 'Not when they know that this isn't for real.' But you wouldn't have guessed it from the way his father and her mother had basked in the congratulatory attention.

And she knew that to outside eyes she would have appeared equally thrilled because she had spent the remainder of the evening with that kiss still burning her lips. He had caught her off guard and had done the one thing which he must have known would have brought hectic colour to her cheeks and left her speechless.

It turned out she had had award-winning skills of deception in spades.

Lest she forget that they were a couple in love, he

had made sure to stick close to her side for the duration of the party. His hand had lain possessively around her waist and she marvelled that no one sought to question this sudden, overwhelming love affair that had smothered the pair of them.

Whatever happened to common sense?

And, whilst she could acknowledge that Leo was a good-looking, sophisticated and very sexy man, how was it that she could have cast aside all her doubts and allowed herself to be so affected by a kiss that had been purely for the benefit of the assembled crowd?

Since then, she had not seen him. He had returned to London to work on deals he needed to close before they left for Australia and she had used the time to hand in her notice, much to the disappointment of the head teacher.

And now, as she stared at the suitcases on the floor in her bedroom in her mother's house, she felt as though she had stepped onto a roller coaster that was picking up speed. It had nudged slowly to the top and she was poised, looking down at the loops stretching ahead of her.

She couldn't stop gazing at the costly engagement ring on her finger and vaguely wondering how she had ended up where she had, all in the space of a week.

But then she knew, didn't she…?

Leo had appealed to the very powerful part of her that had wanted to see her mother's stress alleviated, the part of her that had been frantically worrying about money, about the bank, about how much debt had piled up over the months. The part of her that had been worrying about her future and where she wanted to go with it.

Into this Leo had charged, with heady solutions and

a price to pay…because there was no such thing as a free lunch.

Had she not, reluctantly, felt sympathy for his cause she would have turned her back on his offer, but she was deeply fond of his father and had easily been able to see how the end could justify the means, even though deception was something she found abhorrent. She had also heard enough about Gail Jamieson and about Sean and his constant leeching of his ex-stepfather's bank account to know that Adele would not have a glorious, warm and loving environment if she stayed with her grandmother, who was, from all accounts, even more grasping than her daughter and son-in-law had been.

But, in return, she had had a glimpse of how difficult it was going to be to play the part of loving fiancée because being with Leo was just so unsettling.

She wasn't cool enough to deal with his massive presence. She had never liked the way he treated women and she disapproved of his casual approach to relationships and while neither of these things should have mattered because she and he were only linked by virtue of the charade they were playing, they somehow did.

She heard her mother calling her, carolling that the driver had arrived, courtesy of Leo, who had firmly decreed that a train to the airport wasn't going to do.

She lugged the cases down and found her mother waiting at the bottom of the stairs.

'Are you sure you're going to be all right while I'm gone?' Sammy asked worriedly. 'It will only be for ten days, by which time Leo should have a clear idea of what the outcome of the custody battle is going to be.'

Her mother's thin face was as bright-eyed as Sammy had seen it in a very long time. Which, frankly, was also worrying. She hoped her mother wasn't going to start believing that the pretence was for real. However, this was hardly the time to angst over that when the chauffeur was waiting.

'I'll be absolutely fine, darling. Amy is going to pop over every morning and I don't have any hospital appointments until you're back anyway. You just go out there and, well, enjoy yourself. It's been such a long time since you've had a break.'

'Mum,' Sammy whispered sotto voce as the chauffeur entered and, after a brief cheery smile, headed to the car with her cases. 'This isn't going to be about *having a break*. Remember I told you when I… Well, when I told you what this is all about?'

Her mother's eyes rounded and she smiled reassuringly, 'Of course and you're doing the right thing, darling. Harold is so relieved that this whole business is going to be sorted out once and for all.'

'Well, no one knows what the outcome is going to be,' Sammy pointed out constrainedly.

'It'll be fine with Leo in charge.'

Sammy rolled her eyes, halfway out of the door. 'He's not a knight in shining armour—he can't conquer everything!'

'Harold has a lot of faith in him and, by the way, Sam, you look lovely.'

'Mum, I have to go.' Her face was red. So what if Leo had breezily insinuated that her wardrobe only needed minor tweaks and packages full of beautiful, understated pieces that fitted her perfectly had subsequently arrived at her front door. If he had complained and tried to force her into wearing anything she hadn't wanted to wear then she would have dug her heels in and stood her ground, but he hadn't.

As the car ate up the miles between Salcombe and London, she wondered what he would think when she removed her coat and cardigan to reveal her light-weight cream trousers and her tan tee shirt and when she stashed away her boots, essential against the snow which had been falling when she'd left Devon, and pulled out her cream loafers. She was all covered up in her thick waterproof coat and scarf and gloves, but underneath was evidence of the effort she was making to fit the part.

Of course there would be no male appreciation in his eyes; as he had made clear from the very start, she was the ideal candidate because there would be no temptation for him to come near her. Unless circumstances dictated and he had to for show.

Or, at any rate, something like that.

She was a paid employee and, if it weren't for this weird situation, he certainly wouldn't be seeking her out to spend time in her company.

They made excellent progress and her nerves fluttered as she was helped out of the car with her bags and then, by some prior arrangement only possible, she assumed, with very, very rich and influential people, the chauffeur was permitted to leave his car outside the airport so that she could be delivered to the check-in desk without the hassle of having to manage a trolley herself.

Sammy had never experienced anything like it and although she didn't want to be impressed, she really was.

The crowd parted. People stared and whispered. Someone took a picture. Sammy felt like royalty. She wished she had had the foresight to dump the untrendy coat and scarf before exiting the car.

Cheeks burning, she was relieved to find Leo waiting for her by the first-class check-in desk.

He watched her slow progress towards him. Her hair was loose and it curled and danced around her heart-shaped face, falling in unrestrained ringlets past her shoulders. It was every shade of blond—vanilla streaked with gold with hints of strawberry—and it was brilliantly eye-catching.

The turquoise clarity of her eyes, fringed with dark, dark lashes which were at odds with her blond, blond hair also made him want to stare, he thought distractedly as she abruptly came to a halt in front of him.

'You're here,' he said, lounging indolently against the counter while his driver dealt with the business of the bags on the belt.

'Did you think I wouldn't turn up?'

'Your attitude when we last parted company wasn't reassuring.'

Sammy blushed. She could breathe him in and it was like breathing in some kind of dangerous, mind-altering drug. She stepped back a little.

'I'm glad to see you're wearing the engagement ring.' He took her hand in his and inspected her finger, looking at it from several angles while she fought the temptation to snatch it away.

'I put it on in the car,' she confessed, once she had her burning hand back to herself. 'I didn't want to wear it in front of my mum.' They had checked in and were moving with purpose through the airport, away from the crowds and the duty-free shops and directly towards the first-class lounge. Sammy followed in a daze, eyes darting around her, feeling that sneaky, pleasurable important feeling again because she knew that people were staring sideways at them. He commanded so much attention without even realising it because he looked neither left nor right and was uninterested in everyone around them.

'Why not?'

'She knows that this is just a…a…*charade*, but…'

'But what?'

'I just don't want her to get it into her head that there's any part of this that might actually be for real.'

'No.' Leo looked sideways at her. 'I'm sure she won't.'

'Yes, well, you can never tell,' Sammy continued, pausing only to stare around her at the lounge into which he had led her. It was beyond luxurious, the sort of place where you just knew that nearly everyone was stupidly rich and probably famous. 'Wow,' she couldn't help whispering as they came to a clutch of sofas.

'Wow?' Leo raised his eyebrows, amused at her lack of artifice. She was feisty, outspoken, stubborn as the proverbial mule and would certainly prove to be a challenging assault on his well-ordered world over the next ten days, but no one could accuse her of being anything but glaringly honest in her responses.

'I've never travelled like this in my life before,' Sammy said truthfully. 'In fact, I've only been on a plane twice in my entire life and it was nothing like this.'

'You can take your coat off and sit down.' Leo never paid a scrap of attention to the luxury that surrounded him wherever he went. Now, he glanced around him at the subdued, well-bred, quiet lounge that screamed *exclusivity*. Right about now, any of the women he was accustomed to dating would have stripped off her coat and would have been indulging in the sport of twisting and twirling and making sure that all eyes in the room were focused on her. Sammy was still in her coat. It looked as though she might actually have pulled it more tightly around her.

'You were telling me about your mother getting the wrong idea…' He began removing his laptop from his leather case, absently glancing at the headlines of the newspaper neatly folded on the table in front of the chairs.

He looked up.

The coat was off, as was the scarf. She was bending slightly to unzip her boots.

When he looked at her he could clearly see the outline of her breasts as she leant down. Her tee shirt was figure-hugging, the lightweight trousers lovingly contoured every rounded inch of her bottom and the surprising length of her slim legs. She wasn't looking at him. She was busy shoving the unsightly boots into a bag she had brought with her, replacing them with some cream shoes that complemented the outfit.

Nothing was revealing. There was nothing at all remotely attention-grabbing about what she was wearing. Yet she still managed to grab his attention and hold on to it.

Shoes on and outer layers removed and neatly folded and shoved into her carry-on, aside from the boots, which she had crammed into a canvas bag brought specially for that purpose, Sammy straightened and met his eyes.

For a few seconds she held her breath and wondered whether he would say anything about her outfit. When he didn't, the disappointment felt disproportionate but she pinned a smile on her face anyway.

She brutally reminded herself that there was nothing between them so there was no reason for him to remark on anything she chose to wear. As long as she played her part and gave no one any reason to suspect that there was anything amiss between them, especially when they reached their destination, then conversation would remain perfunctory.

'Yes—' she sat down and tucked her hair behind her ears '—I think that Mum's a little vulnerable because she's been ill. She's always been a strong woman and to have to accept that she wasn't as strong as she thought she was hit her hard.' Sammy frowned. 'It's only recently occurred to me, from a couple of things that Mum's said, that she was worried sick about leaving me single.' She laughed a little self-consciously. 'She seemed to think that if anything happened to her, I might have needed the support of someone by my side.'

'And you think that that worry might lead her to pin her hopes on this becoming more than just a fake engagement?' Leo was trying hard to quell his surging libido, which had suddenly decided to put in an appearance. He wondered why she dressed to hide her body when she had the sort of body that most men would drool over. Unashamedly *feminine* and sexy in its femininity.

'She actually told me that I should enjoy myself in Melbourne because I hadn't had a break in a long time,' Sammy confided.

'And there's no chance of that happening?'

Sammy opened her mouth to ask him how on earth she could possibly relax when she was going to be spending her time there in his company, pretending to be his fiancée.

But she stopped.

Why wouldn't she be able to relax? He would. He would work and when he wasn't working he certainly wouldn't be stressing out because his nerves were all over the place when he was in her company. His stomach wouldn't be doing somersaults when he was in her radius.

'I've spent so long worrying over stuff that I've forgotten how to relax,' she said vaguely, thinking on her feet.

'Then I'll have to change that.'

'What do you mean?'

'Engaged people go places, explore, seek out exciting new adventures.'

'Are you joking?'

'Why would I be joking, Sammy? We have to be convincing and if we spend our free time on opposite sides of the city it won't be long before Jamieson smells a rat.'

'But she's not going to be following us everywhere, is she?'

'Quite frankly,' Leo said with genuine honesty, 'I wouldn't put it past the woman. Think about it. If she loses custody of Adele, she loses access to my money. I owe her nothing. She's not related to me or to my father in any way whatsoever. As long as she can hang on to the child, she is guaranteed an income because neither my father nor, frankly, myself, would want Adele to suffer financial hardship. The tie with my father may not be secured with blood but it's there. So, that being the case, she'll do anything in her power to discredit me and what's the fastest way of discrediting me? By convincing a judge that I'm not the reliable, happily soon-to-be married man I claim to be.'

'I suppose so.'

'So you'll get the break your mother wants you to have,' he told her with silky assurance. 'Now—' he indicated the long counter brimming with delicious snacks '—why don't you go and help yourself? If I'm to have to focus on the custody battle while maintaining our happily engaged façade by mixing in some fun in the sun for the next week and a half, I might as well do as much work as I can while I'm still here.'

Despite what Leo had said about making sure that they stuck to their brief as the loved-up engaged couple, Sammy privately didn't think that anyone in Melbourne would give a hoot whether they looked loved-up or not. And whilst she had heard all sorts of rumours about Gail and her horrendous ways, she honestly couldn't picture the woman creeping around behind them wherever they went, in disguise, with the specific aim of trying to prove them liars.

Exhausted after twenty-two hours of flying, she was dazed as she emerged from the plane. He'd bought every seat in the first-class cabin because sharing space wasn't his 'thing' and it was less hassle than organising his company Gulfstream—and, besides, arriving in full view on a chartered airline worked. It was jaw-dropping extravagance but she had soon discovered that being up in the air for hours and hours and hours on end took its toll, however luxurious the seating arrangements.

Accustomed to functioning wherever he happened to be, and adept at working in the confines of a plane, Leo had not been disconcerted at all. He had pulled out his computer and had spent the majority of the flight working.

At some point, with neither her book or the range of movies netting her attention, she had turned to him and said airily, 'Do you ever get bored?'

'When it comes to work—' he had turned the full wattage of his attention onto her and she had felt, suddenly and inexplicably, like a flower, wilting in the shadows, exposed to the full force of the sun's rays '—I have an inexhaustible supply of energy. I also have to wrap up some pretty important deals before we reach Melbourne. Like I said, fun in the sun is the equivalent of taking time out and taking time out isn't something I can afford to do.'

'When was the last time you had a holiday?'

'You're beginning to sound like my father,' Leo had said wryly. 'Please do me a favour and spare me the long lectures about high blood pressure, premature heart attacks and stress.'

'I wasn't going to start lecturing you about anything,' Sammy had informed him. 'I was just curious and you don't have to think that you have to spend all your spare time with me. In fact, does Ms Jamieson even know exactly when we're due over?'

'You can't imagine that I would make this trip on the off-chance of finding her, do you? I have meetings arranged in advance with her lawyer and I have a team of people at my end, waiting and ready to go. I've made very sure to cage her in. Wouldn't want her to consider bolting.'

For a brief moment, Sammy had almost felt sorry for the woman. She had certainly understood in that moment why his father had had such an unshakeable faith in him securing the outcome that was desired.

He exuded absolute mastery.

But she had still privately thought that, whilst it sometimes paid to be cautious, he was being overcautious when it came to maintaining their charade.

Blistering heat greeted them as they emerged into the soaring summer temperatures. The sky was flamboyantly blue and cloudless and the strength of the heat was formidable. In her tee shirt and slacks, which she had traded on the plane for a set of silk pyjamas, she still felt her skin begin to perspire almost immediately.

She knew that they would be met by a chauffeur. She hadn't known that, along with the chauffeur who was dutifully waiting for them, there would also be a little cluster of paparazzi.

Startled and blinking, she instinctively stepped closer to Leo and felt his arm curve around her as he led her directly to the car waiting for them.

Once inside the air-conditioned space, Sammy craned back, staring at the reporters, then turned to Leo and whispered urgently, 'What on earth were they doing at the airport? I don't get it. We didn't have any of this in England. In fact, other than the people at the party, no one even knows that we're engaged!'

'What gives you that idea?'

'Why would anyone know? There certainly wasn't anyone taking pictures…'

'I've made sure to keep it low-key,' Leo informed her and she looked at him in utter astonishment.

'What do you mean?'

He was sprawled in the seat, leaning against the door, his big body angled to face her. Dressed in grey trousers and a short-sleeved black polo shirt with a tiny discreet insignia embroidered on one side, he was the last word in sophistication. He had *that look*. The look of someone who should be photographed. Rich. Powerful. Influential.

She recalled the way his mouth had felt against hers and quivered.

'I have an excellent relationship with the press, particularly the tabloid press. They're like sharks. They'll cheerfully rip you apart if it takes their fancy. It's always a good idea to keep them onside. I'm wealthy, I'm powerful but I'm not a Hollywood star. The less they print about me, the better, but I accept that my movements are sometimes of interest.' He shrugged. Sammy found it fascinating that he could sit there and talk about a world that was so foreign to her. He really and truly moved in a completely different hemisphere. A world where people were photographed and simple day-to-day things became newsworthy events to be recorded for public consumption.

No wonder he had reasoned that her presence by his side would give his cause gravitas. She was the embodiment of everything that was contrary to all of that—the embodiment of *normality*—just the sort of reassuring thing the lawyers would make note of when it came to sorting out custody of an impressionable young child.

Guilt shook her because this *normality* was only going to last as long as it took for him to have Adele under his wing.

She consoled herself with the thought that whatever was brought to the table by Leo and his wonderful, kind-hearted father was sure to be better than what lay in store for the little girl at the hands of a grasping grandmother, but she still backed away from thinking too hard about the rights and wrongs.

At the end of the day, she thought uneasily, it wasn't her problem.

Besides, whilst the world of extreme wealth was not one she inhabited, she knew that there were very many children of wealthy parents who did very well on a diet of private schools and boarding schools and nannies.

'I know a couple of the reporters,' Leo said as though it were the most normal thing in the world. 'The trick is to see them as humans in their own right and not a collection of pests. Humanise them and they're more likely to humanise *you* in return. At any rate, I spread the word that I was engaged and made it known that a flashy announcement wasn't going to do. I felt that was appropriate, given the circumstances, but no point broadcasting it when it's going to come to an end in due course.'

'No, quite.' She was finding it hard to keep up.

'They listened and did as I asked.'

'People do that, don't they?' she murmured and he looked at her and nodded.

'Different story over here,' Leo informed her. 'Ignore anyone who asks for an interview. I may not be as well known as I am in London but I do have considerable financial interests in this part of the world and...' He flushed darkly and paused, and something about that pause roused her curiosity.

'And what?'

'I did achieve a certain amount of unwanted notoriety for dating a certain Australian actress about a year ago.'

'Really?' Sammy had been so wrapped up in concerns about her mother's health at that time that she doubted she would have been able to remember anything that had been going on around her, never mind what had been unravelling in the gossip pages of tab-loid newspapers.

'Vivienne Madison.'

'*The* Vivienne Madison? Gosh. I had no idea. What happened?'

'I'm surprised you missed out that little slice of my life,' Leo inserted wryly, 'considering you seem to have spotted me in the centre pages of tabloids in the past.'

'I wasn't really with it a year ago,' Sammy admitted. 'Mum was undergoing treatment and I was…in a dif-ferent place. A scary place. I was barely functioning. I mean, I was going to work but taking a lot of time off and I couldn't focus at all. I don't think I glanced at a newspaper once for months.'

'The long and short of it,' Leo said heavily, 'was that she was found with a bottle of pills in a hotel room and the baying Australian press decided to go for me.'

'You mean she tried to commit suicide because you left her?' Immediately, she could feel herself pull back from him, deeply appalled that his way of life, his cav-alier attitude towards women, might have resulted in someone actually attempting to take her own life as a result of being ditched.

Leo read the distaste on her face. Normally, this would not have fazed him. He never saw the need to launch into explanations for his behaviour or to justify decisions he had taken. As long as he stuck to his im-peccable moral code and recognised his own personal truths, who gave a damn what other people thought?

But, for some reason, he didn't like the thoughts he knew were churning around in her head.

'Vivienne Madison was a seriously unstable woman.' He was unfamiliar with the process of explaining himself and found that his words did not come as easily as usual. 'When I became involved with her, I discovered that she had a drinking problem. She was also, I later found out, hooked on painkillers. But she was an amazing actress and managed to hide both those dependencies.' He sighed, his lean, handsome face unusually empathetic, the cold lines temporarily erased. 'She became dependent on me very quickly, although I had told her from the very beginning that I was not interested in settling down. But she was a highly emotional person and her addictions made her even more irrational than she otherwise might have been. I knew that it had to end but I made sure to get her signed up with an excellent counsellor as well as a rehab centre noted for its success rate. I may not have wanted her in my life but I wasn't going to cast her aside like a pile of used rubbish. The truth is that I felt deeply sorry for her.'

Sammy was impressed. That this formidable and ruthlessly controlled man was capable of compassion for a woman he had no longer wanted in his life was an eye-opener.

It didn't *mean* anything, but it certainly afforded her a different take on him. It was peculiarly complimentary to him because she could tell that he was less than comfortable telling this story and was doubtless only doing so in case it came out and she knew nothing about it. As his fiancée, it would be surprising if she was ignorant of what had happened.

'The incident with the overdose was several weeks after we had parted company but that was something the press over here omitted to mention. Later, there was a nondescript apology to me when they discovered that the overdose was in response to a rejection from one of the psychiatrists at the rehab centre. At any rate, my name will be linked to hers forever over here.'

'And is she still in contact with you?'

'In no way, shape or form,' Leo asserted.

That was the end of the conversation. She could see that on his face but it left her thinking that she could almost understand his antipathy towards emotional situations. He had had a substantial amount of experience in dealing with the negative side of them.

'So we have a schedule here,' she said, changing the subject.

'Meetings lined up with lawyers. I expect some sort of compensation will have to be given to Ms Jamieson if custody is awarded to me. It will be a very busy ten days.'

'Not much time for fun in the sun.'

'Tut-tut,' Leo said lazily. 'Is that the right approach for a newly engaged woman to be taking? I'm sure we'll find the time to escape and see some of Melbourne's sights, especially if there are interested parties pursuing us who need to be placated. Like nosy journalists. If Jamieson is playing hardball, then there's every chance she's got in touch with a newspaper and filled them in on what I'm doing over here. It's certainly got the ingredients for a good story, especially with my past association with Vivienne. But don't worry—' he reached out and slid his long brown finger along her arm, sending splinters of awareness skittering through her like quicksilver '—it'll be over in no time at all and you can return to your life.'

CHAPTER FIVE

It DIDN'T TAKE long before the car was pulling up outside a grand hotel and they stepped back out into the searing heat. It felt strange to be in a busy, vibrant city and yet to know that the sea was just a hop and a skip away. Sammy imagined that she could almost smell the salt in the air.

And the people looked different. Relaxed, sunkissed, moving at a slower pace. She had to keep reminding herself that this wasn't the break her mother had told her she needed but she could still feel a holiday spirit pushing through until they were shown up to their massive suite and she gazed around in confusion because there was just the one bedroom.

'Is this it?' she asked, as soon as their bags were deposited and the bellboy had left, quietly closing the door behind him.

Leo, immune to his surroundings as always, was heading to the well-stocked kitchen where he proceeded to fetch them both a bottle of ice-cold water. 'You'll find yourself drinking this by the gallon,' he promised. 'I would recommend that you carry a bottle in your bag whenever you're out. The heat over here can be ferocious and we don't want you getting dehydrated, do we?'

Sammy took the bottle from him. 'Thank you very much for your health tips, Leo, but where is *my* bedroom?'

Leo carried on drinking, looking at her as he drank, then, dumping the empty bottle on the kitchen counter and strolling towards the sitting area, he nodded in the direction of the bedroom.

'What?' She tripped along and watched as he coolly pulled out his computer and flipped it open, attention focused on whatever he had called up to peruse.

'Leo, could you at least look at me when I'm trying to have a conversation?'

'You wanted to know where your bedroom is and I showed you. It's behind me and yes, there's only the one room.'

'But...'

'But what did you expect, Sammy?'

'Not just one bedroom with one bed in it!'

'No?' he drawled coolly. 'Did you think that I would book us into separate rooms? Maybe on different floors? Or why stop there? Different hotels?'

'You're deliberately misunderstanding me.'

'I'm not deliberately misunderstanding you. Frankly, I think you are the one deliberately misunderstanding the situation. Did you honestly imagine that as a newly engaged couple we wouldn't be sharing a bedroom?'

'I hadn't thought about it,' Sammy stuttered.

'Engaged couples tend to share bedrooms these days. There was no chance, after all of this, that I would risk anyone suspecting that all is not what it appears to be in the land of the soon-to-be wed lovebirds.'

He was right, of course. They weren't living in an

era of chaperoned walks in the park and a ban on all forms of physical contact bar holding hands.

She hadn't really thought about that angle at all, just as she hadn't really thought about how open to scrutiny they would be because she had had no idea of the world he occupied.

Sammy dropped into the chair facing him. She wondered how she hadn't really noticed the huge differences between them sooner and then thought that that was probably because she hadn't seen him on enough of a regular basis over the years and, when she *had* seen him, it had always been in the rural setting of his father's house. She had ceased to be awestruck at the mansion in which Harold lived and he was such a lovable and down-to-earth man that, in the setting of his rolling country estate, Leo had been a lot more of an ordinary guy.

But he *wasn't* an ordinary guy. This *wasn't* going to be a low-key two-week situation. He *hadn't* overplayed the amount of attention they might generate.

'We're in this together for the next week and a half, so you might as well get used to it.'

'Thank goodness it's just going to be for a week and a half,' Sammy breathed with sincerity. 'I don't think I could live in it for any longer than that.'

'Oh, really?'

Leo imbued those two simple words with such sarcastic disbelief that she flushed and glared at him.

'I wouldn't want to live in a goldfish bowl,' she asserted dismissively. 'I'd hate to think that there might be people with cameras wherever I went, waiting to get a picture of me.'

'And yet you seemed to be mightily impressed by

the first-class lounge and the first-class cabin and the chauffeur-driven car...'

Sammy blushed, hating him just at that moment because he was right; she really *had* enjoyed that feeling of being treated like royalty.

'That's because it's a novelty. I'd soon tire of it,' she insisted and he shrugged with an expression that indicated that he was suddenly bored with the whole conversation.

'Which is just as well,' Leo drawled, 'considering the novelty isn't going to last very long. It would be a nuisance if you started getting too accustomed to it.'

'Meaning?'

'Like I said to you before, you're ideal for this role because you wouldn't be interested in prolonging it. Indeed, the fact that you don't like this lifestyle could come in very handy when it comes to citing reasons for our break-up. Two people, opposites drawn together by a powerful attraction only, sadly, to discover that opposites, in the end, do not have what it takes to make lasting relationships. But, getting back to the matter of the bedroom... We're sharing it and I'm afraid you're just going to have to deal with that. Let's not forget here that you're not in this because you're an altruistic saint only concerned with my father's welfare. You're in this because the price was right.'

Sammy went bright red. He had sliced through the waffle and got straight to the point and she couldn't dispute the truth of what he was saying.

She also knew that, for what she was being paid, sharing a bedroom was not exactly too high a price to pay. And what, exactly, was her cause for concern, anyway? It wasn't as though he was attracted to her. In fact, she could tell that he was struggling not to let his attention wander back to whatever report she had interrupted. And as soon as they were away from public view, he made no attempt to come near her or to even look at her as though she belonged to the female sex.

She was only his type when she had to be, which was when they were being observed.

She stood up stiffly. 'Okay. Fair enough.'

Leo's dark-eyed gaze narrowed. So she had bought into a situation and was now discovering that it came with certain clauses she might not have taken into account. He felt a degree of sympathy for her, even though he had no intention of revealing that because, as far as he was concerned, when you put your signature on the dotted line you agreed to all the terms and conditions.

But she wasn't like the women he was accustomed to dating. Naturally, she would have had experience of sharing a bed with a man—she wasn't a teenager, after all—but he was a virtual stranger and she was weirdly disingenuous.

Yet, after her initial appalled reaction, she had accepted it without further ado.

'You're perfectly safe with me,' he told her roughly and Sammy paused, her heartbeat suddenly accelerating as their eyes met.

She didn't know what to say and even if there had been anything remotely resembling a coherent thought in her head she wouldn't have been able to vocalise it because her mouth was dry and her vocal cords had stopped working.

'You don't have to worry,' he explained into the deafening silence, 'that I'm going to lunge for you in the middle of the night. I would offer to sleep on the sofa but it seems a ridiculous amount of hassle to make a sofa up with whatever spare linen we can rustle up from a cupboard, only to *unmake* it first thing in the morning.'

'I'm not complaining.' Sammy finally found her voice and was pleased that it sounded relatively normal. 'I was just a little taken aback, that's all.' She told herself that this was a job, as he had made sure to remind her, and part of the job would be to sleep next to him. No big deal. She would be well and truly covered up. It wasn't as though her change of wardrobe had extended to a collection of French knickers and frilly negligees. It would be as unthreatening as if she were sleeping next to a potted plant.

'If you don't mind, I think I'll go have a bath now, freshen up. What are our plans for tomorrow?' She was still furiously trying to quieten her nerves at the prospect of sharing a bed with him and pretending that he was the equivalent of a potted plant.

Leo afforded her his sole undivided attention for a few seconds. 'I expect,' he said slowly, 'that it will involve you meeting the Jamieson woman at some point. My lawyers have emailed me over the proposal they've put to her lawyers and instinct tells me that she's not going to be over the moon. That's in the afternoon. Tomorrow morning, I suggest we visit a few shops.'

'Why?'

'Is that your response to the offer of going shopping?' Leo was amused.

'I don't like shopping,' Sammy admitted. She tilted her chin at a defiant angle. 'You can probably see for yourself why!'

'Come again?'

Sammy spread her hands down in a sweeping gesture and laughed. 'I'm not exactly built like a model. You, of all people, should be able to see that for yourself, considering you only date models. And actresses who have model bodies.'

'What does that have to do with anything?' Leo was genuinely bewildered and Sammy was already regretting her impulse to put herself down but, when it came to her appearance, it was something that had always come as second nature. If you laughed at yourself first, then it deflected other people from laughing at you.

'When you have a figure like mine, twirling in front of mirrors in changing rooms is a bit of an ordeal,' she said lightly, scuttling in small steps towards the bedroom door. 'You probably wouldn't understand,' she embellished, more embarrassed by the second.

'And that would be because...?'

'You must know that you're a good-looking guy!' She wondered how the conversation had strayed so quickly from her simple enquiry as to what the plans were for the following day. 'I don't suppose mirrors pose a problem for you. Anyway—' she brushed aside the conversation, uncomfortable under his perceptive gaze '—you were talking about shopping. Why are we going shopping? There are loads of other things I'd rather be doing.'

'I'm in complete agreement with you there. However, you're going out with me now, we're engaged and it would seem odd for you to be seen wearing cheap off-the-peg clothes.'

Sammy's mouth dropped open. 'You said you weren't interested in telling me what I could or couldn't wear.'

'And I'm not, although I confess that I'm relieved you

took the decision yourself to put the jeans and baggy tops on the back burner while we're out here.'

'So if you don't care what I wear, then what's the shopping expedition all about?' she bristled, fired up at an implied insult behind the suggestion. 'I'll bet you've never hinted to any of those women you've been out with in the past that you wanted to take them shopping because you didn't like their choice of clothing!'

'That's a thought,' Leo murmured, remembering what she had said about not liking shopping experiences. He didn't get why she would feel self-conscious of her body because there was an earthy voluptuousness about her that was powerfully attractive.

His eyes wandered.

She had slender legs, and a waist that was a handspan slim, but her breasts were generous and her hips were downright sinful in their curves, fashioned to be contoured by a man's hands.

He looked away, frowning at his brief loss of self-control.

'Maybe—' he thought of his exes and their minimalist approach to clothing '—I should have steered some of my past girlfriends to items of dress that weren't the size of paper tissues. A diet of relentlessly non-existent clothing can get very boring for a guy after a while.'

'You don't mean that.' But she was foolishly touched that he had made an effort to counteract any offence she might have taken by indulging in a little white lie.

'It's not about *what* you choose to wear. It's about the *quality* of what you choose to wear.'

'I can't afford to blow my savings on clothes,' Sammy told him abruptly.

'You probably could,' Leo countered with cool, restrained honesty, 'when this little charade is over. But that's by the by. What I'm saying is that any woman of mine would be expected to be wearing the very best. The very best in twinsets and pearls, if that happened to be her choice.'

Sammy stared at him and then she burst out laughing. 'You have got to be kidding!'

Leo frowned. 'Why would I be kidding?'

'Leo, I'm not the kind of girl who expects any man to buy her clothes for her! That's incredibly old-fashioned.'

'And what sort of girl would you be describing?' he enquired with the sort of shuttered expression that would have signalled a warning to her across the bows had she not still been smirking at the concept of a man paying for what she wore.

'Oh, just an airhead who traipses along from shop to shop, happy for you to dip into your wallet to fund her wardrobe.'

'Have you ever,' he asked, 'been treated to a shopping spree by one of these chauvinistic dinosaur guys you don't approve of?'

'Well…'

'So that's a *no*. Maybe you should give it a try before you start passing judgement. The fact of the matter is this, as my fiancée, you would be treated like a queen. There's no way I would countenance you going out in cheap supermarket bulk-buy clothes. You would wear the very best, in whatever you chose to wear.'

'I didn't get my outfits in a supermarket.'

'You know where I'm going with this, Sammy. Were this real, I would want you to be wearing the very best. It would give me pleasure to indulge you.'

Sammy went bright red. The deep, sexy timbre of

his voice conjured up an image of this big, powerful man entranced enough with a woman to be possessive, generous and proud.

'But it isn't real.' She headed straight back down to earth before wayward images in her head could start giving her a thrill that would have been utterly inappropriate.

'No,' Leo agreed smoothly, 'it isn't. But, since that's not the image we're aiming to project, you're just going to have to subject yourself to the torture of the shopping trip.' He raised his eyebrows and looked at her speculatively. 'Who knows…maybe you'll enjoy it more than you expect. And if at the end of this you're too proud to keep the clothes you've bought you can always hand them back to me. A charity shop would be more than happy to take the discards.'

Sammy couldn't dwell on any of that for long because she was wandering back off to the appalling prospect of sharing a bed with him. Somehow she had convinced herself to forget about that while they had been sparring but her apprehension swamped her all over again as she locked herself in the bathroom and took her time having the longest bath in living memory, while listening out to hear whether he had entered the bedroom.

Her very-respectable pyjamas were neatly folded on the little circular table in the enormous bathroom. She only wished she weren't so nervous because her nerves prevented her from enjoying what had to be the most luxurious bathing experience of her life. The bathroom was a vision of pale marble, oversized fluffy towels, a walk-in wet room and a bath big enough to stage a concert.

Just like that, she thought back to him asking her whether she had ever been treated to a shopping spree by a guy. She was very quick to condemn the thought of it, and she knew that she wasn't going to *have fun* choosing clothes which someone she barely knew was going to feel obliged to pay for, but, that said, here she was, enjoying the splendour of a hotel he was paying for.

What did that say? She had always prided herself on her ability to stand on her own two feet. From an early age, she and her mother had presented a united front, soldiering on after her father's premature death. She had learned how to carry the weight of responsibility on her shoulders and that had been truly put to the test when her mother had fallen ill.

She had also learned not to depend on something as frivolous as her looks to get her through and, yes, she had privately nurtured some scorn for those women who relied on their appearance to provide the rungs on the ladder they could use to clamber upwards.

She wasn't going to turn to crafty feminine traits to see her through!

But something about Leo made her feel feminine. She found herself responding to his blatant masculinity in ways that were girlish and light-headed. She had wanted him to compliment her on her choice of dress and she could only blame the bizarre nature of the situation for fostering unwanted responses.

She listened carefully at the bathroom door before pushing it open into the adjoining bedroom. She was fully dressed, bathrobe on for good measure, but in fact she need not have worked herself up into a lather because he wasn't in the bedroom. The vast four-poster bed, bigger than a normal king-sized bed, was untouched.

She wasn't about to hazard a peek outside to see what he was doing or even whether he was still in the suite. She might be covered from head to toe but there was something about being dressed in pyjamas...

She dived into the bed, burrowed down so far to one side that she was inches away from tumbling off, hunkered down for the long haul and eventually fell asleep.

When she woke, daylight was doing its best to wriggle past the floor-to-ceiling curtains, which were still tightly drawn.

And Leo was nowhere to be seen, although his side of the bed had definitely been slept in.

She had no idea when he had got into bed and no idea when he had got out of it. It was after nine and she freshened up in a rush, changing into a summery dress, a cheap and cheerful addition to her wardrobe, and a pair of canvas espadrilles. She combed her hair loosely over one shoulder so it fell in soft waves and tentatively left the sanctuary of the empty bedroom.

Leo had been on the verge of waking her because time was moving on but, whilst he rarely suffered from jet lag, he accepted that she might need to sleep off the disruption to her body clock.

He was also strangely reluctant to venture into the bedroom.

By the time he had finally made it to bed, she had been fast asleep, her breathing soft and even. As his eyes had adjusted to the darkness, he could see that she had kicked off the duvet, just as he could see that her prim and proper top had ridden up and, from the angle in which she was lying, he could just about make out the soft swell of the underside of her breast.

He had felt like a voyeur.

Riveted to the spot, he had felt himself harden and, for the first time in his life, he had been unable to control his wayward libido as he had remained glued to the spot, staring at that sliver of pale skin, barely visible at all.

He had seen more of the naked female form than most men but he couldn't recall the last time he had been held captive by a glimpse of a breast.

Thinking about those few seconds, when he had barely been able to breathe, was enough to ensure he remain just where he was, at the desk by the window, waiting for her to emerge.

'You're up.' He pushed himself away from the desk and folded his hands behind his head.

She looked fresh and very, very young. Her pale hair flowed over one shoulder and caught the sun pouring through the huge windows, brightening the strands to a silvery white. She looked wholesome and sexy at the same time, although he was certain that she was utterly unaware of how appealing the combination was.

'I'm sorry I overslept. How long have you been up?'

'Three hours.'

'You should have woken me.' But she was relieved that he hadn't. She shied away from thinking about him shaking her until she opened drowsy eyes and looked at him, both in the same bed, warm from their shared body heat. 'I'm ready to go now, anyway.'

'Breakfast?'

'I'm not hungry.' She was starving but nobly decided to ignore her hunger rather than risk those cool, assessing eyes watching her as she tucked into a plate full of food.

'Sure?'

Sammy nodded, walking towards her handbag, which she had left in the sitting area on a chair. She stole a sideways glance at him as he rose elegantly to follow her to the door, casting a last look at the suite before opening the door for her.

She could see why he was taking her shopping. Next to him, her clothes shrieked *bargain basement* and whilst he really didn't seem to mind what kind of clothes she chose to wear, he certainly cared about the price of them.

Outside, she breathed in the heat, revelling in the sun as it poured down on her shoulders, and, as they were ferried to the most expensive shopping street in the city, she looked left and right at the enormous diversity of the architecture.

Old and new jostled side by side. Coffee shops spilled onto pavements. There were elements of the past in the gracious Victorian buildings and arcades and elements of the ultra-modern in spacious glass and chrome buildings that housed offices and shops.

The yellow taxis and glimpses of trams held her rapt attention because it was all so different in ways she couldn't quite put her finger on.

They entered an ornate arcade and he took her hand in his, linking his fingers with hers.

It didn't matter how many times she reminded herself that this was a business arrangement, she still couldn't stop herself from reacting to him and she was doing it now. Heat flooded her body and she knew that her face was red because all she could focus on was the feel of his cool fingers entwined with hers.

They hit the first shop, which, under normal circumstances, would have been way out of her price range. She didn't need to peruse the racks of clothes to establish that. She could tell at a glance from the lack of price tags and the elegant glacial beauty of the two shop assistants.

It was a large boutique, white and clinical, with a high-tech spiral staircase leading to an upper area.

Sammy hesitated by the door and felt him gently tug her in. 'Where's the excitement?' he murmured, leaning down, his breath warm against her ear.

'I'm not sure this is the sort of place that would stock anything I would like...'

'You haven't looked.'

'I can tell from the racks.' She smiled weakly at the saleswoman whose eyes briefly scanned her then moved on to Leo.

'Nonsense!' He firmly ushered her forward and Sammy watched, entranced, as he charmed the blonde beauty. Somewhere along the line, she got the impression that the other woman had recognised him, although, of course, it would have been totally out of order for her to have said anything. The actress he had dated was world famous. It wouldn't have surprised her if half of Melbourne recognised him.

'Now, darling...' he turned to her, dark eyes shielded '...take your pick.' He leaned down and gently cupped the side of her face in his hand, his fingers grazing her hair, which was as soft as silk and smelled of flowers. He lingered for a few seconds, startled by how much he was enjoying the feel of it, slippery under his fingers. 'If you feel the clothes here are a little too modern or revealing for you, then say the word.'

She was only twenty-six years old but he made her

feel like a granny. Who could blame him, though? There was no denying her outfits had an old-fashioned flavour about them. It was brought sharply home to her just how much she had grown accustomed to hiding her figure behind baggy and unrevealing clothes. Comfort dressing was obviously a habit that she had become used to.

The soothing, patronising tone of his voice got her back up and she pursed her lips before smiling tightly at the shop assistant.

'Why don't you go and have a wander?' She reached up on tiptoe to cup his face just as he had done hers, going one step further and pressing her lips against his cheek. 'You don't want to spend your time sitting here looking at your watch while I try on outfits, do you? That'll be really boring for you.'

The show of loving familiarity was all for the benefit of their attentive spectators but Sammy still wasn't prepared when he curved both arms around her and drew her closely against him, angling her so that their bodies were neatly pressed together, his legs squarely planted apart to accommodate her between them.

Breathless, Sammy's eyes widened. Her whole body tingled and she was aware of herself, of every tiny pore and every strand of fine hair on her skin, in a way she had never been in her life before.

She shivered, as helpless in his embrace as a leaf being whipped along in a force ten gale. Instinctively, she leaned into him, overwhelmed with a sudden craving that shook her to the very core. This was much more than a kiss—this was the feel of his hard masculinity against her and it sent flames of desire licking through every part of her body.

Panicked, she flattened her hands against his chest but she wasn't allowed to push him back.

With a deep-throated growl of masculine satisfaction, Leo kissed her.

He wasn't into public displays of any sort, least of all when there was an audience, and there was very much an audience in the shop. Indeed, he had heard the sound of the door opening as more people entered but even that was not sufficient incentive to tear himself away from her.

What had started out as a little lesson to teach her that if she wanted to touch him to make a point then he was going to touch her right back to make an even bigger point had turned into something altogether different.

Way too different.

He drew back, releasing her abruptly, and it took a few seconds for his sudden withdrawal to register and, when it did, Sammy stepped smartly back, shaken to the core.

How had that happened? How had she *let* it happen? For a few long, long moments it had felt as though that kiss were the real thing, as though he were a real boyfriend. She just hoped that he hadn't sensed it. She smiled brightly at him but her eyes were unfocused.

Leo was looking at her narrowly. Had she intended to draw him into that kiss? His instinct was to have said no, but the way she had responded, throwing herself into it...

He had felt the yielding softness of her body beneath the cheap cotton dress, had felt the fullness of her breasts pushing against him. She had known just how to get to him with that little teasing taunt, just how to up the ante so that, for a minute there, he had well and truly lost sight of the fact that she wasn't one of his lovers.

She made a big song and dance about not liking the world of money, paparazzi and untold luxury into which she had been thrown but he knew women and he had never met one whose head hadn't been turned by the glimmer of what his money could buy them. In fairness, most of them had needed no persuasion to kick back and enjoy what he could give them, but because she had started reluctant didn't mean that she would end up that way.

He hoped she wouldn't start getting ideas because that would be inconvenient.

And, just in case she *did*, even if the thought was just a shadow, a barely formulated shadow at the back of her brain, then he would have to cool the shows of ardour.

Certainly no more loss of self-control, which was what had regrettably happened just then.

'I like the way you're learning to play to the audience,' he murmured, low enough for her to hear and with an intimate smile that would convey to anyone who might be looking that sweet nothings were being whispered. Typical of a couple besotted with one another.

'Learning to play... Yes, well.'

'You're a quick study.' He dealt her a slashing smile and she smiled tightly back. 'No more cold war. No more protesting...I like it. It'll make this a whole lot easier.' He stood back and smiled at the saleswoman, who was managing to keep her distance without losing her quarry. 'Take care of her.' He gave her a little reassuring squeeze and waited until the blonde had approached them with an ingratiating smile.

'Darling—' Sammy looked up at him with a smile

that oozed sugary sweetness '—don't make me sound so helpless!' She patted his cheek and their eyes met—hers blue, pushing the boundaries, his dark, knowing just what she was up to.

'I can't think of anyone less helpless than you,' Leo murmured with heartfelt sincerity. 'I'll return for you in an hour. Think that will be long enough for you?'

'Oh,' Sammy said breezily, 'I might have bought the entire shop by then!'

Their eyes tangled and she could see exactly what he was thinking.

Bought the entire shop? Hardly. You don't like shopping, you don't care about clothes... You'll head for the least daring racks and you'll be done in under fifteen minutes.

Sammy smiled. 'I think,' she said slowly, batting her lashes and frowning in a faraway manner, finger tapping the side of her mouth, head tilted to one side, 'I might actually need a little longer. Why don't we meet at Giles King's offices at three?' Was this what being assertive with a man was like? It felt good, particularly when Leo frowned, caught on the back foot by a suggestion he hadn't anticipated.

It dawned on her that he was accustomed to calling the shots in every single area of his life. As far as he was concerned, he was paying her for her participation in this charade and he didn't expect her to do anything but follow his lead. She smiled brightly at him.

'You don't know where his offices are,' Leo pointed out.

'I think I'm smart enough to make my way there. I know the name of his firm.' She turned to the blonde, who was watching this exchange with fascinated interest. 'Men. They really *do* like to think of us as the weaker species, don't they?'

'I would never dream of being so cavalier where you are concerned, my sweet.' Leo wasn't sure whether to be amused by these antics, impressed by her ingenuity because she was putting on a show of loving familiarity that would have taken some beating, or uneasy because he wasn't on familiar ground and he had no idea where she was heading with this show of independence.

Then he relaxed.

Where could she possibly be going? As always, he had everything under control and, in the meantime, well, who ever said that life had to be predictable *all* of the time?

He thought that he might just start enjoying the next week and a half...

CHAPTER SIX

IT WAS A mad rush. Who knew that choosing some clothes and having bits and pieces done could actually take up so much of a person's time?

She'd whizzed through the shop, enjoying the heady feeling of having the snooty saleswoman bend over backwards to make sure she got exactly what she wanted.

Before they'd left the hotel, with Sammy still in protest mode at being told that her clothes were too cheap to be seen in when she was supposed to be engaged to him, he had urged her to buy whatever she wanted.

He already had details of her bank account and he had told her that if she didn't want him handing over his credit card to a salesperson because it went against her feminist instincts then she was free to use her own—he would ensure sufficient money was deposited into her account to cover all costs. He'd named a sum that had stunned her into silence and had shrugged when she had told him that she wouldn't know how to spend that amount of money because surely a few items of clothing couldn't cost very much.

Her plan had been to select the least outrageously expensive items of clothing and, likewise, the least flamboyant.

Plans, she discovered, could change in a heartbeat.

At the end of forty-five minutes in the boutique, and another forty-five minutes in two other boutiques farther along in the shady, exclusive arcade, she was weighed down by several bags, and two hours after that the hands holding those bags had been manicured and the feet shod in some rather delightful sandals, which were far more attractive than her canvas shoes and the hair... She felt like a million dollars.

But it had been an almighty rush. She hadn't been able to stop for food and, without breakfast, her stomach was intent on reminding her that sustenance was a lot more important than appearance.

And, for the first time in her life, Sammy didn't agree. She just had time to dash to the hotel, dump all the bags, change clothes and make sure she looked the part before she was back out to the car, which was on permanent standby just for her.

Now, with barely seconds to spare, she gazed at the graceful Victorian building that housed the law firm Leo was using to represent his interests.

Drawing in a deep breath, she purposefully strode towards the grey brick building, checked in at reception and was shown towards a conference room on the first floor.

Tension knotted her stomach. Nerves at the thought of the meeting that lay ahead and nerves at the new look she was sporting and how that new look would be received.

Did she look silly? she wondered.

She had felt so confident in the shop but then the saleswoman was in the business for a reason; she was adept at flogging very expensive clothes to women and part of her tactics would involve lavish praise and over-the-top compliments.

She told herself that instead of focusing on her silly clothes she should focus instead on what really mattered, which was the fate of a five-year-old girl whose life could be changed forever by what went on in that conference room.

This wasn't her. This person in shiny, expensive new clothes, seeking other people's approval and admiration. This wasn't her and it wasn't how she had been brought up!

Chin up, priorities firmly back in place, she took a deep breath and confidently entered the room, brushing past the young girl who had stepped back, holding the door open for her.

She only faltered for a second.

The room was absolutely enormous and there was nothing old-fashioned about the decor. A long, sleek table, so highly polished that it was as reflective as a mirror, dominated the central area, long enough to seat twenty people comfortably. To the back was a small circle of chairs and one wall was taken up with a white screen for presentations. There was a laptop in front of every chair. By the window, a sideboard, of the same highly polished wood as the conference table, housed coffee and tea-making facilities and plates of biscuits and tiny cakes, none of which appeared to have been touched.

Sammy took in all of this in a matter of seconds but, even as she was absorbing the surroundings, she remained entirely focused on the people sitting at that long conference table.

Leo easily dominated the group of eight. He was

sprawled back in his chair, which he had pushed away from the table, and his face was thoughtful and shuttered. He looked exactly like what he was—a lean, dangerous predator out to win.

But her eyes lingered on him for only a few moments because almost immediately she noticed the woman sitting directly opposite him and she knew, without having to be told, that this was Gail Jamieson.

She was small. Even sitting, Sammy could tell that she was no taller than five-two, maybe less, and she was the sort of woman who made jaws drop and caused heads to turn.

Her hair was a big bouffant and very blond, and her face tried desperately to belie her age, but the work she'd had done, rather than making her seem younger than her years, had somehow managed to age her.

Her eyes were wide and unblinking, her skin unnaturally line-free and her lips were pillowy and painted a bright fuchsia-pink, perfectly matching the colour of her formal suit which, likewise, matched her high stilettos.

She sought Leo, who had risen to greet her, and when he enfolded her in a brief embrace she wanted to stay there because she knew that the second she was released she would be in the firing line of Gail and her bank of representatives.

She had come out to play hardball and she wasn't going to pretend otherwise.

The conversation, the discussion of technicalities, voices being raised, Gail stridently talking over her lawyer and Leo responding coldly and with the sort of utter self-composure that should have been seen as a warning of armoury ready and poised for action passed in a blur and before she knew it the meeting was over.

As Sammy followed Leo—who was talking in a low, urgent voice to one of his lawyers—out of the room, Gail strode towards her.

'Funny,' Gail said, tugging Sammy to a stop, 'Sean never mentioned you when he spoke about his step-brother.'

'Er...'

'And he spoke about Leo *a lot*. But never mentioned you. Not once. Funny that, wouldn't you say?'

'Why is it funny?' Sammy finally found her voice. She darted a look at Leo, who had not noticed that she had been held back. He had his hands in his pockets and she could see from his body language that he was one hundred per cent focused on whatever was being said to him.

'Because...'

Bright pink nails dug into Sammy's arm. When Sammy looked down she was skewered by light blue, unblinking eyes.

'Because he followed everything Leo did, and I mean *everything*. Knew who Leo was going out with almost before he was going out with them! But he never mentioned you. Not once. So I'm just curious as to how it is that Leo's suddenly engaged to be married. To someone he didn't know from Adam two months ago.'

'Love.'

Leo's voice was deep and dark and held just the tiniest hint of menace.

Sammy felt his arm around her waist and she leant into him, relieved beyond belief that he had interrupted what showed promise of being a difficult exchange.

'Ever experienced that, Gail? Or has the love of a good deal always won out over the love of a good man?'

Gail's lips pursed. Her ample bosom heaved. Every strand of heavily dyed blond hair seemed to bristle with rage.

'Over my dead body,' she spat, 'are you going to get the kid. And don't think that you can fool me into thinking that you're suddenly Mr Respectable because you happen to show up here with some woman wearing an engagement ring.'

'I hope this isn't the sound of you spoiling for a fight,' Leo drawled. 'Because I don't like fighting but if I have to, I always emerge the winner.'

The pack of lawyers had disappeared, shooting off in separate directions.

'I've brought that kid up like she was my own!'

'Then I shudder to think what sort of upbringing your daughter was subjected to,' Leo informed her coldly. 'From what I've unearthed about you, a life of alcohol with a revolving door of unsuitable younger men hardly sounds like a woman who should have possession of a child.'

'Adele relies on me. I'm all she's known since she was born. Louise and Sean had their problems and I had the kid in my care more regularly than they did.'

'I have neither the inclination nor the time to get into an argument with you. If you want a fight, then fight through our lawyers. Don't ever let me find you trying to sideline my fiancée into any sort of conversation or, worse, trying to intimidate her in any way whatsoever. Do you read me loud and clear?'

He hadn't bothered to look in Gail's direction when he said this and his voice was calm and perfectly modulated but, even so, Sammy felt a shiver of apprehension on behalf of the other woman should she decide to ignore the warning.

And Gail must have felt the same. Her bravado evaporated as they stepped back outside into the sweltering heat and the pulsing throng of people in shorts and tee shirts.

'I don't want to fight either.' Her voice was plaintive. 'If it comes to it, I just want what's fair for me and all the time I've put in with the kid. If it weren't for me...'

'I've already heard that tale of self-sacrifice.' Leo's arm was still draped possessively over Sammy's shoulders and he was looking at Gail now, through narrowed eyes. 'It failed to impress me the first time and it fails to impress me now.'

Sammy found that she had been holding her breath and she expelled it in one long, shuddering sigh of relief as the older woman merged into the crowds, a dollop of bright pink that was visible as she weaved along the pavements, finally vanishing round a corner.

'Wow,' she said weakly. 'She's a force of nature.'

'She's an idiot for thinking she can win this.'

'She scared me,' Sammy confessed. 'I understand now why you felt you had to show up here with me in tow. I thought you had been exaggerating.'

His arm was still around her and she was suddenly self-conscious of how she looked. She had been talked into a long skirt that was light and fell beautifully to her ankles in various tie-dyed shades of apricot and grey. It was the height of modesty but the top twinned to go with it lovingly curved over her full breasts, dipping to expose just a hint of cleavage. The overall effect was one that made her look sexy and respectable at the same time. She had twirled in front of that mirror in the boutique and marvelled that she even had the ability to pull off a look like that.

She had thought that she would be excruciatingly self-conscious walking into that room in the lawyer's office but, in fact, she had barely been aware of what she was wearing.

'I hadn't expected her there.' There had been other things Leo hadn't been expecting, the way his *fiancée* looked in that outfit being one of them. She'd walked into that room and every head had turned in her direction and his stomach had clenched as he'd taken in those darting, quickly concealed looks of appreciation from the men in the room. Including his own top lawyer who was fifty if he was a day, short and balding. Hope, he had thought grimly, certainly sprang eternal. Which hadn't made him any the less annoyed.

'I think—' he found his eyes straying to the sway of her heavy breasts and had to force himself to look away '—she decided that if she caught everyone on the hop then she might have the element of surprise.'

As if by magic, their car was pulling to the kerb, slowing for them to hop in, which was a blessed relief because it was so hot and humid. The long skirt was far cooler than trousers or anything shorter or tighter, but Sammy had still started perspiring within moments of leaving the lawyer's air-conditioned office.

Resting against the seat with her eyes closed for a couple of seconds, Sammy then turned to look at Leo. 'I barely took in what was going on. I was very nervous.'

'Legal back and forth,' Leo said drily. 'I've sat through enough meetings with lawyers to know that it's a very delicate rally that gets played in any situation where two sides are trying to meet.'

'*Are* you trying to meet? I mean—in the middle with Gail?'

Leo dealt her a cool sideways smile. 'I'm prepared to make some concessions. Louise and Sean made lousy parents and there's some truth in what she says, that the care of Adele fell on her shoulders more than should have been necessary. I've done extensive background checks on the woman, however. And, whilst she was technically in charge of her granddaughter, everything she says has to be taken with a pinch of salt. She's been demanding and receiving vast sums of money from my father and, well, you can see for yourself where some of that money has gone. There have been some plastic surgeons rubbing their hands in glee every time she's phoned to make an appointment. I know down to the last penny where the money's gone.' He shrugged. 'But if she doesn't put up a fight, then I'm willing to leave her with some cash.'

'She doesn't believe that this is a real engagement,' Sammy mused cautiously.

Her body tensed then flamed as he ran his eyes very, very slowly over her. She hadn't thought he'd noticed what she was wearing and then she'd decided that it wasn't her place to feel disappointed if he hadn't commented because there was no reason for him to. He'd noticed. It was there in the heat of his brooding, fabulous eyes. By the time he had finished his leisurely inspection of her, her face was bright red and she would have told him in no uncertain terms that *looking at her like that* wasn't part of the arrangement except she had enjoyed every heat-filled second of that visual appraisal.

'Maybe she had her doubts when the news was first broken to her that I was no longer going to fit into the role of inveterate womaniser and unsuitable guardian which she had hoped for… Maybe she showed up here today with the express purpose of making sure her law-yers got on board with her way of thinking…but I think it's fair to say that after today…'

'I know what you're saying,' Sammy told him, break-ing eye contact to find that the palms of her hands were slippery with perspiration and that had nothing to do with the temperature in the car. 'You were right. It would have looked peculiar if I had been wearing my department store clothes. Especially given that the woman looks as though she would be able to tell de-signer from fake without any trouble at all.'

'So good thinking. You chose just the right mix of daring and prudish. No one could doubt that you were a respectable teacher with just the right amount of sex appeal.'

'To attract a man of your high standards?' He'd no-ticed her but only insofar as she had chosen the right clothes for the job at hand. She gave a tinkling laugh that implied that she knew exactly what he meant.

'You're putting words into my mouth.' He wondered whether she was aware of just how incredibly erotic that alluring mix of daring and prudish actually was. He had given his lawyer some background details on her so they were all predisposed to think of her as highly respectable, moral, responsible—a shining example of just the sort of woman any man would bring home to his mother.

That said, had she looked too much like the moral, respectable teacher, they would all have been a bit be-mused because how could a guy reasonably go from an actress whose face graced billboards to a teacher who was camera-shy and modestly dressed? Gail was astute. She would have sniffed out a phoney from a hundred paces and Sammy, resentful in borrowed clothing, would have been easily sniffed out. Better she be comfortable than bristling with transparent resentment.

But her choice of dress had been nothing short of inspired.

When they arrived back at the hotel he suggested dinner at one of the several excellent restaurants in the hotel. She could take her pick.

Sammy had forgotten all about her hunger pangs. Now, they resurfaced with a vengeance and no sooner had they sat down and bread was brought to them than she tucked in. To heck with pretending that she had the appetite of a sparrow, she thought.

'I'm ravenous,' she confessed, resisting the urge to help herself to more bread. 'What were you talking to your lawyer about? When we were leaving?'

'I don't think I've ever heard any woman admit to being ravenous.'

'I used to try dieting when I was younger but I gave up after a while. If you're hungry, I don't see the point of starving yourself.'

Sammy thought that since theirs was a phoney relationship based on necessity on both sides, there was no need to try and be someone she wasn't. She'd been out with guys in the past and she'd always been conscious of trying hard to be as ladylike as possible, which, in restaurants, had meant ordering healthy salads and dishes with weird ingredients that sounded good for you. But she wasn't out to impress Leo and he certainly wasn't open to being impressed by her. For him, she was a means to an end. She didn't have to edit her personality at all. She was the hired help. He touched her when he had to and when he looked at her, the way he had done just then, his dark eyes lazy and speculative, the only thing he was speculating about was how convincing she would be in her choice of clothing and whether there was anything else she could do to make sure he got what he had come to get.

'Watching their weight is part of some women's livelihoods.' He was fascinated by the enthusiasm with which she was working her way through her hearty starter of aubergine *parmigiana*.

'Of course it's important to be healthy. This is delicious. I don't do much eating out in expensive restaurants. On a teacher's salary, cheap and cheerful is usually all I can afford, and especially with the money problems Mum's been having.'

'As you know, my father offered her money countless times.'

'She's proud. She would never accept anything from your dad. I was surprised when she seemed to be all for this charade, though. I think it's a relief for her to know that I'll be getting something I've wanted for a really long time out of it and that it's not just about making sure that the mortgage is paid off.'

Plates were cleared. Wine was poured. She looked the most relaxed he had seen her since they had arrived in the country and he assumed that that was because the first steps had been taken towards resolving what they had come for.

The wine was also having its effect. She was on her second glass. He didn't think that she would be someone accustomed to drinking much alcohol.

Funny, he had known her for a long time and yet

he felt as though he was getting to know her for the *first* time.

She had ordered a pie for her main course. It arrived with much fanfare and he couldn't help grinning as she tucked into it, taking a few seconds first to appreciate the mouthwatering beauty of the golden pastry and the rich red wine gravy bubbling through the crusty lid.

Sammy could feel his eyes on her but when he spoke it was to say, pensively, 'I'm beginning to realise that a woman who doesn't enjoy her food is probably not a woman worth going out with.'

'What do you mean?' Sammy looked at him, her wide, bright blue eyes startled.

'There's something extremely sensual about food, wouldn't you agree? About someone who appreciates the pleasure of eating.'

Confused, Sammy, fork poised in mid-air and mouth half-open, was excruciatingly aware of Leo watching her as she ate a mouthful of the delicious beef and celeriac pie.

Leo watched her. It was an intoxicating sight. She was so unlike any woman he had ever been attracted to before. He could imagine that she was the sort of woman who came with all sorts of fairy-tale daydreams and unrealistic fantasies about happy-ever-after and soulmates. The sort who secretly collected bridal magazines and dreamed of having a dozen kids. A woman who came fully equipped with high moral values, which was why, he was forced to concede, she was so disapproving of him.

Disapproving but not immune.

With instincts that barely registered on any kind of conscious scale, Leo knew that.

It was there in the tide of colour that flooded her cheeks whenever he looked at her for a second longer than was strictly necessary.

Like now.

It was there in the way she lowered her eyes and half turned away when she was caught looking at him.

And it had been there in her reaction to him every single time he had touched her.

She'd quivered, as if her whole body had suddenly come alive with an undercurrent of electricity over which she had no control.

Sammy cleared her throat and frantically tried to find something innocuous to say to break the sudden electric tension stretching between them.

'You…you were going to tell me what you were chatting to your lawyer about. When Ms Jamieson got me to one side. Um…'

'Was I?'

'Stop…stop looking at me like that.'

'Like what?' Leo raised his eyebrows in amused query.

Squirming because she was so out of her comfort zone, Sammy licked her lips nervously and looked away. 'Is there something you want to say about, um, about the way I look?'

'Yes,' Leo said gravely and Sammy's eyes flew towards him in sudden consternation.

'You said that my choice of dress was…that you liked what I had selected to wear.'

'Do you want honesty from me?'

'I don't know. Maybe not.' Sammy was blushing furiously.

'Okay.' Leo shrugged.

The conversation resumed on less contentious matters. Leo had been to the country several times, although only to Melbourne twice, and over the rest of the meal he proved a witty companion, full of interesting anecdotes about the places he had been. She truly began to appreciate the extent of his vast wealth as he told her about the properties he owned, scattered across the globe. She listened, asked questions and kept thinking, *did she want his honesty?* What did he think he had to be *honest* about?

'You might as well tell me,' she said in a rush, putting down her fork next to the chocolate brownie dessert she was halfway through.

Leo had known that sooner or later she would ask him to explain what he had meant, although if she hadn't he had resolved not to push the issue. He was attracted to her and there was a danger in that situation. He had agreed to this charade, and to his father's choosing her as a candidate to help pull it off, because he had known that she would be a safe proposition. Sex complicated things and he had not wanted complications. Eventually persuaded by his father to undertake this mission, he had come to the conclusion that in and out as fast as possible would be his approach. Complications of any sort were to be avoided at all costs.

He signalled for the tab to sign but didn't take his eyes off her face. 'There is a small bar area farther along from the restaurant. They serve very good coffee.'

Sammy nodded. 'Just say what you have to say,' she half pleaded, tripping along beside him as he led the way to the cosy sitting area which, presumably, he had used before when he hadn't been in the suite with her. It was a perfect place to work in peace. Secluded, quiet, tucked away in a spot that was far from noise and crowds.

The fact that he was shying away from telling her what he had to tell her said something. It said that he knew she wouldn't be happy with whatever it was he had to say. Maybe his lawyer had said something to him during that little chat they had had when the meeting had come to a close.

She felt like a trainee about to be told that she hadn't, unfortunately, passed her probation because her work had not been up to scratch.

'When I agreed to do this—' he waited until she was sitting and then sat opposite her, adjusting his chair to accommodate the length of his body '—I decided that you were as ideal as it got for the job.'

'I know.' Defensiveness had crept into her voice. 'You knew how to get to me because of Mum. You knew that the money would be invaluable and you knew that my dream was to start my own freelance business so you had a good idea of what you could put down on the table to ensure I was left without much of a choice.'

'Spare me the victim speech, Sammy. You could have said no. We all have choices.'

'You thought I was convincingly *ordinary*,' she elaborated with grudging honesty. 'Have you decided that I'm just *too* ordinary? Because I don't know how I can overcome that. I can't turn into someone I'm not.'

Leo looked at her for so long that she began to fidget. 'You're not what I'd expected,' he said silkily. 'I'm seeing things I never saw before when we happened to bump into one another in the past.'

Sammy's mouth ran dry. She opened her mouth to

say something but nothing emerged. She had no idea where he was going with this. She felt as though she had deliberately jumped into the path of an unstoppable train and would have to live with the consequences. If she could break eye contact she might be able to do something sensible like stand up and leave, but she couldn't seem to do anything but stare.

'There's something about you,' he murmured roughly, his sharp eyes taking in every small reaction in her expressive face. He'd never made a pass at any woman without knowing the outcome in advance. In fact, he'd seldom had to make passes at all. But this was different and he felt a swift adrenaline rush as he contemplated laying his cards on the table without fully knowing how she would react.

He wanted her. It made no sense and it was a nuisance, but she appealed to him in ways that were visceral and primitive and beyond his control.

He knew that he could keep trying to impose common sense but wouldn't it just be easier to scratch that itch? They were both adults and he suspected that she was as interested in exploring the chemistry between them that had blown up as he was. The fact that he wasn't *entirely* sure, instead of being a turn-off, had fired up his libido even more.

'Something about me?' Sammy squeaked.

'You're sexy,' Leo admitted in a roughened undertone. 'I can't seem to look at you without wondering what it would be like to take your clothes off.'

Sammy was having severe trouble breathing. Was he joking? Was this some kind of sadistic lead up to something really offensive he wanted to say?

'Of course I'm not,' she breathed shakily and he

reached out and played with her fingers, toying with them and sending her scattered nerves every which way.

'And not just when you decide to make the most of your fantastic figure,' Leo assured her. 'So this has created a situation I hadn't banked on having to deal with.' He shot her a crooked smile that sent her blood pressure doing all sorts of irregular things. 'We're sharing a bed,' he told her bluntly, 'and I'm not going to beat around the bush. I want you. And I sense you want me, too.'

'Do you?' Sammy's voice was barely audible. 'I… I don't…'

'No?' He leaned forward suddenly, catching her by surprise. He reached out, hand curving at the nape of her neck, and drew her towards him. It was as if she had been hovering like a satellite circling a magnetic force which was warm and bright and irresistible and now that magnetic force was pulling her in and she wanted to go.

She could barely gasp before his mouth covered hers and his kiss was long and gentle and she fell into it with the ease of a hapless swimmer getting caught in a whirlpool. It just sucked her in. She closed her eyes, shifted closer, knew that she should push him back but couldn't find the strength.

He thought that she was sexy.

Her fingers trembled as they came into contact with his dark hair. This was the riskiest thing she had ever done in her entire life. Nothing else came close. He was so out of her league that they barely inhabited the same planet and yet here she was, kissing him and never wanting that kiss to stop.

She moaned softly.

This was her fantasy guy, the guy who had played a starring role in her adolescent daydreams.

A guy any woman would give her right arm to find herself in a clinch with—just like this one.

A guy who wasn't hers.

Cold, brutal reality asserted itself and she tore herself away from the embrace. She was shaking like a leaf. Her lips felt swollen and bruised from where he had kissed her and she had to resist wiping the back of her hand across them.

This wasn't about love or even affection. She was in a make-believe situation with a make-believe fiancé who would never have looked at her twice under normal circumstances.

Suddenly he found her sexy?

Hilarious. She had met him countless times over the years and he had never found her sexy on any of those occasions. Maybe his eyes had changed over time, maybe he needed specs.

Overcome with mortification at how easily she had leapt to that kiss, she was brutal with herself as she wrapped her arms around her body and looked at him.

'I don't want to…I'm not interested…'

'Sure about that?'

'And I think it's best we just put that behind us and remember that we're…remember that this isn't *real*.'

'The engagement isn't real,' Leo affirmed in a low, husky voice. 'My wanting to get you into bed, on the other hand, couldn't be more real.' He abruptly sat back and relaxed into his chair. 'But if you want to kid yourself that it's a one-way street, then that's fine by me. Moving on to what you asked me, I was talking to my lawyer about Adele. We meet her tomorrow.'

Head spinning from the change of subject, Sammy could only stare at him. He'd drawn her in only to suddenly drop her from a great height and he couldn't have been clearer in telling her that he might fancy her, and she still found that impossible to imagine, but he could take her or leave her at the end of the day. It was up to her.

Her brain struggled to focus on what really mattered. 'Tomorrow.'

'She will be delivered here to the hotel at lunchtime. It's been quite an achievement and Gail fought tooth and nail against it but she lost. She only found out when she spoke to her lawyer after the meeting today.'

He stood, waiting for her to follow suit. They were about to head for the bedroom, for the king-sized bed that would suddenly feel as big as a matchbox after what he had said. Her skin tingled at the prospect of getting into it with him.

'Don't worry,' he murmured, reading her mind or maybe her expression of full-blown panicked apprehension, as they headed for the bank of lifts to take them to their suite. 'I've never forced myself on a woman and I don't intend to start now. I have work to do when we get back and by the time I get into that bed you will already be sound asleep. Unless, of course, you decide that sex between two consenting adults who are attracted to one another is worth exploring…' He laughed when she pointedly ignored him and grazed his finger along her cheek, keen eyes watching the heat of her reaction.

'Sweet dreams,' he called as she disappeared into the bedroom but before she could shut the door on him. 'And don't forget—we're engaged… It's only natural to take things to their final conclusion!'

CHAPTER SEVEN

LEO HAD THROWN down his gauntlet. He'd been nothing but truthful when he had told her that being attracted to her had been an unforeseen curveball. She had skittered away like a Victorian maiden, shrieking with pious moral outrage, but then he'd kissed her and she had melted into his arms. He had needed no further evidence that she would be his.

Naturally, he wasn't going to pursue her.

He had been taken aback when they reached the suite to discover that she seemed to be sticking to her *hands off* moral high ground. She had stood in front of the bedroom door, like a bouncer on a mission to deter unwanted riff-raff, and informed him that she would be having a bath and perhaps he could make good on his promise to work until she had fallen asleep.

She had actually used the term *make good*, while he had stared at her as it had slowly dawned on him that she might just be sticking to her guns.

Leo had been genuinely confused. He'd taken the rash decision to bypass common sense and lay his cards on the table and, having done so, he had been gratified to find that the attraction worked both ways.

So where was the problem?

He had hit the bedroom an hour and a half after she had disappeared and had found her barricaded on her side of the bed, with two of the sausage-shaped cushions separating them.

He had woken at five-thirty, as he always did, wherever in the world he happened to be, and she had given no indication that she was awake. Her back had resolutely been turned to him and she hadn't moved a muscle as he'd made for the bathroom, showered, dressed and then exited the bedroom.

For the first time in living memory, Leo was finding it impossible to concentrate on work.

He kept looking at the closed bedroom door as the time ticked by. What was she doing? Was she up? Getting dressed? Abseiling down the side of the building in an attempt to get away from him?

He was distracted and he didn't like it. He was making himself a cup of coffee when the bedroom door finally opened so he remained where he was, lounging against the kitchen wall, cup in hand, watching her over the rim of it as he sipped his coffee.

'Get you some?' He raised the mug towards her and Sammy nodded politely.

Whilst she felt as though the bags under her eyes were as big as suitcases and just as obvious, he looked as fresh as a daisy.

And as drop-dead gorgeous as she'd hoped he wouldn't.

She'd heard him the second he had slipped out of the bed and every nerve in her body had tensed. Then he'd run his shower, not even bothering to shut the bathroom door fully behind him, and she'd sneaked a surreptitious glance at him, peeking out from where she was safely cocooned under the sheets and blanket. Her heart had almost stopped beating. He had taken his jeans into the bathroom with him and he was as indecently clad as any human could be whilst wearing trousers.

The top button was undone, the zip slightly down and, in the back light from the bathroom, she could make out every detail of his sinewy and completely bare upper half. The jeans rode low down lean hips and as he padded to the chest of drawers, quietly retrieving a tee shirt, she was treated to perfection in motion. He'd slipped the tee shirt over his head and she had squeezed her eyes tightly shut and drawn her breath in sharply because watching the ripple of muscle was just too much.

She had felt light-headed. How on earth was she going to be able to keep him at arm's length? No, more to the point, how on earth was she going to keep *herself* away from him at arm's length?

She'd never been so tempted by anyone in her entire life and she couldn't understand how it was that someone like him, who had absolutely *none* of the qualities she looked for in a man, would be the person to tempt her.

She had waited until he had shut the bedroom door behind him, then she had nodded off briefly before waking up and listening to make sure that he was well and truly absorbed in his work outside.

She'd felt like a thief, hiding out in a closet, forced to keep perfectly silent or else risk being caught red-handed with the family heirlooms.

Except what did she have to be sneaky about?

She'd kissed him back but then she'd pulled away and let him know in no uncertain terms that she was not up for a romp in the hay. She had stood her ground and she had retired to bed rather proud of herself.

The trouble was that her body refused to play along. She'd never found herself in the position of having to exercise denial when it came to a guy and denial physically *hurt*. Between her legs had throbbed and her breasts had ached. Her whole body had felt as though it needed to be touched and, lying in the darkness, her mind had been filled with images of him caressing her, taking her...

But Sammy knew that she couldn't allow herself to forget that this was a game. It would be dangerous to start blurring the edges between fiction and reality.

Consequently, she had dressed for the day ahead in the most sensible of the outfits she had bought.

It was going to be baking hot outside. She wasn't sure what the plans for the day were but she assumed that he would spend the morning working. At any rate, she would encourage him to do so, which would leave her free to explore the city until Adele was dropped off at midday.

She was wearing pale blue flip-flops, loose-fitting cotton trousers, also pale blue in colour, and a loose-fitting sleeveless top, patterned with a riot of tiny flowers that stopped at the waist so that when she moved a little sliver of tummy was visible. She had tied her hair in a high ponytail and escaped tendrils framed her heart-shaped face.

Leo took his time looking at her and when she blushed, he grinned and shrugged.

'I won't touch. At least not unless the occasion demands it.' He held his hands up in a gesture of mock surrender. 'But,' he drawled, 'I never promised that I wouldn't look.'

He turned around, fixed her a mug of coffee and sauntered towards her. Her blue eyes were wary but stubborn and he liked that.

'You shouldn't look at me like that,' Sammy said shakily.

'I can't help it.' He handed her the mug but he didn't move back. Instead, he remained towering over her, crowding her.

'I'm not going to sleep with you.'

'Did you hear me ask?'

'No, but…'

'I'm not going to pretend that I don't want to, though,' he said pensively, sipping the excellent coffee, amused when she shimmied away from him. He wondered whether she was scared that she might be driven to touch if she stayed too close to him.

His whole body went into overdrive when he imagined her coming to him, unable to fight the force of their mutual attraction.

'What are your plans for the day?' Sammy thought that if she didn't change the conversation he would carry on looking at her with those brooding, amazing, fabulously sexy eyes and she would go up in flames.

'*My* plans?'

'I thought as we aren't due to meet Adele until lunchtime that you might want to get some work done.'

'Why would you think that?'

'Because you obviously have a lot on your plate. I mean, you don't get to bed until very late and you're up early so that you can catch up.'

'A wild number of misconceptions in that statement,'

Leo said lazily. 'I'm my own boss. I'm not a hamster on a treadmill, running furiously for fear of getting left behind. And yes, I don't happen to need much sleep but I assure you that I would be more than happy to hit the sack early and get out of it late if the incentive was right...'

'Will you stop doing that!' But it turned her on. Why bother to pretend otherwise? She *liked* the way his eyes on her made her feel. She *enjoyed* the slow, crazy burn she got when he talked like that, saying things that made her feel sexy and feminine, which were two things she had never felt in her life before. He was the equivalent of a slab of wicked, wicked chocolate. You wanted it so much but you knew that you had to fight the temptation because one bite wouldn't be enough and it certainly wouldn't be good for you.

'I wouldn't dream of leaving you to your own devices today,' he said, pocketing his cell phone and heading towards the door. 'We'll get breakfast, then do some city exploring and get back here in time to meet Adele.'

Sammy knew when she was beaten. She hoped he wouldn't wage his devastating assault on her senses. She found herself fast-forwarding to conversations they might or might not have. She braced herself to keep pushing him back.

She was disproportionately disappointed when the morning passed with him being the perfect gentleman.

He held her hand but he didn't try to kiss her. He looked at her, but those looks didn't linger longer than necessary. She had expected to spend three hours rigid with tension but he seduced her into talking about herself and, afterwards, she couldn't imagine how he had done that.

How had he managed to bypass her guard?

'Are you nervous?' she asked as they were making their way back to the hotel.

'About what?' Leo looked at her with a frown. It had taken more willpower than he knew he possessed not to touch her.

'Seeing Adele.'

'The only thing I'm nervous about is this custody battle not going in my favour. My father wouldn't recover.'

'Have you spoken to him?' Sammy's voice softened for she was hugely fond of the elderly man.

'Two emotionally charged emails and one phone call where he sounded as though a nervous breakdown wasn't far away. This has to work out. There's no choice.'

'Do you have much experience of children?'

'Is that a necessity?'

'It helps.'

'I don't.' He turned to her as they entered the cool of the hotel lobby. 'So it's just as well that I have someone by my side who can make up for my shortfall, isn't it?'

He looked past her and then pulled her close to him and dropped a kiss on her head.

Sammy had followed his eyes and almost immediately her heart went out to the child sitting on one of the long grey sofas in the lobby, next to a man she recognised as one of the lawyers from the other side.

Adele was a pretty little thing, with long dark hair caught in two braids which ended in pink ribbons, neatly tied into bows. They matched her dress and her shiny patent plastic shoes. She was sitting ramrod straight, her hands folded on her lap and next to her was a bright pink bag. Not a backpack but a handbag. Her face was small and serious and she looked terrified.

Leo hadn't seen her for well over a year. Suddenly, the enormity of his undertaking was brought home to him. This wasn't a deal. There was no company involved, no stock market to follow in the wake of a deal, no factory that might or might not need to be closed, no redundancies to be handled and workforce to be relocated. This was a living, breathing child and he tensed.

Sammy felt it. He had faltered. No one would have noticed, but *she* did. She looped her arm through his without looking at him, took a deep breath and headed directly for the little girl who was primly sitting on the grey sofa.

'Hi.' She ignored the lawyer, who had risen and taken Leo to one side so that they could have a confab. 'I'm Sammy.' She knelt down so that she was on eye level with Adele. She was accustomed to young children. She was comfortable around them and she knew how to make them feel comfortable around her. It was part and parcel of being a good teacher.

Leo watched her. The lawyer was busily telling him about the arrangements that had been secured for the day and the outcome of the long meeting they had the day before. Leo heard everything but his attention was riveted to the woman kneeling in front of the little girl. All her natural warmth was on show. She was very tactile, was resting her hand on Adele's arm, and he could see the way the child was being drawn into whatever she was being told.

Compared to her, his girlfriends of the past, with their frantic self-absorption, now struck him as somewhat brittle.

There was an earthy, engaging and entirely uncontrived sexiness about his fake fiancée that kept turning him on. He dragged his attention away to finalise details of handing Adele back to the lawyer and then, lawyer gone, he joined the twosome, standing above them until Sammy straightened.

Introductions were made. Adele stared at him with huge navy blue eyes and noticeably cringed back.

'What now?' Leo asked roughly, on the back foot for the first time in his life.

Sammy gave Adele's hand a tiny reassuring squeeze. 'Leave it to me.' She stood on tiptoe and impulsively kissed the side of his mouth because he looked uncertain and weirdly vulnerable and she liked that. She liked knowing that, for the first time in his life, probably, he wasn't quite in control of a situation.

They had Adele for lunch and the remainder of the afternoon, and Sammy allowed the little girl to choose what she wanted to do. They lunched at a popular restaurant where everything was geared towards children, from what was on the menu to the colouring books and games they could enjoy while they waited for their food.

Then they went to the Melbourne Aquarium.

'Do you do stuff like this often?' Sammy asked casually at one point during the day, and Adele shook her head and whispered that sometimes Sarah would take her out but mostly she stayed in and played with her toys.

'Sarah?'

'The girl who looks after me,' Adele said. 'Nana Gail doesn't have much time because she goes out a lot and she's busy all the time.'

Leo tried to involve himself but he was so clearly

making an effort that it had the opposite effect of scaring Adele away. The bigger the effort he made the more alarmed she seemed to get. And the more frustrated he became. By the end of the day, there was a tentative hug from Adele for Sammy and a polite handshake for Leo. Pink plastic bag dangling on her tiny wrist and feet beautifully turned out because, she had confided haltingly, she did ballet lessons three times a week because it suited her grandmother who met friends for early evening drinks then, she looked like a miniature queen politely bidding one of her subjects goodbye.

'Well, that was a complete fiasco,' was the first thing Leo said as they headed up to the suite. 'I need a drink. Actually, scratch that. I need several drinks.'

Sammy was on a high. She had had a wonderful time. She had been as nervous as a kitten about meeting the lawyers, about meeting Gail and about the whole pretend charade, and Adele had been a shining light, returning her to her comfort zone. And it had felt good to find herself in the leading role for the first time, rather than tumbling around on a roller coaster ride into which she had suddenly been plunged.

'It wasn't a fiasco,' she said, stepping into the lift and then turning to him as they were whooshed up to their suite. 'It went really well.'

'It went really well for *you*,' Leo amended, lounging against the mirrored panel, thumbs hooked on the waistband of his jeans. 'You're obviously a natural when it comes to children.'

'It's my job. Besides, I really liked her. She's been through a rough time. That's why she's so quiet and scared. I can't imagine what it must have been like having two very young and irresponsible parents and then, when they're no longer around, having to cope with a grandmother who clearly doesn't particularly want her around.'

'You're really...' He looked at her, head tilted to one side until colour crawled into her cheeks.

'I'm really *what*?'

Leo opened the door with his key card and pushed it, stepping back so that she could brush past him. She smelled of sun and the outside—a flowery, healthy, clean, natural smell that filled his nostrils, making him want to take a step back and close his eyes.

'Caring.' He took up where he'd left off.

Over the years, he had heard all about her from his father, who was her number one fan. It had mostly gone in one ear and out the other. But he remembered things he had been told now, about how good she was at her job, how popular she was with her pupils, the sort of girl who took in stray animals and nursed them back to rude health. Privately, it had all sounded like the perfect description of a bore with whom he couldn't possibly have anything in common. Pious and saintly, which had always been the image he had been fed, couldn't have been further from the sort of person who could engage his attention.

But she was nothing like that image he had built in his head. She didn't set about drawing attention to herself like most women he knew were prone to doing, but she was still curiously capable of holding his attention in ways he didn't really get.

And she was naturally empathetic. He had seen that for himself with Adele today, if it hadn't already been apparent.

She was feisty but caring, argumentative and stubborn as a mule but had what it took to gain the trust of a suspicious five-year-old. She didn't strut her stuff and blushed like a teenager. He couldn't imagine anyone less likely to make a pass at him, even if she wanted to. She believed in true love and was seriously romantic.

In all respects, she managed to tick none of the boxes that he had always thought counted when it came to women.

But the more he was in her company, the more turned on he was by her.

Sammy thought that he had succeeded in turning *caring* into *as boring as watching paint dry*.

'You mean I'm dull!' She laughed off the knot of hurt that tightened inside her.

He was pouring himself something from the well-stocked minibar and she accepted a glass of wine because she was still smarting from the *dull as dishwater* description she had read into his words.

It wasn't yet six-thirty. She guessed that the plan would be for them to go somewhere for dinner. After two nights, she no longer felt awkward about the whole sharing a bed situation. He seemed to have an amazing ability to detach. He might tell her that he found her sexy, but he didn't feel any compulsion to follow through.

Thank heavens, was what she firmly told herself.

'You're anything but dull.' Leo had opted for red wine over his instinctive choice of something a lot harder and he looked at her as he sipped it.

The day's outing had done great things to her satiny skin, which was fast acquiring a pale gold colour and turning her blond hair even blonder. The ponytail had disappeared at some point during the day and her hair now tumbled in curls and ringlets over her shoulders. She was the picture of health, the perfect image of someone who didn't care about what the weather was doing to her make-up or her hairstyle. Once he'd started staring, he found that he couldn't stop and he had to physically turn away and prowl towards the floor-to-ceiling window that overlooked a park that was bathed in the last of the sunshine.

'I just want to say…' He frowned and tried to locate the right words.

'What?' The wine was delicious and Sammy wandered to where he was standing and absently looked outside before turning her attention to him.

'I want to thank you.' His voice was gruff and she gazed at him, bewildered.

'Thank me for what?'

'You took charge today.' He drained his glass, twirled it thoughtfully between his fingers and then gently placed it on the squat glass table next to him. 'Quite honestly, I'm not sure how things would have gone if you hadn't been there.'

'You would have… You…er…'

'I can tell you're confused because you can't decide which of the many things I did today made just the right impression on Adele. You're spoilt for choice.'

Sammy blushed and laughed because he was incredibly endearing when he was being self-deprecating.

'You would have coped. I have a lot of experience when it comes to dealing with young children and you don't have any. I guess it was always going to be easier for me. I also don't have any emotional investment in the situation whereas you do.'

'That's a very generous take on the situation. I like that about you.'

'What do you mean?'

'You give the benefit of the doubt to people.'

'And you don't?' Her heart was beating like a jack-hammer because the conversation was so personal. She liked the feeling of playing with fire. She liked not caring whether she got burnt or not.

'I really want to make love to you.'

Sammy froze. Her eyes widened and her breathing slowed to a near stop. His voice was thick with intent.

'I mean,' Leo continued huskily, 'we could carry on pretending that there's nothing between us. I could work out here until I'm certain that you're asleep and then I can creep into the bed and wake up before you start surfacing from your beauty sleep and we can both kid ourselves that we haven't shared the same bed at all and that, even if we did, it doesn't matter because we're just two business associates on a job and that if there's some chemistry then we can choose to ignore that. I can make sure not to look at you for too long and only touch you when we're in public. I can pretend that I don't feel you tremble when I do touch you. I can pretend that you don't sigh softly when I kiss you. The alternative, however...'

He allowed that to stretch out into the silence between them while he continued to pin her to the spot with his eyes.

'This isn't real.' Sammy heard the desperation in her voice as she tried to cling to sanity.

'We're not really engaged,' Leo agreed in a rough-ened undertone. 'And we won't really be walking up the aisle with stars in our eyes. But *this*...' he cupped the side of her face with his hand and then caressed her smooth skin, dropping his finger to her mouth and tracing the outline of her lips '...*this* is real.'

'We shouldn't...'

'You're preaching to the converted,' Leo confessed with raw honesty. 'I know that making love isn't what either of us had planned. I know I'm probably the last guy in the world you would actively hunt down...' He wasn't even aware of leaving a pause after he said that but he was piqued when she didn't rush to fill it with a denial.

'I'm not the kind of girl who falls in bed with someone.'

'No.' Her skin was so soft and silky. It was torture trying to suppress his very natural urge to take and conquer.

'In fact,' she said awkwardly, 'I'm not the type of girl who has ever fallen into bed with someone.'

His hand stilled and he frowned as his brain tried to compute what she had just said. And failed. Was she admitting to being a virgin? A woman in her twenties?

'You're kidding.'

Sammy stared off into the distance. If her heart were to beat any faster she would be in danger of it cracking a couple of ribs. She'd always known that she would have to have this conversation with whatever guy she eventually fell into bed with, but in her head the conversation had never been with a man like Leo. In her head the conversation had always been with a kind, gentle guy who would clasp her hand and understand where she was coming from because he, like her, if not a virgin, would have been discriminating with his women.

Leo enjoyed women unabashedly. He took what he

wanted, always drawn to the prettiest and the most tempting, and he moved on quickly from one to another.

The fact of her virginity was just something else that separated them.

Actually, there were so many things separating them that she could start counting now and probably not reach the end of the list by the time they left the country.

'Why would I be kidding?'

'Because...' Leo was lost for words. 'Because... How old are you?'

'Twenty-six.'

'You're *twenty-six* and you've *never* slept with a man?'

Sammy flushed but she wasn't ashamed of that and never had been. She'd never been part of any crowd, growing up, who had giggled and ticked off the days on a calendar before they could lose their virginity and, once she had left her teens behind, the subject had never arisen with her girlfriends. If anything, she had seen enough broken hearts from friends who had become hopelessly involved with the wrong type of guy to have known that when she did decide to sleep with a man it would be with the right man.

What a joke, as it turned out.

Because she wanted to sleep with *this one* and *wrong* didn't begin to describe the category he fell into.

'Why not?' Leo asked bluntly. He still couldn't get his head round that idea but now he was looking at her in a slightly different light. *A virgin?*

'Because it just never happened,' she muttered under her breath, red as a beetroot and furiously wishing she had never said anything. She should have just carried on keeping him at arm's length and not softened at that glimpse of vulnerability.

'I get it…' Leo said slowly, his beautiful mouth curving into a smile of lazy intent. 'You thought that sex was something you could control. You'd fall in love and sex would follow as a tidy little afterthought. You believed that love and sex came as a package deal…'

'I never said that.'

'But you're attracted to me and that doesn't compute.' He'd never experienced any woman fighting an attraction to him. 'You've discovered that lust doesn't necessarily go hand in hand with love, and you've found out that it's powerful enough to make minced meat of common sense. Welcome to the real world.'

'There's nothing real about what we have.'

'You can keep fiddling around with words, Sammy, but you still won't be able to turn the chemistry between us into something else because it makes you feel uncomfortable.'

'This is crazy!' she burst out, looking at him with agitation. 'It doesn't make any sense. It would be madness to…to…'

She didn't get to finish the sentence.

Because he pulled her towards him and kissed her and he kept on kissing her until all thought faded away and what was left was pure sensation.

CHAPTER EIGHT

AT THIS STAGE in the proceedings, Leo would have marked his boundary lines out very clearly. He didn't feel that he needed to with Sammy, though. She got them. She had entered this contract with her eyes wide open and she knew him for the man he was—a man who wasn't going to ever offer her anything but the gratification of a physical need.

She wasn't a woman rushing to climb into bed with him as a prelude to trying to stake a claim. She was a woman who had done her best to avoid climbing into bed with him and staking a claim was the last thing on her mind.

She wasn't losing her virginity to him because he was the man she had been looking for all her life. She was losing her virginity to him because, like a minnow caught in a riptide, she just couldn't help herself.

The chemistry between them, for all sorts of reasons he couldn't understand, was overpowering.

'Sometimes crazy is good,' he broke away to rasp. Without giving her time to find an answer to that observation, he picked her up and she gave a soft little gasp because they were heading for the bedroom and that king-sized bed.

She'd definitely overestimated her ability to hang on to her self-control when he was around!

If they'd buried this and not brought it out in the open, she might have been safe but, as it stood…

She spread her hand flat against his chest and felt the hardness of muscle. If she stopped to think about whether it had anything to do with love or affection or wanting to discover more about her, then she would go mad. It was all about sex and lust and he was right— she had never predicted how powerful a physical urge could be.

He deposited her on the bed and then stood back and looked down at her with an expression of masculine satisfaction.

'Hot day out there…'

'Huh?'

'I'm thinking we should start with a bath. How does that sound?'

'Maybe we should just get it over and done with.' Sammy looked at him anxiously and he burst out laughing.

He raked his fingers through his hair and gazed at her with lively amusement. 'That's the first time any woman has ever said that to me. *Maybe we should just get it over and done with*…' He shook his head and dropped onto the bed to sit next to her and she scrambled up so that she was hugging her knees, her eyes wide with a mixture of apprehension and hot longing.

Both did unheard of things to his body. His erection was so hard it was painful. He had no idea how he was going to get through a leisurely bathing session but sating their needs fast and hard was going to have to wait.

'Is this the first time you've ever made love to a virgin?' she asked quietly and he touched her cheek briefly.

'It is, but don't be scared, Sammy. I'll be gentle. I just need to make sure of one thing—I need to know if this is really what you want.' His voice was utterly serious. This wasn't quite what she had expected. She had summed Leo up as the typical wealthy, good-looking businessman who could have any woman he wanted and so took without thinking of consequences. She'd assumed that he was selfish sexually, happy to pick up and discard women without any thought to whether he left them with broken hearts or not.

His account of what had happened behind the scenes with Vivienne Madison had subtly changed that opinion but perhaps her opinion had been changing before that.

Assailed by a moment of confusion, her mind went blank for a few seconds and then she slowly began processing that the three-dimensional man was nothing like the cardboard cut-out she had had in her head.

'Really what I want?' she parroted weakly.

'You've spent your life saving yourself for the right man,' Leo told her roughly. 'I'm not the right man for you and I never will be. I'm not on the lookout for love—I don't have time for the complication of emotions. If I were to describe my ideal life partner, it would be someone whose view of the institution of marriage was similar to my own. A man like me would be no good for you any more than a woman like you would suit a man like me.'

Sammy hugged her knees tighter to her chest. She was being given an out. She looked at him, chin tilted mutinously at an angle. 'You were right,' she told him.

'I thought sex and love went together. I hadn't banked on being swept off my feet by…by…lust.'

Leo was impressed because it was brave of her to admit that. It would have been much easier to have buried her head in the sand, stuck it out here for the next week and then pocketed the money and put the whole thing down to experience rather than facing up to something she found uncomfortable and bewildering.

'Is that you telling me that you want this?'

Sammy nodded and he grinned. 'You're going to have to do better than that, Sammy.' He sifted his fingers through her hair and gently tugged her towards him. His kiss was long and deep, their tongues meshing, driving her wild.

'Let me hear you say it…' he encouraged, breaking apart to look at her.

'I…I want this.' Sammy felt heady and reckless. She felt as though she had one foot hanging off the side of a precipice. In a minute she would leap into the air and free fall. She was terrified and excited all at once.

'In that case, stay right where you are.'

He padded off to the en suite bathroom, where she heard the sound of the bath being run. When she thought about the two of them in that bath she shivered. But she wasn't going to back out.

Her mind was frantically trying to deal with images of them together when he reappeared at the bathroom door, leant against the door frame and gazed at her with his arms folded.

'Rule number one,' he drawled, 'is to relax.' He strolled towards her and she followed his lazy progress with wide blue eyes. 'Rule number two is to stop thinking that what we're about to do will be anything but exquisite. And rule number three…' he ran his fingers through her hair and gently tilted her face upwards so their eyes met, his reassuring, hers needing reassurance '…is that you trust me.' He stood back and held out one hand and she took it mutely and then he led her to the bathroom, where the bath was a mass of fragrant bubbles.

'Now…' Leo positioned her in the middle of the bathroom and stood back, gazing at her with the eyes of a connoisseur. It was an exaggerated pose, finger lightly resting on his mouth, head tilted back, eyes half closed, and she wanted to laugh, which relaxed her.

'What are you doing?'

'Where to start?' he murmured. 'With your top, I think…'

'No—no!' She hurriedly stepped back and hooked her fingers under the stretchy fabric. 'I can do that myself.'

'Should I turn my back and only look around when you're safely concealed under a metre of bubbles?'

'Hardly a metre!'

'You're not going to get away that lightly,' he teased, enjoying the novelty of a woman who wasn't flinging herself at him. He walked towards her and when she opened her mouth he gently placed one finger over her lips. 'Now, remember those rules of mine?'

Sammy nodded meekly.

'Okay. Let's focus on rule number three, which is *trust me*.' He lightly tapped her hands away from the top to replace them with his own and slowly, tantalisingly slowly, he pulled the top over her head, keeping his eyes on her face, and then he tossed it on the chair by the door.

Sammy's mouth was dry. 'I know I'm not exactly skinny,' she breathed huskily and he tutted under his breath. 'My breasts are way too big,' she continued, just in case she hadn't already made it perfectly clear that making love to her wasn't going to be like making love to one of his superslender models or waif-thin actresses, and not just because she was a virgin.

Leo was finding it very hard to step back from the searing urge to rip her bra off and feel those lush breasts for himself. The last thing his aching erection needed was a description from her about just how generous they were in size.

'You're perfect,' he ground out, briefly closing his eyes to get a grip.

Sammy would have launched into a question and answer session about his definition of *perfection* because she had eyes in her head and knew that *perfect* was the last thing she was, but he had slid his hands behind her back and was unclasping her bra.

She gasped and squeezed her eyes tightly shut as the bra joined her top on the chair. Her body was as rigid as a plank of wood but not for long, as he curved big hands around her breasts and then, slowly and expertly, rubbed his thumbs over the stiffened peaks of her nipples.

Leo wasn't sure he was going to be able to keep up the pretence of the sophisticated lover in control of the situation when he felt as though he was on the brink of exploding. He was hard as a rock and throbbing. When he looked down to those heavy, abundant breasts with their circular pink nipples, he could easily have been a horny adolescent on the verge of losing his virginity. That was how turned on he was.

He continued to massage them, to play with her nipples, while she moaned softly under her breath, as if a little embarrassed to be making any noise at all.

Her inexperience hit him like a dose of adrenaline and he fumbled, in a very uncool way, with her trousers, which he somehow managed to get down her legs without his usual aplomb.

She stepped out of them. Sammy's eyes were still squeezed shut and, whilst everything was melting, she just didn't quite know what she should do next. Her whole body went up in flames when she thought of those fabulous dark eyes scrutinising her body. She took a peek and daringly made some halting attempts to get him to the same state of undress as she was.

'Shh…' Leo murmured, as though she had spoken. He stayed her hand.

'This feels weird,' Sammy said shyly. Their eyes met and he nodded. He had never made love to a virgin in his life before. Had she ever seen a man naked? He was well built. Would his sheer size intimidate her? He stepped back and began undressing, his dark eyes fixed on her as she watched him with unabashed fascination. Without thinking, she had covered her breasts with her arm. It was curiously erotic.

Shirt off, he began unzipping his trousers.

Sammy couldn't take her eyes off him.

He was the most sensationally beautiful man she had ever seen and all of a sudden she knew, with some kind of unerring instinct, that she had been looking at him all her life. He'd never noticed *her*, but she had spent her life noticing *him*.

And now here she was…

She was so turned on that she had to briefly close

her eyes and, even with her eyes closed, she could still see his image imprinted on her retina. Broad bronzed shoulders, muscled arms, narrow waist and washboard-hard stomach.

When she opened her eyes he was stepping out of the trousers and she gasped, her mouth forming a perfect oval, and Leo grinned.

'I can't remember the last time I had such a dramatic reaction from a woman at the sight of my naked body,' he drawled wryly.

Sammy's cheeks were burning. Her eyes flicked down to his substantial, impressive manhood and then back to his face. He was still grinning.

'Don't worry—' he read her mind without her having to say what was on it '—male and female bodies are engineered to fit together.'

He urged her into the bath. It was huge, big enough for them both, but he knelt at the side and lavished his attention on her, taking his time as he soaped her, massaging her neck until her bones turned to water and then moving on to massage her breasts until she was so relaxed she just wanted to sigh and moan and enjoy the intense pleasure of his hands on her.

Her self-consciousness had disappeared some time between sinking into the hot water and hearing the sound of him lathering soap between his hands.

By the time his big hands were moving over her breasts, her legs were limp and her eyelids fluttered as he worked his way down her body, urging her to sit up so that he could soap her back, his thumbs pressing against her spine in a way that was quite, quite delicious.

'Enjoying?' he whispered and she nodded and muttered something that was meant to signify a resounding *yes*.

'Still nervous?' he questioned, and she flicked drowsy eyes at him.

'Not so much,' she confessed. 'You're good at this, aren't you?'

'I've never been in this position before. It's as new to me as it is to you.'

'But you have heaps of experience.'

'There's another rule I should have added,' Leo mused. 'I should have added the *no chatting* rule.'

'I mean—' Sammy ignored him completely '—I always imagined that when I was, well, in this position… You know what I mean, that it would be with someone less…er…'

'There would be something a little weird about a guy in his mid to late twenties who was still a virgin. Or am I being a little fanciful here? Now, stop talking!'

His hands moved over her body, massaging gently, exploring gently, finding her inner thighs and separating them…also gently. His caresses were unhurried and measured and she physically felt herself relaxing more and more until all the apprehension had seeped out of her.

She received his finger with a shiver as it slid between her legs. Maybe it helped that she was covered in warm, sudsy water. Or maybe because the lighting was dimmed in the bathroom and her eyes were closed so that she couldn't see that lean, beautiful face. Or maybe she was just, weirdly, relaxed. She didn't understand how or why but she was. Everything was happening so slowly.

Leo stroked her between her legs, building up the

rhythm. He knew that this would be achingly intimate for her, and he half wondered whether some kind of prudish instinct would kick in and she would push his questing hand away, but she didn't and he was inordinately pleased by that.

It mattered to him that she open herself to him and that was what she was doing. Her breathing quickened and her cheeks became flushed with hectic colour. She was moving in the bathtub, bucking ever so slightly so that the water lapped around her, enabling him to see the slick wetness of her big breasts rising and falling. He kept up his gentle but insistent rhythm until, with a deep groan, she arched up and spasmed against his finger.

Sammy was shocked and mortified at the way she had just *let go*. She had been so caught up in the waves of pleasure rolling over her that she would not have been able to stop herself if she had tried.

When she opened her eyes, he was smiling and she struggled up into a sitting position. 'I'm sorry…' She could barely get the words out. He stroked her face, stood up and helped her to her feet.

'You should be,' he admonished, 'because I'm so turned on I feel as though I'm about to explode. I had planned this bathing experience to be very long and very leisurely but I'm going to have to revise that plan.'

'Why's that?' She smiled shyly because she knew what he was saying and yet she could hardly believe it.

'Fishing?' Leo grinned, outrageously masculine in his nakedness. If he didn't have her, and have her fast, he wasn't going to be responsible for whatever his body decided to do.

'Yes,' Sammy confessed honestly. He helped her out of the tub and wrapped her in a towel and she was be-mused to find herself suddenly settling onto the over-sized bed—the same bed which had filled her with dread when she had first arrived.

Leo laughed. 'I like that,' he confided, and she looked at him with a puzzled expression. 'The way you have of saying exactly what's on your mind,' he elaborated. 'You don't care what impression you make.'

'And that's a good thing?' Sammy asked lightly.

'Refreshing. The women I date have always taken great care to say what they thought I wanted them to say.'

'I thought all men liked women who agreed with them.'

'Maybe,' Leo murmured, 'or maybe that's just a lazy response. Now, enough talk.' He sank onto the mattress and guided her hand to his throbbing erection, draw-ing in his breath sharply as she wrapped her fingers around him.

She asked him what to do. She was anxious that he enjoy himself. Her frank honesty and hesitancy was refreshing.

'Don't worry about me,' he told her roughly. 'This is about *you*. I want this first time for you to be special. I want you to remember it forever.'

Sammy's heart swelled as he angled her underneath him, pinned both her hands together above her head with one hand and then instructed her to leave them there.

If he was as turned on as she was, then his whole body would be on fire, just as hers was, and yet he was willing to sublimate his urges so that he could take his time with her. He nuzzled the side of her neck and she wriggled and sighed, her eyelids fluttering as he then proceeded to work his way downwards, sprinkling a trail of delicate, feathery kisses along her collarbone, then lower to the soft swell of her breasts.

She opened one eye and the sight of his dark head, the intimacy of where it was placed just there by her nipple, made her stifle a squeak of edge-of-the-seat excitement.

She closed her eyes. She felt like the cat that nabbed the cream. His mouth edged down to her nipple and he suckled on it, drawing it in and teasing it with the tip of his tongue. Sammy groaned out loud. Her hands itched to burrow into his dark hair and propel him harder against her sensitive nipple but instead she clasped her fingers together and squirmed as he continued to send her body to heaven. She was still tingling between her legs and the tingling was building momentum, wanting satisfaction all over again.

He caressed her breasts, torturing her by taking his time as he explored first one then the other. He licked her nipples, traced them with his flicking tongue, nipped them and sucked them until she barely recognised the low, shuddering moans coming from her.

Those moans grew deeper when he cupped her between her legs and very gently pressed down in lazy circular movements.

Leo felt her impatience, felt her body yearning to receive him and he wanted nothing more than to yield to the siren call of desire, to satisfy his driving need to feel her tight and hot around his hard, painfully erect manhood.

It took immense willpower to leave her breasts so that he could taste the flat planes of her stomach, so that he could circle the delicate indentation of her belly button with his tongue, so that he could breathe in the musky, sexy scent of her womanhood.

He knelt between her legs and took his time, first licking the soft underside of her thighs and then, when her panting was raspy and hoarse, gently inserting his tongue along the crease and then delving deeper to taste her wet, slick sweetness.

Sammy bucked against him. She couldn't keep her hands obediently clasped above her head and instead curled her fingers into his dark hair, driving his mouth deeper against her so that the starbursts of pleasure became sharper and sharper until she was rolling on a tide of pure sensual delight.

She hitched her legs up, intensifying the pleasure, and then cried out when he inserted two fingers into her so that he was caressing her with his mouth and his fingers.

Leo could feel self-control slipping fast. He wanted and *needed* to be inside her.

'I need you *now*.' He barely recognised the shaky tenor of his voice. He reared up and their eyes met. Sammy nodded wordlessly. Even in the midst of searing passion, she noted that he took time out to put on a condom. She was a virgin so perhaps he assumed that she wasn't on the Pill or maybe, even if she *was* for whatever reason, he was a man who never took chances.

He had brought her to the brink and had taken her to a place where nerves at taking him inside her had miraculously vanished. Yes, she still registered that this was going to be a whole new experience for her, but she literally couldn't wait to feel the bigness of him inside her.

He ran a finger along her, delved briefly into her

wetness, then nudged her tentatively with the tip of his shaft.

'Leo…' She whispered his name in a voice that was halfway between a gasp and a plea. Her hands were on his shoulders, her body arched up, ripe and ready, as he edged into her, inch by glorious inch.

The feeling was exquisite. Sammy had never actually dwelled on what sex might *feel* like. It had always been a blurry, rosy image wrapped up in the comforting haze of love with a capital *L*. There was nothing blurry or rosy about this. The sensation of his hardness plunging into the very depths of her was mind-blowingly erotic and raw. She pushed against him and that was all Leo needed to ramp up his rhythm. He thrust deeper and harder and felt her whole body quiver around him, their bodies fused.

Sammy was scarcely aware of a brief twinge of discomfort. His need mirrored her own and it was proof of his mastery that he had been able to get her to a point of relaxing enough, trusting enough, to give herself to him without fear of stepping into the unknown.

The feel of her tightness was amazing, as was the heat of her body, the lushness of her feminine curves, the naked desire that had darkened her eyes and caused her nostrils to flare.

He held on, tuned in to her every whimper and cry, knowing just how to drive and angle his big body to intensify the sensations pouring through her as her cries became higher, more uncontrolled.

Her whole body tensed and arched up and only then did he allow himself to let go. The timing was impeccable as their bodies convulsed in unison. It was the most sensual experience Leo could remember having and he wondered whether the fact of her virginity had been a mental turn-on as well as a physical one.

Sagging against him, utterly spent, Sammy wondered what happened next in this scenario. She hadn't given that a moment's thought. She'd been way too busy rushing into Leo's arms. Now, her nudity embarrassed her and she made tiny movements to distance herself from him and put the sheets between their damp bodies. Leo wasn't having any of it.

'Don't tell me that you're going to go all modest on me,' he murmured, firmly lifting the sheets she had tried to stuff between them and pulling her close against him so that she was in no danger of pretending that what had happened had been a blip she could swipe away. 'I've seen you naked now so trying to cover up is just shutting the stable door after the horse has bolted.' He grinned and lay back flat, tugging her onto him and then draping his arm over her.

Sammy quivered. Her automatic instinct was to analyse what had happened and discuss what would happen next. This was a big deal for her. It was slowly trickling into her that the lines between what was real and what wasn't had become blurred. Where did that leave her? She had handed her virginity to Leo. What did that mean? Was this the beginning to an affair? She'd never considered herself to be *affair material*. Or maybe this was just a one-night stand, something that had happened because they had both been overwhelmed.

She knew that he was not being afflicted by similar internal angst. He wasn't confusing lines or frantically wondering what happened next. When it came to sex, Leo was a man who lived in the moment. He had wanted her, she had wanted him and one and one made two—it was as simple as that.

If she told him that this was a one-off, a mistake, then she knew that he would shrug those broad shoulders of his and put it down to experience. Their charade would continue unimpeded.

And for her...

Would it be so bad for her to snatch a little bit more of this while it lasted? Instead of reacting like Chicken Little with the sky falling down? Leo was offering *fun* and the fact that they were supposedly engaged was an added bonus because it just added verisimilitude to the charade. What was wrong with fun?

She had had a hellish year and a half and now she had a chance to lighten up and enjoy herself for a little while. Where was the crime in that?

His phone buzzed and he rolled to his side and she watched his broad, tanned, muscled back as he read whatever message had been texted to him.

Daringly, she traced a pattern with the tip of one finger. It was probably the least wanton gesture she could have made but she was gratified when he moved and then turned back to her and swung her against him.

'Nice,' Leo growled, turning back to her and catching her finger, sucking it, while keeping his dark eyes firmly fixed on her face. 'I can tell you're destined to be an excellent pupil.'

'What makes you say that?' For someone as forbidding as he was, she was discovering that he could be incredibly engaging.

'You've already picked up rule number four before I've even had a chance to tell you what it is.'

'Have I? What is it?'

Still grinning, Leo primly tucked the sheet under her breasts and circled one of her nipples with his finger. Instantly, it peaked into hot arousal. He moistened his finger and returned it to her nipple and absorbed the little reactions of her exquisite body.

'You're making the first move,' he drawled. 'I like that, but before we have fun—' he settled her against him '—we're going to go downstairs and have something to eat and then we're going to talk about tomorrow.'

'Why?' She flashed him a reckless smile. 'Weren't you the one who mentioned something about no chatting? Wasn't that one of your rules?'

'Like I said, a fast learner. But you're going to have to be the teacher for a while,' he told her wryly. 'The text I just received was from my lawyer. We're going to have Adele solidly for the next four days. A test, it would appear, to judge whether she can adapt to us.'

'Day and night?'

Leo nodded. 'I gather that this is Gail's attempt to throw her granddaughter in at the deep end to prove a point, after which she will repeat her case for having the child stay in Melbourne with her, while she continues to collect even more money from me, no doubt, than she already does, unless she can convince the court that Adele is incompatible with my lifestyle, whether you're on my arm or not, then her case is over and the money will stop.'

'My goodness! And how on earth is it going to be possible to prove anything at all? Is she going to have spies with binoculars peering from behind the bushes and writing reports on what we're doing?'

'A child psychologist will establish how well Adele

is likely to cope in the UK and how comfortable she feels around us. So…'

Sammy could see a flicker of anxiety in the depths of his bitter-chocolate eyes although his voice remained neutral.

'So?'

'So I propose we escape to somewhere a little less busy. Head to the coast. I can get my lawyer to source somewhere we can rent. A villa by the sea.'

Without crowds around them and a deadline to meet before Adele was returned to her grandmother, it was going to be much harder for their charade to hold water, especially with a child. Sammy knew, from experience, that most children were a heck of a lot sharper than adults thought when it came to assessing situations and people. Leo wouldn't have to pretend to be in love with her for the sake of lawyers and the public at large. This was going to be a much more difficult task.

'And,' she said slowly, 'you want me to teach you how to relate to Adele? How on earth can I teach you something like that?'

'I didn't come this far to fail at the final hurdle.' He slid out of the bed, prowled naked towards the window, then returned and leaned over her, caging her in, his arms on either side of her body.

'Children aren't like adults,' Sammy told him softly. 'They don't judge and they respond the more natural and open you are with them.'

'Then natural and open is what I will have to be.'

Sammy gazed at him and she thought that it was going to be a lot more complicated for him than merely being natural and open. He would have to relinquish his desire to control everything around him. He would have to go with the flow.

Somehow the thought of that made it easier for her to accept that she wanted him even if it meant stifling her urge to analyse where that *want* would take her. They would both be functioning out of their comfort zone.

She laughed and then sobered up when she saw that he was dead serious. 'Sometimes, it's hard to believe that you and your father share the same genetic pool.'

Leo slipped back into bed. 'I know,' he said drily. 'I guess I'll just have to learn how to operate a little on his emotional level for a while.'

'Is that going to be possible for you?'

Leo didn't answer. The enormity of this undertaking was hitting home—and hitting home hard. To leave Adele in the care of her grandmother would be a disaster but bringing her back with him was going to require changes to his life he had not considered in depth. Would he be able to cultivate an emotional bond with the child? He'd had a good childhood, he thought, even though he had hardened over time as he had watched the destructive path his father's emotional excesses had taken him down.

He relaxed.

He might have trained himself to put his emotions on ice when it came to the opposite sex—he had seen for himself the catastrophes that could occur to the hapless bugger who wore his heart on his sleeve—but there was no reason to think that he wouldn't make a perfectly acceptable guardian to Adele and, besides, what he lacked his father would make up for in spades.

'Perfectly possible.' He smiled lazily. 'Especially with you at my side, applying a little discipline whenever you notice me slipping up.' He dropped a kiss on her parted mouth and the kiss deepened until she was throbbing between her legs for him. He pulled back. 'I'll get the ball rolling for somewhere by the sea.' He flicked on his cell phone and began scrolling through his address book. 'And you can get dressed and start thinking of ways of turning me into a good little boy who can pass the next big test.'

CHAPTER NINE

SAMMY LAY BY the pool, her eyes hidden behind the oversized sunglasses she had bought two days previously, shortly before they had collected Adele from her grandmother's lawyer.

Everything had to be done by the book.

'One foot out of place,' Leo had said grittily, 'and she'll run screeching to her lawyers that we're flouting the rules.'

In the past couple of days she had heard things about Gail Jamieson that had conclusively done away with any lingering doubts about what they were doing. Leo had clearly been loath to part with the information but maybe because they were now more than just partners in a business arrangement he had felt inclined to open up.

Pillow talk.

'Sean was a weak man,' he had told her pensively late at night after their first successful day with Adele, the little girl tucked safely in bed hours earlier. 'An only child, spoiled and indulged, with almost no discipline, and I tend to agree with my father that he found himself swept along on a riptide over which he had no control whatsoever. He was completely taken in by Louise and it wasn't hard for him to fall off the bandwagon completely after his mother died. From his communications with my father, it would appear that whilst he knew well enough that neither he nor Louise were equipped to take care of the child they had produced, neither was Gail. There were stories of her leaving the baby unattended while she went out at night and, on one occasion, an actual admission to hospital when Adele was little more than a toddler, after her *falling down some stairs*—although Sean hinted that some corporal punishment had been inflicted by the grandmother.'

·'Why on earth didn't he take Adele and leave?'

'Because,' Leo had told her with a wry grimace, 'he was a drug addict. His best intentions were never going to come to anything. Nor could we have undertaken a snatch and grab rescue mission. No, the only way my father felt he could help was to send money over to make Adele's life more comfortable and to sponsor rehabs that never seemed to come to anything.'

'If Gail has been responsible for physical abuse, then surely that would make it easy for you to...'

'Hearsay,' he had told her bluntly. 'To outside eyes, she is the grandmother who rose to the occasion when her daughter couldn't look after her own child.'

Now, looking at Adele in her swimming costume at the side of the pool, Sammy could make sense of the child's personality.

Since they had arrived at the villa, which was an exquisite masterpiece of modernism with spectacular views down to the Surfers Paradise Coast, Adele had barely spoken to Leo at all. She was a cautious, watchful five-year-old, without any of the spontaneity she should have had at her age. There was no running around, no bursts of laughter, no mess made, no noisy intrusions into adult conversations.

Her clothes were neatly worn and never seemed to get dirty. She was the most background child Sammy had ever encountered and her heart went out to her.

And it went out to Leo because she could tell that he was trying hard. Unfortunately, whilst his questions were politely answered, there was minimal eye contact made and absolutely only essential interaction. Now, he was doing lengths, his lean, well toned bronzed body cutting a swathe through the crystal-clear water while Adele stared out into the distance as she clutched the side of the pool.

Sammy could predict the way the rest of the day would go because she was sure that it would follow the pattern of the other days they had had in the villa.

They would enjoy the sun and the swimming pool and then venture down to the town for something to eat and take in another of the local sights. Yesterday had been a stroll on the beach, where they had watched surfers ride the soaring waves. The day before they had paid a visit to the animal park, where Adele had been encouraged to pat a koala, which she had seemed to enjoy. Today they would do something else, some other fun activity, which would end up leaving Leo restless and frustrated because he would, yet again, fail to break through the wall of Adele's politeness.

She smiled as Adele caught her eye and then levered herself up and began walking over. She was wearing a plain black swimsuit and had not removed her bright pink plastic beach shoes, which sloshed as she approached.

'I thought you were going to be a little fishy again—'

Sammy grinned '—and show me how you could do those flips underwater.'

Adele smiled and dropped her eyes. 'Leo's in the pool,' she said in a whisper and Sammy reached out and held the child's hands in hers.

'You can't let him be the only fish,' she said with a smile. 'Besides, you make a much prettier fish than Leo. Maybe today we could get you a nice fishy swimsuit. Would you like that? Something nice and colourful? And maybe an inflatable for the pool, as well?'

'Nana might get angry.' Adele chewed her lip anxiously. 'She says it's important not to ask for things. I can only have things if I don't ask for them.'

Sammy's ears pricked up because Adele rarely mentioned her grandmother. 'What if you *do* ask?' she questioned gently. 'Does your grandmother get cross?'

Adele shrugged and remained silent.

'You know,' Sammy said quietly, 'that you have a lovely grandpa over in England who really wants to meet you.'

Adele slid a sideways look at Sammy. 'Nana says that no one wants me but her.'

'Now I *know* that's not true.' She was still smiling, her voice soft and encouraging, but her heart clenched at the behind-the-scenes picture being painted. 'You have a very, very loving grandpa who would burst into tears if he heard you say that.'

Adele's eyes brightened. 'Old people don't cry!' she giggled.

'Just wait till you meet your uncle Leo's dad,' Sammy confided. 'He's a big softie. But maybe you *should* be cautious,' she mused thoughtfully. 'He's famous for hugging a lot. He might just get hold of you and never let you go. You'd be wrapped up in a big bear hug for the rest of your life!'

'How would I eat?' Adele giggled again. It was an unusual sound.

'Your uncle Leo would have to sneak you titbits.'

'How would I go to the bathroom?'

'You'd be allowed to go to the bathroom but you'd have to follow that trail of bread back to his arms.'

'Like Hansel and Gretel.'

'*Just* like Hansel and Gretel.'

'Running away from the bad witch.'

'Who is the bad witch?'

Adele shrugged and her face grew serious, and Sammy knew when to leave things alone.

Later, she repeated the conversation to Leo. It was a little after eight in the evening and Adele was asleep. She never kicked up about going to bed. Indeed, she had to be persuaded on night one to stay up beyond six and as soon as Leo had looked at his watch, at a little after seven, she had jumped to her feet, her teddy clutched to her chest, ready to head upstairs.

She never asked for a bedtime story. She never asked for anything.

'It's almost as though she's too scared of the response she might get.'

'Does that surprise you?' Leo looked at her. The sun had worked magic on her skin, turning her flawless, milky whiteness a toasted golden colour. He couldn't get enough of her. Hours were spent in anticipation of bedding her as soon as they were together. He guiltily wondered whether he was devoting the amount of attention he should have to his little charge when his thoughts always seemed to be wrapped up in images of Sammy and her hot, willing body under his, when his eyes seemed to follow her every small movement. Right now, with the meal finished, he took his time as he watched her over the rim of his wine glass.

She wasn't wearing a bra.

He'd told her that just the thought of being able to reach under her top and feel her glorious breasts was enough to make him harden and she had teasingly threatened to dispense with the bra, a threat he had been extremely keen to take her up on.

'You're looking at me.' Sammy blushed. Her nipples tightened into hard pebbles and she felt that wonderful, familiar dampness between her legs. She had never thought that her body could respond to anyone the way it responded to Leo. His eyes on her made the hairs on the back of her neck stand on end, made her skin prickle as though someone had run a feather over it. The sound of his voice, deep and dark and velvety, could trigger a series of graphic images in her head that made her pulses quicken and her heart beat faster.

She blinked as her sluggish brain began to make all sorts of connections that had been there all along, waiting to be unearthed.

She'd agreed to a phoney relationship and then had agreed to a sexual one because she had been unable to deny her body the thing it seemed to crave.

She'd been swept along on a rosy wave of thinking that she was having fun and not doing anything that any girl her age wouldn't have done. Namely, falling into bed with a hot guy she found irresistible. She was only acting her age!

Had she been especially vulnerable because Leo had

been an adolescent crush? Had that added to the thrill? She hadn't stopped to question it.

Of course, it wasn't going to last and that was fine. They were as different as chalk and cheese and if fate hadn't thrown them together then their paths would never have crossed in the way that they had. They would have remained two people who met now and again and exchanged a bit of this and that conversation.

In time, she would have met someone to settle down with. Mr Right. He would have been reliable, kind and with a gentle sense of humour. In keeping with the fact that she had never placed much importance on looks and bearing in mind that she was never going to be asked to sashay down any catwalk, he would have been pleasant enough looking. No gargoyle but no movie star.

So what was she doing falling in love with a billionaire who was out of her reach? A guy who wasn't into commitment, who had thought nothing of throwing money at her to get what he wanted and who had not once mentioned having any feelings for her even though they were sleeping together?

Because fall in love with him she had. Hook, line and sinker, and now the thought of returning to life as she knew it held no appeal, even though she would be getting everything she had dreamed of that money could buy, including the freelance career she craved.

It was a nightmare. What on earth would he think if he could read her thoughts? If he could see into her heart? He was having a fling and she was busy experiencing the greatest love of her life.

'You make me want to stare,' Leo confided roughly.

'Huh?'

'Penny for them.'

'Penny for what?'

'Whatever it is that's going through your head.' He smiled lazily, the smile of the predator sure of its willing prey. 'Is it me?'

Sammy blinked. Her heart was thumping so fast that her ribcage felt threatened. She tried to match his sexy smile with one of her own. It wobbled. 'You're so egotistical.'

'Come and sit next to me.' He patted the space next to him. 'I can't look without touching.'

'Adele's upstairs!'

'And have you ever known a child to sleep as soundly as she does?' Leo asked drily. 'When I looked in on her half an hour ago she was snoring like a trooper.'

Besides, the way the house was designed, it was unlikely that they would be disturbed. It was a clever configuration of all glass at the front, so that every bit of the spectacular view was captured, from the soaring surf of the ocean to the vast blueness of the sky, an uninterrupted panorama because the house was built into the side of a cliff. On the lower floor, everything was open-plan. When one of the immense glass panes was opened, the sea breeze reached every corner of the house. On the veranda, which was railed in with steel, the view was breathtaking.

They were in the snug, which was the only enclosed room on the lower floor and was on a raised, floating mezzanine that afforded them a bird's-eye view of the entire floor but, thanks to one-way glass, no one inside could be seen. A useful office space, Sammy assumed, from which family life could be observed whilst absolute privacy within was maintained.

Not, as Leo had pointed out, there was the slightest

chance of Adele surprising them. It was apparent that surprising anyone was something she had been trained never to do.

'We were talking about Adele.' But her voice was tellingly feeble.

'I can't talk with you sitting so far away.'

'Don't be silly.'

'Shall I come and get you? Do you want a demonstration of my caveman capabilities?'

Sammy could think of nothing she wanted more but now her every move was invested with the pain of knowing that all too soon this would be gone. She padded the few feet separating them and sat primly next to him and he pulled her so that she was sprawled against him, lying on top of him but on her back, her body cradled between his powerful thighs.

He slipped his big hands under her tee shirt and she released a sigh of pure pleasure as he massaged her breasts, rolling his fingers over the stiffened peaks of her nipples and rubbing until the wetness between her legs made her want to wriggle.

'We were talking about Adele,' Leo reminded her.

'I... Yes...' Sammy panted. His erection was pressed like a rod of steel against her back, tangible proof of how much he was turned on. 'She... It's a difficult situation for her but, in a strange way, it's, um, actually... I can't think when you're doing that...'

'Playing with your breasts? I'd quite like to take them into my mouth. Think you could flip over so that I can taste them?'

'Leo!'

'You know you want to.'

She did and so much more besides. She flipped over

and arched up over him so that her breasts quivered tantalisingly above his mouth and she flung her head back and closed her eyes as he took his time suckling on her nipples, feasting on them, in no great rush. Eyes shut, teeth clenched, she endured the exquisite agony of being teased until she couldn't stand it any more, at which point she settled back down in her original position between his legs, breathing hard and fast.

She wriggled into a comfortable position and her legs dropped open.

'Take off the shorts,' Leo commanded softly into her ear.

Sammy wriggled out of them but when she made to remove the lacy briefs he stayed her hand. Her body was on fire. This was what he did to her. He took away her ability to think and to behave sensibly. He'd done that from the start and he would carry on doing it until he walked away from her. Until they walked away from one another. Except he would continue having an effect on her long after she had disappeared from his life. She couldn't imagine how it would feel to see him the way she had before, in passing glimpses, with Adele.

He pressed his hand flat between her legs, over her knickers, and caressed her until she was moving against his hand, wanting those lazy movements to pick up tempo.

Then he slipped his hand under the lacy cotton. When he inserted his finger and began stroking, she felt like passing out because it felt so good. Her breathing quickened as she savoured the feel of him touching her, the even rhythm as his finger slid up and down, pushing against her core.

He moved and began licking her, revelling in her

wetness on his mouth, sliding his tongue into her and feeling the gasp she uttered transmitted directly to his own body, stirring him up. He wouldn't let her come against his mouth like this. But he would fire her almost to the point of no return and then take her.

Their bodies were slick with perspiration when, as she balanced precariously on the cusp of coming against his mouth, he levered her off, pausing only to don contraception while she watched him impatiently, cupping herself between her legs with her hand to alleviate the ache there. Their eyes tangled and he smiled because he knew exactly what she was thinking and what she was feeling.

He nudged at her sensitive opening and then eased himself inside her, his girth filling her up, and when he began to thrust in deep, rhythmic strokes she could only close her eyes and let sensation carry her away.

Their bodies moved as one. Sammy couldn't imagine that sex could ever feel as glorious as this with anyone else, but then how could it when she had given her heart away to him? She came, her body stiffened and then arched up as it splintered into a thousand heavenly pieces and she felt his own orgasm matching her own.

She was as limp as a rag doll as he rolled off her so that they were lying side by side, shoulders and arms lightly touching, both of them staring up at the ceiling. She idly wondered whether the size of the sofa in the room, wider than a single bed, had been fashioned with this sort of activity in mind. Work and play in soundproof silence, invisible to outside eyes. There was something a little naughty about the design of the room and its position inside the house.

She turned onto her side to say something of the sort

to him, only to find him staring at her intently, expression speculative.

'What?'

'I expect you're going to be a little shocked at what I'm about to say.'

'What? What are you about to say?' He was so long in answering that her heart had time to gather pace and her nerves had time to start jangling and her brain had time to work out a thousand possible scenarios.

'Will you marry me?'

Sammy's mouth dropped open and she stared at him. She wondered whether her ears had been playing tricks on her but the way he was staring at her, his dark eyes serious with intent, made her pause.

Piercing happiness shot through her. She hadn't dared hope that he might have returned her love! He had been so adamant in his opinions on commitment. He had been so clear-cut when he had laid down the rules of this charade. But if she had been wrong-footed by Cupid, then who was to say that he hadn't been, as well?

'Marry you?'

'I can see that my proposal is shocking but—' he slid off the sofa, flexing his muscles, and slung on his trousers, zipping them up but not bothering with the top button and not bothering with his shirt, then he returned and perched on the sofa next to her '—I don't think I considered this whole thing when I embarked on my mission to rescue Adele from her grandmother.'

'What do you mean?'

'My father was desperate to make sure that his granddaughter was brought to England. He'd read between the lines of Sean's infrequent communications to fear the worst and I was inclined to agree with him.

The fact that Sean wanted the child to live in England was another argument for the defence, so to speak.'

Sammy was barely following what he was saying. She was too busy wondering where the marriage proposal had been buried. The breathless excitement that had raced through her was giving way to confusion.

'Yes…'

'I expected,' Leo confessed, 'that the difficult part would be getting the grandmother to acquiesce. In other words, I had focused exclusively on winning the custody battle and, with that in the forefront of my mind, all other considerations had taken a back seat.'

'Okay…' It seemed ridiculous that he had put his trousers back on while she remained on the sofa in her birthday suit, so she, likewise, stuck on her shorts and her tee shirt although she could still smell the tang of sex on her body and could still feel the powerful throb of him inside her.

She sat up straight, hands primly on her knees, and watched him.

'Of course, I did understand that having a child around would alter the dynamics of my life.'

'Did you really?'

Leo grimaced. 'I deserve your sarcasm,' he conceded with a graceful gesture of rueful surrender. 'I was naïve.'

'You're way too accustomed to having everything your own way.'

'I also thought that Adele would be…less stubborn. I have no experience with young children but, in my head, I naturally assumed that this would, indeed, be a rescue mission and the object of the rescue would be overjoyed at being saved.'

'And instead,' Sammy filled in slowly, 'you got a little girl with problems and anxieties. And despite the fact that remaining in this country with her grandmother will probably be the worst thing for her, despite the fact that she probably, from the sounds of it, doesn't even *enjoy* living with her, it's still all she's ever known and she's going to cling to the familiarity.'

'I frighten her,' Leo said bluntly. 'The second I try to engage her in conversation, she clams up. The minute I get too close, even if I'm obeying your teacher theory of stooping down to her level, she looks as though she's going to have a panic attack.'

'She just needs to get used to you and she will. Wait and see.'

'Whilst I deeply appreciate your stirring words of encouragement,' Leo said wryly, 'I don't have a great deal of time left over here before the case is decided one way or another. If the outcome is that she is allowed to come back with me, and I very much think that it will be a favourable outcome, then it doesn't give me much time for the bonding process to be solidified.' He looked at her speculatively. 'She likes you. She feels safe with you.'

Sammy didn't say anything. The marriage proposal and that brief flare of thrilling, wonderful joy had withered fast. She knew where he was going and it made her feel faint.

'And so you want to marry me because marrying me would make your life easier with Adele.'

Leo flushed darkly. 'That's not quite how I would have put it.'

'Then how would you have put it?'

'What started as a necessary charade to win this

custody battle has stopped being a charade. We're lovers and we both know the sex between us is amazing. On top of that, you have won Adele over. She trusts you and it would certainly make things easier for her if you were to be around when we return to London. Provided, of course, that we return mission accomplished,' he amended dutifully.

'You've paid me a great deal of money,' Sammy said coolly. 'You could just have asked me to stick around for a couple of weeks until she settled in to life over there.'

'I could have,' Leo admitted, 'but it occurred to me that marriage might be no bad thing. I cannot expect to resume my old life as I knew it with a child on the scene.'

'So what you're proposing is a business arrangement.' Sammy's voice had dropped from cool to positively freezing.

'Since when can sex ever be classified as part of a business arrangement?'

Restlessness consumed her and she paced the room, prowling to stand by the glass pane overlooking the living area, distractedly appreciating the fabulous symmetry of the house while she fought down the hurt and anger of being offered a marriage of convenience.

'I don't suppose it's occurred to you that I might want a little bit more for myself than a marriage of convenience?'

Leo's jaw clenched. He wondered whether he had approached this matter in the right way but how else could he have broached the subject? And why was she now attacking him? He had asked her to marry him. It was a proposal that made sense and not just for him but for her, as well. They got along and the sex was great.

She would make a terrific surrogate mother to Adele. Was the prospect of all of that, with unlimited money thrown in for good measure, so appalling?

She was a virgin when she had met him. So obviously the man of her dreams had not sauntered by waving a wedding ring in his hand and patting a cushion in preparation for his bended knee, and surely she was practical enough to wonder whether such a man existed anyway.

Whatever line of reasoning he used, Leo knew that he was aggrieved because he had offered her marriage, the single thing he had never offered any other woman, and she had turned him down, which no other woman—not one, not a single one—would have done.

'You only want to marry me because it makes sense.' Bitter disappointment made her sound shrill. She hated herself for actually imagining, even for a second, that he had been about to follow up on his marriage proposal with a confession of love. She had truly forgotten the game they'd been playing. She'd truly forgotten that he hadn't jumped into bed with her for any other reason than passing lust and, now that they were lovers, she made sense as a wife because of the relationship she had fostered with his charge.

'Remind me what's wrong with a marriage based on good sense,' Leo gritted. 'Look at my father's disastrous union with Sean's mother and Sean's disastrous union with Adele's mother. The list could go on and on and on. Emotions have a nasty habit of sabotaging good intentions.'

'No.' It would be pointless going into lots of reasons why she wouldn't marry him but for her the biggest one was that he just didn't love her and, when it came to spending the rest of her life with someone, love had to be on the menu.

And he could quote as many disastrous unions as he wanted—that was *his* learning curve, not hers.

He wanted her to be a fixture in his life because he would be inheriting a small child and having Sammy around would enable him to return to his normal life without too much difficulty. She would be there to take the brunt of the childcare away from him. She would be working freelance and could so devote her time to ensuring that Adele settled in as best she could. Leo might have sidelined work a little whilst he was in Melbourne but as soon as his feet hit British soil he would once again immerse himself in his job and if she were around as the dutiful wife he would be unfettered by having to compromise his time.

Marrying her was the lazy, selfish solution to a complex situation he had not given much thought to.

She could understand that he might think that he was conferring a great honour on her because the women he dated would all have probably walked on a bed of burning embers to get to the other side if the ring had been on offer. He wasn't to know that she was in love with him. He wasn't to know that the thought of being with someone who couldn't love her back would have been torture.

Plus, whilst he might be attracted to her now, what was to say that he wouldn't lose interest in a few weeks' time? Without love there to provide the necessary glue to a relationship, would he consider it acceptable to have affairs with women because he had married a woman to basically look after his charge? How could the commitment ever be there between two people locked in a marriage that was an arrangement? When would she start to become a liability? In time, he would form a firm bond with Adele and her usefulness would be at an end. Would he then start regretting his impulsive proposal?

The arrangement he had proposed had more holes than a colander but she still felt sick because she knew that if she turned him down then what remained of their stay in Melbourne would be awkward and stilted and she had become so accustomed to the easy, sexy, flirty rapport they had developed.

But turn him down she would.

'I can never marry you,' she explained quietly. 'I want more from life than being harnessed to someone for all the wrong reasons. If you're worried about how Adele will adjust if you win this fight and get custody of her, then you just need to employ a nanny.' She looked him straight in the eye. 'If you employ a good-looking one, you might even find that you want to hop into bed with her. You really don't have to stick a ring on my finger to get what you want. Now, if you'll excuse me, I think I'll go have a shower…and an early night.'

CHAPTER TEN

LEO STARED, SCOWLING, at the computer in front of him. The office was, as was usual late in the evening, quiet. Under normal circumstances, he would have relished the peace and solitude to catch up on the enormous amount of work that required his undivided attention.

Unfortunately, normal circumstances had not been in evidence for some time now.

And yet current circumstances couldn't have been more *normal* in the great scheme of things. He had won custody of Adele. The child psychologist had done a thorough job, had spent time assessing Adele through the child-friendly means of drawing, paper tasks and games. Unbeknown to Leo, it emerged that some testing had previously taken place and had indicated some areas of concern with her grandmother. These areas of concern were not in evidence when it came to Adele's experiences with Leo and Sammy. The process of bonding had begun and the psychologist had been gratified to note that, thanks to her interpretation of the various tasks set, under that quiet five-year-old's exterior was a child who was tentative but keen to face the future with a couple who would allow her to be a child without fear of reprisal. Ironically, the act they had instigated had convinced everyone that the love between them would provide just the security that Adele needed.

Furthermore, the parting of ways between the child and her grandmother had been less nightmarish than expected, thanks to the vast amount of cash he had gifted the woman. Along with assurances that contact would be maintained between her and her granddaughter, with one trip a year being paid for so that they could physically meet. With defeat staring her in the face, Gail had tactfully backtracked from her belligerent stance to become the epitome of helpfulness.

That had been over two months ago.

He had, before even leaving Melbourne, instructed his PA to supervise the redecorating of the room Adele would call her own and, with money thrown at the project, it had been completed in record time.

A week after the agreement had been reached, they had arrived back at his penthouse apartment to a wonderfully child-friendly environment.

Sammy had even gone beyond the call of duty and stayed on the scene for a couple of weeks after they'd returned.

Leo's scowl deepened. She'd thrown his marriage proposal back in his face, politely told him that circumstances had altered and she would no longer feel comfortable being his lover and had then proceeded to act as though nothing had ever happened between them. She had blanked out the amazing sex and turned into a distant friend, acting the part she had been hired to play. She had spent the remainder of their time at the villa keeping Adele occupied, smiling and chatting politely to him and reading her book in the evenings, out on the front deck that gave on to the spectacular ocean views.

He hadn't been able to comprehend why she had turned him down.

What he *did* comprehend, what had become patently clear over time, as she had gradually extricated herself out of his life, was that she had left some kind of ridiculous void.

She was on his mind all the time.

He couldn't focus.

There were many times he wanted to talk to her about Adele, ask her opinion on the child's progress. He knew she'd have been pleased at how *his* progress with Adele had been and he caught himself wishing she was around to congratulate him, with that warm smile that he missed so much.

He had got a top child psychologist on board to come for little 'chats' three times a week, so that he could spot any problems in the making, of which there were, thankfully, none. She would have approved of that. He had taken his time and, with Sammy's help during those first couple of weeks, had employed a young nanny who worked part-time at the school into which Adele had been enrolled. He had made a big effort to try and curtail his working hours and he had spent every weekend with his father, who had been over the moon to have his granddaughter back in England.

Indeed, this was the first late night he had had at the office and only because Adele was in the country staying with his father for a long weekend.

He would be joining at lunchtime the following day.

It irked him to acknowledge that he couldn't stop wondering whether Sammy had spent the day with Adele and his father. He knew that she was building up her fledgling career as a freelance artist because his father had told him so in passing.

Pride had prevented him from asking for more detailed information.

But pride made a very cold bedfellow and his bed was the coldest it had been since he had reached adulthood. He had no interest in inviting any woman to share it.

With a groan of pure frustration, Leo glanced at his watch to register that it was a little after eight and he had managed to achieve very little on the work front.

This couldn't continue. Accustomed to assuming that for every single problem there was a solution, Leo made his mind up on the spot. It would take him several hours to get down to Devon but the only way he would ever get the wretched woman out of his head was if he actually confronted her.

They had parted company with too many things left unsaid behind the polite smiles and courteous, remote conversation and cornflower-blue eyes that had refused to quite meet his.

He needed to tell her…

Leo's mind braked to a halt and he frowned because he had to dig deep to find the answer to that and digging deep when it came to anything emotional was not in his nature.

So instead he focused on the logistics of getting down to Devon on a Friday evening, debating whether to get his driver to do the honours so that he could try and work in the back of the limo, or else driving himself.

Moving and thinking at the same time, he opted to drive down himself.

He enjoyed driving and being behind the wheel of his high-performance sports car might just clear his head.

There was no need to pack for he kept a wardrobe in his room at his father's house so he didn't have to return to his apartment.

He hit the road and as soon as he cleared the chaos of late-evening London traffic his head also began to clear. Just leaving London behind induced a rush of freedom and he realised that this, at least in part, was down to the fact that he was going to do something about the messy tangle of emotions that had afflicted him ever since Sammy had walked out of his life.

In the morning he would talk to her.

He would pay her a civilised visit. He would ask her how she was doing. Ask to see the studio, maybe talk about her work. Having a civilised conversation with her would fill the nagging hole she had left in his life. It would remove her from the pedestal on which she had somehow managed to get herself placed and he would once again see her for what she was—a nice, uncomplicated and rather ordinary young woman who was ill suited to have any place in his fast-moving, high-octane London life.

She had been a temporary blip and because of the way things had ended, because she had been the one to walk away, he had been left with his nose out of joint.

Wounded pride and a dented ego were curable ailments but he would have to re-establish some sort of normality between them instead of the frozen silence that currently existed.

Frankly, he just felt that he needed to see the woman to get a grip on his wayward emotions.

Adele would be pleased to see him and he found himself smiling. Every shy smile she directed at him was worth its weight in gold.

He had never had much of a paternal streak in him and he had accepted that having the child in his life would be the equivalent of taking on an honourable duty, but Leo was beginning to taste the sweet beginnings of unconditional, uncomplicated love.

He was discovering that there was nothing boring in looking at a three-line story written in oversized letters that were misspelt. Nor was it a waste of his time fumbling to try to braid her hair and secure the braid with the bright pink ribbons she seemed to like so much. She still didn't talk much but she no longer darted into hiding whenever he appeared. The nanny and the psychologist had worked miracles but the miracle had really started in Melbourne, under the attentive eye of Sammy.

Thoughts flitted through his head as he steadily burned up the distance between London and Devon.

He didn't allow any of them to settle for too long. He knew that at one point he toyed with the crazy notion that the only way he would get her out of his system would be if he slept with her again.

It was beyond incomprehensible because he couldn't conceive of ever chasing behind any woman who had turned him down, especially one who had turned him down when the offer had gone way past the bedroom door and up the aisle in a church.

But the memory of her responsive, hot body still burned a hole through all his attempts at shutting down the temptation to try it on with her again.

He was barely aware of the darkness gathering as he drove fast and smooth past Bristol and into the West Country.

He was also barely aware that he had bypassed the usual route to his father's mansion and was instead following the less travelled road to where Sammy lived with her mother.

He knew the route.

He had taken it on two occasions, the first when they had both arrived down in Devon with Adele and had taken her first to see the grandfather she had never known and then to Sammy's mother. The second time he had managed to find some excuse to take his little charge there. It had been only two weeks previously and Sammy had not been there. He had made a point of not asking where she was.

Leo found himself parked outside the cottage, which was in predictable darkness at a little before midnight, and he honestly couldn't work out at what point his plans for a civilised chat first thing in the morning had changed.

Sammy heard something outside and woke up instantly, although it took her a few seconds to register exactly what it was she was hearing. When she *did* register the source of the noise, she was too alarmed and, frankly, confused to do anything but sit up in bed and hold her breath.

Just in case she had imagined the whole thing and she had, in fact, been awakened by a bad dream. One of the many that plagued her largely restless nights since she had returned to Devon.

Her life should have been a bed of roses. Leo had fulfilled all the financial obligations as promised and more. She now had a fabulous studio in which to work, was right there for her mother, whose health was improving hourly because there were no money worries distressing her to bring her down and cause her sleepless nights. She had arranged a part-time teaching job at a nearby school, just so that she could continue having adult company because freelance work could be a solitary career. Two evenings a week, she went into the school and helped with additional lessons for some of the children. The atmosphere at the school was lively, the teachers were young and she loved it there.

But behind the smiles and cheerful façade of the perfect life, she couldn't stop thinking about Leo and the brief relationship they had shared.

She knew that she'd done the right thing in turning down his marriage proposal but, where that clear-cut decision should have helped her move on, she seemed caught in a halfway house of muddled emotions and dissatisfied longings. And she also missed Adele. They had formed a bond in the time they had spent together and, although she had seen her a few times since she had returned to pick up the pieces of her life in Devon, she wished that she could see the child more, could play more of a part in her growing life.

The sound of something hitting her window snapped her back to the present and she warily sidled towards the window, making sure not to turn on any lights in the room, and pulled back just enough of the curtain to peer out without being seen.

Her heart began to thump and her mouth went dry because although she hadn't known *what* she had been expecting, it certainly hadn't been Leo.

And definitely not Leo, the epitome of everything that was an alpha male, throwing pebbles at her window. How did he even know *which* window was hers? And then she worked out that it wouldn't have been difficult. The cottage was tiny and only her mother would have occupied, for health and mobility reasons, the bedroom on the ground floor.

She yanked back the curtains and raised the sash window.

'Leo!' For a few seconds her brain seized up. 'What the heck are you doing?'

Good question, Leo thought. He shoved his hands into his pockets and glared up at her, his midnight-black eyes narrowing on her face with the sort of accusation that had Sammy's bewilderment turning to sudden anger.

How dare he show up at her house and throw her into turmoil when turmoil was exactly what she was so desperate to run away from? What gave him the right to mess with her head by just appearing out of nowhere? And why was he here anyway?

At midnight?

When the whole world was asleep?

She flew down the stairs, as silent as a ghost for fear of waking her mother, which was unlikely because she was nothing if not a deep sleeper. Still, it was better to take no chances. When she had returned, mission accomplished, engagement off, she had had the sneaking suspicion that her mother had been disappointed. Although when she had lightly raised the subject, her mumbling concerns had been laughingly waved aside.

But were her mother to wake up and find her daughter caught in a mysterious tryst with Leo, then who knew what idiotic ideas she might start conceiving?

Which brought her right back to wondering what he was doing on her doorstep, as she pulled open the door and, not seeing him there, carefully stepped out into the night.

Dressed in just her thin oversized tee shirt and with only fluffy bedroom slippers on her feet, the cool early spring air instantly made her shiver. She wrapped her arms around her body and tentatively circled to the side of the house to find him leaning against the wall, so tall, so lean and so ferociously masculine that she felt the breath catch in her throat.

'L-Leo,' she stammered, taken aback by his body language and by the sideways glance he slung in her direction at the sound of her approach. 'What on earth are you doing here?' Her breathing was raspy and uneven, her heart thundered inside her, her eyes were riveted to his lean face, drinking him in the way a starving man might eye up a banquet.

His lack of self-control in ending up here, bringing her outside by a thirteen-year-old's ploy of throwing stones at her window, slammed into him with the force of a sledgehammer and made him stiffen in automatic self-defence.

He had never done anything like this before or ever acted with such a lack of discipline and even now, as his gaze swept over her scantily clad body, he could feel his self-control drop another notch.

'Going to invite me inside?' He pushed himself off the wall but kept his hands firmly in his pockets. 'I decided not to ring the doorbell in case your mother was sleeping.'

'Why are you here?' she breathed shakily.

'I...' He looked away. 'I had to talk to you.'

'At *this* hour?'

'I drove straight down from London,' he said in a non sequitur.

'You could have just called me.'

On the back foot yet again, he bunched his fists and fought down his instinctive urge to try to take command of the situation in any way he could think.

'I needed to see you. I needed to talk to you face-to-face and I thought that if I phoned you, you might be tempted to ignore my call. I wasn't taking any chances.' His glare challenged her to take issue with what he had said but Sammy was so shocked at his raw honesty that she could only stare at him.

She spun round, heart beating fast, and led the way back into the house. She was scarcely conscious of the fact that she was dressed in next to nothing or that the stiffened peaks of her nipples were poking against the soft jersey cotton of her tee shirt.

She'd tried hard to forget the impact he had on her but just seeing him here now, as she shut the kitchen door behind her and leant against it, was reminding her of her aching weakness for him—a weakness she didn't want.

'Surely whatever you have to say could have waited until tomorrow. Is it to do with Adele? I know you've been looking at schools for her in London.'

Don't let your imagination run away with you.

Don't start reading anything behind that intense, disconcerting expression on his face.

'How do you know that?'

'Because your father told me.' Face flaming red, she turned her back on him to put the kettle on for some coffee, hands shaking.

'You've been talking to my father about me?' Leo asked quickly and, he was forced to admit to himself, hopefully.

'No!' Sammy spun round to face him and leaned

against the counter by the sink, arms folded, very conscious now of her legs on display. 'He mentioned it in passing. I can't think of any reason for you to have just shown up here unless you had some pressing need to ask my advice on schools since I taught in one for quite a while. And that doesn't make sense anyway! That's the sort of thing that could easily have waited until tomorrow. Why won't you just tell me what brought you here?' The atmosphere had shifted and her skin warmed as his eyes roved over her and suddenly she just *knew* why he had come under cover of darkness, *knowing* that he would find her mother fast asleep!

Except surely he wasn't arrogant enough to think that because *she* had been the one to walk away from him that the scales wouldn't be balanced until she warmed his bed again and *he* was the one to walk away? The way he always walked away from women? It seemed incredible but why else would he have descended here at this hour of the night? She truly couldn't think of any other explanation and was frankly appalled when she actually gave houseroom to the tempting idea of taking him up on any advances he might make because she just missed him so much.

'I…' Leo surprised himself by faltering. 'I had to,' he said in a driven undertone and Sammy's brow pleated in consternation. 'You turned down my marriage proposal.'

'You came all the way here and threw stones at my window to tell me *that*?'

'I told you why I didn't ring the doorbell.'

'But I still don't know why you're here.'

And it's not fair to spring yourself on me because I'm not strong enough to withstand your impact.

'I haven't been able to stop thinking about you.' His fabulous dark eyes held hers. 'I couldn't believe it when you turned me down.'

'Because you're so accustomed to getting your own way,' Sammy said painfully, lowering her eyes and sipping some of the coffee. She noticed that her hands were shaking a little and hoped that he hadn't noticed that, as well. Every nerve and sinew and pore in her body was reacting to his presence, putting her on hyperalert and touching her in places she didn't want. It wasn't fair!

'You can't just show up here and say stuff like that!'

'It's the truth. You make me lose sleep.' He groaned, impatient with the way he suddenly couldn't find the right words to express what he wanted to say. 'When you rejected me I thought that it was something I would be able to shrug off without too much difficulty. I had never let my emotions get in the way of my private life. I had always known where my priorities were. My father had set me a good example when it came to being wary of the pitfalls of acting on impulse and flinging yourself into situations because you were being guided by your heart and not your head. The truth is that I've been thinking about you every day. And every day I managed to convince myself that common sense would reassert itself and I would actually be able to get on with my work and with my life…'

Sammy fought down a wave of disappointment because he was simply confirming what she had already concluded for herself. He had been driven to show up because he hadn't been able to accept the reality of being turned down, especially when it had involved something as serious as a marriage proposal.

'I'm not going to fall into bed with you because…

because you miss me,' she said on a hitched breath and Leo flushed. Yes, he missed her. Another weakness of which he was not proud but a weakness, he now realised, he had never had a hope in hell of combating.

He found that he was hesitant to ask her whether *she* missed *him*. What if her answer was *no*? Never before had Leo felt himself treading carefully on such uncertain ground.

Lush lashes shielded his gaze as he lowered his eyes. Sammy itched to reach out to him and she knew that it was just the effect he had on her. He made her want to touch.

'It's not just about missing you.' He recognised what was at the very heart of the restless turmoil that had been undermining his usual single-minded focus for the past few months. 'It's more than that. I feel things for you.'

'You feel *things* for me? What sort of *things*?' Sammy refused to be drawn into feeling hopeful because she had been down that road once and wasn't going to be lured down it again.

'I need you in my life, Sammy.'

'You think you need me because of Adele.'

'This has nothing to do with Adele. My relationship with her is improving by the day. I—no, this is to do with how I feel about you. You came into my life for reasons I could never have predicted and you changed my life and all my priorities. You're warm and funny and smart and all those things should have alerted me to the real reason why I proposed to you.'

'What real reason?' Sammy drew in an expectant breath and held it.

'I love you, Sammy. I fell in love with you out there

in Melbourne but I didn't wake up to that because I had always associated falling in love with the kind of excesses I had witnessed, not just in my father and my stepbrother, but in friends, as well.'

'You love me?'

'I love you with all my heart.' His dark eyes were intense with emotion. 'I'd locked away the simple truth that my father adored my mother. I'd sidelined it because the impact of my father's second marriage occurred when I was older and perhaps that's why it was the example I processed more easily. He lost a fortune to that woman who used him ruthlessly and took advantage of his emotional nature. Indeed, he only went into that marriage because he hadn't been able to cope with my mother's death. All in all, I'd resolved from an early age to approach life a lot more phlegmatically than my father had always been prone to do. So when I started loving you it was easy for me to write it off as lust. Lust was something I could deal with. I should have known the minute I proposed to you that I should sit up and take notice.'

'I turned you down because I needed you to love me,' Sammy said, heart full. She reached across the table and they linked fingers. 'I knew that I had fallen for you and I knew that if all you wanted was a suitable mother figure for Adele then it would just be a matter of time before you got fed up having me around and started regretting the fact that you were stuck with me if we married. You don't know how many times I asked myself whether I made the right decision to turn you down.' She grimaced. 'I had to keep reminding myself that you didn't love me and that I would end up getting terribly hurt because you didn't. When you showed up here tonight…' She looked at him with love in her eyes. 'I actually thought that you might have come to try to seduce me. And, if you had, I knew I would have been so tempted to have just caved in.'

'Will you marry me, Sammy? Because I can't live without you. Because you give my life shape and meaning.'

Tears glimmering in her eyes, Sammy smiled and moved round the table to sit on his lap and entwine her hands tightly round his neck. 'I will.'

The following day they announced their engagement— their *real* engagement—to Adele and their parents. They had expected surprise and had anticipated a few seconds of shock. Instead, Sammy's mother exchanged a smug smile with Leo's father.

'I told you,' she said comfortably.

'You win.' Harold chuckled. 'Remind me,' he told his son, beaming, 'never to make a bet with a woman again. This lady never doubted that you'd end up together.'

Adele, sitting pressed between the adults, looked at them for a few seconds and then said tentatively, her little face alive with pleasure, 'When you get married, can I wear pink?'

* * * * *

Alekos was offering Sara what might be her only opportunity to meet her blood relations. Common sense doused her excitement. 'It would look strange if you took your PA to a private engagement.'

'Possibly, but you wouldn't be there as my PA. You would accompany me as my date. My mistress,' he explained, when she stared at him uncomprehendingly.

For a third time Sara's heart jolted against her ribs. 'We agreed to forget about the kiss we shared last night.' She flushed, hating how she'd sounded breathless when she had intended her voice to be cool and crisp.

His eyes gleamed like hot coals for a second, before the fire in those dark depths was replaced by the faintly cynical expression that Sara was more used to seeing.

'I don't remember agreeing to forget about it,' he drawled. 'But I'm suggesting that we *pretend* to be in a relationship. If people believe you are my girlfriend it will seem perfectly reasonable for you to be with me.'

Chantelle Shaw lives on the Kent coast and thinks up her stories while walking on the beach. She has been married for over thirty years and has six children. Her love affair with reading and writing Mills & Boon stories began as a teenager, and her first book was published in 2006. She likes strong-willed, slightly unusual characters. Chantelle also loves gardening, walking and wine!

Books by Chantelle Shaw

Mills & Boon Modern Romance

To Wear His Ring Again
A Night in the Prince's Bed
Captive in His Castle
At Dante's Service
The Greek's Acquisition
Behind the Castello Doors

Wedlocked!

Trapped by Vialli's Vows

Bought by the Brazilian

Mistress of His Revenge
Master of Her Innocence

The Howard Sisters

Sheikh's Forbidden Conquest
A Bride Worth Millions

The Chatsfield

Billionaire's Secret

The Bond of Brothers

His Unexpected Legacy
Secrets of a Powerful Man

Visit the Author Profile page at
millsandboon.co.uk for more titles.

ACQUIRED BY HER GREEK BOSS

BY
CHANTELLE SHAW

First Published in Great Britain 2017
By Mills & Boon, an imprint of HarperCollins*Publishers*
1 London Bridge Street, London, SE1 9GF

© 2017 Chantelle Shaw

ISBN: 978-0-263-92509-8

Printed and bound in Spain
by CPI, Barcelona

ACQUIRED BY
HER GREEK BOSS

For Pippa Roscoe,
Thank you for being a wonderful editor,
for giving great advice, for the laughs we've shared
and your understanding (and occasional tear-mopping)
when I've struggled with a book!
Best wishes always,
Chantelle

CHAPTER ONE

'CAN I HELP YOU?' Alekos Gionakis said curtly, when he strode into his office on Monday morning and found an unknown woman making coffee with his espresso machine.

In the past month he'd had four temporary PAs, all of whom had proved inadequate to the task of organising his hectic schedule. But this morning his super-efficient personal assistant was due back at work after her holiday and Alekos was looking forward to his life running smoothly again. The idea that Sara might have delayed her return for some reason, and he would have to manage for even one more day with yet another temp, cast a dark cloud over his mood.

His rapier glance skimmed over the woman's hair that fell in loose waves around her shoulders and seemed to encompass every shade of brown from caramel to latte. Her delightfully curvaceous figure was packaged in a dusky pink blouse and a cream pencil skirt that was a good two inches shorter than knee length.

Moving his gaze lower, Alekos felt a jolt of masculine appreciation at her shapely legs, which were enhanced by her high-heeled shoes with cut-out sections at the front that revealed her bare toes. He noticed her toenails were varnished a flirty shade of hot pink that was more suited to a beach than to Gionakis Enterprises' prestigious offices in Piccadilly.

'Good morning, Alekos.'

He frowned at the sound of the familiar voice. Low-toned and melodious, for some reason it made him think of a cool, clear mountain stream.

'Sara?' Her *voice* was recognisable, but everything about his PA's appearance was definitely not. His brain was not playing tricks on him, Alekos realised when she turned her head. Even though she was standing several feet away from him, he was struck by the intense green of her eyes. They were her only remarkable features—or at least that had been true when Sara's style of workwear for the past two years had been a navy blue skirt and jacket, which she'd teamed with a plain white shirt, buttoned primly all the way up to her throat in the summer, or a black roll-neck sweater in colder weather.

Smart, practical and frankly unnoticeable was how Alekos would have described his PA's appearance before she had inconveniently decided to take a month's holiday in Spain. When he'd objected, she had reminded him that she hadn't used any of her annual leave since she'd started working for him, apart from one day to attend her mother's funeral. Sara had looked even more washed out than she usually did. Alekos was not renowned for his sensitivity, but he'd acknowledged that caring for her terminally ill mother must have been a strain and he'd reluctantly agreed to her taking an extended holiday.

He had vaguely imagined her on a scenic coach tour of Spain to visit places of historical and architectural interest. He knew she liked history. No doubt the majority of the other people on the tour would be pensioners and she would strike up a friendship with a spinster, or perhaps a widow who was travelling alone and who would be grateful for Sara's innately kind nature.

Alekos's rather cosy picture of his PA's holiday plans had been disrupted when she'd told him that she was going away on a YFS trip—which stood for Young, Free and Single. As their name suggested, the tour operator specialised in holidays for people in the twenty-something age bracket who wanted to spend every night clubbing, or partying on a beach. The media often reported scenes of drunken debauchery by Brits in Benidorm. When he had pointed out that a better name for the holiday company would be AFS—Available For Sex—Sara had laughed and, to Alekos's astonishment, told him she was looking forward to letting her hair down in Spain.

His eyes were drawn back to her hair. He visualised her as she had looked every weekday for the past two years. She had always worn her nondescript brown hair scraped back from her face and piled on top of her head in a no-nonsense bun that defied gravity with the aid of an arsenal of metal hairpins.

'You're wearing your hair in a new style,' he said abruptly. 'I was trying to work out why you look different.'

'Mmm, I had it cut while I was away. It was so long, almost waist length, and I was fed up of having to tie it up all the time.' She ran her fingers through the silky layers of her new hairstyle. In the sunshine streaming through the window, her hair seemed to shimmer like gold in places and Alekos felt an unexpected tightening sensation in his groin.

'And I finally ditched my glasses for contact lenses. Although I must admit they're taking a while to get used to.' Sara sounded rueful. 'My new contacts make my eyes water sometimes.'

Alekos was relieved that she wasn't fluttering her eyelashes at him seductively, but she was blinking presumably because her contact lenses felt strange. Without the thick-rimmed glasses he was used to seeing her wearing, her cheekbones were more noticeable and her face was prettier than his memory served him.

He wondered if she'd had some sort of surgical procedure to her lips. Surely he would have remembered the fullness of her lips—and, *Theos,* that faint pout of her lower lip that tempted him to test its softness with his own mouth. He forced his mind away from such a ridiculous idea and reminded himself that this was Miss Mouse, the name that one of his legion of leggy blonde mistresses had unkindly christened Sara.

The nickname had suited her plain looks but not her dry wit that frequently amused Alekos, or her sharp mind and even sharper tongue that he had come to respect, because Sara Lovejoy was the only woman he had ever met who wasn't afraid to state her opinion—even if it was different to his.

'I'll put your coffee on your desk, shall I?' Without waiting for him to reply, Sara walked across the room and placed a cup of coffee on the desk in front of Alekos's chair. He could not help himself from focusing on the sensual undulation of her hips as she walked, and when she leaned across the desk her skirt pulled tighter across the curves of her buttocks.

Alekos cleared his throat audibly and tightened his fingers on the handle of his briefcase as he moved it in front of him to hide the evidence that he was aroused. What the blazes was the matter with him? For the first time in a month he had woken in a good mood this morning, knowing that Sara would be back and between them they would clear the backlog of work that had built up while she'd been away.

But work was the last thing on his mind when she turned to face him and he noticed how her pink silk shirt lovingly moulded the firm swell of her breasts. The top two buttons on her blouse were undone, not enough to reveal any cleavage but more than enough to quicken his pulse as he visualised himself removing her shirt and her lace-edged bra that he could see outlined beneath the silky material of her top.

He forced his gaze away from her breasts down to her surprisingly slim waist and cleared his throat again. 'You…er…appear to have lost some weight.'

'A few pounds, as a matter of fact. I expect it was down to all the exercise I did while I was on holiday.'

What sort of exercise had she done on a young, free and single's holiday? Alekos was not usually prone to flights of imagination but his mind was bombarded with pictures of his new-look PA discarding her inhibitions and enjoying energetic nights with a Spanish Lothario.

'Ah, yes, your holiday. I hope you enjoyed yourself?'

'I certainly did.'

Her grin made him think of a satisfied cat that had drunk a bowlful of cream. 'I'm glad to hear it,' he said tersely. 'But you are not on holiday now, so I'm wondering why you've come to work wearing clothes that are more suitable for the beach than the office.'

When Alekos spoke in that coldly disapproving tone, people tended to immediately take notice and respond with the respect he commanded. But Sara simply shrugged and smoothed her hand over her skirt.

'Oh, I wore a lot less than this on the beach. It's perfectly acceptable for women to go topless on the beaches in the French Riviera.'

Had Sara gone topless? He tried to banish the vision of his prim PA displaying her bare breasts in public. 'I thought you went to Spain for your holiday?'

'I changed my plans at the last minute.'

While Alekos was registering the fact that his ultra-organised PA had apparently changed her holiday destination on a whim, Sara strolled towards him. Why had he never noticed until now that her green eyes sparkled like emeralds when she smiled? He was irritated with himself for thinking such poetic nonsense but he could not stop staring at her.

Along with her new hairstyle and clothes, she was wearing a different perfume: a seductive scent which combined spiky citrus with deeper, exotically floral notes that stirred his senses—and stirred a lot more besides, he acknowledged derisively when he felt himself harden.

'So, where do you want me?' she murmured.

'What?' He stiffened as a picture leapt into his mind of Sara sprawled on the leather sofa with her skirt rucked up around her waist and her legs spread wide, waiting for him to position himself between her thighs.

Cursing beneath his breath, Alekos fought to control his rampant libido and realised that his PA was giving him an odd look. 'Shall I sort out the pile of paperwork on my desk that I presume the temp left for me to deal with, or do you want me to stay in here and take notes from you?' she repeated patiently.

She put her hands on her hips, drawing his attention to the narrowness of her waist that served to emphasise the rounded curves of her breasts. 'I understand that the temp I arranged to cover my absence only lasted a week, and HR organised three more replacements but you dismissed them after a few days.'

'They were all useless,' he snapped. Glancing at his watch, Alekos discovered that he had wasted ten minutes ogling his PA, who normally did not warrant more than a five second glance. He felt unsettled by his awareness of Sara as an attractive woman and was annoyed with himself for his physical response to her. 'I hope you are prepared for the fact that we have a ton of work to catch up on.'

'I guessed you'd have me tied to my desk when I came back to work,' she said airily.

Alekos's eyes narrowed on her serene expression, and he was thrown by the idea that she knew the effect she was having on him. His mental vision of her tied, face down, across her desk made his blood sizzle. He felt confused by his inability to control his response to her.

This was dull, drab Sara—although, admittedly, he had never found her dull when she'd made it clear, soon after he'd promoted her from a secretary in the accounts department to his PA, that she wasn't going to worship him like most women did. But her frumpy appearance had been one reason why he had chosen her. His position as chairman of GE demanded his absolute focus and there was no risk of him being distracted by Miss Mouse.

Alekos had become chairman of the company, which specialised in building luxury superyachts, two years ago, following the death of his father, and he had decided that Sara's unexciting appearance, exemplary secretarial skills and excellent work ethic would make her his ideal PA.

He walked around his desk, lowered his long frame into his chair and took a sip of coffee before he glanced at her. 'I need to make a few phone calls and no doubt you will have plenty of stuff to catch up on, so come back in half an hour and bring the Viceroy file with you.'

'Aren't you forgetting something? The word *please*,' Sara reminded him crisply when he raised his brows questioningly. 'Honestly, Alekos, no wonder you frightened off four temps in as many weeks if you were as surly with them as you're behaving this morning. I suppose you've got woman trouble? That's the usual reason when you come to work with a face like thunder.'

'You must know by now that I never allow my relationships to last long enough for women to become troublesome,' Alekos said smoothly. He leaned back in his chair and gave her a hard stare. 'Remind me again, Sara, why I tolerate your insolence?'

Across the room he saw her eyes sparkle and her mouth curve into a smile that inexplicably made Alekos feel as if he'd been punched in his gut. 'Because I'm good at my job and you don't want to sleep with me. That's what you told me at my interview and I assume nothing has changed?'

She stepped out of his office and closed the door behind her before he could think of a suitably cutting retort. He glared at the space where she had been standing seconds earlier. *Theos*, sometimes she overstepped the mark. His nostrils flared with annoyance. He could not explain the odd sensation in the pit of his stomach when he caught the drift of her perfume that still lingered in the room.

He felt rattled by Sara's startling physical transformation from frump to sexpot. But he reminded himself that her honesty was one of the things he admired about her. He doubted that any of the three hundred employees at Gionakis Enterprises' London offices, and probably none of the three thousand staff employed by the company worldwide, would dream of speaking to him as bluntly as Sara did. It made a refreshing change to have someone challenge him when most people, especially women, always said yes to him.

He briefly wondered what she would say if he told her that he had changed his mind and wanted to take her to bed. Would she be willing to have sex with him, or would Sara be the only woman to refuse him? Alekos was almost tempted to find out. But practicality outweighed his inconvenient and, he confidently assumed, fleeting attraction to her, when he reminded himself that there were any number of women who would be happy to help him relieve his sexual frustration but a good PA was worth her weight in gold.

The day's schedule was packed. Alekos opened his laptop but, unusually for him, he could not summon any enthusiasm for work. He swivelled his chair round to the window and stared down at the busy street five floors below, where red London buses, black taxis and kamikaze cyclists competed for road space.

He liked living in England's capital city, although he much preferred the current June sunshine to the dank drizzle and short days of the winter. After his father's death it had been expected by the members of the board, and his family, that Alekos would move back to Greece permanently and run the company from GE's offices in Athens. His father, Kostas Gionakis, and before him Alekos's grandfather, the founder of the company, had both done so.

His decision to move the company's headquarters to London had been mainly for business reasons. London was closer to GE's growing client list in Florida and the Bahamas, and the cosmopolitan capital was ideally suited to entertain a clientele made up exclusively of millionaires and billionaires, who were prepared to spend eye-watering amounts of cash on a superyacht—the ultimate status symbol.

On a personal front, Alekos had been determined to establish himself as the new company chairman away from his father's power base in Greece. The grand building in Athens which had been GE's headquarters looked like a palace and Kostas Gionakis had been king. Alekos never forgot that he was the usurper to the throne.

His jaw clenched. Dimitri should have been chairman, not him. But his brother was dead—killed twenty years ago, supposedly in a tragic accident. Alekos's parents had been devastated and he had never told them of his suspicions about the nature of Dimitri's death.

Alekos had been fourteen at the time, the youngest in the family, born six years after Dimitri and after their three sisters. He had idolised his brother. Everyone had admired the Gionakis heir. Dimitri was handsome, athletic and clever and had been groomed from boyhood to take over running the family business. Alekos was the spare heir should the unthinkable happen to Dimitri.

But the unthinkable *had* happened. Dimitri had died and Alekos had suddenly become the future of the company—a fact that his father had never allowed him to forget.

Had Kostas believed that his youngest son would make as good a chairman of GE as his firstborn son?

Alekos doubted it. He had felt that he was second best in his father's eyes. He knew that was still the opinion of some of the board members who disapproved of his playboy lifestyle.

But he would prove those who doubted his abilities wrong. In the two years that he had been chairman the company's profits had increased and they were expanding into new markets around the globe. Perhaps his father would have been proud of him. Alekos would never know. But what he knew for sure was that he could not allow himself to be distracted by his PA simply because her sexy new look had stirred his desire.

Turning away from the window, he opened a document on his laptop and resolutely focused on work. He had inherited the company by default. He owed it to Dimitri's memory to ensure that Gionakis Enterprises continued to be as successful as it had been when his father was chairman, and as Alekos was sure it would have been under his brother's leadership.

Sara ignored a stab of guilt as she passed her desk, piled with paperwork that required her attention, and hurried into the bathroom. The mirror above the sink confirmed her fears. Her flushed cheeks and dilated pupils betrayed her reaction to Alekos that she had been unable to control.

She felt as though she had been holding her breath the entire time she had been in his office. Why was it that she'd managed to hide her awareness of him for two years but when she had set eyes on him this morning after she hadn't seen him for a month her pulse-rate had rocketed and her mouth had felt dry?

The sensation of her heart slamming against her ribcage whenever she was in close proximity to Alekos wasn't new, but she had perfected the art of hiding her emotions behind a cool smile, aware that her job depended on it. When Alekos had elevated her to the role of his PA over several other suitably qualified candidates for the job, he had bluntly told her that he never mixed business with pleasure and there was no chance of a sexual relationship developing between them. His arrogance had irritated Sara and she'd almost told him that she had no intention of copying her mother's mistake by having an affair with her boss.

During the eighteen months that she had worked in the accounts department before her promotion, she'd heard that the company's board members disapproved of Alekos's playboy lifestyle, which attracted the wrong type of press interest, and she understood why he was determined to keep his relationship with his staff on a strictly professional footing. What Alekos wanted from his PA was efficiency, dedication and the ability to blend into the background—and plain, conservatively dressed Sara had fitted the bill perfectly.

In truth she would have worn a nun's habit to the office if Alekos had required her to because she was so keen to secure the job. Her promotion to personal assistant of the chairman of Gionakis Enterprises had finally won her mother's praise. For the first time in her life she had felt that she wasn't a disappointment to Joan Lovejoy. The surname was a misnomer if ever there was one because, as far as Sara could tell, there had been no love or joy in her mother's life.

She'd wondered if her mother had loved the man who'd abandoned her after he had made her pregnant. But Joan had refused to reveal Sara's father's identity and only ever made a few oblique references to him, notably that he had once been an Oxford don and it was a pity that Sara hadn't inherited his academic brilliance.

Sara had spent most of her life comparing herself to a nameless, faceless man who had helped to create her but she had never met—until six weeks ago. Now she knew that she had inherited her green eyes from her father. He was no longer faceless, or nameless. His name was Lionel Kingsley and he was a well-known politician. She'd been stunned when he had phoned her and revealed that there was a possibility she might be his daughter. She had agreed to a DNA test to see if he was really her father but she had been sure of the result before the test had proved it. When she looked into a mirror she saw her father's eyes looking back at her.

For the first time in her life she felt she was a whole person, and so many things about herself suddenly made sense, like her love of art and her creativity that she'd always suppressed because her mother had pushed her to concentrate on academic subjects.

Lionel was a widower and had two grown-up children. Her half-siblings! Sara felt excited and nervous at the thought of meeting her half-brother and half-sister. She understood Lionel's concern that his son and daughter from his marriage might be upset to learn that he had an illegitimate daughter, and she had told herself to be patient and wait until he was ready to acknowledge publicly that he was her father. Finally it was going to happen. Lionel had invited her to his home at the weekend so that he could introduce her to Freddie and Charlotte Kingsley.

Sara had seen pictures of them and discovered that she bore a striking resemblance to her half-siblings. But the physical similarities between her and her half-sister did not apply to their very different dress styles. Photographs of Charlotte wearing stylish, figure-hugging clothes had made Sara realise how frumpy she looked in comparison. The smart suits she wore to the office reflected the importance of her role as PA to the chairman of the company and she had reminded herself that if Alekos had wanted a decorative bimbo to be his PA he wouldn't have chosen her.

The new clothes she had bought while she had been on holiday did not make her look like a bimbo, Sara reassured herself. The skirt and blouse she was wearing were perfectly respectable for the office. Shopping in the chic boutiques on the French Riviera where her father owned a holiday villa had been a revelation. Remembering the photos she'd seen of her stylish half-sister had prompted Sara to try on colourful summery outfits. She had dropped a dress size from plenty of swimming and playing tennis and she loved being able to fit into skirts and dresses that showed off her more toned figure.

She ran her fingers through her new layered hairstyle. She still wasn't used to her hair swishing around her shoulders when she turned her head. It made her feel more feminine and, well...*sexy*. She'd had a few blonde highlights put through the front sections of her hair to complement the natural lighter streaks from where she had spent a month in the French sunshine.

Maybe it was true that blondes *did* have more fun. But the truth was that meeting her father had given her a new sense of self-confidence. The part of her that had been missing was now complete, and Sara didn't want to fade into the background any more. Travelling to work on the Tube this morning, she'd wondered if Alekos would notice her changed appearance.

She stared at her flushed face in the mirror and grimaced. All right, she had *hoped* he would notice her, instead of treating her like a piece of office furniture: functional, necessary but utterly uninteresting.

Well, she had got her wish. Alekos had stopped dead in his tracks when he'd seen her and his shocked expression had changed to a speculative gleam as his eyes had roamed over her. Heat had swept through her body when his gaze lingered on her breasts. She felt embarrassed thinking he might have noticed that her nipples had hardened in a telltale sign that he excited her more than any man had ever done.

Her decision to revamp her appearance suddenly seemed like a bad idea. When she'd dressed in dowdy clothes she hadn't had to worry that Alekos might catch her glancing at him a dozen times a day, because he rarely seemed to notice that she was a human being and not a robot. Remembering the hot, hard gleam in his eyes when she had been in his office just now sent a tremor through her, and a little part of her wished she could rush back home and change into her safe navy blue suit. But when she'd returned home from her holiday she'd found that all her old clothes were too big, and she'd packed them into black sacks and donated them to a charity shop.

There was no going back. The old Sara Lovejoy was gone for ever and the new Sara was here to stay. Alekos would just have to get used to it.

CHAPTER TWO

AT EXACTLY NINE THIRTY, Sara knocked on Alekos's door and took a deep breath before she stepped into his office. He was sitting behind his desk, leaning back in his chair that was half turned towards the window, and he was holding his phone to his ear. He spared her a brief glance and then swung his gaze back to the window while he continued his telephone conversation.

She ordered herself not to feel disappointed by his lack of interest. Obviously she must have imagined that earlier he had looked at her with a glint of desire in his eyes. Just because she had a new hairstyle and clothes did not mean that she had become Alekos's fantasy woman. She knew his type: elegant blondes with legs that went on for ever. In the past two years a steady stream of models and socialites had arrived in his life and exited it a few months later when Alekos had grown bored of his affair with them.

Sara had hoped she would be able to control her reaction to Alekos but her heart leapt wildly in her chest as she studied his profile. Slashing cheekbones, a square jaw shadowed with dark stubble and eyes that gleamed like polished jet all combined to give him a lethal magnetism that women invariably found irresistible. His thick black hair had a habit of falling forwards across her brow and she was tempted to run her fingers through it. As for his mouth… Her eyes were drawn to his beautiful mouth. Full-lipped and sensual when he was relaxed and utterly devastating when he smiled, his mouth could also curve into a cynical expression when he wished to convey his displeasure.

'Don't stand there wasting time, Sara.' Alekos's voice made her jump, and she flushed as she registered that he had finished his phone call and had caught her out staring at him. 'We have a lot to get through.'

'I was waiting for you to finish your call.' She was thankful that two years of practice at hiding her reaction to his smouldering sensuality allowed her to sound calm and composed even though her heart was racing. The way he growled her name in his sexy accent, drawing out the second syllable… Sa*raaa*…was curiously intimate—as if they were lovers. But of course they were not lovers and were never likely to be.

She forced herself to walk unhurriedly across the room, but with every step that took her closer to Alekos's desk she was conscious of his unswerving gaze. The unholy gleam in his eyes made her feel as if he were mentally undressing her. Every centimetre of her skin was on fire when she sat down on the chair in front of his desk.

It would be easy to be overwhelmed by him. But when she had been promoted to his PA she'd realised that Alekos was surrounded by people who always agreed with him, and she had decided that she could not allow herself to be intimidated by his powerful personality. She'd noted that he did not have much respect for the flunkeys and hangers-on who were so anxious to keep on the right side of him.

She had very quickly proved that she was good at her job, but the first time she had disagreed with Alekos over a work issue he'd clearly been astounded to discover that his mousy assistant had a backbone. After a tense stand-off, when Sara had refused to back down, he had narrowed his gaze on her determined expression and something like admiration had flickered in his dark eyes.

She valued his respect more than anything because she loved her job. Working for Alekos was like riding a roller coaster at a theme park: exciting, intense and fast-paced, and it was the knowledge that she would never find a job as rewarding as her current one that made Sara take a steadying breath. She could not deny it was flattering that Alekos had finally noticed her, but if she wanted to continue in her role as his PA she must ignore the predatory glint in his eyes.

She held her pencil poised over her notepad and gave him a cool smile. 'I'm ready to start when you are.'

Her breezy tone seemed to irritate him. 'I doubt you'll be so cheerful by the time we've finished today. I'll need you to work late this evening.'

'Sorry, but I can't stay late tonight. I've made other plans.'

He frowned. 'Well, change them. Do I need to remind you that a requirement of your job is for you to work whatever hours I dictate, within reason?'

'I'm sure I don't need to remind you that I have always worked extra when you've asked me to,' Sara said calmly. 'And I've worked *unreasonable* hours, such as when we stayed up until one a.m. to put together a sales pitch for a sheikh before he flew back to Dubai. It paid off too, because Sheikh Al Mansoor placed an order for a one-hundred-million-pound yacht from GE.'

Alekos's scowl did not make him any less gorgeous; in fact it gave him a dangerous, brooding look that turned Sara's bones to liquid.

'I can stay late every other night this week if you need me to,' she went on in an effort to appease him. Alekos's bad mood threatened to spoil her excitement about meeting her father after work. Lionel Kingsley's high profile as an MP meant that he did not want to risk being seen in public with Sara. As they couldn't go to a restaurant, she had invited him to her home and was planning to cook dinner for him before he attended an evening engagement.

'Oh, I can't stay late on Friday either,' she said. 'And actually I'd like to leave an hour early because I'm going away for the weekend.' She remembered the plans she'd made to visit her father at his house in Berkshire. 'I'll work through my lunch hour to make up the time.'

'Well, well.' Alekos's sardonic drawl put Sara on her guard. 'You go away for a month and return sporting a new haircut, a new—and much improved, I have to say—wardrobe, and now suddenly you have a busy social life. It makes me wonder if a man is the reason for the new-look Sara Lovejoy.'

'My personal life is none of your business,' she said composedly. Technically, she supposed that a man was the reason for the change in her, but she had not met a lover, as Alekos had implied. She had enjoyed getting to know her father when he had invited her to spend her holiday at his villa in the south of France but she had promised Lionel that she wouldn't tell anyone she was his daughter.

Deep down she felt disappointed that her father wished to keep their relationship secret. It was as if Lionel was ashamed of her. But she reminded herself that he had promised to introduce her to her half-siblings on Friday, and perhaps then he would openly welcome her as his daughter. She pulled her mind back to the present when she realised Alekos was speaking.

'It will be my business if your work is affected because you're mooning over some guy.'

Sara still refused to rise to Alekos's verbal baiting. She tapped the tip of her pencil on her pad and said with heavy emphasis, '*I'm* ready to start work when you are.'

Alekos picked up a client's folder from the pile on his desk, but he did not open it. Instead he leaned back in his chair, an unreadable expression on his handsome face as he surveyed her for long minutes while her tension grew and she was sure he must see the pulse beating erratically at the base of her throat.

'Why did you change your holiday plans and go to France rather than Spain?'

'The holiday company I'd booked with cancelled my trip, but a…friend invited me to stay at his villa in Antibes.'

'Would this friend be the man whose voice I heard in the background when I phoned you with a query from the Miami office a week ago?'

Sara tensed. Could Alekos possibly have recognised her famous father's voice?

'Why are you suddenly fascinated with my private life?'

'I'm merely concerned for your well-being and offering a timely reminder that holiday romances notoriously don't last.'

'For goodness' sake!' Sara told herself not to be fooled by Alekos's 'concern for her wellbeing'. His real concern was he did not want his PA moping about or unable to concentrate on her work because she'd suffered a broken heart. 'What makes you think I had a holiday romance?'

He trailed his eyes over her, subjecting her to a thorough appraisal that brought a flush to her cheeks. 'It's obvious. Before you went on holiday you wore frumpy clothes that camouflaged your figure. But after spending a month in France you have undergone a transformation into a frankly very attractive young woman. It doesn't take a detective to work out that a love affair is probably the cause of your new-found sensuality.'

'Well, of course *you* would assume that a *man* is the reason I've altered my appearance.' Sara's temper simmered. 'It couldn't be that I decided to update my wardrobe for *me*.' His cynical expression fuelled her anger but she also felt hurt. Had she really looked so awful in her navy blue suit with her hair secured in a neat bun, as Alekos had said? It was pathetic the way her heart had leapt when he'd complimented her new look and told her she was attractive.

'You are such a male chauvinist,' she snapped. Ignoring the warning glint in his eyes, she said furiously, 'I suppose you think I altered the way I dress in the hope of impressing you?'

The landline phone on his desk rang and Sara instinctively reached out to answer it. Simultaneously Alekos did the same and, as his fingers brushed against hers, she felt a sizzle of electricity shoot up her arm.

'Oh!' She tried to snatch her hand away, but he snaked his fingers around her wrist and stroked his thumb pad over her thudding pulse.

'When you dressed to come to work this morning, did you choose your outfit to please me?' His black eyes burned like hot coals into hers.

Sara flushed guiltily. 'Of course not.' She refused to admit to herself, let alone to Alekos, that for the past two years she had fantasised about him desiring her. She stared at his chiselled face and swallowed. 'Are you going to answer the call?' she said breathlessly.

To her relief, he let go of her wrist and picked up the phone. She resisted the urge to leap out of her seat and run out of his office. Instead she made herself stroll across the room to the coffee machine. The familiar routine of pouring water into the machine's reservoir and inserting a coffee capsule into the compartment gave her a few moments' breathing space to bring herself under control.

Why had she goaded Alekos like that? She had always been careful to hide her attraction to him but he must have noticed how the pulse in her wrist had almost jumped through her skin because it had been beating so hard, echoing the thudding beat of her heart.

She could not put off carrying their coffees over to his desk any longer, and she was thankful that Alekos did not glance at her when he finished his phone call and opened the file in front of him. He waited for her to sit down and pick up her notepad before he began to dictate at breakneck speed, making no allowances for the fact that she hadn't taken shorthand notes for a month.

It set the tone for the rest of the day as they worked

together to clear the backlog that had built up while Sara had been away. At five o'clock she rolled her aching shoulders and went to the bathroom to brush her hair and apply a fresh coat of rose-pink lip gloss that was her new must-have item of make-up.

In Alekos's office she found him standing by his desk. He was massaging the back of his neck as if he felt as tired from their busy day as she was. She had forgotten how tall he was. He had inherited his six-foot-four height from his maternal grandfather, who had been a Canadian, he'd once explained to Sara. But in every other aspect he was typically Greek, from his dark olive complexion and mass of black hair to his arrogant belief that he only had to click his fingers and women would flock to him. The trouble was that they did, Sara thought ruefully.

Alekos was used to having any woman he wanted. She told herself it was lucky that there had been no repeat of the breathless moments that had occurred earlier in the day, when rampant desire had blazed in his eyes as he'd trapped her wrist and felt the giveaway throb of her sexual awareness of him.

He must have heard his office door open, and turned his head in her direction. They had played out the same scene hundreds of times before, and most days when she came to check if he needed her to do anything else before she went home he did not bother looking up from his computer screen as he bid her goodnight. But he was looking at her now. She watched his hard features tauten and become almost wolf-like as he stared at her with a hungry gleam in his eyes that excited her and filled her with illicit longing.

Something tugged in the pit of her stomach, tugged

hard like a knot being pulled tighter and tighter, as if an invisible thread linked her body to Alekos. And then he blinked and the feral glitter in his eyes disappeared. Perhaps it had never been there and she had imagined that he'd stared at her as if he wanted to devour her?

'I'm just off now.' She was amazed that her voice sounded normal when her insides were in turmoil. 'I'll finish typing up the report for the shareholders first thing tomorrow.'

'Did you remember that we are attending the annual dinner for the board members on Thursday evening?'

She nodded. 'I'll bring the dress I'm going to wear for the dinner to work and get changed here at the office like I did for the Christmas party.'

'You had better check with the restaurant that they won't be serving seafood. Orestis Pagnotis is allergic to it and, much as I'd like to have the old man off my back, I'd better not allow him to risk suffering a possibly fatal reaction,' Alekos said drily.

'I've already given the restaurant a list of the dietary requirements of the guests.' She smiled sympathetically. 'Is Orestis still being a problem?'

He shrugged. 'He's one of the old school. He joined the board when my grandfather was chairman, and he was a close friend of my father.' Alekos gave a frustrated sigh. 'Orestis believes I take too many risks and he has the support of some of the other board members, who fail to understand that the company needs to move with the times rather than remain in the Stone Age. Orestis's latest gripe is that he thinks the chairman should be married.'

Alekos muttered something in Greek that Sara guessed was not complimentary about the influential board member. 'According to Orestis, if I take a wife it will prove that I have left my playboy days behind and I will be more focused on running GE.'

Her heart dipped. 'Are you considering getting married?'

Somehow she managed to inject the right amount of casual interest into her voice. She knew he had ended his affair with a stunning Swedish model called Danika shortly before her holiday, but in the month she had been away it was likely that he had met someone else. Alekos never stayed celibate for long.

Perhaps he had fallen in love with the woman of his dreams. It was possible that Alekos might ask her to organise his wedding. She would have to pin a smile on her face and hide her heartache while she made arrangements for him and his beautiful bride—she was certain to be beautiful—to spend their honeymoon at an exotic location. Sara pulled her mind away from her unwelcome thoughts when she realised Alekos was speaking.

'I'll have to marry eventually.' He sounded unenthusiastic at the prospect. 'I am the last male Gionakis and my mother and sisters remind me at every opportunity that it is my duty to produce an heir. Obviously I will first have to select a suitable wife.'

'How do you intend to *select a suitable wife*?' She could not hide her shock that he had such a cavalier attitude towards marriage. 'Will you hold interviews and ask the candidates, who are your potential brides, to fill out a detailed questionnaire about themselves?' She was aware that her voice had risen and Alekos's amused smile infuriated her further.

'Your suggestion is not a bad idea. Why are you so outraged?' he said smoothly.

'Because you make marriage sound like a…a cattle market where finding a wife is like choosing a prize heifer to breed from. What about love?'

'What about it?' He studied her flushed face speculatively. 'Statistically, somewhere between forty and fifty per cent of marriages end in divorce, and I bet that most of those marriages were so-called love matches. But with such a high failure rate it seems sensible to take emotion out of the equation and base marriage on social and financial compatibility, mutual respect and the pursuit of shared goals such as bringing up a family.'

Sara shook her head. 'Your arrogance is unbelievable. You accuse some of GE's board members of being stuck in the Stone Age, but your views on marriage are Neolithic. Women nowadays don't sit around twiddling their thumbs and hoping that a rich man will choose them to be his wife.'

'You'd be surprised,' Alekos murmured drily. 'When I decide to marry—in another ten years or so—I don't envisage I'll have a problem finding a woman who is willing to marry a multimillionaire.'

'Well, I wouldn't marry for money,' Sara said fiercely. Deep inside her she felt an ache of regret that Alekos had trampled on her silly dream that he would one day fall in love with her. Realistically, she knew it would never happen but hearing him state so emphatically that he did not aspire to a marriage built on love forced her to accept that she must get over her embarrassing crush on him.

'You would prefer to gamble your future happiness on a fickle emotion that poets try to convince us is love? But of course love is simply a sanitized word for lust.'

'If you're asking me whether I believe in love, then

the answer is yes, I do. Why are you so sceptical, Alekos? You once told me that your parents had been happily married for forty-five years before your father died.'

'And therein proves my point. My parents had an arranged marriage which was extremely successful. Love wasn't necessary, although I believe they grew to be very fond of each other over the course of their marriage.'

Sara gave up. 'You're just a cynic.'

'No, I'm a realist. There is a dark side to love and I have witnessed its destructive power.'

A memory slid into Alekos's mind of that fateful day twenty years ago when he'd found Dimitri walking along the beach. His brother's eyes had been red-rimmed and he'd wept as he'd told Alekos he had discovered that his girlfriend had been unfaithful. It was the last time Alekos had seen Dimitri alive.

'Love is an illusion,' he told Sara harshly, 'and you would do well to remember it before you rush to give away your heart to a man you only met a few weeks ago.'

After Sara had gone, Alekos walked over to the window and a few minutes later he saw her emerge from the GE building and walk along the pavement. Even from a distance he noted the sexy wiggle of her hips when she walked and a shaft of white-hot lust ripped through him.

He swore. Lusting after his PA was so unexpected and he assured himself that his reaction to Sara's transformation from dowdy to a very desirable woman was down to sexual frustration. He hadn't had sex since he'd split from his last mistress almost two months ago.

'What are you looking for?' Danika had asked him when he'd told her their affair was over. 'You say you don't want permanence in a relationship, but what do you want?'

Right now he wanted a woman under him, Alekos thought, conscious of his erection pressing uncomfortably against the zip of his trousers. A memory flashed into his mind of Sara leaning across his desk with her skirt pulled tight over her bottom. He imagined her without her skirt, her derrière presented for him to slide her panties down so that he could stroke his hands over her naked body. In his fantasy he had already removed her blouse and bra and he stood behind her and slid his arms round her to cup her firm breasts in his hands...

Theos! Alekos raked his hand through his hair and forced his mind away from his erotic thoughts. Sara was the best PA he'd ever had and he was determined not to damage their excellent working relationship. She was the only woman, apart from his mother and sisters, who he trusted. She was discreet, loyal and she made his life easier in countless ways that he had not fully appreciated until she had taken a month's holiday.

If he made her his mistress he would not be able to continue to employ her as his PA. Office affairs did not work, especially after the affair ended—and of course it would end after a few months at most. He had a low boredom threshold and there was no reason to think that his surprising attraction to Sara would last long once he'd taken her to bed.

Alekos turned his thoughts to the party he was due to attend that evening. Perhaps he would meet a woman who would hold his attention for more than an hour. He received many more invitations to social functions than he had the time or the inclination to attend, but he had a particular reason for accepting an invitation to a party being given by a wealthy city banker. Alekos knew that a Texan oil baron would be included on the guest list. Warren McCuskey was looking to buy a superyacht to keep his wife, who was twenty years younger than him, happy, and Alekos was determined to persuade the billionaire Texan to buy a yacht from GE.

From his vantage point at the window he continued to watch Sara standing in the street below. She seemed to be waiting for someone. A large black saloon car drew up alongside her, the rear door opened and she climbed into the car before it pulled away from the kerb.

He was intrigued. Why hadn't Sara's 'friend' got out of the car to greet her? Earlier, she had been oddly secretive about her boyfriend. And what was the real reason for her attractive new look? Alekos couldn't remember the last time a woman had aroused his curiosity and it was ironic that the woman who had fired his interest had been under his nose for the past two years.

CHAPTER THREE

ON THURSDAY EVENING, Alekos checked the gold watch on his wrist and frowned when he saw that he and Sara needed to leave for the board members' dinner in the next five minutes. Usually when she accompanied him to work functions she was ready in plenty of time. He was annoyed that she had not been waiting for him when he'd walked out of the private bathroom next to his office, where he had showered and changed.

He wondered what she would wear to the dinner. He remembered that a few months ago it had been a particularly busy time at work and Sara had stayed at the office until late, only dashing off to change for the staff Christmas party ten minutes before it was due to start. She had emerged from the cloakroom wearing what he had supposed was a ball gown, but the long black dress had resembled a shroud and had the effect of draining all the colour from her face.

He had been tempted to order her to go and buy something more cheerful. The shop windows were full of mannequins displaying party dresses for the festive season. But then he'd remembered that Sara was grieving for her mother, who had recently died. For once he had studied her closely, and her pinched face and the shadows beneath her eyes had evoked a faint tug of sympathy for his PA, who reminded him of a drab sparrow.

Alekos turned his thoughts to the present. The board members' dinner was a prestigious event that called for him to wear a tuxedo, but he refused to be clean shaven. He glanced in the mirror and grimaced as he ran his hand over the trimmed black stubble on his jaw. No doubt his nemesis Orestis Pagnotis would accuse him of looking more like a pirate than the chairman of a billion-pound company.

Behind him the office door opened and Sara stepped into the room. His jaw dropped as he stared at her reflection in the mirror, and he was thankful he had his back to her so that she couldn't see the betraying bulge of his erection beneath his trousers.

The drab sparrow had metamorphosed into a peacock. Somewhere in Alekos's stunned brain he registered that the description was all the more apt because her dress was peacock-blue silk and the long skirt gave an iridescent shimmer when she walked. The top of the dress was high-necked and sleeveless, leaving her shoulders bare. A sparkling diamanté belt showed off her slender waist.

From the front, the dress was elegant and Alekos had no problem with it. But when Sara turned around to check that the espresso machine was switched off, he saw that her dress was backless to the base of her spine. A hot haze of desire made his blood pound through his veins.

'You can't wear that,' he rasped, shock and lust strangling his vocal cords. 'Half the board members are over sixty and I know for a fact that a couple of them have weak hearts. If they see you in that dress they're likely to suffer a cardiac arrest.'

She looked genuinely confused. 'What's wrong with my dress?'

'Half of it is missing.'

'Well, technically I suppose that's true. But I don't suppose the sight of my shoulder blades will evoke wild lust in anyone.'

Don't bet on it, Alekos thought grimly. He would not have believed that a woman's bare back could be so erotic. The expanse of Sara's skin revealed by the backless dress invited him to trace his fingertips down her spine and then spread his hand over her tempting nakedness.

Theos, what he actually wanted to do was stride over to her, sweep her into his arms and ravish her thoroughly and to their mutual satisfaction on top of his desk. That particular fantasy had been a common theme for the past four days, which had frankly been torturous. Sara had turned up for work each morning wearing outfits that had sent his blood pressure soaring. Her stylish skirts and blouses had hugged her curvy figure without being too revealing, and somehow the hint of her sexy figure beneath her clothes was much more exciting than if she had worn a miniskirt and boob tube.

He checked the time again and realised they would have to leave immediately or risk being late for the dinner. 'God knows what the board members will make of you dressed like a glamour model in a men-only magazine,' he growled as he held the door open and then followed Sara into the corridor. 'You know how conservative some of them are.' He shoved his hands into his pockets out of harm's way, but he could not control the hard thud of his heart, or the hard throb of another part of his anatomy, he acknowledged derisively.

'Nonsense, they'll think I'm wearing a perfectly nice dress,' she said serenely. 'The board members like me. They know I work hard and I would never do anything that might harm the company's image.'

Alekos had to admit she was right. Even his main critic Orestis Pagnotis approved of Sara and had remarked to Alekos that he should consider marrying someone as sensible and down-to-earth as his PA.

The trouble was that Sara no longer looked like his sensible PA. She looked gorgeous and unbelievably sexy, and while Alekos certainly had no thoughts of marrying her he couldn't deny that he wanted her—badly. He was not used to denying himself. But the rules he had made about not getting personally involved with any member of his staff meant that she was forbidden. To a born rebel like himself the word *forbidden* acted like a red rag to a bull. It was a fact of life that you wanted most what you couldn't have, Alekos brooded when they were in the car on the way to the dinner. It was also true that rules were made to be broken.

The restaurant was at a five-star hotel on Park Lane and a private dining room had been booked for the board members' dinner.

'Alekos!' A high-pitched voice assaulted Alekos's ears as he walked into the private function suite, and he swore silently when a young woman ran over to him and greeted him enthusiastically by kissing him on both his cheeks.

'Zelda,' he murmured as he politely but firmly unwound her arms from around his neck. Orestis Pagnotis's granddaughter was as exuberant as a young child but there was nothing childlike about the eighteen-year-old's physical attributes. Alekos was surprised that Orestis had allowed his granddaughter to wear a gold clingy dress with a plunging neckline. But he knew that Zelda was her grandfather's favourite grandchild—a fact she used shamelessly to get her own way.

Zelda had developed a crush on Alekos the previous year when he had spent a few days meeting with some of GE's senior board members aboard the company's flagship yacht, *Artemis*. One night, Alekos had found the teenager waiting for him in his bed. He had managed to persuade her to return to her own cabin and had done his best to avoid her since then.

But the gods were ganging up against him tonight, he decided as Zelda linked her arm possessively though his and he had no choice but to escort her into the salon, where champagne cocktails and canapés were being served. He looked around for Sara and his temper did not improve when he saw her chatting with the new whiz-kid CFO. Paul Eddis was in his early thirties, and Alekos supposed that women might consider his blond hair and rather delicate facial features attractive. Sara certainly looked happy in his company, and Eddis was staring at her with a stunned expression on his face as if he couldn't believe his luck that the most beautiful woman in the room was giving him all her attention.

The evening went from bad to worse when they were called to take their places for dinner and Alekos discovered he was seated next to Zelda. Sara had arranged the seating plan and he'd specifically asked her to put him on a different table from Zelda. Had Sara decided to have a joke at his expense? Alekos glared across the room to where she was sitting at another table. But she was facing away from him and white-hot fury swept through him when he noticed the waiter ogling her bare back.

He forced himself to eat a little of his cheese soufflé, which was as light as air but tasted like cardboard in his mouth. 'Shouldn't you be at school, studying for exams?' he muttered to Zelda as he firmly removed her hand from his thigh.

'I've left school.' She giggled. 'Well, the headmistress insisted I leave because she said I was a bad influence on the other girls. But I don't need to pass exams because I'm going to be a model. Pappoús is paying for me to have my portfolio done with a top photographer.'

'If you don't behave yourself, perhaps your grandfather will refuse to fund your modelling career.'

'Oh, Pappoús will give me anything I ask for.' Zelda leaned closer to Alekos. 'If I don't behave, will you punish me?' she said artfully.

He would like to punish his PA for putting him through an uncomfortable evening. Alekos's furious black gaze bored into Sara's shoulder blades. And yes, they could send a man wild with desire, he discovered. The hellish meal ended eventually but as the band started up and he strode away from the table—ignoring Zelda's plea to dance with her—he was waylaid by Orestis Pagnotis.

The older man glared at Alekos with his gimlet gaze. 'Keep away from my granddaughter. Zelda is an innocent young woman and I will not allow you to corrupt her, Alekos. I've always been concerned that your womanising ways would bring the company into disrepute. I'm sure I don't need to remind you that you need the support of *every* member of the board to implement the changes you want to make within GE.'

Alekos struggled to keep his temper under control. 'Are you threatening me?'

'I suggest you think hard about what I've said,' Orestis warned.

Sara stood up as Alekos approached her table. 'What's wrong? You don't look like you're enjoying the party.'

'I wonder why that is?' he snapped. 'Do you think it could be because you placed me next to Zelda Pagnotis at dinner, after I'd expressly asked you to seat her away from me? Or perhaps it's because Orestis believes that I have designs on his granddaughter, who he thinks is as innocent as a lamb, incidentally.'

'I didn't seat you next to her.' Sara looked puzzled. 'When we arrived I even popped into the dining room to check that the seating plan had been set out as I had organised it… Zelda must have switched the name cards around.'

Alekos's frustration with Orestis's manipulative granddaughter, and his anger with Orestis for threatening to withhold his support at the next board meeting, turned to a different kind of frustration as he stared into Sara's guileless green eyes. Across the room he saw Zelda heading purposefully in his direction. He caught hold of Sara's hand.

'Dance with me,' he ordered, pulling her towards him. She gave him a startled look, but Alekos was too stunned by the fire that ignited inside him when he felt her breasts pressed against his chest to care.

It was impossible to believe that this was the same Sara who had held herself stiffly and ensured that no part of her body touched his when he'd felt duty-bound to ask her to dance with him at the Christmas party. This Sara was soft and pliant in his arms and he was conscious of the hard points of her nipples through his shirt and the surprising firmness of her thighs beneath her silk dress as she moved with him in time to the music.

'I noted that you made sure you were sitting next to Paul Eddis at dinner,' he bit out. The memory of watching Sara leaning her head towards the CFO when they had sat together for the meal evoked an acidic sensation in his gut. *Theos*, was it *jealousy* that had made him want to walk over to Eddis and drag the guy out of his seat? Alekos had never been possessive of a woman in his life, but he felt a burning urge to drape his jacket around Sara's shoulders and hide her naked back from view. 'You are meant to be on duty this evening, not flirting with other members of GE staff, or the waiters.'

Twin spots of colour stained her cheeks and he could tell she was fighting to control her temper. The thought excited Alekos more than it should. He wanted to disturb her composure like she disturbed him.

'I haven't flirted with anyone. You're being ridiculous.'

'Am I?' Alekos succumbed to the demon called temptation and slid his hand up from her waist to her spine. The bare skin of her back was as smooth as silk but, unlike cool silk, her skin was warm and as he spread his fingers wide he felt the heat of her body scald him. 'You must be aware that every man in this room desires you,' he taunted her.

Her eyes widened and he thought he might drown in those mysterious deep green pools. 'Even you?' she taunted him right back.

Her refusal to be cowed by him had earned Alekos's

respect when she'd been his prim, plain secretary. But now her sassy tongue shattered the last vestiges of his restraint.

'What do you think?' he growled as he pressed his hand into the small of her back so that her pelvis came into contact with his. The hard ridge of his arousal could leave her in no doubt of the effect she had on him.

'Alekos…' Sara licked her dry lips. Her intention had been to remind him that they were on the dance floor in full view of GE's board members and senior executives. But, instead of sounding crisply efficient in her best PA manner, her voice emerged as a breathy whisper as if she were starring in a soft porn movie, she thought disgustedly.

'Sara,' he mocked, mimicking her husky tone. The way he said her name in his sexy accent, curling his tongue around each syllable, made her toes curl. When she had danced with him at the Christmas party she'd been so tense, terrified he would guess he was all of her fantasies rolled into one. But he'd caught her off guard when he'd pulled her into his arms just now. Dancing with him, her breasts crushed against his broad chest and her cheek resting on the lapel of his jacket, was divine. Beneath her palm she could feel the hard thud of his heart and recognised that its erratic beat echoed her own.

Every day at the office for the past four days had been a refined torture as she'd struggled to hide her awareness of him. It had been easier when he hadn't noticed her, but since she had returned to work after her holiday she'd been conscious of a simmering sexual chemistry between her and Alekos that she had tried to ignore. To be fair, he had seemed as if he was trying to ignore it too and a lot of the time they had been so stiff and polite with each other, as if they were strangers rather than two people who had built up a comfortable working relationship over two years.

But sometimes when she'd stolen a glance at Alekos she'd found him staring at her in a way that made her uncomfortably aware of the heaviness of her breasts and the molten heat that pooled between her thighs. That heat was inside her now, flooding through her veins and making each of her nerve endings ultra-sensitive. She was intensely conscious of his hand resting on her bare back. His touch scorched her skin as if he had branded her, and when she stumbled in her high-heeled shoes he increased the pressure of his fingers on her spine and held her so close that she could feel the muscles and sinews of his hard thighs pressed up against hers.

'Sara…look at me.' His voice was low and seductive, scraping across her sensitised nerves. Impossible to resist. She jerked her gaze upwards as if she were a marionette and he had pulled her strings. Her heart lurched as she was trapped by the dark intensity of his eyes. This had been building all week, she realised. Every searing glance they had shared had throbbed with sexual tension that was now threatening to erupt.

His face was so near to hers that she could feel his warm breath graze her lips. She had never been so close to his mouth before and, oh, God, its sensual curve compelled her to lean into him even closer and part her lips, inviting him to cover her mouth with his.

But she must not allow Alekos to kiss her. Certainly not in front of the board members of GE and the senior executives. Her sudden recollection of their situation shattered the spell he had cast on her. It was acceptable for Alekos to dance with his PA, but not to ravish her in public as the sultry gleam in his eyes warned her that he wanted to do.

The band finished playing and Sara took the opportunity to step away from him, murmuring an excuse that she needed to visit the ladies' room. She resisted the urge to glance back at him as she hurried across the dance floor but she felt his dark eyes burning between her shoulder blades, exposed by her backless dress. Luckily, the bathroom was empty and she stood at a basin and held her wrists under the cold tap to try and cool her heated blood. Thank goodness she had stopped him before he had actually kissed her.

The dull ache in the pit of her stomach mocked her for being a liar. She had wanted him to kiss her more than she'd wanted anything in her life. But her common sense reminded her that if he *had*, they would have crossed the line between employer and employee into dangerous territory.

She knew she couldn't put off returning to the party for much longer but she whiled away a few more minutes by checking her phone for messages. Her heart missed a beat when she saw that she had a text from her father.

Five minutes later, Sara stared at her white face in the mirror and willed herself not to cry. Not now, when she must go back and smile and chat to the party guests as her job demanded. She would have to wait until later, when she was alone, before she could allow her tears to fall. She read Lionel's text one more time.

After considerable thought I have decided that it would be unfair to tell Frederick and Charlotte that they have a half-sister at this time. They were very close to their mother and are still mourning her death. The news that many years ago I was unfaithful to my wife will, I fear, be a great shock to my son and daughter. I hope you will understand my decision. It is not my intention to upset you, Sara, but I must protect Freddie and Charlotte and allow them time and privacy to grieve for their mother. Unfortunately, my position as an MP and public figure means that any revelation that I have an illegitimate daughter would attract a great deal of press interest.

In other words, her father had decided that protecting the feelings of the children from his marriage was more important than publicly acknowledging that *she* was his daughter, Sara thought painfully.

Was it because she was as much of a disappointment to her father as she had been to her mother? All her feelings of self-doubt came flooding back. Maybe she wasn't clever enough, or pretty enough, for her famous father.

And maybe, Sara thought grimly, she should have worn the boring black ball gown to the dinner that she'd bought last year specifically to wear to work functions. The dress was a sensible classic style that did not draw attention to her. Instead tonight she'd worn a daring dress that she had secretly hoped would capture Alekos's attention. What had she been hoping for? Did she really want an affair with Alekos when she knew it would mean the end of her job? She'd felt the evidence of his desire for her when he had held her close while they were dancing. But she did not kid herself that his interest in her would last any longer than with his numerous other mistresses.

Alekos wasn't her knight in shining armour. And neither was her father, she acknowledged bleakly. Her mother had taught her that the only person she could rely on was herself. It was a lesson she was determined not to forget.

'Where the hell have you been hiding for the last twenty minutes?' Alekos demanded when Sara joined him at the bar. 'I looked everywhere for you.'

'Why, did you need me for some reason?'

'You should know I need my PA to be on hand at all times,' he growled. While Sara had done her disappearing act from the party he'd been forced to hide behind a pillar to avoid Zelda Pagnotis. Alekos feared no man, but an eighteen-year-old girl who was determined to get her claws into him spelled trouble. Sara sat down on a stool and he wondered if he had imagined that she seemed determined not to make eye contact with him.

'Do you want a drink?' He caught the barman's attention and ordered an orange juice, which he knew was Sara's usual choice of drink.

'Actually, I'd like a whisky and soda, please,' she told the barman. 'Make it a double.'

Alekos gave her a close look and noted her face was pale. Tension emanated from her and he wondered if she was in the grip of the same sexual tension that made his muscles feel tight and his blood thunder through his veins. He had tried to convince himself he'd imagined the chemistry that had simmered between them on the dance floor. But his body clenched as he breathed in her perfume. His reaction to her, the way his manhood jerked to attention beneath his trousers, mocked his assumption that his fascination with her was a temporary aberration.

He frowned when she picked up her glass and threw back her drink in a couple of gulps. 'Is something the matter? You seem on edge.'

'I've got a headache,' she muttered.

'If you didn't before, you soon will have after downing a double whisky,' he said drily.

She slid off the bar stool and picked up her purse. 'Seriously, I...I don't feel well and I need to go home.'

Out of the corner of his eye, Alekos spotted Zelda making her way over to the bar. 'I'll drive you,' he told Sara quickly.

She shook her head. 'I'll call a cab. You don't need to leave the party early on my account.'

'It's fine.' He didn't tell her he was glad of an excuse to leave. 'You are my responsibility and of course I'll take you home if you're not feeling well.'

Alekos had driven himself and Sara to the dinner party in his sports car, and so he hadn't had a drink. As soon as they had escaped the busy roads of central London and reached the motorway he opened up the powerful engine. Twenty minutes later, he turned off into a quiet suburb and drew up outside the nondescript bungalow where she lived.

'Thank you for the lift,' she said when he walked round the car and opened her door.

'No problem.'

On the few previous occasions when he had driven her home, she had asked him in for coffee but he had always declined. Tonight she did not issue an invitation but, perversely, Alekos was curious to see inside her home, thinking that he might learn more about the woman who had worked closely with him for two years but about whom, he realised, he knew very little.

'Goodnight.' Sara turned to walk away from him, but she caught her heel on an uneven paving slab and stumbled. *'Ouch.'*

'Are you all right? That's what comes of knocking back a double whisky when you're not used to drinking spirits,' he told her impatiently.

'I've just twisted my ankle a bit. *Alekos…*' her voice rose in protest when he scooped her up into his arms and strode down the garden path to the front door '…really, it's nothing. I'm fine.'

'Give me your key.'

He heard her mutter something beneath her breath but she obviously realised it was pointless to argue with him and dug inside her handbag and gave him a key. He shifted her in his arms so that he could open the front door and carried her into the narrow hallway.

'You can put me down now.' She wriggled in an attempt to make him set her on her feet. The friction of her breasts rubbing against his chest had a predictable effect on Alekos's body. The hunger he had tried to ignore since he had danced with her at the party ignited into an inexorable force that burned in his gut.

'You shouldn't walk in high heels if you've sprained your ankle.'

'I don't suppose it is sprained.' Tension edged into her voice. 'It was kind of you to bring me home but will you please go now?'

He ignored her request and continued walking down the hall, past the sitting room and a small functional kitchen. Both rooms were painted an insipid beige which matched the beige carpet. There were two doors on the opposite side of the hall. 'Which is your room?'

'The second door. I can manage now, thanks,' Sara said when he shouldered the door and carried her into her bedroom. She flicked the light switch and Alekos was surprised by the room's décor. The walls were covered with murals of exquisite, brightly coloured flowers and the floral theme extended to the curtains and bedspread. The single bed was piled with stuffed toy bears and a large pink rabbit, which he guessed were relics from her childhood. The room was a vibrant and startling contrast to the otherwise characterless house.

'You obviously like flowers,' he murmured. 'Who painted the murals?'

'I did.'

'Seriously?' He was amazed. 'You're very talented. Did you study art?'

'No,' she said shortly. 'My mother thought I would be wasting my time going to art school. It was her idea that I trained as a secretary because it's a more reliable career.'

Sara wished Alekos would leave. She considered struggling to force him to put her down, but his arms around her were like iron bands and she did not relish an undignified tussle. It was bad enough that he believed she had been affected by alcohol and it was the reason she had tripped and hurt her ankle. He had probably only carried her into the house because he'd felt it was his duty not to leave her sprawled in the gutter. But she did not want him in her bedroom. It was her personal space, and when her mother had been alive it had been the only place where she had been able to indulge the creative side of her nature that she'd recently discovered she had inherited from her father.

Her father who had refused to tell her half-siblings that she was his daughter.

Every word of the text her father had sent her was imprinted on her memory. She told herself it was understandable that Lionel Kingsley cared more about his children from his marriage than for the illegitimate daughter whose existence he had only been aware of for a few months. But it felt like a rejection and it hurt. She had no other family. Her mother had grown up in a children's home, and after Joan had died Sara had felt completely alone until she had met her father.

The tears she'd managed to hold back while she had been at the party filled her eyes and slid down her face. She brushed them away with her hand and swallowed a sob but she felt so empty inside, knowing that she would not now meet her half-brother and half-sister at the weekend. And maybe never, she thought bleakly. Perhaps her father regretted finding out about her.

'Sara, why are you crying? Does your ankle hurt?' Alekos sounded terse. Sara knew he hated displays of emotion as much as she hated displaying her emotions in front of anyone. Even when her mother had died she'd accepted Alekos's rather stilted words of sympathy with quiet dignity and had sensed his relief that she'd kept her emotions out of the office.

But she could not stop crying. Perhaps the whisky she'd drunk at the party had loosened her grip on her self-control. Her father's text had left her utterly bereft and the sense of loneliness that she'd always felt—because she'd never had a strong emotional bond with her mother—now overwhelmed her and she turned her face into Alekos's chest and wept.

Somewhere in her haze of misery she acknowledged that the situation was undoubtedly Alekos's worst nightmare. She remembered an occasion when one of his ex-lovers whom he'd recently dumped had stormed into his office in floods of tears and accused him of breaking her heart. Alekos had literally shuddered in disgust at his ex's undignified behaviour. What must he think of her? Sara wondered. But her tears kept coming. It was as though a dam inside her had burst and allowed her pent-up emotions to escape.

She expected Alekos to stand her on her feet before he beat a hasty retreat from the house. But he didn't. Instead he sat down on the edge of her bed and cradled her in his lap. She was aware of the muscled strength of his arms around her, and the steady beat of his heart that she could hear through his chest was oddly comforting. It was a novelty to feel cared for, even though she knew Alekos's show of tenderness wasn't real. He did not care about her. He'd reminded her when he'd offered to drive her home from the party that she was a member of his staff and therefore his responsibility.

But it was nice to pretend for a few minutes that he actually *meant* the gentle words of comfort he murmured. His voice was softer than she'd ever heard it, and she could almost fool herself that it was the intimate voice of a lover caressing her senses like the brush of velvet against her skin. Gradually her harsh sobs subsided and as she drew a shaky breath she inhaled the spicy musk of Alekos's aftershave mixed with an indefinable male scent that was uniquely him.

In that instant she became conscious of his hard

thighs beneath her bottom and the latent strength of his arms around her. Heat flared inside her and she felt a sensuous heaviness in her breasts and at the molten heart of her femininity.

She could not have said exactly when she sensed a change in him, only that she became aware that his breathing became irregular and his heartbeat beneath her ear quickened and thudded hard and fast. Desire stole through her veins as she lifted her head away from his chest. Her heart lurched when she saw the fierce glitter in his eyes.

'Sara—' His voice throbbed with a raw hunger that made her tremble as she watched him lower his face closer to hers. She stared at his mouth. His sensual, beautiful mouth. So often she had imagined him kissing her with his mouth that promised heaven. 'You're driving me crazy,' he growled before he covered her lips with his and the world went up in flames.

CHAPTER FOUR

HE HAD WANTED to kiss Sara all evening. All week, if he was honest, Alekos admitted to himself, remembering how he had barely been able to keep his hands off her at the office. By the end of each day his gut had felt as if it were tied in a knot, and punishing workouts at the gym after work had failed to relieve his sexual frustration.

There was only one way to assuage the carnal hunger that ignited inside him and made him shake with need. The ache in his groin intensified when Sara parted her lips beneath his and her warm breath filled his mouth. He kissed her the way he'd fantasised about kissing her when he'd first caught sight of her wearing her backless dress. At the party he'd struggled to concentrate on his conversations with the other guests, when all he could think about was running his hands over Sara's naked back. Now he indulged himself and stroked his finger-tips up her spine before he clasped her bare shoulders and pulled her even closer to him.

If she had offered the slightest resistance, perhaps he would have come to his senses. But his heart slammed into his ribs when she wound her arms round his neck and threaded her fingers into his hair. Her eager response decimated the last vestiges of his control, and he groaned as he dipped his tongue into her mouth and tasted her. She was nectar, sweet and hot and utterly intoxicating. In the far recesses of his mind Alekos was aware that he should stop this madness. Sara was his secretary, which meant she was off-limits. But it was impossible to associate the beautiful, sensual woman who had driven him to distraction over the past few days with his plain PA who had never warranted a second glance.

She shifted her position on his lap and he groaned again as her bottom ground against his rock-hard erection. He couldn't remember the last time he had felt so turned on. He felt as if he was going to explode and the faint warning voice inside his head was drowned out by the drumbeat of his desire to feel Sara's soft curves beneath him.

He manoeuvred her so that she was lying on the bed and he stretched out on top of her before capturing her mouth once more and kissing her with a deepening hunger that demanded to be appeased. Trailing his lips down her throat, he slid his hand behind her neck into the heavy silk of her hair and discovered that three tiny buttons secured the top of her dress. Three tiny buttons were all that prevented him from pulling the top of her dress down and revealing her ripe breasts that had tantalised him when they had been pressed against his chest. Urgency made his fingers uncooperative. He swore beneath his breath as he struggled to unfasten the buttons and something soft fell across his face.

Lifting his head, Alekos found himself eye to eye with a large pink rabbit. The incongruousness of making love to a woman on a narrow single bed adorned with stuffed animals catapulted him back to reality.

This was not any woman. This was Sara, his efficient, unflappable PA, who apparently had an unexpected liking for cuddly toys. He was only here in her bedroom because she had shockingly burst into tears.

Usually, when faced with a weeping woman, Alekos's instinct was to extricate himself from the situation as quickly possible. But Sara's tears had had an odd effect on him and inexplicably he'd found himself trying to comfort her. He had no idea why she had been crying. But he remembered that in the car when he'd driven her home she had read a text message on her phone and had looked upset.

Memories pushed through the sexual haze that had clouded Alekos's mind. Sara had hurried out of the office at the beginning of the week to meet someone. She had admitted she'd spent her holiday with a male 'friend' at his villa, and she had returned from the French Riviera transformed from a frump into a gorgeous sexpot. At the start of this evening she had seemed happy, but something had happened that had caused her to act out of character and she'd gulped down a double whisky as if it was no stronger than milk.

The most likely explanation Alekos could think of for Sara's distress was that her holiday romance was over. So what the hell was he—*the consolation prize*? He rolled away from her and sat up, assuring himself he was glad he had come to his senses before any harm had been done. Before he'd made the mistake of having sex with her. A kiss was nothing and there was no reason why they couldn't put it behind them and continue with their good working relationship as they had done for the past two years.

He stared at her flushed face and her kiss-stung

mouth that tempted him to forget everything and allow
the passion that had sizzled between them moments
ago to soar to its natural conclusion. But apart from all
the other considerations to them sleeping together—
and there were many—Alekos did not relish the idea
that Sara wanted someone else and he was second best.
Theos, he'd spent much of his life feeling second best
to his dead brother and believing that, in his father's
opinion, he was inferior to Dimitri.

'Alekos.' Sara's soft voice made his gut clench. She
sat up and pushed her hair back from her face. She
looked as stunned as he felt, and oddly vulnerable. For
a moment he had the ridiculous idea that having a man
in her bedroom was a new experience for her. 'We…we
shouldn't have done that,' she said huskily.

He was well aware of that fact, but he was irritated
she had pointed it out. 'It was just a kiss.' He shrugged,
as much to emphasise the unimportance of the kiss to
himself as well as to her. 'Don't look so stricken, Sara.
It won't happen again.' Anger with himself for being
so damned weak made him say harshly, 'It wouldn't
have happened at all if you hadn't practically begged
me to kiss you.'

'I did no such thing.' Fiery colour flared on her
cheeks. 'You kissed me. One minute you were comforting me because I was upset, and the next…'

Alekos did not want to think about what had happened next. Remembering how he had explored the
moist interior of Sara's mouth with his tongue, and
the little moans she had made when he had kissed her,
caused his erection to press uncomfortably against the
restriction of his trousers.

'Ah, yes, you were upset—' he focused on the first

part of her sentence '—I'm guessing that the reason you were crying was because your holiday lover has dumped you. Your eagerness to kiss me was because you're on the rebound from the guy in France who has rejected you.'

'There was no holiday lover,' she said tightly. 'The "guy in France" was my *father*. I spent my holiday at his villa.' Sara's bottom lip trembled. 'But you're right to think I feel rejected. I'm starting to believe my father regrets that he got in contact with me. Until recently I didn't know about him, or that I have a half-brother and half-sister.' Tears slid down her cheeks. She gave a choked sob and covered her face with her hands, and so did not see Alekos's grim expression.

He had never seen Sara cry until tonight and his abhorrence of emotional displays meant that he really didn't want to stick around. But the fact that she was crying in front of him suggested something serious had happened to upset her. Why, even when she had come to work one Monday morning just before Christmas and told him that her mother had died at the weekend she had kept her emotions in check.

He felt an odd tug in his chest as he watched Sara's body shudder as she tried to regain control of herself. Ignoring a strong temptation to leave her to it, he pulled the dressing table stool next to the bed and sat down on it before he handed her some tissues from the box on the bedside table.

'Thanks,' she said indistinctly. Her tears had washed away most of her make-up, and again Alekos was struck by her air of innocence that he told himself he must have imagined.

'What did you mean when you said you think your

father regrets contacting you? Had there been a rift be-tween the two of you?'

She shook her head. 'It's complicated. I met my fa-ther for the first time six weeks ago. When my holiday plans to Spain fell through he invited me to stay at his villa in Antibes. He wasn't there for the whole time, but he came to visit me and we began to get to know each other. I pretended to anyone who asked that I was em-ployed as a housekeeper at the villa because my father was worried about the media.' Her voice broke. 'I'm a scandal from his past, you see, and he doesn't want his other children to find out about me.'

'But why would the media be interested in your fa-ther?'

'Because he's famous. I promised I would keep my relationship to him secret until he is ready to publicly acknowledge that I am his illegitimate daughter.'

She was her father's shameful secret, Sara thought mis-erably. And from the text that Lionel had sent her ear-lier, it seemed as though she would remain a secret and never meet her half-siblings. She hadn't revealed her father's identity to anyone, not even her closest friend, Ruth, who she had known since they were at primary school. But the truth about her father that at first had been such a wonderful surprise had become a burden she longed to share with someone.

She blinked away yet more tears. Her head ached from crying and she wished she could rest it on the pil-lows. But if she did that, Alekos might think she was inviting him to lie on the bed with her and kiss her again. She darted a glance at him and heat ran through her veins as she remembered the weight of him pressing her into the mattress and the feel of his muscular thighs as he'd ground his hips against her pelvis.

Of course she hadn't 'practically begged him to kiss her', as he'd accused her, she assured herself. But she hadn't stopped him. She bit her lip. Alekos had been the one to draw back, and if he hadn't… The tugging sensation in the pit of her stomach became a sharp pull of need as her imagination ran riot and she pictured them both naked, their limbs entwined and his body joined with hers.

She flushed as her eyes crashed into his glittering dark gaze and she realised that he was aware she had been staring at him.

'Why did you only meet your father for the first time recently?'

'He wasn't part of my life when I was growing up.' She shrugged to show him it didn't hurt, even though it did. 'My mother was employed as my father's secretary when they had an affair. He was married with a family, but he decided that he wanted to try and save his marriage and ended his relationship with Mum. She moved away without telling him that she was pregnant. She refused to talk about him and I have no idea why, in the last week of her life, she wrote to him and told him about me.'

She sighed. 'My father found out about me six months ago, but his wife was ill and he waited until after she had died before he phoned and asked if we could meet. He said he was glad he had found me. He'd assumed that my mother had told me his identity. Now I'm wondering if his reason for finding me was because he feared I might sell the story about my famous father to the newspapers. If the press got hold of the story it could damage his relationship with his children from his marriage. And I imagine the scandal that he'd had an affair, even though it was years ago, might harm his political career.'

Alekos's brows rose. 'Your father is a politician?'

Sara felt torn between her promise to protect her father's identity and what she told herself was a selfish need to unburden her secret to *someone*. But to Alekos? Strangely, he was the one person she trusted above all others. The tabloids made much of his playboy reputation, but she knew another side to him. He was dedicated to GE and worked hard to make it a globally successful business. He was a tough but fair employer and he was intensely protective of his mother and sisters. He guarded his own privacy fiercely, but could she trust that he would guard hers?

'It's vital that the story isn't leaked to the media,' she cautioned.

'You know my feelings about the scum who are fondly known as the paparazzi,' he said sardonically. 'I'm not likely to divulge anything you tell me in confidence to the press.'

She snatched a breath. 'My father is Lionel Kingsley.' It was the first time she had ever said the words aloud and it felt strange. Alekos looked shocked and she wondered if she had been naïve to confide in him. Now he knew something about her that no one else knew, and for some reason that made her feel vulnerable.

He gave a low whistle. 'Do you mean the Right Honourable Lionel Kingsley, MP—the Minister for Culture and the Arts? I've met him on a few occasions, both socially and also in his capacity as Culture Secretary, when I sponsored an exhibition of Greek art at the British Museum. As a matter of fact he was a guest at a party I went to earlier this week.'

'It sounds as though you have a lot more in common with my father than I do,' Sara muttered. She didn't move in the exalted social circles that Alekos and Lionel did, and she would definitely never have the opportunity to meet her father or her half-siblings socially. She tried to focus on what Alekos was saying.

'What has happened to make you think your father regrets finding you?'

'I was supposed to go and stay at his home at the weekend so that I could meet my half-siblings. But Lionel has decided against telling Freddie and Charlotte about me. It's only two months since their mother died. They were very close to her, and he's worried about how they will react to the news that he had been unfaithful to his wife.'

She pressed her hand to her temple, which had started to throb. 'I get the impression that I'm a complication and Lionel wishes he hadn't told me he is my father. His name isn't on my birth certificate and there's no possibility I could have found out I'm his daughter.'

She swung her legs off the bed and stood up. Alekos also got to his feet and her small bedroom seemed to be dominated by his six-feet-plus of raw masculinity.

'You should go,' she said abruptly, feeling too strung out to play the role of polite hostess. 'What happened just now...when we kissed...' her face flamed when he said nothing but looked amused, damn him '...obviously it can never happen again. I mean, you have a strict rule about not sleeping with your staff. Not that I'm suggesting you want to sleep with me,' she added quickly, in case he thought she was hinting that she hoped he wanted to have an affair with her.

Hot with embarrassment, she ploughed on, 'It was an unfortunate episode and I blame my behaviour on the whisky I drank earlier.'

'Rubbish.' Alekos laughed softly. 'You're not drunk. And I haven't had a drink all night. Alcohol had nothing to do with why we kissed. It was chemistry that ignited between us and made us both act out of character.'

'Exactly.' Sara seized on his words. 'It was a mistake, and the best thing we can do is to forget it happened.'

He deliberately lowered his eyes to her breasts, and she fought the temptation to cross her arms over her chest and hide her nipples that she was aware had hardened and must be visible jutting beneath the silky material of her dress. Somehow she made herself look at him calmly.

'Do you think it will be possible to forget the passion that exploded between us?' he murmured.

'It has to be, if I am going to continue as your PA.' She sounded fiercer than she had intended as she fought a rising sense of panic that the memory of Alekos kissing her would stay in her mind for a very long time. 'And now I really would like you to leave. It's late, and I'm tired.'

He checked his watch and said in an amused voice, 'It's a quarter to ten, which is hardly late. We left the dinner early because you said you were feeling unwell.'

To her relief he said no more and walked over to the door. 'I'll see myself out. And Sara—' his gaze held hers and his tone was suddenly serious '—your secret is safe with me. For what it's worth, I think your father should feel very proud to have you as his daughter.'

Alekos's unexpected compliment was the last straw for Sara's battered emotions. She held on until she heard the front door bang as he closed it behind him before she gave in to the tears that had threatened her composure since he had *stopped* kissing her.

Yes, she was upset about her father, but she was horrified to admit that she was more hurt by Alekos's rejection. She couldn't forget that he had been the one who had come to his senses. But what did her tears say about her? Why was she crying over a man who hadn't paid her any attention for two years? He had only noticed her recently because she'd revamped her appearance.

Alekos's interest in her was a passing fancy, but he could very easily break her heart if she allowed him to. She wished she *had* been drunk tonight, she brooded. At least then she could forgive herself for responding to him the way she had. Instead she only had her foolish heart to blame.

It took all of Sara's willpower to make herself stroll into Alekos's office the next morning and give him a cheerful smile before she turned her attention to the espresso machine.

His eyes narrowed when she walked over to his desk and placed a cup of coffee in front of him. She had resisted the urge to wear the beige dress that still lurked in the back of her wardrobe—a remnant of her previous dreary style. Out of sheer bravado she had chosen a bright red skirt and a red-and-white polka-dot blouse. Red stilettos and a slick of scarlet lip gloss completed her outfit. Her layered hairstyle flicked the tops of her shoulders as she sat down composedly and waited for him to give her instructions for the day.

'You're looking very perky. I trust you are feeling better?'

The gleam in his dark eyes was almost her undoing, but she had promised herself that she wouldn't let him rattle her and so she smiled and said coolly, 'Much better, thank you. I'm just sorry that you had to leave the dinner early last night because of me.'

'I'm not,' he murmured. The gleam turned to something darker and hotter as he skimmed his gaze down from her pink cheeks to her dotty blouse, and Sara was sure he was remembering the passion that had exploded between them in her bedroom.

She was conscious of the pulse at the base of her throat beating erratically and said hurriedly, 'Shall we get on? I thought you wanted to go through the final details for the Monaco Yacht Show.'

Alekos's sardonic smile told her he had seen through her distraction ploy, but to her relief he opened the folder in front of him. 'As you know, GE is one of the top exhibitors at the show, and we will be using the company's show yacht to give tours and demonstrations to potential clients interested in buying a superyacht. I've heard from the captain of *Artemis* that she has docked in Monaco and the crew are preparing her for the show. You and I will fly out to meet the rest of the sales team, and we will stay on board the yacht.'

For the rest of the morning, work was the only topic of conversation and if Sara tried hard she could almost pretend that the events of the previous night hadn't happened. It helped if she didn't look directly at Alekos but on the occasions when she did make eye contact with him the glittering heat in his gaze caused her stomach to dip. Alekos had called it *chemistry*, and its tangible presence every time she stepped into his office simmered between them and filled the room with a prickling tension that seemed to drain the air from Sara's lungs.

She was relieved when he left for a lunch appointment and told her he did not expect to be back until later in the afternoon. But, perversely, once he had gone she missed him and couldn't settle down to her work because she kept picturing his ruggedly handsome face and reliving the feel of his lips on hers. It was just a kiss, she reminded herself. But deep down she knew that something fundamental had changed between her and Alekos. She had hidden her feelings for him for two years, but it was so much harder to hide her desire for him when he looked at her with a hungry gleam in his eyes that made her ache with longing.

He returned just before five o'clock and seemed surprised to find her still at her desk. 'I thought you wanted to leave early tonight.'

'I'm not going to visit my father at his home in Berkshire now, so I thought I might as well catch up on some filing,' she said in a carefully controlled voice. She was embarrassed that she had cried in front of Alekos last night and was determined to hide her devastation over her father's change of heart about introducing her to her half-siblings.

His speculative look gave her the unsettling notion that he could read her thoughts. 'I've been thinking about your situation and I have an idea of how to help. Come into my office. I'm sure you would rather not discuss a personal matter where anyone walking past could overhear us.'

Sara didn't want to have a personal discussion with him anywhere, but he held open his office door and she could not think of an excuse to refuse. Besides, she was intrigued that he had actually thought about her. 'What idea?' she said as soon as he had shut the door.

He walked around his desk and waited until she was seated opposite him before he replied. 'On Sunday evening I have been invited to the launch of a new art gallery in Soho.'

'I'm up to speed with your diary, Alekos.' She hid her disappointment that he had brought her in to discuss his busy social schedule. But why would he be interested in her problems?

He ignored her interruption. 'The gallery's owner, Jemima Wilding, represents several well-established artists, but she also wants to support new talent and the gallery's launch will include paintings by an up-and-coming artist, Freddie Kingsley.'

Sara's heart gave an odd thump. 'I didn't know that my half-brother was an artist.'

'I believe Freddie and Charlotte both studied art at Chelsea College of Art. Charlotte is establishing herself as a fashion designer. She will be at the gallery launch on Sunday to support her brother, along with Lionel Kingsley.'

'Why are you telling me this?' She could not keep the bitterness from her voice. Alekos was emphasising what she already knew—that she did not belong in the rarefied world that her father and half-siblings, and Alekos himself, occupied.

'Because my idea is that you could accompany me to

the gallery launch to meet your half-siblings. I realise you won't be able to say that you are related to them, but you might have a chance to talk to your father in private during the evening and persuade him to reveal your true identity.'

Her heart gave another lurch as she tried to imagine meeting Freddie and Charlotte. Would they notice the physical similarities she shared with them? Probably not, she reassured herself. They were unaware that they had an illegitimate half-sister. Alekos was offering her what might be her only opportunity to meet her blood relations. Common sense doused her excitement. 'It would look strange if you took your PA to a private engagement.'

'Possibly, but you wouldn't be there as my PA. You would accompany me as my date. My mistress,' he explained when she stared at him uncomprehendingly.

For a third time Sara's heart jolted against her ribs. 'We agreed to forget about the kiss we shared last night.' She flushed, hating how she sounded breathless when she had intended her voice to be cool and crisp.

His eyes gleamed like hot coals for a second before the fire in those dark depths was replaced by a faintly cynical expression that Sara was more used to seeing. 'I don't remember agreeing to forget about it,' he drawled. 'But I'm suggesting that we *pretend* to be in a relationship. If people believe you are my girlfriend it will seem perfectly reasonable for you to be with me.'

'I can see a flaw in your plan.' Several flaws, as it happened, but she focused on the main one. 'You have made it clear that you would never become personally involved with any member of your staff. If we are seen together in public it's likely that the board members of

GE will believe we are having an affair. They disapprove of your playboy reputation and might even decide to take a vote of no confidence against you.'

'That won't happen. As you said yourself, the board members approve of you. They think you are a good, stabilising influence on me,' he said drily.

Sara remembered the many glamorous blondes Alekos had dated in the past. 'I'm not sure your friends would be convinced that you and I are in a relationship,' she said doubtfully.

'They'd have been convinced if they had seen us together last night.' His wicked grin made her blush. 'The plan will work because of the sexual chemistry between us. There's no point in denying it.' He did not give her a chance to speak. 'It is an inconvenient attraction that we might as well use to our advantage.'

So she was an inconvenience! It was hardly a flattering description. 'Why are you willing to help me meet my half-siblings? You've never taken an interest in my personal life before.'

He shrugged. 'You're right to guess I am not being entirely altruistic. Zelda Pagnotis will also be at the gallery launch. She is a friend of Jemima Wilding's daughter, Leah. You saw how Zelda followed me around at the board members' dinner, how she changed the name cards around so that she was seated next to me.' Frustration clipped his voice. 'Her crush on me is becoming a problem, but if she believes that you are my girlfriend it might persuade her to move her attention onto another guy.'

'Are you saying you need me to protect you from Zelda?'

'Orestis thinks I want to corrupt his granddaughter,'

Alekos growled. 'Of course nothing could be further from the truth, but I guarantee Orestis won't disapprove of you being my mistress. He's more likely to be relieved.'

'But why don't you flaunt a genuine mistress in front of Zelda? There must be dozens of women who would jump at the chance to go on a date with you.'

'I don't happen to have a girlfriend at the moment. If I invite one of my exes to the gallery launch there's a risk they will read too much into it and believe I want to get back with them.'

'What it is to be Mr Popular,' Sara murmured wryly. Alekos's arrogance was infuriating, but he had a point. In the two years that she had been his PA she'd realised that women threw themselves at him without any encouragement from him.

He hadn't needed to encourage her to kiss him last night. She flushed as she remembered how eagerly she had responded to him. But he had called a halt to their passion even though he must have sensed that she wanted him to make love to her. Now he was asking her to pretend to be in love with him, and she was afraid she would be too convincing.

'What do you think of my idea, Sara? It seems to me that it will be an ideal solution for both of us.'

She looked into his dark eyes and her heart gave a familiar swoop. 'I need time to think about it.'

He frowned. 'How much time? I'll need to let Jemima know that I am bringing a guest.'

Sara refused to let him browbeat her into making a decision. Although she longed to meet her half-siblings she was worried about how her father might react to seeing her at a social event. 'Phone me in the morning and I'll give you my answer,' she said calmly. She stood up and walked over to the door, but then hesitated and turned to look at him.

'Thank you for offering to help me meet my half-siblings. I appreciate it.'

Alekos waited until Sara had closed the door behind her before he strode over to the drinks cabinet and poured himself a double measure of malt Scotch. Her smile had hit him like a punch in his gut. He'd always known he was a bastard, and Sara had confirmed it when she'd said that she appreciated his help.

He raked his hair off his brow. Sara had no idea that her revelation about her father's identity was a very useful piece of knowledge that he intended to use to his advantage. His keenness to attend the gallery launch had nothing to do with an interest in art and everything to do with business. Alekos knew that the Texan oil billionaire Warren McCuskey was on the guest list. He also knew that McCuskey and Lionel Kingsley were close friends.

The story went that many years ago both men had been amateur sailors competing in a transatlantic yacht race, but the American had nearly lost his life when his boat had capsized. Lionel Kingsley had been leading the race but had sacrificed his chance of winning when he'd gone to McCuskey's assistance. Three decades later, Warren McCuskey had become one of the richest men in the US and the person who had the most influence over him was his good friend, English politician Lionel Kingsley—who, astonishingly, happened to be Sara's father.

Alekos was aware that networking was a crucial part

of business, and the best deals were forged at social events where the champagne flowed freely. He'd heard that McCuskey was considering splashing out some of his huge fortune on a superyacht. At the party on Sunday evening, Sara would want to spend time with her father, and it would be an ideal opportunity for him to ingratiate himself with the Texan billionaire.

He took a swig of his Scotch and ignored the twinge of his conscience as he thought of Sara and how he planned to use a fake affair with her for his own purpose. All was fair in love and business, he thought sardonically. Not that he knew anything about love. GE was his top priority and he had a responsibility, a *duty*, to ensure that the company was as successful as it would undoubtedly have been under Dimitri's leadership. He secretly suspected that his brother had thrown his life away because of a woman. But Alekos would never allow any woman close to his heart and certainly not to influence his business strategy.

CHAPTER FIVE

THE LIMOUSINE CAME to a halt beside the kerb and Alekos prepared to step out of the car, when Sara's voice stopped him.

'I don't think I can go through with it.' Her voice shook. 'You didn't say the press would be here.'

He glanced out of the window at the group of journalists and cameramen gathered on the pavement outside the Wilding Gallery. 'There was bound to be some media interest. Jemima Wilding is well-known in the art world and naturally she wants exposure for her new gallery. I suspect she leaked the names on the guest list to the paparazzi,' he said drily.

The chauffeur opened the door but Sara did not move. 'Doesn't it bother you that photos of us arriving together might be published in the newspapers and give the impression that we are...a couple?'

'But that's the point.' Alekos stifled his impatience, realising he needed to reassure her. When he'd phoned Sara on Saturday morning, she had said she would pretend to be his mistress and accompany him to the gallery launch. Now she seemed to be having second thoughts. 'You want to meet your half-siblings, don't you?' he reminded her of the reason she had agreed to his plan.

'Of course I do. But I'm worried my father will be angry when he sees me. He might think I came here to-night to put pressure on him to tell Charlotte and Freddie about me.'

'Then we will have to put on a convincing act that you are my girlfriend and you are at the party with me.'

'I suppose so.' She still sounded unsure. Alekos watched her sink her teeth into her soft lower lip and was tempted to soothe the maligned flesh with his tongue. But such an action, although undoubtedly enjoyable, would be wasted here in the car where they couldn't be seen.

Glancing out of the window again, he noticed a young woman, wearing a skirt so short it was not much more than a belt, standing in the glass-fronted lobby of the gallery. He gritted his teeth. Zelda Pagnotis was an irritating thorn in his side, but unless he took drastic action to end her crush on him the teenager could become a more serious problem and cause a further rift between him and her grandfather.

'Thank you, Mike,' Alekos said to the chauffeur as he climbed out of the car and held out his hand to Sara. After a few seconds' hesitation she put her fingers in his and stepped onto the pavement. She stiffened when he slid his arm around her waist and escorted her over to the entrance of the art gallery. As Alekos had predicted, the paparazzi took pictures of him and Sara, and she pressed closer to him and put her head down as the flashbulbs went off around them when they walked into the building.

A doorman stepped forwards to take her coat. It had been raining earlier when the car had collected her from her house and Alekos hadn't seen what she was wearing beneath her raincoat until now.

Theos! He tore his eyes from her and glanced around him, thinking he had spoken out loud. But no one was looking at him. He returned his gaze to her and stared. 'Your dress...'

'Is it all right?' Her tongue darted out to moisten her lips. The gesture betrayed her nervousness and sent a shaft of white-hot desire through Alekos. 'Is my dress suitable?' she said in an undertone. 'Why are you staring at me?'

'It's more than suitable. You look incredible.' He ran his eyes over her bare shoulders, revealed by her emerald silk strapless dress, down to the rounded curves of her breasts that made him think of ripe peaches, firm and delicately flushed, tempting him to taste them. Lowering his gaze still further, he noted how the design of the dress drew attention to her slim waist before the skirt flared over her hips and fell to just above her knees.

Forcing his eyes back up her body, he noted how her layered hair swirled around her shoulders when she turned her head, and the hot ache in his groin intensified when he imagined her silky hair brushing across his naked chest as he lifted her on top of him and guided her down onto his hard shaft.

'Theos.' This time he spoke aloud in a rough voice as he curved his hand behind her neck and drew her towards him. He saw her eyes widen until they were huge green pools that pulled him in.

'Alekos,' she whispered warningly, as if to remind him that they were not alone in the lobby. But she didn't pull away as he lowered his face towards hers.

'Sara,' he mocked softly. And then he covered her mouth with his and kissed her, long and slow, and then deep and hard when she parted her lips and kissed him back with a sweet intensity that made his gut twist and made him want to sweep her up in his arms and carry her off to somewhere where they could be alone.

The low murmur of voices pushed into his consciousness and he reluctantly lifted his head and snatched oxygen into his lungs. Sara looked as stunned as he felt, but he had no intention of admitting that what had just happened was a first for him. He had *never* kissed a woman in public before. As he stepped away from her he caught sight of Zelda Pagnotis hurrying out of the lobby wearing a sulky expression on her face.

'First objective of the evening completed,' he told Sara smoothly, keen to hide the effect she had on him. 'Zelda can't doubt that we are having an affair. I've just spotted Lionel Kingsley and his son and daughter. Are you ready to meet your half-siblings?'

Sara could feel her heart hammering beneath her ribs as she walked with Alekos into the main gallery. She was excited that in a few moments she would meet her half-brother and half-sister for the first time, but she was still reeling from the sizzling kiss she had shared with Alekos.

While she'd been in his arms she had forgotten where they were, or why he had brought her to the art gallery. But when he had lifted his mouth from hers, she'd seen Zelda Pagnotis walk past them and realised that Alekos had deliberately kissed her in view of the teenager. *First objective completed.* She recalled his words ruefully. What an idiot she was to have believed that he'd kissed her because he desired her.

She looked ahead to the group of people Alekos was heading towards and her heart beat harder when she saw her father. Lionel was frowning as he watched her approach and her hesitant smile faltered. *She shouldn't have come.* The last thing she wanted to do was alienate her father. Her steps slowed and she felt a strong urge to run out of the gallery, but Alekos slipped his arm around her waist and propelled her forwards.

A tall woman with purple hair detached from the group and greeted them. 'Alekos, darling, I'm so glad you were able to come this evening. That was quite an entrance you made,' she said in an amused voice that made Sara blush. 'You must be Sara. I'm Jemima Wilding. I'm so pleased to meet you. Alekos, I think you and Lionel Kingsley have met before.'

'We have indeed.' Lionel shook Alekos's hand. 'Your financial support of the Greek art exhibition last year was much appreciated. But actually we met very recently at a party earlier this week.' He glanced at Alekos's hand resting on Sara's waist. 'You were un-accompanied on that occasion.'

'Yes, unfortunately Sara had another commitment,' Alekos said smoothly. He tightened his arm around Sara's waist as if he guessed that her heart was fluttering like a trapped bird in her chest. 'This is Sara Lovejoy.'

To Sara, the silence seemed to last for ever and stretched her nerves to the snapping point. But in reality Lionel Kingsley hesitated infinitesimally before he shook her hand. 'I am delighted to meet you... Miss Lovejoy.'

'Sara,' she said thickly. Her throat felt constricted and she smiled gratefully at Alekos when he handed her a flute of champagne from a passing waiter.

Lionel introduced the other people in the group, starting with a stockily built man with a rubicund face. 'This is my good friend Warren McCuskey, who flew to London from Texas especially so that he could attend the gallery launch and support my son Freddie's first exhibition.'

Sara greeted Warren with a polite smile, but her heart was thumping as Freddie Kingsley stretched his hand towards her. She prayed no one would notice her hand was trembling as she held it out to him.

Her half-brother smiled. 'Pleased to meet you, Sara.'

'I...' Emotion clogged her throat as Freddie closed his fingers around hers. His handshake was firm and his skin felt warm beneath her fingertips. Her secret drummed in her brain. Freddie was unaware that the blood running through his veins was partly the same as her blood. She swallowed and tried to speak but the lump in her throat prevented her.

Alekos moved imperceptibly closer, as if he understood that her emotions were balanced on a knife-edge. There was something comforting about his big-framed, solid presence at her side and, to her relief, she could suddenly breathe again.

'It's lovely to meet you,' she told Freddie softly. Her half-brother was taller than she had imagined, his brown hair curled over his collar and his smile was wide and welcoming. She looked into his green eyes and recognised herself.

He gave her a puzzled look. 'Have we met before? Your face seems familiar.'

'No, we've never met.' Sara was conscious of her father standing a few feet away and wondered if she was the only person in the group who could sense Lionel's tension.

Freddie shrugged. 'You definitely remind me of someone but I can't think who. Are you interested in art, Sara?'

'Very. I'd love to see your work.'

She followed Freddie over to where six of his paintings were displayed against a white wall. Even to her untrained eye she could tell that he was a gifted artist. His use of intense colour and light made his landscapes bold and exciting.

'My brother is very talented, isn't he?'

Sara turned her head towards the voice and discovered her half-sister standing next to her.

'I'm Charlotte Kingsley, by the way. I really like your dress.' Charlotte grinned and murmured, 'I really like your gorgeous boyfriend too. And he seems very keen on you. Even when he is talking to other people he can't keep his eyes off you. Have the two of you been together long?'

'Um…not that long.' Sara experienced the same difficulty speaking that had happened when she'd met Freddie. She felt an instant connection with Charlotte which made her think that maybe they could become friends. But perhaps her half-siblings would hate her if they learned that she was the result of Lionel Kingsley's affair with her mother.

She chatted for a few minutes and then slipped away to a quiet corner of the gallery, needing to be alone with her churning emotions. It was obvious that Charlotte and Freddie were deeply fond of each other. Sara felt a pang of envy as she watched them laughing together. Her childhood had been lonely because her mother hadn't encouraged her to invite school friends home. She had longed for a brother or sister to be a companion, unaware that growing up in Berkshire had been her half-sister, who was a year older than her, and her half-brother, three years her senior.

Tears gathered in her eyes and she quickly blinked them away when Lionel walked over to join her. She glanced around the gallery, searching for Alekos. Her instinctive need for his protection was a danger that she would have to deal with later. She saw him chatting with the Texan, Warren McCuskey, and her heart gave a silly skip as she realised that Alekos must have purposely given her and her father a few minutes of privacy.

'Sara, it's good to see you.' Lionel's smile allayed her concern that he was annoyed she had come to the party. 'I had no idea you were dating Alekos Gionakis. I thought you worked for him?'

'I'm his PA, but recently we…we've become close.' She felt her face grow warm. Lying did not come naturally to her. But she had to admit that Alekos's idea for her to pretend to be his girlfriend had allowed her to meet her half-siblings, and maybe she had a chance of persuading her father to reveal her identity to Freddie and Charlotte.

'Gionakis is an interesting man. He is knowledgeable of the arts but I've heard that he's a ruthless businessman.' Lionel lowered his voice so that he couldn't be overheard by anyone else. 'Sara, if Joan had told me she was pregnant I would have offered her financial support while you were a child. I regret that you did not grow up in a family.'

'I have a half-brother and half-sister who are my family, and I would love to get to know Charlotte and Freddie if only you would tell them I am your daughter,' Sara replied in a fierce whisper.

Her father looked uncomfortable. 'I will tell them when the time is right. Maybe if they got to know you first it would help when I break the news that I once cheated on their mother.' He looked round and saw Alekos approaching. 'Does Gionakis know of our relationship?'

Sara hesitated. 'Yes. But I know Alekos won't say a word to anyone,' she said hurriedly when Lionel frowned.

'You must love him to trust him so much.'

Love Alekos! Sara found she could not refute her father's comment. Her heart gave a familiar lurch as she watched Alekos walk towards her. He looked outrageously sexy, wearing a casual but impeccably tailored light grey suit and a black shirt, unbuttoned at the neck. His thick hair was ruffled as if he'd raked it off his brow several times during the evening, and the dark stubble shading his jaw added to his dangerous magnetism.

Of course she was in love with him; she finally admitted what she had tried to deny to herself for two years. She loved Alekos, but he'd told her he did not believe in love. Just because you loved someone didn't mean you could make them love you back. Her mother had discovered the truth of that when she had fallen in love with Lionel Kingsley.

'I told you my plan would work.' Alekos knew he sounded smug but he didn't care. He'd had a couple of drinks at the gallery launch and, although he was certainly not drunk, he felt relaxed and pleased with how the evening had gone. He leaned his head against the plush leather back seat of the limousine as they sped towards north London. His thoughts were on Warren McCuskey. The Texan billionaire was definitely interested in buying a superyacht and Alekos had used all his persuasive powers to convince him to commission a yacht from GE. He was confident he was close to finalising a deal with McCuskey. He could taste success, smell it.

He could also smell Sara's perfume. The blend of citrusy bergamot and sensual white musk, that had tantalised him every day at the office, filled the dark car and his senses. Suddenly he didn't feel relaxed any more. He felt wired up inside, the way Sara always made him feel lately. He was conscious of the hard thud of his heart and the even harder ache of his arousal that jerked to attention and pushed against the zip of his trousers.

'I don't think Zelda will continue to be a problem now that she believes you are my mistress,' he drawled, more to remind himself of the reason why he had spent most of the evening with his arm around Sara's waist. She'd fitted against his side as if she belonged there. He frowned as he remembered how, every time he'd leaned towards her, he'd inhaled a vanilla scent in her hair that he guessed was the shampoo she used.

'Good. That's one problem solved at least.' She sounded distracted.

Alekos glanced at her sitting beside him. She had put her coat on before they'd left the gallery, but it was undone and he could see the smooth upper slopes of her breasts above the top of her dress. 'Is there another problem?' he said abruptly.

'There might be.' She flicked her head round to look at him and her hair brushed against his shoulder, leaving a trail of vanilla scent. 'Alekos, we need to talk.'

Talking to Sara was not uppermost in his mind. But if he told her of his erotic thoughts about her she would probably slap his face. The car pulled up outside her house. 'Invite me in for coffee and you can tell me what's troubling you.'

'All right,' she said after a moment's hesitation. 'But I only have instant coffee. Will that do?'

As Alekos followed her into the house he regretted his suggestion. He detested the insipid brown liquid that the English insisted on calling coffee. But, more pertinently, he couldn't understand why he had suggested to Sara that she could confide in him what he assumed was a problem with her private life. He was about to tell her not to worry about the coffee but she showed him into the sitting room, saying, 'I'll go and put the kettle on.'

It was difficult to imagine a room more characterless than the one he was standing in. The neutral décor was joyless, as if whoever had chosen the beige furnishings had found no pleasure in life. It was a strangely oppressive room and Alekos retreated and walked down the bungalow's narrow hallway to the kitchen.

Sara had taken off her coat and she looked like a gaudy butterfly in her bright dress against the backdrop of sterile worktops and cupboards. She had also slipped off her shoes and he was struck by how petite she was without her high heels. The sight of her bare feet with her toenails varnished a flirty shade of pink had an odd effect on him and he felt his gut twist with desire. He searched for something to say while he struggled to control his rampant libido.

'How come your bedroom is so colourful, while the rest of the house is...' he swapped the word *drab* for '...plain?'

'My mother didn't like bright colours. Now Mum has gone I've decided to sell the house. The estate agent advised me not to redecorate because buyers prefer a blank canvas.' She placed a mug on the counter in front of him. 'I made your coffee extra strong so it should taste like freshly ground coffee.'

Alekos thought it was highly unlikely. But remembering Sara's brightly coloured bedroom brought back memories of his previous visit to her home when he had kissed her and passion had ignited between them. There was barely enough space for the two of them in the tiny kitchen but he didn't want to suggest they move into the sitting room, which was as welcoming as a morgue. He sipped his coffee and managed not to grimace. 'What did you want to talk about?'

'Lionel thinks it would be a good idea if I could mix with Charlotte and Freddie socially so they can get to know me before he tells them I am their half-sister. He intends to use his association with you—namely your support of art projects—to invite us both to his villa in Antibes, where he's planning to celebrate his birthday.' Sara tugged on her bottom lip with her small white teeth, sending Alekos quietly to distraction as he imagined covering her lush mouth with his.

'Go on,' he muttered.

'I couldn't tell my father that I had pretended to be your girlfriend tonight so I could meet my half-siblings. Lionel believes we are genuinely in a relationship and we would have to continue the pretence if you accept his invitation.'

'Who else has your father invited to his villa?'

'Charlotte and Freddie and my father's close friend Warren McCuskey. By the way, thanks for chatting to Warren at the gallery while I spoke to my father privately.'

'You're welcome.' Alekos ignored the irritating voice of his conscience, which reminded him he was an unprincipled bastard. It was a fact of life that you couldn't head a multimillion-pound business and have principles. He'd seized his chance to grab McCuskey's undivided attention while Sara was talking to Lionel. 'When is your father's birthday?'

'Next weekend. I'd mentioned that we will be in Monaco for the yacht show and he said that Antibes is only about an hour's drive away. But I did warn him that we will be busy with the show and might not have time to visit him.'

'Our schedule for the three days of the show is hectic. But how about if I arranged a birthday lunch for your father and his guests aboard *Artemis* for next Sunday? That way we can catch up on paperwork in the morning, and you'll be able to spend time with Lionel and your brother and sister in the afternoon.' It would also be an ideal opportunity to give Warren McCuskey a demonstration of GE's flagship superyacht, but Alekos kept that to himself.

'Would you really be prepared to do that on my behalf?' Her smile stole his breath and he shrugged off the niggling voice of his conscience. Sara caught her lower lip between her teeth again. 'But will you mind having to keep up the pretence that I am your girlfriend?'

Alekos dropped his gaze from her mouth to the delectable creamy curves of her breasts cupped in her silk dress, and he was surprised that the thud of his heart wasn't audible. 'I think I can put up with pretending that we are lovers,' he drawled.

He smiled when he heard her breath rush from her lungs as he wrapped his arm around her waist and drew her towards him so that she was pressed against his chest, against his heat and the hardness of his arousal that ached. *Theos,* he had never ached so badly for a woman before.

'Alekos,' she whispered. Her green eyes were very dark and he saw her uncertainty reflected in their depths as he lowered his head. 'What are you doing?'

'Rehearsing for when we meet your father,' he growled before he slanted his mouth over hers and kissed her like he'd wanted to do, like he'd been burning up to do since he had kissed her in the lobby of the art gallery. The difference was that that had been for Zelda Pagnotis's sake, or so Alekos had assured himself. But this time it was lust, pure and simple, that made him cup Sara's jaw in his palm and angle her head so that he could plunder her lips and slide his tongue into her mouth to taste her sweetness.

Without her high-heeled shoes she was much smaller than him and Alekos lifted her up and sat her on the kitchen worktop, nudging her thighs apart so that he could stand between them. The fact that she let him gave him the licence he needed to capture her mouth and kiss her again, hard this time, demanding her response as the fire inside him burned out of control.

Her shoulders were silky smooth beneath his hands. He traced his fingers along the delicate line of her collarbone before moving lower to explore the upper slopes of her breasts. Touching wasn't enough. He had to see her, had to cradle those firm mounds in his hands. With his lips still clinging to hers, he reached behind her and unzipped her dress. The green silk bodice slipped down and he helped it on its way, tugging the material until her breasts popped free. His breath hissed between his teeth as he feasted his eyes on her bare breasts, so pale against his tanned fingers, and at their centre her nipples, tight and dusky pink, just waiting for his tongue to caress them.

With a low growl Alekos lowered his mouth to her breast and drew wet circles around the areola before he closed his lips on her nipple and sucked. The soft cry she gave turned him on even more and he slid his arms around her back and encouraged her to arch her body and offer her breasts to his mouth. Every flick of his tongue across her nipple sent a shudder of response through her and when he transferred his attention to her other breast and sucked the tender peak she made a keening noise and dug her fingers into his hair as if to hold him to his task of pleasuring her.

He was so hard it hurt. His erection strained beneath his trousers as he shifted even closer to her, forcing her to spread her legs wider so that her dress rode up her thighs and he pressed his hardness against the panel of her knickers. Knowing that a fragile strip of lace was all that hid her feminine core from him shattered the last of his restraint and he groaned and cupped her face in his hands.

'Let's go to bed, Sara *mou*. This kitchen is not big enough for me to make love to you comfortably.' He doubted that her single bed would offer much more in the way of comfort and remembering her collection of child's soft toys strewn on her bed was a little off-putting. But the only other room was that soulless sitting room and he quickly dismissed the idea of having sex with her there.

He eased back from her and looked down at her naked breasts with their reddened, swollen nipples. 'Come with me,' he said urgently. If he did not have her soon he would explode.

Bed! Sara stiffened as Alekos's thick voice broke through the haze of sexual excitement he had created with his mouth and his wicked tongue. When he had sucked her nipples she'd felt an electrical current arc from her breasts down to the molten core of her femininity. She'd been spellbound by his magic, enthralled by the myriad new sensations induced by his increasingly bold caresses. But his words brought her back to reality with a thud.

On the opposite wall of the kitchen she could see her reflection in the stainless steel cooker splashback that her mother had religiously polished until it gleamed. Dear heaven, she looked like a slut, with her bare breasts hanging out of the top of her dress and the skirt rucked up around her thighs. She pictured Joan's disapproving expression and shame doused the heat in her blood like cold water thrown on a fire.

'Men only want one thing,' her mother had often told Sara. *'Once you give them your body they quickly lose interest in you.'*

Sara assumed that was how her father had treated her mother. It was certainly true of Alekos. She knew about all the gorgeous blondes who had come and gone in his life, because he'd given her the task of arranging an item of jewellery from a well-known jewellers to be sent to his mistresses when he ended his affair with them. Who would choose a pretty trinket to be sent to a mistress who was also his PA? She didn't know whether to laugh or cry.

'We can't go to bed,' she told him firmly. 'You know we can't, Alekos. We shouldn't have got carried away like we did.' She watched his expression turn from puzzlement to shock at her refusal before his eyes narrowed to black slits that gleamed with anger.

'Why not?' he demanded, his clipped tone betraying his frustration. 'We are both unattached, consenting adults.'

'I work for you.'

He dismissed her argument with a careless shrug of his shoulders. 'This evening we gave the impression that we are having an affair and tomorrow's papers will doubtless carry pictures of us arriving at the art gallery together.'

'But we were only pretending to have a relationship. You don't really want me.'

'It's patently obvious how much I want you,' Alekos said sardonically. 'And you want me, Sara. Don't bother to deny it. Your body doesn't lie.'

She followed his gaze down to her bare breasts and silently cursed the hard points of her nipples that betrayed her. Red-faced, she yanked the top of her dress back into place. 'We can't,' she repeated grittily. But her resolve was tested to its limit by the feral hunger in his eyes. 'If we had an affair, what would happen when it ended?'

'I see no reason why you couldn't carry on being my PA. We work well together and I wouldn't want to lose you.'

Alekos wouldn't want to lose her as his PA, but that was all. She could not risk succumbing to her desire for him because she would find it impossible to continue to work for him after they were no longer lovers. It would be torture to know he was dating other women after he'd finished with her. And she *would* know. In the two years she had been his PA she'd learned to recognise the signs that he was having regular sex.

She felt emotionally drained from the evening. Meeting her half-siblings had made her long to be part of a family. But she certainly wasn't going to sleep with Alekos to ease the loneliness she had felt all her life. 'I think you had better leave,' she told him huskily, praying he wouldn't guess she was close to tears.

'If you really want me to go, then of course I accept your decision,' he said coldly, sounding faintly incredulous that she had actually rejected him. 'But in future I suggest you do not respond to a man so fervently if you don't intend to follow it through.'

'Are you accusing me of leading you on?' Her temper flared. 'That's a foul thing to suggest and grossly unfair. You came on to me.'

'And you hated every moment when we were kissing, I suppose?' he mocked. 'It's a little too late to play the innocent victim, Sara.'

'I'm not trying to imply that I'm a victim.' But if he knew how innocent she really was he would run a mile, she thought grimly. She suddenly remembered that they had travelled from Soho to her house in Alekos's limousine. 'If I had invited you to stay the night, what would your chauffeur have done? Would he have slept in the car?'

Alekos shrugged. 'We have an arrangement. Mike

knows to wait for a while…' He did not add anything more but Sara understood that his driver had been instructed to leave after a couple of hours if Alekos went into a woman's house and did not reappear. No doubt it was an arrangement that had been used on many occasions. Sara got on well with Mike and she would have felt so embarrassed if she'd had to face him after Alekos had spent the night with her. It brought home to her that she could not sacrifice her job, her reputation and her self-respect for a sexual liaison with her boss.

But when she followed Alekos down the hall and he opened the front door she had to fight the temptation to tell him that she had changed her mind and wanted him to stay and make love to her. Love had nothing to do with it, she reminded herself. At least not for Alekos. And she had sworn she would not make her mother's mistake and fall in love with a man who could never love her.

'Goodnight,' she bid him in a low voice.

'Sleep well,' he mocked, as if he knew her body ached with longing and regret that would make sleep impossible. As she watched him stride down the path she thought that at least she would be able to face him in the office tomorrow morning with her pride intact.

But pride was a poor bedfellow she discovered later, as she tossed and turned in her single bed. Her nipples still tingled from Alekos's ministrations and the insistent throb between her legs was a shameful reminder of how close she had come to giving in to her desire for him.

CHAPTER SIX

MONACO WAS A playground for millionaires and billionaires, and for the last three days the tiny principality had hosted the iconic yacht show, which this year had taken place in June rather than its usual date in September. Some of the world's most impressive superyachts were moored in the harbour, the largest and most spectacular being the two-hundred-and-eighty-foot *Artemis* from leading yacht brokerage and shipyard, Gionakis Enterprises.

On Sunday morning, Alekos made his way through Port Hercules in the sunshine. Now that the show was over, the huge crowds that had packed the waterfront had gone and his route to where *Artemis* was moored was no longer blocked by yacht charter brokers, who had been keen to tour the vessel and discover the superlative luxury of her interior.

Gone too were the glamour models and hostesses who were synonymous with the prestigious show. Monaco surely boasted more beautiful women wearing minuscule bikinis that revealed their tanned, taut bodies than anywhere else in the world, Alekos thought cynically. He could have relieved his sexual frustration with any of the numerous women who had tried to catch his eye, but there was only one woman he wanted and she had studiously kept out of his way.

After the frenzy of the past three days, Alekos's preferred method to unwind had been to go for a fifteen-mile run along the coast. Now he felt relaxed as he boarded *Artemis* and walked along her deck, with nothing but the cry of gulls and the lap of water against the yacht's hull to break the silence. His sense of calm well-being was abruptly shattered when he entered the small saloon which he had been using as an office and found Sara sitting at a desk with her laptop open in front of her.

She was dressed in white shorts and a striped top and her hair was caught up in a ponytail with loose tendrils framing her face. Without make-up, the freckles on her nose were visible and she looked wholesome and utterly lovely. Alekos felt his gut twist.

'Why are you working already? I told you I was planning to go for a run and you could have a lie in this morning.'

'I woke early and decided to get the report about the show typed up,' she said, carefully not looking directly at him. 'I thought you wouldn't be back for another hour or so.'

'Is that why you started work at the crack of dawn, hoping to have finished the report before I came back, so that you could avoid me like you've done since you arrived on Wednesday?'

She flushed. 'I haven't avoided you. We've worked together constantly every day.'

'During the day we were surrounded by other people, and you took yourself off to bed immediately after dinner every evening. I can't believe you usually go to bed at nine p.m.,' he said drily.

The colour on her cheeks spread down her throat and Alekos wondered if the rosy blush stained her breasts. 'I was tired,' she muttered. 'The past few days have been incredibly busy.'

'I don't deny it. And because I came to Monaco a couple of days before you did, this is the first chance we have had to discuss what happened after we attended the art gallery launch last week.'

Now she did look at him, her eyes so wide and full of panic that she reminded him of a rabbit caught in car headlights. 'There's nothing to discuss. We...we got carried away, but it won't happen again.'

'Are you so sure of that?' Alekos deliberately lowered his gaze to the hard points of her nipples, outlined beneath her clingy T-shirt, and grinned when she crossed her arms over her chest and glared at him. He did not know why he took satisfaction from teasing her but he suspected it was to make him feel less bad about himself. He couldn't comprehend why he had come on to her so strong last Sunday evening. It was not his style. And she had rejected him! *Theos*—that was a first for him.

What was it about Sara that fired him up as if he were a hormone-fuelled youth instead of a jaded playboy who could take his pick of beautiful women? All week he had racked his brain for an answer while he'd been alone each night in the opulent master suite on *Artemis*, whereas at last year's show he'd enjoyed the company of two very attractive—not to mention inventive—blondes.

The only reason that made any sense—but did not make him feel good about himself, he acknowledged grimly—was simply that he wanted Sara so badly because she had turned him down. He wanted to see her sprawled on his bed, all wide-eyed and flushed with sexual heat, and he wanted to hear her beg him to make love to her because his ego couldn't deal with rejection.

She was watching him warily, and for some reason it angered him. She had been with him all the way the other night, right up until he'd suggested they go to bed. Even though she had said no, he'd sensed he could have persuaded her to change her mind. But he'd never pleaded with a woman to have sex with him before, and he had no intention of starting with his PA, who clearly had a hang-up about sex.

He leaned across the desk and tugged her arms open. Ignoring her yelp of protest, he drawled, 'It will help to make the pretence that we are lovers more convincing if you drop the outraged virgin act when your father and his guests arrive.'

Her eyes flashed with anger and she clamped her lips together as if to hold back a retort. Alekos wondered how much resistance she would offer if he attempted to probe her lips apart with his tongue. Lust swept like wildfire through him and he abruptly swung away and strode over to the door, conscious that his running shorts did not hide the evidence of his arousal.

'As you are so keen to work, you may as well type up the financial report for the shareholders. It will keep you busy until lunchtime, and as you are so averse to my company you won't want to join me for a swim in the pool, will you?' he murmured, and laughed softly at her fulminating look.

They had lunch on one of the yacht's four decks, sitting at a table set beneath a striped canopy that provided shade from the blazing Mediterranean sun. Lionel Kingsley, his son and daughter and Warren McCuskey had boarded *Artemis* at midday, and Alekos had instructed the captain to steer the yacht out of the harbour and drop anchor a couple of miles off the coast.

They were surrounded by blue, Sara thought as she looked around at the sparkling azure ocean which met a cornflower blue sky on the horizon. A gentle breeze carried the faint salt tang of the sea and lifted the voices and laughter of the people sitting around the table. She popped her last forkful of the light-as-air salmon mousse that the chef had prepared for a main course into her mouth and gave a sigh of pleasure.

After her run-in with Alekos earlier in the morning, her nerves had been on edge at the prospect of them having to act as though they were a couple. She'd fretted about the lunch, knowing that she had lied to her father about being Alekos's girlfriend and, even worse, not being truthful to Charlotte and Freddie that she was their half-sister.

But she need not have worried. Alekos had been at his most urbane and charming, although his eyes had glinted with amusement and something else that evoked a molten sensation inside her when he'd slipped his arm around her waist as they had walked along the deck to greet Lionel and his party. 'Showtime, Sara *mou*,' Alekos had murmured before he'd kissed her mouth, leaving her lips tingling and wanting more, even though she knew the kiss had been for the benefit of the interested onlookers.

Recalling that kiss now, she ran her tongue over her lips and glanced at Alekos sitting across the table from her. Heat swept through her when she discovered him watching her through narrowed eyes, and she knew that he was also remembering those few seconds when his lips had grazed hers. She tore her gaze from him when she realised that Charlotte was speaking.

'An office love affair is so romantic. When did you and Alekos realise that there was more to your relationship than you simply being his PA?'

'Um...' Sara felt her face grow warm as she struggled to think of a reply.

'It was a gradual process,' Alekos answered for her. 'Obviously, Sara and I work closely together and to begin with we were friends before our friendship developed into something deeper.'

He sounded so convincing that Sara almost believed him herself. It was true that friendship had grown between them over the last two years. But that was where fact ended and her fantasy that he would fall in love with her began, she reminded herself.

Keen to change the subject, she turned to Freddie. 'Tell me what it was like at art school. It must have been fun. I would have loved to study for an art degree.'

'Why didn't you, if it is a subject that you say you have always been interested in?'

She shrugged. 'My mother wanted me to find a job as soon as I'd finished my A levels. There was only the two of us, you see, and she struggled to pay the bills.'

'Couldn't your father have helped?'

Sara froze and was horribly aware that her father had broken off his conversation with McCuskey and was waiting tensely for her to respond to Freddie's innocent question.

'No...he...wasn't around.'

'Luckily for me, Sara joined GE,' Alekos said smoothly. 'I realised as soon as I met her that she would be an ideal person to organise my hectic life.' He rang the little bell on the table and almost instantly a steward appeared, pushing the dessert trolley. 'I see that my chef has excelled himself with a selection of desserts. My personal recommendation is the chocolate torte.'

Following his words, there was a buzz of interest around the table over the choice of dessert and the awkward moment passed. Sara gave Alekos a grateful look.

'After lunch I thought you might like to use the jet skis,' he said to Charlotte and Freddie. 'Or if you prefer an activity that involves less adrenalin there is snorkelling equipment, or the glass-bottomed dinghy is a fun way to view marine life.'

'You've got one heck of a boat here, Alekos,' McCuskey commented. 'Is it true there is a helipad somewhere on the yacht?'

'The helipad is on the bow and there is a hangar below the foredeck which is specially designed. I could give you a tour of *Artemis* if you'd like to see all of her many features.'

'I surely would,' the Texan said enthusiastically.

Sara had never had as much fun as she did that afternoon. The sea was warm to swim in and, with Charlotte and Freddie's help, she soon got the hang of snorkelling. Alekos joined them later in the day and when they took the jet skis out Sara rode pillion behind him and hung on tightly to him as they sped across the bay. With her arms wrapped around his waist and her cheek resting on his broad back, she allowed herself to daydream that it was all real—that she and Alekos were lovers and her half-siblings accepted her as their sister.

'Dad and Warren are driving back to Antibes. But

Charlotte and I are meeting up with some friends in Monte Carlo this evening,' Freddie said as they stood on deck and watched the glorious golden sunset. 'Why don't you and Alekos come with us?' He put his head on one side as he studied Sara's face. 'It's bugging me that you remind me of someone, but I can't think who.'

Alekos slid his arm around her waist. 'What do you say, *agapi mou*? Would you like to go to a nightclub?'

'Yes. But I don't mind if you'd rather not,' she said quickly, unaware of the wistful expression in her eyes.

'I want to do whatever makes you happy,' he assured her.

Sweet heaven, he was a brilliant actor, but it was all pretend, Sara reminded herself firmly. She must not allow herself to be seduced by the sultry gleam in Alekos's dark eyes and the velvet softness of his voice that made her wish for the moon even though she knew it was unreachable.

Monte Carlo at midnight was a blaze of golden lights against a backdrop of an ink-black sky. Sara followed Alekos out of a nightclub that apparently was *the* place to be seen and to see celebrities. She had spotted a famous American film star and a couple of members of a boy band, but she'd only had eyes for Alekos.

They had met up with Charlotte and Freddie's friends, and Alekos had arranged for their group to use a private booth in the nightclub. He had stayed close to her all evening, draping his arm around her shoulders when they had sat in the booth drinking cocktails, and drawing her into his arms on the dance floor so that her breasts were crushed to his chest and she was conscious of his hard thigh muscles pressed against her through the insubstantial black silk dress she had chosen to wear for a night out.

He led her over to a taxi and opened the door for her to climb inside. 'My feet are *killing* me,' she complained as she flopped onto the back seat.

Alekos slid in beside her and lifted her feet onto his lap. 'Your fault for wearing stilts for shoes,' he said, inspecting the five-inch heels on her strappy sandals. Sara caught her breath when he curled his fingers around her ankles and unfastened her shoes before sliding them off her feet. While they had been in the nightclub they had continued the pretence of being lovers in front of her half-siblings. But now it seemed way too intimate when he trailed his fingertips lightly up her calves. 'Did you enjoy yourself tonight?'

'It was the best night of my life,' she said softly. 'And the best day.' Her eyes were drawn to him. In the dark taxi his chiselled profile was shadowed and the sharp angles of his face were highlighted by the glow from the street lamps. 'Thank you for making it possible for me to spend time with Charlotte and Freddie, and with my father earlier today. I hope you weren't too bored showing Warren McCuskey around *Artemis*. I guessed you had offered to give him a tour of the yacht so that I could have time alone with Lionel.'

'Yeah, I'm all heart,' he drawled. His oddly cynical tone made Sara dart a look at him, but the taxi drew up to the jetty and he climbed out of the car. She couldn't face putting her shoes back on, and while she stood contemplating whether to walk the short distance along the jetty in bare feet Alekos scooped her up in his arms and carried her up the yacht's gangway.

'Thanks.' She silently cursed how breathless she

sounded and hoped he couldn't feel the erratic thud of her heart. 'You can put me down now.'

He continued walking into the main saloon before he lowered her down. She curled her toes into the soft carpet. Every sensory receptor on her body felt vitally alive and she was intensely aware of Alekos, of the spicy scent of his aftershave, the heat of his body and the smouldering gleam in his dark eyes. It all felt like a wonderful dream—staying on a luxurious yacht, spending time with her half-siblings and dancing the night away with a man who was so handsome it hurt her to look at him.

'I wish tonight didn't have to end.' She blurted out the words before she could stop herself and flushed, thinking how unsophisticated she sounded.

'It doesn't have to end yet. Will you join me for a nightcap?'

'Um…well, I shouldn't. It's late and we both have to be up early in the morning. You're flying to Dubai to visit Sheikh Al Mansoor, and my flight to London is at ten a.m.'

'I realise that it's three hours past your bedtime,' he said drily. 'But why not live dangerously for once?'

Alekos had simply invited her to have a drink with him. This was not a defining moment in her life, Sara told herself firmly. 'All right.' She ignored the warning in her head that sounded just like her mother's voice, and sided with the other voice that urged her to stop hiding from life and *live*. 'Just one drink.'

'Sure. You don't want to overdose on excitement.' He gave her a bland smile as he ushered her out of the main saloon and towards the stairs that led to the upper decks.

When she hesitated he murmured, 'There is champagne on ice in my suite.'

Sara had never been in the master suite before and its opulent splendour took her breath away. The décor of the sitting room and the bedroom she could see beyond it was sleek and ultra-stylish while the colour scheme of soft blue, grey and white was restful. Not that she felt relaxed. Quite the opposite as she watched Alekos slip off his jacket and throw it onto a chair before he strolled over to the bar. His white silk shirt was unbuttoned at the throat, showing his dark olive skin and a glimpse of black chest hairs. His hair fell across his brow and the dark stubble on his jaw gave him a rakish look that evoked a coiling sensation in the pit of her stomach.

The sliding glass doors were open and she stepped outside onto the private deck and took a deep breath. On this side of the yacht facing away from the port there was only dark sea and dark sky, lit by a bright white moon and stars like silver pins studding a black velvet pincushion.

Alekos's footfall was silent but she sensed he was near and turned to take the glass of pink fizz he handed her. 'Kir Royale, my favourite drink.'

'I know.' He held her gaze. 'Why were you looking sad?'

Sara sighed. 'Charlotte and Freddie both talked a lot about their happy childhoods, and how much their parents loved each other. Lionel's wife suffered from multiple sclerosis for several years and he cared for her devotedly until her death two months ago.' She bit her lip. 'If Lionel reveals that I am his daughter, all their memories of growing up in a happy family will be tainted by the knowledge that their father cheated on their mother.'

She placed her glass down on a nearby table and curled her hands around the deck rail, staring into the empty darkness beyond the boat. 'I'm afraid that my half-siblings will hate me,' she said in a low voice.

'I don't believe anyone could hate you, Sara *mou*.'

The gentleness in Alekos's voice was unexpected and it tore through her. 'I'm not *your* Sara.'

He smiled at her fierce tone. 'Aren't you?' He uncurled her fingers from the rail and turned her to face him. Sara trembled when he drew her unresisting body closer to his—so close that she could feel his heart thundering as fast as her own.

Of course she was his. The thought slipped quietly into her head. It wasn't complicated; it was really very simple. She had been his for two years and she could not fight her longing for him when he was looking at her with undisguised hunger in his eyes that made her tremble even more.

'I want you to be mine, and I think you want that too,' he murmured. She felt his lips on her hair, her brow, the tip of her nose. And then his mouth was there, so close to hers that she felt his warm breath whisper across her lips, and she couldn't deny it, couldn't deny him when it would mean denying herself of what she wanted more than anything in the world—Alekos.

Maybe it was because she had made him wait that explained the wild rush of anticipation that swept through him, Alekos brooded. And perhaps it was the lost, almost vulnerable expression on her lovely face moments ago that had elicited a peculiar tug on his heart.

The haunted look in her eyes should have warned him to back off while he still retained a little of his sanity. But it was too late. His desire for her was too strong for him to fight. Sara had driven him to the edge of reason for too long and the feel of her soft curves pressing against his whipcord body, and the little tremors that ran through her when he smoothed his hand down her back and over the taut contours of her bottom decimated his control.

He took possession of her mouth and gave a low growl of satisfaction when she parted her lips to allow his tongue access to her sweetness within. This time she would not reject him. He felt her desperation in the way she kissed him with utter abandon, and her response fuelled his urgency to feel her naked body beneath his.

He liked the little moan of protest she made when he ended the kiss and lifted his head to stare into her green eyes with their dilated pupils. She was so petite he could easily sweep her up in his arms, but he stepped back and held out his hand. 'Will you come and be mine, Sara?'

He liked that she did not hesitate. She put her fingers in his and he led her into the bedroom. His heart was pounding faster than when he'd gone for a fifteen-mile run that morning. And he was already hard—*Theos*, he was so hard; his body was taut with impatience to thrust between her slim thighs. The sight of her wearing a bikini when they had swum in the sea earlier in the day had driven him to distraction, and he had suggested using the jet skis to hide the embarrassing evidence of his arousal that his swim shorts couldn't disguise.

Most women would have played the temptress and given him artful looks as they performed a striptease for his benefit. Sara simply stood at the end of the bed

and looked at him with her huge green eyes. Her faint
uncertainty surprised him. She was, after all, a modern
single woman in her mid-twenties and he assured himself that this could not be new for her. It was difficult to
picture her as the drab sparrow who he had barely noticed in his office but, remembering the old style Sara,
he thought it was likely that she hadn't had many lovers.

But he did not want her to be shy with him. He
wanted her to be bold and as eager as he was. His hunger for her was so intense and he sensed that this first
time would not last long. He needed her with him all
the way, which meant that he must turn her on by using
all his considerable skill as a lover.

'I want to see you,' he said roughly. The bedside
lamps were switched off but the brilliant gleam from
the moon silvered the room and gave her skin a pearles-
cent shimmer as he pulled the straps of her dress down,
lower and lower until he had bared her breasts.

'*Eísai ómorfi.* You are beautiful,' he translated, realising he had spoken in Greek. His native tongue was the
language of his blood, his passion, and he groaned as
he cradled her breasts in his hands, testing their weight
and exploring their firm swell before he was drawn in-
exorably to their dusky pink crests that jutted provoca-
tively forwards, demanding his attention.

She shivered when he flicked his thumb pads over
her nipples, back and forth before he rolled the tight
nubs between his fingers until she gave a low cry that
corkscrewed its way right into his gut. Giving her pleasure became his absolute focus but when he lowered
his head to her breast and closed his mouth around her
nipple, sucking hard, she bucked and shook and her un-

disguised enjoyment of what he was doing to her drove him to the brink.

'Sara, I have to have you now. I can't wait,' he muttered as he straightened up and sought her lips with his, thrusting his tongue into her mouth to tangle with hers. Next time he would take it slow, he promised himself. But he was fast losing control and the drumbeat of desire pounding in his veins demanded to be assuaged.

He would have liked her to undress him, maybe knelt in front of him to pull his trousers down and then taken him in her mouth. His body jerked at his erotic fantasy and he swore beneath his breath. There was no time for leisurely foreplay and he fought his way out of his clothes with none of his usual innate grace, while she stood watching him, her eyes widening when he stepped out of his boxers. She stared at his rock-hard arousal, and the way she swallowed audibly made him close his eyes and offer a brief prayer for his sanity.

'Alekos...' she whispered.

'If you have changed your mind. Go. Now,' he gritted.

'I haven't. It's just...' She broke off and ran her fingertips lightly, almost tentatively over his proud erection.

He grabbed her hand and lifted it up to his chest where his heart was thundering so hard he knew she could feel it. 'Playtime's over, angel.' He tugged her dress over her hips and it slithered to the floor. A pair of black lacy knickers were all that hid her femininity from him and he dealt with them with swift efficiency, sliding them down her legs before he lifted her and laid her on the bed.

The strip of soft brown curls between her thighs partially shielded her slick heat from his hungry gaze. He lifted her leg and hooked it over his shoulder, then did the same with her other leg, and his laughter was deep and dark when she gasped in protest.

'Beautiful,' he growled. She was splayed in front of him, open and exposed, and he had never seen anything as exquisite as he lowered his head and placed his mouth over her feminine heat.

'*Oh.*' She jerked her hips and clutched his hair. It crossed his mind that maybe she hadn't received pleasure this way before, and the possessive feeling that the thought elicited rang a faint alarm bell in his mind. He had never felt possessive of any woman and Sara was no different than any of the countless lovers he'd had since his first sexual experience when he was seventeen.

She squirmed beneath him. 'You can't...' She sounded scandalised, but there was something else in her guttural cry, a note of excitement that made Alekos smile.

'Oh, but I can,' he promised. And then he bent his head once more and probed his tongue into her slick heat, straight to the heart of her. Her hoarse moans filled his ears and her sweet feminine scent swamped his senses. She tasted of nectar and he licked deeper, sliding his hands beneath her bottom to angle her hips so that he could suck the tiny nub of her clitoris.

The effect was stunning. She gave a keening cry, bucking and writhing beneath him so that he gripped hold of her hips and held her fast while he used his tongue to drive her over the edge. She shattered. And watching her climax, her fingers clawing at the satin bedspread as her body shook, fired his blood and his need.

Theos, he had never *needed* a woman before. His

brother had been needy for the woman who had broken his heart, but Alekos had learned from Dimitri's death that needing someone was a weakness that made you vulnerable. Although he was loath to admit it, right now he needed Sara the same way he needed to breathe oxygen.

Somehow, Alekos retained enough of his sanity to take a protective sheath from the bedside drawer and slide it over his erection. And then he positioned himself between her spread thighs once more and his need was so fierce and consuming that the flicker of apprehension in her eyes did not register in his mind. Not until it was too late.

He could hear the sound of his ragged breaths and his blood thundering in his ears. His fingers shook as he stroked them over her moist opening and found her hot and slick and ready for him. He was so close to his goal and with a groan he thrust his way into her and froze when he felt an unmistakable resistance.

She could not be a virgin.

But the evidence was there in the sudden tension of her muscles and the way she went rigid beneath him. His brain told him to halt and withdraw, but his body was trapped in the web of his desire. A sense of urgency that was more primitive and pressing than logical thought overwhelmed him. His shock at discovering her innocence was followed by an even greater shock as he realised that he was out of control. His body was driven by a fearsome need that drove him to move inside her and push deeper into her velvet heat.

Somewhere in the crazy confusion of his mind he was aware that she had relaxed a little and she flattened her hands against his chest and slid them up to his shoulders, not pushing him away but drawing him down onto her. She shifted her hips experimentally to allow her internal muscles to accommodate him, and just that small movement blew his mind. With a sense of disbelief Alekos felt his control being stretched and stretched. Everything was happening too fast. He closed his eyes and fought against the heat surging through his veins, but he couldn't stop it… He couldn't…

He let out a savage groan as his control snapped and he came hard, his body shuddering with the force of his climax. Even as the tremors still juddered through him, shame at his lack of restraint lashed his soul. How could he have been so weak? How could Sara have made him so desperate?

And what the hell was he going to do with her now?

CHAPTER SEVEN

'WHY DIDN'T YOU tell me it was your first time?'

Alekos's voice sounded...odd, not angry exactly, but not pleased either. And perhaps his gruff tone was to be expected, Sara acknowledged. He had been anticipating a night of passion with a sexually experienced mistress, but instead he'd found himself making love to a woman whose sexual experience could be documented on the back of a postage stamp.

'It was my business,' she said huskily, finding it hard to speak past the lump that inexplicably blocked her throat.

'But now you have made it my business too.' He said something in Greek that she thought it was best she did not understand. 'I'm sorry I hurt you.' He sounded remorseful and again there was that odd tone in his voice that was not quite anger but might have been regret.

'You didn't really. I mean, just a bit at first but then it was...okay.'

'You should have told me,' he said more harshly this time.

She sighed. 'I was curious.' Not the full truth but it would do. She wanted to cry—perhaps every woman felt emotional after her first sexual experience—but she was determined to wait until she was alone before she let her tears fall.

Alekos's weight was heavy on her, pressing her into the mattress and making her feel trapped. She didn't want to look at him, but there was nowhere else *to* look when his body was still joined with hers. His dark eyes that only moments ago had blazed with desire were now chips of obsidian and his beautiful mouth was compressed into a hard line. It was impossible to believe that his lips had ever curved into a smile of sensual promise.

She pushed against his chest. 'Can we talk about this some other time, and preferably not at all? We're done, aren't we?' She bit her lip. 'To be honest, I don't understand why people make sex such a big deal.'

She could not hide the disappointment in her voice. The discomfort she'd experienced when Alekos had pushed his powerful erection into her had only lasted a few moments. The stinging sensation had faded and been replaced with a sense of fullness that had begun as pleasant, and when he'd moved, and pushed deeper, had become a tantalising throb that she had wanted to continue.

But it had ended abruptly. Alekos's ragged breaths had grown hoarser before he'd made a feral growl that sounded as if it had been ripped from his throat as he had slumped forwards and she'd felt his hot breath on her neck.

He was still on top of her. Still *inside* her. There was too much of him for her fragile emotions to cope with, and now he was frowning, his heavy brows meeting above his aquiline nose.

'No, we are not done, Sara *mou*. Nowhere near.'

'I'm not your Sara.'

He laughed softly and the rich sound curled around her aching heart. Tenderness from Alekos was something she hadn't expected and it was too beguiling for her to bear right now.

'I have indisputable proof that you are mine. Am I hurting you now?' he murmured. He shifted his position very slightly and she felt something bloom inside her, filling her once more so that her internal muscles were stretched. While she was stunned by the realisation that he was hardening again, he bent his head and captured her mouth in a slow, sensual kiss that started out as gentle and, when she responded because she couldn't help herself, became deeper and more demanding.

She was breathless by the time he trailed his lips over her cheek to her ear and nipped her lobe with just enough pressure that she shivered with pleasure that was not quite pain. He moved lower, kissing his way down her throat and over the slopes of her breasts before he flicked his tongue across one nipple and rolled the other peak between his fingers, making her gasp at the sheer intensity of the sensations he was creating.

He played her body the way a skilled musician wrung exquisite notes from an instrument, his touch now light, now masterful, and always with the utmost dedication to giving her pleasure. And all the while he moved his hips unhurriedly, sometimes in a gentle rocking motion, sometimes circling his pelvis against hers.

Each movement resulted in his erection growing harder within her and stretching her a little more, filling her until she was only aware of Alekos—the warmth of his skin, the strength of his bunched shoulder muscles beneath her hands, the power of his manhood pushing into her, pulling back, pushing into her, pulling back, in a steady rhythm that made her want more of the same.

He looked down at her and his mouth curved into a slow smile as he slid his hands beneath her bottom and encouraged her to arch her hips to accept the thrust of his body.

'Does that feel good?'

'Yes.' It felt amazing but she was suddenly shy, which was ridiculous, she told herself, when she was joined with him in the most intimate way possible.

'Tell me if it hurts.'

'It doesn't.'

'Tell me what you want.'

Oh, God, how could she tell him that his relentless rhythm was driving her mad? How could she tell him what she wanted when she didn't know? She stared up at his handsome face and thought she would die of wanting him. 'I want you to move faster,' she whispered. 'And harder. Much harder.'

'*Theos*, Sara…' He gave a rough laugh. 'Like this?' He thrust deep and, before she had time to catch her breath, he thrust again. 'Like this?'

'Yes…*yes*.'

It was unbelievable, indescribable. And so beautiful. She learned his rhythm and moved with him, meeting each thrust eagerly as he took her higher, higher. He possessed her utterly, her body and her soul, and he held her at the edge, made her wait a heartbeat before he drove into her one final time and they exploded together, her cries mingled with his hoarse groan as they shattered in the ecstasy of their simultaneous release.

Sara came down slowly. A heavy lethargy stole through her body, making her muscles relax and block-

ing out the hundreds of thoughts that were waiting in
the wings of her mind, preparing to lambast her with
recriminations. Alekos moved away from her and moments later she heard a click that she guessed was the
door of the en suite bathroom closing. She wondered
if it was her cue to leave. What was the protocol when
you had just lost your virginity to your boss?

Oh, God, it was better not to think of that. Better not
to think at all, but to keep her eyes closed and that way
she could pretend it had all been a dream. Hovering
on the edge of sleep, she was aware that the mattress
dipped and she breathed in the elixir that was Alekos—
his aftershave, sweat, the heat of his body.

In her dream she turned towards his warmth and
curled up against him, her face pressed to his chest so
that she felt his rough chest hairs against her cheek. In
her dream he muttered words in Greek that she didn't
understand as he slid his arm beneath her shoulders and
pulled her close to him.

Alekos knew he was in trouble before he opened his
eyes. The brush of silk on his shoulder and a faint vanilla scent were unwelcome reminders of his stupidity.
Lifting his lashes, he confirmed that the situation was as
bad as it could get. Not only had he had sex with Sara,
but she had slept all night in his bed. *Theos*, in his *arms*.

He hardly ever spent an entire night with a lover.
Sharing a bed for sleeping suggested a level of intimacy
he did not want and could lead to mistaken expectations
from a woman that she had a chance of being more than
his mistress. Last night he had intended to leave Sara
in his bed and go and sleep in another cabin.

He could not explain to himself why he had climbed

back into bed after he'd visited the bathroom. Alarm bells had rung in his head when she'd snuggled up to him, all soft and warm and dangerously tempting. He'd been tired and had closed his eyes, promising himself he would get up in a couple of minutes, and the next he'd known it was morning.

He swore beneath his breath. Sara was still asleep and he carefully eased his arm from beneath her. The sunlight filtering through the blinds played in her hair and made the silky layers burnish myriad shades of golden brown. With her English rose complexion and her lips slightly parted she looked innocent, but of course she wasn't, thanks to him, he acknowledged grimly.

What had he been thinking when he'd made love to her, not just once but twice? But that was the trouble. *He hadn't been capable of rational thought.* His actions had been driven by desire, by his need for Sara that in the crystal clarity of the-day-after-the-night-before shamed him. Discovering that she was a virgin should have immediately prompted him to stop having sex with her. But he had been unable to resist the slick, sweet heat of her body, and he'd come—*hell*, he'd come so hard. Even now, remembering the savage intensity of his release caused his traitorous body to stir.

Failing to satisfy a lover was a new experience for him and Sara's obvious disappointment had piqued his pride. He grimaced. His damnable pride was not the only reason he'd set out to seduce her a second time. He'd convinced himself it was only fair that he should gift her with the pleasure of an orgasm. Despite her inexperience, she had been a willing pupil and he'd found her ardent response to his lovemaking irresistible.

It was that thought that compelled him to slide out

of bed and move noiselessly around the bedroom while he dressed. In his mind he replayed the last conversation he'd had with his brother when he was fourteen.

'Why are you so upset just because your girlfriend cheated? You can easily find another girlfriend. Women love you.'

'No other woman could ever replace Nia in my heart,' Dimitri had said. 'When you are older you'll understand, Alekos. One day you will meet a woman who gets under your skin and you'll be unable to resist her. It's called falling in love and it's hellish.'

He wouldn't visit hell for any woman, Alekos had vowed years ago as he'd watched his brother weeping. Love had brought Dimitri to his knees. Had it also been ultimately responsible for his death? The question had haunted Alekos for twenty years.

There was no danger he would fall in love with Sara. But his weakness last night served as a warning he could not ignore. He didn't know why she had chosen to lose her virginity with him, and he did not want to know what hopes she might be harbouring about them making their pretend affair a reality.

One thing he knew for sure was that he needed to get the hell off the yacht before she woke up. A short, sharp lesson might be brutal but it was best to make it clear that all he'd felt for her was lust. He still felt, he amended when she moved in her sleep and the sheet slipped down to reveal one perfect rose-tipped breast. She was peaches and cream and he wanted to feast on her again. The strength of his desire shocked him and he strode over to the door, resisting the urge to look back at her.

Sara would probably expect to find him gone when she woke up. She knew he was planning to fly to Dubai to take part in a charity polo match organised by his friend Sheikh Al Mansoor. Kalif had brought one of his cousins to Monaco to visit the yacht show, and the three of them would fly to Dubai on the Prince's private jet. There was no reason why he should feel guilty for abandoning Sara, Alekos assured himself. After all, she was his PA and she had arranged his diary around his ten-day trip to stay at Kalif's royal palace.

Deep down, Alekos acknowledged that he was running away, and the unedifying truth did not make him feel good about himself. He was running scared, his conscience taunted him. Sara had made him lose control and it had never happened before. No woman had ever got under his skin and he hoped—*no*, he was sure—that distance would allow him to put his fascination with her into perspective. He'd responded to the chemistry between them. That was all. When he returned to the London office in ten days' time she would no doubt be as keen as him to forget about their night of passion.

Sara was woken by a *thud-thud* noise that she recognised was a helicopter's rotor blades. She opened her eyes and frowned as she looked around her. This was not her cabin on *Artemis*. This was... *Dear, sweet heaven!* Memories of the previous night flooded her mind. Last night she'd had sex with Alekos and he had not been pleased when he'd discovered it was her first time.

She turned her head on the pillow and, finding she was alone in the bed, assumed he was in the bathroom. Her thoughts flew back to last night. It had been over fairly quickly and she'd felt underwhelmed by the experience. But then Alekos had made love to her a second time, and nothing she'd ever read about sexual pleasure came close to the incredible orgasm that had exploded through her body like an electrical storm and left her shaking in its aftermath.

It had been just as good for Alekos. His harsh groan before he'd slumped on top of her had told her he'd reached his own nirvana. But what would happen now? Where did they go from here?

It suddenly seemed a good idea to get dressed before she faced him. Muscles she'd been unaware of until this morning tugged as she slid out of bed and scooped up her dress and knickers from the floor where they had scattered. The memory of his hands on her body and his mouth on her breasts and—*dear God*—between her legs when he'd bestowed a shockingly intimate caress, caused heat to bloom on her cheeks and she felt even hotter inside.

When he'd realised she was inexperienced he had tempered his passion with tenderness that had captured her heart and made her hope— *No*, she must not go down that road, she told herself firmly. Just because Alekos had made love to her with exquisite care and made her feel beautiful and desirable, she must not hope he might fall in love with her. *But he might*, whispered a little voice in her head.

The sound of rotor blades was becoming fainter, as if the helicopter was flying away. Sara frowned. Who could have been delivered to the yacht by helicopter? As far as she was aware, no guests were expected. Alekos was taking a long time in the bathroom. Struck by a sudden sense of foreboding, she knocked on the bathroom door and when he didn't answer she tried the handle and found it unlocked and the room empty. She ran over to the sliding glass doors and out onto the deck.

Looking up, she saw that it was the *Artemis* helicopter flying away from the yacht and her heart dropped faster than a stone thrown into a pool as she realised that Alekos must be on board.

She remembered she'd arranged for the pilot to fly him to the airport at Nice, and from there he would travel to Dubai. Of course she wouldn't have expected him to change his plans, but why hadn't he at least woken her to say goodbye? Because he was reluctant to face her after last night, she thought bleakly. She felt sick to think that Alekos had used her for sex. She heard her mother's voice: *'Once you've given a man what he wants you won't see him for dust.'*

Choking back a sob, Sara hurried back to her own cabin on the deck below, praying she wouldn't bump into any of the yacht's crew. She had things to do: clothes to pack, paperwork to stow in her briefcase before she was due to leave *Artemis* and travel to the airport with members of GE's sales team. Keeping busy stopped her from brooding on the fact that Alekos had abandoned her.

Laden with her suitcase and laptop, she descended to the main deck and forced a smile when she saw her father's friend Warren McCuskey walking up the gangway onto the yacht.

'I'm afraid you have just missed Alekos. He left early for an appointment.'

'Not to worry. I'll call him with the news he's been wanting to hear.' The Texan laughed. 'I've gotta hand it to your guy—he's a damned good salesman. When I met him a couple of months back I happened to say that my wife, Charlene, fancied us having a boat, and since then Gionakis hasn't missed a chance to try and persuade me to buy a yacht from GE. The day after we met at the art gallery in London he invited me to visit *Artemis* while she was in Monaco. By lucky coincidence I'd arranged to stay at Lionel's place in Antibes.'

'Did you say you had met Alekos *before* the gallery launch?' Sara strove to sound casual while her brain reminded her that Alekos did not operate on 'lucky coincidences'. He'd known Warren would be staying at her father's villa because she'd told him.

'Sure. And, like I said, he used every opportunity to use his sales tactics on me. But what really sold me on the idea of buying a yacht from his company was when he said that you are Lionel's daughter.'

Warren mopped his sunburned brow with a handkerchief and so did not notice the colour drain from Sara's face. 'Lionel is my closest friend, and if Gionakis is going to be his son-in-law I'll be happy to buy a boat from him.'

'Alekos told you that he and I are getting married?' she said faintly.

'Not in so many words. But I can tell when a fella is in love. He couldn't keep his eyes off you at lunch yesterday. I was impressed with this yacht and I've decided to buy her.'

'You want to buy *Artemis*?' Sara was stunned. The superyacht's price was two hundred million dollars, making her one of the most expensive yachts ever built. Alekos had seen a business opportunity when she'd told him that Lionel Kingsley was her father. No wonder he had suggested they could pretend to be having an affair so that she could attend functions with him and socialise with her father. He had been aware that Warren McCuskey was Lionel Kingsley's close friend; it was fairly common knowledge.

Alekos had been *so* helpful talking to Warren to give her time alone with her father, she thought cynically. She had believed his offer to help her had been genuine, out of kindness. But Alekos wasn't *kind*. He was a ruth-less businessman and, unforgivably, he had betrayed her secret and told Warren that Lionel was her father.

Idiot, she thought bitterly. Why had she given herself to Alekos, knowing he was a notorious womaniser and heartbreaker? The answer—that she was in love with him—filled her with self-disgust. Did she really have so little self-worth to love a man who only loved himself?

'If you speak to Alekos, will you pass on a mes-sage?' Warren said.

'Oh, I'll give him a message, don't you worry.' She disguised her sardonic tone with a bland smile. The Texan would be shocked if he knew she intended to tell Alekos he was an arrogant, manipulative bastard. Beneath her outwardly calm exterior she was seething. Alekos had played her for a fool but she would never give him the chance to humiliate her again.

After the cloudless blue skies and golden sunshine of Monaco, the typical British summer weather of rain and a chilly wind that whipped along Piccadilly did nothing to lift Sara's spirits. It was strange to be back in the office without Alekos and she felt annoyed with herself for missing him as she tried to focus on work.

'Sara, do you have a minute?' Robert Drummond, the CEO, stopped by her desk on Friday afternoon.

'Of course. What's up, Bob?' She noticed he seemed tense. 'Can I get you a coffee?'

'No, thanks. Remind me, when will Alekos be back?'

'He's due in the office next Wednesday. His trip to

Dubai is a private visit but I can contact him if necessary.' She hadn't heard from Alekos since they had left Monaco but she had not expected to, and luckily there had been no work issues that required her to phone him.

The CEO frowned. 'Keep this to yourself. There has been some unusual trading activity of the company's shares in recent days. It's probably nothing to be concerned about but I'll keep my ear to the ground and talk to Alekos when he's back.'

After Bob had gone, Sara drummed her fingertips on her desk, wondering if she should call Alekos. She was still his PA for now and it was her job to alert him of anything that might affect the company. Her phone rang and her heart leapt into her throat when she saw his name on the caller display.

'Sara, I need you to come over immediately.' Alekos's sexy Greek accent was more pronounced than usual, making the hairs on her body stand on end. Damn the effect he had on her, she thought bitterly.

'You want me to come to Dubai?' She was pleased that she sounded cool and composed.

'I returned to London earlier than planned,' he said tersely. 'I'm working from home. I've sent Mike to collect you, so go and wait in the car park for him.'

She stared at the envelope on her desk containing her letter of resignation. The sooner she gave it to Alekos the better.

'Sara—' he sounded impatient, and nothing like the sensual lover who had spoken to her tenderly when he'd made love to her '—did you hear me?'

'Yes.' She dropped the envelope into her handbag. 'I'm on my way.'

CHAPTER EIGHT

ALEKOS'S LONDON HOME was a penthouse apartment next to the river with stunning views of the Thames, Tower Bridge and the Shard.

His valet opened the door to admit Sara into the hallway and her tension racked up a notch when she heard a female voice from the sitting room. Did he have a woman here? Maybe someone he'd met in Dubai. It was only four nights ago that he had slept with *her*. She was tempted to hand the letter in her bag to the valet and ask him to deliver it, but just then the sitting room door opened and Alekos's mother came out to the hall. When she saw Sara she burst into tears.

'No, no, Sara,' she sobbed, 'you must not allow Alekos to work. The doctor said he has to rest.'

Sara had met Lina Gionakis a few times and had found her to be charming but excitable. She frowned. 'Doctor? Is Alekos unwell?'

'He could have died,' Lina said dramatically.

'Rubbish.' Alekos's gravelly voice made Sara's pulse race as she followed his mother into the sitting room and her gaze flew to him, sprawled on a sofa by the window. He was wearing faded denim jeans, a cream shirt undone to halfway down his chest and no shoes.

She dragged her eyes from the whorls of black hairs that grew thickly on his chest and stared at his bare feet. There was something curiously intimate about seeing his feet that reminded her of when he'd stripped in front of her before he had undressed her in his bedroom on *Artemis*.

Pink-cheeked, she jerked her gaze up to his face and did a double take when she saw he was wearing a black eye patch over his right eye.

'Polo,' he said drily, answering her unspoken query. 'I was hit in the eye with a mallet during a match.'

'The doctor said you are lucky you were not blinded in your eye.' Lina wrung her hands together. 'Promise me you will wear a helmet and faceguard in future. What if you had fallen from your horse? A head injury can be fatal. Polo is such a dangerous sport and you know I couldn't bear it if I lost another son.'

'Mana, I am not a child.' Alekos was clearly struggling to control his impatience with his mother and he looked relieved when the valet returned with a tea tray. 'Sit down and Giorgos will serve you tea and cakes while I go over a few things with Sara.'

He strode out of the room and Sara followed him into his study. 'Is your eye injury serious?'

'Not really. The blow from the mallet caused a blood vessel in my eye to rupture and my vision is blocked by a pool of blood covering the iris and pupil. The condition is called a hyphema and it shouldn't result in long-term harm.' He shrugged. 'It's fairly painful and I have to use eye drops and wear the patch for a few weeks. But I'll live,' he added sardonically.

'Your mother is very upset. What did she mean when she said she couldn't bear to lose another son?'

Alekos leaned his hip against the desk and folded his arms across his chest. But, despite his casual air, Sara sensed a sudden tension in him. 'I had an older brother,' he said abruptly. 'Dimitri died…in an accident when he was twenty-one. My mother still mourns him and, as you saw just now, she is terrified of losing me or one of my sisters.'

'I'm not surprised after such a tragic event. You've never mentioned your brother to me.'

'Why would I?'

Why, indeed? she thought painfully. Alekos was an intensely private man who guarded his personal life and his family. He would not choose to confide in his PA, not even one he'd had sex with. It was a timely reminder that she meant nothing to him and she opened her handbag and gave him the letter.

'What's this?'

'My formal notice of resignation. I can't continue to work for you after we…' Colour flooded her cheeks. 'After what happened a few nights ago.'

'We had sex,' he said bluntly. 'It's too late now to be embarrassed about it.'

'But I am embarrassed. We both behaved unprofessionally and that's why I have to leave my job.'

'*Theos*, Sara.' Impatience was etched onto his hard features. 'Why are you getting so worked up because we spent one night together? It didn't mean anything.'

She felt a knife blade pierce her heart. 'You made that very clear when you left the next morning without saying a word.'

Dark colour streaked along his cheekbones. 'You were asleep.'

'*You made me feel like a whore.*' She drew a shuddering breath and would have laughed at his astonished expression if she hadn't wanted to cry. 'It would have been less insulting if you'd left a cheque for my sexual services on the pillow.'

'You wanted me as much as I desired you,' he said grimly. 'Don't pretend you were the innocent one in this.'

Alekos's words hung in the air. He must have thought she was a freak when he'd discovered she was a twenty-four-year-old virgin, she thought painfully. She had been stupidly naïve to have fallen for the well-practised seduction routine of a playboy. 'When you read the letter, you will see that I have requested to leave earlier than the three months' notice my contract stipulates. It will be easier if I go as soon as possible.'

She turned and walked over to the door, but his harsh voice made her hesitate.

'Damn it, Sara. Where's your loyalty? You can't leave me now when I need you.'

'I'm sorry about your eye, but you said there will be no long-term damage.' She fought the insidious pull on her emotions. Alekos did not need her; he simply wanted to avoid the inconvenience of having to employ another PA. 'And how dare you throw my loyalty in my face after you showed me no loyalty at all?' She breathed hard as her anger with him exploded. 'I told you that Lionel Kingsley is my father in absolute confidence. How could you betray my secret to Warren McCuskey?'

'I didn't…'

She ignored him and continued. 'You were determined to sell a yacht to Warren and you knew that Lionel has a lot of influence over him. When you learned that I was Lionel's daughter you suggested we could pretend to be a couple so I could meet my half-siblings. But the real reason was to give you access to Warren, and your manipulation worked,' she said bitterly. 'One reason why Warren has decided to buy *Artemis* is because you let him think you are in love with me—his best friend's secret daughter.'

'I didn't tell him.' Alekos's voice was as sharp as a whiplash and made Sara flinch. 'Warren asked me if I knew you were Lionel's daughter, and I said yes because it would have looked odd if you hadn't told me when we were supposedly in a relationship.'

She looked at him uncertainly. 'Then how did Warren know?'

'It's likely that Lionel confided in his closest friend.'

Sara had to acknowledge the truth of what Alekos said but it didn't ease the hurt she felt. 'You still used my relationship with my father to your advantage to promote GE.'

He did not deny it. 'There is no room for sentiment in business. Which is why I need you to carry on being my PA, for now at least.' He straightened up and walked towards her, and his face was grimmer than Sara had ever seen it.

'GE is the target of a hostile takeover bid. In the past few months a large amount of company shares have been bought, seemingly by several smaller companies. I received a tip-off that these companies are all owned by one individual who has accumulated a significant number of GE's shares. In business, an unwanted takeover bidder is known as a black knight. If the black knight acquires fifty-one per cent of GE's shares he will be able to appoint a new management team and board of directors, and effectively take over the company.'

'Do you know how close the black knight is to acquiring fifty-one per cent?'

'Too damned close. It will be more difficult for him now he's out in the open. Instead of buying up shares stealthily through his various companies, he will have to try to persuade GE's shareholders to sell stock to him.'

'Are you saying that if this black knight does manage to buy enough shares, you could lose the company that your grandfather set up?' Looking closely at Alekos, Sara saw evidence of the strain he was under in his clenched jaw and the two grooves that had appeared on either side of his mouth. Despite his cavalier treatment of her, she felt a tug on her soft heart. 'There must be something you can do to stop him.'

'There are various strategies which I am already putting in place, but my best hope—only hope, to be brutally honest—is if I can convince the shareholders, many of whom are board members, not to sell their shares and remain loyal to me.' He raked his hair off his brow. 'As you are aware, I haven't always had the support of every member of the board. In fact, the black knight is a board member.'

'Orestis Pagnotis,' Sara guessed.

'Actually, no, it's Stelios Choutos. He doesn't like the new direction I am taking GE and his takeover bid is backed by an American hedge fund. Fortunately, Warren McCuskey's decision to buy *Artemis* will win me a lot of support from shareholders. An injection of two hundred million dollars into the company's coffers couldn't have come at a better time.'

'I'm sorry about your problems, but I still intend to

resign. I don't see what use I can be.' Sara's heart jolted when Alekos moved to stand between her and the door. The patch over his eye made him look even more like a pirate and his rugged good looks were a dangerous threat to her peace of mind.

'I need to have people around me who I can rely on and trust. If you are really determined to walk away from your job for no good reason I'll allow you to leave after you've served one month's notice. The future of GE will have been decided by then,' he said grimly. 'I'll pay you a full three months' salary. But in return I will expect you to be at my call constantly while I fight to save my company.'

Sara warned herself not to be swayed by his admission that he trusted her. But didn't she owe Alekos her loyalty while GE was under threat? She bit her lip, torn between feeling it was her duty to help him and the knowledge that if she stayed in her job and saw him every day it would be harder to fall out of love with him.

'All right,' she agreed before she could change her mind. 'I'll stay on for one month. But I want six months' salary.'

The extra money would pay for the college art course she wanted to do. Instead of having to wait until she had sold her mother's house, she would be able to start the art course in the new term in September. She had never made any demands on Alekos and had put him on a pedestal, always doing her best to please him. The result was that he'd treated her badly. He had made it clear that she did not matter to him, and she realised that she had wasted two years of her life loving him when he did not deserve her love. It was time she started to value herself, Sara decided.

'I guess I shouldn't be surprised that you are as mercenary as most other women,' Alekos said in a hard voice. 'I've admitted I need your help.'

'There is no room for sentiment in business,' she quoted his words back to him coolly. 'If you want me, you're going to have to pay for me.'

Alekos felt as if his head was going to explode. His eye injury had caused him to suffer severe headaches, but he hadn't taken any of the strong painkillers he had been prescribed because they made him feel drowsy and he'd needed to have all his wits about him at a crucial meeting with a group of shareholders.

He pinched the bridge of his nose to try and control the pain in his head. Behind him, the staccato click of stiletto heels on the marble-floored foyer of GE's offices in Athens sounded as loud as gunshots. He dropped his arm as Sara came to stand beside him and saw her frown when she darted a glance at his face.

He knew he did not look his best. For the past two weeks he'd survived on patchy meals, not enough sleep and too much whisky, while he'd criss-crossed the globe to meet with shareholders and tried to persuade them to back his leadership of GE. Since Stelios Choutos had issued GE with a formal notice of an intended takeover bid the battle lines had been drawn. Shareholders either supported the company's current chairman or the disgruntled board member Stelios. So far, Stelios was winning.

Now Alekos had brought the battle to GE's birthplace in Greece. He stared at the blown-up photographs on the wall of his grandfather and founder of the company, Theo Gionakis, his father, Kostas, and brother,

Dimitri. Failure was not an option he would consider. But maybe he *was* second best, as he was certain his father had thought. He wasn't the true Gionakis heir. Self-doubt congealed in the pit of his stomach.

'Why are there photos of your grandfather, your father and your brother above the reception desk, but not a picture of you?' Sara asked.

'They are all dead,' he said bluntly. 'The photo gallery is of past chairmen. Although my brother never actually became chairman, my father had his picture placed here after Dimitri died.' Alekos's jaw clenched. 'If my brother had lived to take over from my father, maybe GE would not be under threat.'

'Surely you don't believe that?'

'I have no way of knowing whether I am as good a chairman as I have no doubt Dimitri would have been.'

He felt Sara's eyes on him but he carefully avoided her gaze. It was easier, he'd found, if he did not look directly at her. That way his heart did not thump quite so hard and he could kid himself that the effect she had on him was a temporary aberration. For the past two weeks he had spent virtually every waking hour with her while they had worked together to save the company. When he was alone in bed at night it was his fantasies about making love to her, fuelled by erotic memories, rather than worry about GE that kept him awake.

He glanced at a message on his phone. 'The helicopter is waiting for us on the helipad. Let's go.'

'Go where?' she asked as they rode the lift up to the roof of the building. 'I know you have a home in Athens, and I assumed I would check in to a hotel.'

'You will stay with me. It'll be easier if you are on the same premises when we have to work late,' he countered the argument he could see brewing in her green eyes. *Theos*, she could be stubborn. But he was damned glad she was on his team.

Sara had impressed him with her dedication to GE. She'd accompanied him on his tour of cities around Europe, as well as to the US and the Far East. They had clocked up thousands of air miles to visit GE's shareholders and at every boardroom meeting, every dinner, every long evening spent in hotel bars Sara had invariably charmed the shareholders with her warmth and grace and personable nature.

She was an asset to the company and he did not want to lose her as his PA. He dismissed the thought that he did not want to lose her at all. She was not his, and perhaps this inexplicable possessive feeling was because he had been her first lover.

They boarded the helicopter and it took off, flying over Athens and out over the coast. 'I thought we were going to your house?' Sara said.

'We are. It's down there.' Alekos pointed to a small island just off the mainland. 'I own the island. Its name is Eiríni, which means *peace* in Greek.'

The helicopter hovered above the many trees that covered the island. From the air, Eiríni appeared like an emerald jewel set amid a sapphire-blue sea and some of his tension eased. This was home, his private sanctuary, and it occurred to him that Sara was the only woman, apart from his mother and sisters, who he had ever brought here. When they landed, he pulled in deep breaths of the fresh sea air mingled with the sweet scent of the yellow mimosa bushes that lined the path leading up to the house. But, as always, the scent that filled his senses was the evocative fragrance that was Sara.

He led her from the baking sun into the cool entrance hall of the house, where they were met by his housekeeper. 'Maria will show you to your room,' he told Sara. 'Feel free to explore or use the pool and we'll meet for dinner in an hour.'

She took a small bottle of pills out of her bag and gave it to him. 'You left your painkillers on your desk back in Athens. If I were you, I'd take the necessary dose and try to rest for a while.'

Her soft voice washed over him like a mountain stream soothing his throbbing head and her gentle smile made something twist deep inside him. He wanted to lie on a bed with her and pillow his head on her breasts. But that was too needy, he thought grimly. Needing someone made you vulnerable.

'Stop fussing—you sound like my mother.'

'If I had been your mother when you were growing up, I would have sent you to your room until you'd learned some manners.'

The softness had gone from her voice and Alekos heard a note of hurt that her cool tone couldn't hide. *Theos*, what the hell was wrong with him that he couldn't even be civil? As Sara turned to follow the housekeeper he caught hold of her arm.

'I'm sorry.' He raked his hair off his brow. 'I'm under a lot of strain, but that's no excuse for me to take my bad mood out on you.'

She held his gaze, and he had a feeling she knew his secret fear that his father had been right to doubt his abilities. 'You're a good chairman, Alekos, and I believe you will win the backing of the shareholders.'

'Let's hope you're right,' he said gruffly.

* * *

When Alekos woke it was dark, and a glance at the bedside clock showed it was ten p.m. *Ten!* He jerked upright and discovered that his headache had mercifully gone. After showering, he had taken Sara's advice and swallowed a couple of painkillers before he'd stretched out on the bed for twenty minutes. That had been three hours ago. She must have thought he'd abandoned her—again.

Leaving her on *Artemis* when he'd rushed off to Dubai had not been his finest hour, he acknowledged. He had been stunned to discover she was a virgin, but what had shaken him even more was the intensity of the emotional and physical connections he'd felt with her when they had made love.

He stood up, thinking he should get dressed and go and find her. Maybe it was the painkillers that had caused his sleep to be fractured with unsettling dreams about his brother, but a more likely reason was his ever-present dread that he could lose GE, which should have been Dimitri's by birthright.

His trousers were on the chair by the window. He was about to put them on when he happened to glance at the beach. The full moon shone brightly on the sand and on Sara. Alekos frowned as he watched her walk along the shoreline. She was wearing a long floaty dress, and when a bigger wave swirled around her ankles she stumbled and fell. *Theos*, what was she doing going into the sea alone at night? He stared across the beach and his heart crashed into his ribs when he could no longer see her.

Swearing, he tore out of his room and took the stairs

two at a time. The back door was open and he ran outside and sprinted across the sand. 'Sara, *Sara…*' His breath rattled from his lungs when he saw something in the shallows. It was her dress. *'Sara?'* He ploughed through the waves. 'Where are you?'

'I'm here.' She swam out from behind some rocks and stood up and waded towards him. 'What's the matter?'

Her calm tone turned his fear to fury. *'What the hell are you doing swimming on your own in the dark?'* he bellowed as he splashed through the water and grabbed hold of her arm. 'You bloody fool. Don't you have *any* common sense?'

'*Ow!* Alekos, you're hurting me. Why shouldn't I swim? It's not dark—there's a full moon.' She tried to pull free of him but he tightened his grip and dragged her behind him back to the shore. She kicked water at him. 'Let go of me. You're a control freak, do you know that?'

He tugged her closer to him so that her breasts, barely covered by her wet bra, were pressed against his heaving chest. Alekos's lungs burned as if he'd run a marathon. His dream about Dimitri was jumbled in his mind with the reality of seeing Sara disappear into the sea.

'I won't have another death by drowning on my conscience.'

She stopped struggling and stared at him, her green eyes huge and dark in the moon shadow. 'What do you mean?'

He silently cursed his emotional outburst. He knew he should shrug it off and walk back to the house, but inexplicably he found he wanted to tell Sara the terrible secret that had haunted him since he was a teenager. He trusted her implicitly, but he did not want to think of the implications of that right now.

He exhaled heavily. 'My brother drowned in the sea.' Sara drew a sharp breath as he continued. 'He'd gone swimming alone at night and his body was discovered washed up on the beach the next day.'

'Oh, God, how awful. Do you know how it happened? Maybe he had an attack of cramp.'

'Dimitri was a strong swimmer and a superb athlete.' Alekos released Sara's arm and dropped down onto the sand where the waves rippled onto the beach. He loved the sea but he hated it too for taking his brother from him. He hated himself more for his failure. 'It was my fault,' he said harshly. 'I could have saved Dimitri.'

She sat down on the sand next to him. 'Do you mean you were both swimming when your brother got into trouble? I know you would have done your best to save his life,' she said softly.

He shook his head. 'I wasn't with him. At the inquest his death was recorded as an accident. But...' he swallowed hard '...I believe Dimitri took his own life.'

Again she inhaled sharply. 'Why do you think that?'

'Because he told me he wanted to die. My brother was heartbroken when he found out his girlfriend had cheated on him, and he said to me that he didn't want to live without her.' Alekos raked his hair off his brow with an unsteady hand as his mind flew back to the past. Aged fourteen, he hadn't understood why Dimitri had cared so deeply for a woman.

'You'll understand when you fall in love,' Dimitri had told him. *'You'll find out how love catches you when you least expect it and eats away at you until you can't*

think or sleep or eat for thinking about the woman you love. And when you find out that she doesn't love you, love destroys you.'

Alekos had vowed when he was a teenager that love would never have a chance to destroy him like it had Dimitri. But for twenty years he'd felt guilty that he had not taken his brother's threat to end his life seriously and he hadn't sought help for Dimitri. His parents had been devastated by their oldest son's death and Alekos hadn't wanted to add to their grief by revealing that he believed Dimitri had committed suicide.

'I had spoken to my brother earlier on the day that he died, and he told me he felt like walking into the sea and never coming back. But I didn't take him seriously. I assumed he'd get over Nia and go back to being the fun, happy guy my brother was—until he fell in love.'

Alekos's jaw clenched. 'Love destroyed him, and I did nothing to save him.' He tensed when Sara put her hand on his arm. Her fingers were pale against his darkly tanned skin. She did not say anything but he sensed compassion in her silence and it helped to ease the raw feeling inside him.

'My memories are of him laughing, always laughing,' he said thickly. 'But on that day I found him crying. I was shocked but I still didn't do anything. I should have told my parents that Dimitri had suicidal thoughts. I didn't understand how my amazing brother, who everyone loved, could really mean to throw away his life and hurt his family over a goddamned love affair.'

'I don't believe you could have done anything, if your brother was determined to take his life,' Sara said gently. 'He may have had other problems you didn't know about. Young men in particular often find it hard to talk about things. But you don't know for certain that he did commit suicide. Presumably he didn't leave a note as the inquest recorded an accidental death.'

'He told me what he intended to do but I've never confided to anyone what I'm convinced was the real reason for Dimitri's death.'

'And so you have kept your guilt a secret for years, even though you don't know for sure that you have anything to feel guilty about. Dimitri's death *could* have been an accident. But even if it wasn't, you were in no way to blame, Alekos. You were young, and you were not responsible for your brother.'

Sara stood up. 'We should go back to the house. It must be late, and there is another meeting with shareholders tomorrow.' She brushed sand from her legs. 'I'm going for a quick swim to wash off the sand but I'll stay close to the shore.'

'I'll come with you.' He jumped up and followed her into the sea. The water was warm and its silken glide over his skin cleansed his body and his mind. The fact that Sara had not judged him and had tried to defend him helped him to view the past more rationally. *Could* it simply have been a terrible coincidence that Dimitri had died soon after confiding that he was depressed? Alekos had never considered the possibility before because he'd blamed himself when he was fourteen and he'd carried on blaming himself without questioning it.

He swam across the bay and back again, once, twice, he lost count of how many times as he sought to exorcise his demons, cutting through the water with powerful strokes until finally he was out of breath.

He watched Sara wading back to the beach. Her impromptu swim meant that she was in her underwear and

her wet knickers were almost see-through so that he
could make out the pale globes of her buttocks. When
she turned to look for him, he saw in the moonlight
her dark pink nipples through her wet, transparent bra.

Desire coiled through him, hardening him instantly
so that he was glad he was standing waist-deep in the
water. But he couldn't remain in the sea all night. He
knew from her stifled gasp that she had noticed the
bulge beneath his wet boxer shorts when he walked towards her. As he drew closer to her he watched her pupils dilate until they were dark pools, full of mystery
and promise, and he asked the question that had been
bugging him since the night they had spent together.

'Why did you choose me to be your first lover?'

CHAPTER NINE

SARA KNEW THAT telling Alekos the truth was not an option. Even if she was brave enough, or foolish enough, to admit she loved him, the revelation was not something he would want to hear. She understood him better now that he had told her about the nature of his brother's death. Living with the belief that Dimitri had taken his own life because of a failed love affair explained a lot about Alekos's opinion of love.

'Love is simply a sanitized word for lust,' he'd once sneered. The truth was that he blamed love for his brother's death as much as he blamed himself for not preventing Dimitri's suicide—if it *had* been suicide.

She frowned as she examined her own past that, like Alekos, she had allowed to influence her for far too long.

'I grew up being told by my mother that men only want women for one thing. Mum never revealed who my father was but she made it clear that she blamed him for abandoning her when she fell pregnant with me.'

She paused, remembering the brittle woman who she had called Mum and yet she'd never felt any kind of bond between them. Her mother's unplanned pregnancy had resulted in an unwanted child, Sara thought painfully. When she'd been old enough to start dating she had never allowed things to go too far, and when guys had dropped her because she refused to sleep with them it had reinforced her mother's warning that men only wanted sex. 'I'm sure she had loved my father and I think she continued to love him up until her death. I'm certain she never had another relationship after Lionel went back to his wife.'

She stirred the wet sand with her toes. Alekos was standing very close and she was agonisingly aware of him. The moonlight slanted over his broad shoulders and made the droplets of water clinging to his chest hairs sparkle. 'When I finally met my father I realised that he wasn't a bad person. He admitted he'd made a mistake when he'd had an affair with my mother. But she'd known he was married and so it was her mistake too.'

Sara made herself look directly at Alekos. He still had to wear the eye patch and, with a day's growth of dark stubble covering his jaw, he looked more like a pirate than ever. Dark, dangerous and devastatingly attractive. 'I had sex with you because I wanted to. You didn't coerce me or pretend that it meant anything to you—and that's fine because it didn't mean anything to me either.'

'But why me?' he persisted. 'Why not Paul Eddis, for instance? You seemed pretty friendly with him at the board members' dinner.'

She shrugged. 'Paul is a nice guy, but there was no spark between us like there was between you and me.'

'*Was?*' Alekos said softly. 'I would not use the past tense.' He curved his arm around her waist and tugged her into the heat of his body. The effect on her was electrifying and she was mortified, knowing he must feel the hard points of her nipples. Her brain urged her to step away from him but her body had other ideas and she was trapped by her longing for him when he lowered his head towards her.

'Is this the spark you referred to?' he growled. He kept her clamped against him while he ran his other hand down her spine and lower, sliding his fingers beneath the waistband of her knickers to caress her bare bottom. 'Sexual chemistry enslaves both of us, Sara *mou*.'

She couldn't deny it, not when her body shook, betraying her need for him as he covered her mouth with his and kissed her deeply, hungrily, making the spark ignite and burn. He'd called it *chemistry* and she told herself that was all it was. His story about his brother had touched her heart, but it had also shown her that Alekos would not fall in love with her because he despised love and maybe he was afraid of it.

She could end this now. But why deny herself what she so desperately wanted? Alekos was an incredible lover. True, she had no one to compare him to, but instinctively she knew that when they'd made love it had been magical for him too. She had already decided to leave her job and she had two weeks left to serve of the month's notice period they had agreed on.

Why shouldn't she make the most of the time she had with him and then walk away with her head held high? Her mother had spent her life loving a man she couldn't have. There was no way she was going to do the same, Sara vowed. Knowing that Alekos would never love her freed her from hope and expectation and allowed her to simply enjoy his skill as a wonderful lover.

And so she kissed him back with a fervour that revealed her desire and made him groan into her mouth when she traced her fingertips over his chest and abdomen, following the arrow of black hairs down to where his wet boxer shorts moulded the burgeoning length of his arousal.

His hands were equally busy as he unfastened her bra and peeled the sodden cups away from her breasts so that he could cradle their weight in his palms. 'Beautiful,' he muttered before he bent his head and took one nipple into his mouth, sucked hard until she cried out, and her cry echoed over the empty beach. Then he transferred his lips to her other nipple and flicked his tongue across the tender peak while simultaneously he slid his hand into the front of her knickers and pushed his finger into her molten heat.

Her legs buckled and he tightened his arm around her waist and lowered her onto the sand, coming down on top of her so that his body covered hers. She was aware of him tugging her panties off and her excitement grew when he jerked his boxers down and his erection pushed into her belly. His ragged breaths filled her ears and his male scent swamped her senses. She licked his shoulder and tasted sea salt.

'Open your legs,' he said hoarsely.

She wanted to feel his length inside her and she shared his impatience. But his voice broke through the sexual haze clouding her brain and she remembered something vital.

'We can't here. I'm not on the pill.' Not even her overwhelming desire for Alekos was worth risking an unplanned pregnancy.

He tensed and swore softly as he lifted himself off

her and pulled up his boxers before he held out his hand and drew her to her feet. 'I can't go back to the house naked,' she muttered as he began to lead her up the beach. 'One of the staff might see me.'

'None of them sleep here. There is a small fishing village on the island and all the staff return to their own homes every evening.' He scooped her up in his arms and strode across the sand. 'So, are you going to sleep with me, Sara *mou*?' His sensual smile did not disguise the serious tone of his voice.

'I hope not.' She grinned when he frowned. 'I'll be very disappointed if all we do is sleep.'

Laughter rumbled in his big chest. 'Do you know the punishment for being a tease?' He proceeded to tell her exactly how he intended to punish her, so that by the time he carried her into his bedroom and laid her on the bed Sara was shivering with anticipation and a wild hunger that grew fiercer when he slid a protective sheath over his erection and positioned himself between her thighs.

He drove into her with a powerful thrust that made her catch her breath as she discovered again his size and strength. He filled her, fitted her so perfectly as if he had been designed exclusively for her. She pushed away the dangerous thought and concentrated on learning every inch of his body, running her hands over his chest and shoulders, his long spine and smooth buttocks that rose and fell in a steady rhythm.

She arched her hips to meet each thrust as he plunged deeper, harder, faster, taking her higher with every measured stroke. He was her joy and her delight, her master and tutor. Her love.

Terrified she might say the words out loud, she

cupped his face between her hands and kissed his mouth.

'Ah, Sara.' His voice sounded oddly shaken, as if he too felt a connection between them that was more than simply the joining of their mouths and bodies. Don't look for things that are not there, Sara told herself. Enjoy this for what it is—fantastic sex.

Alekos showed her how fantastic, how unbelievably amazing sex could be when he slid his hands beneath her bottom and lifted her hips to meet his devastatingly powerful thrust that hurtled her over the edge and into ecstasy. It was beyond beautiful, and she sobbed his name as pulses of pleasure radiated out from deep in her pelvis. The fierce spasms of her orgasm kept shuddering through her while he continued to move inside her. His pace was urgent now as he neared his own release. And when he came, it was with a groan torn from his throat as his body shook so hard that she wrapped her arms around him and held him tight against her heart.

Another week passed, as tense and turbulent as the weeks preceding it, as Alekos fought to save the business his father had entrusted to him. In many ways it was the worst time of his life. Endless meetings with shareholders at GE's offices in Athens, strategy meetings with his management team and, hanging over him, the possibility he refused to consider—that he might fail. It *should* have been the worst time of his life and the fact that he could smile—*Theos,* that he could actually be happy—was totally down to Sara.

At work she was a calming presence, offering thoughtful and intelligent suggestions when he asked her advice—which he had found himself doing more and more often. She charmed the shareholders and the board members liked and trusted her. Sara was an asset in the office as his PA, and when they returned to Eiríni each evening she delighted him in her role as his mistress.

Often they walked down to the village and sat on the small harbour to watch the fishing boats unload the day's catch. Later they would return to the house and eat dinner served on the terrace by his housekeeper before they went to bed and made love for hours until exhaustion finally claimed them. Alekos was waiting to grow bored of Sara, but when he woke each morning and studied her lovely face on the pillow beside him he felt an indefinable tug in his chest and a rather more predictable tug of sexual hunger in his groin that he assuaged when he woke her and she was instantly aroused and ready for him.

'Why do you think your father would blame you for GE's problems when you yourself told me that hostile takeover bids are a common threat to businesses?' she asked him one day, after he'd confided that he felt he had let his father's memory down.

'He doubted my ability to run the company as successfully as he believed Dimitri would have done.' Alekos rubbed a towel over his chest after he'd swum in the pool. He sat down on a lounger next to where Sara was sunbathing in a tiny green bikini which his fingers itched to remove from her shapely body that drove him to distraction.

It was Sunday, and after six crazily busy days of working he had decreed that today they would not leave the island. In truth, he would have been happy not to leave the bedroom they now shared, but Sara had murmured that they couldn't spend *all* day having sex.

'Why do you think your father compared you to your brother?'

He shrugged. 'Dimitri was the firstborn son and my father groomed him for his future role as chairman of GE from when he was a young boy. My relationship with my father was much more distant. I was the youngest of his five children, the second son. When Dimitri died and I became my father's heir he made it obvious that I was second best. Sometimes,' he said slowly, 'I wondered if he wished that I had died and Dimitri had lived.'

Sara sat up and faced him, her green eyes bright and fierce. 'I'm sure that's not true. It must have been a difficult time for all the family, but particularly for your parents who were grieving for their son. It sounds like he was very popular.'

'Everyone loved Dimitri.'

'Especially you. I think you were very close to your brother,' she said softly.

'I idolised him.' Images flashed into Alekos's mind: Dimitri teaching him to sail, the two of them kicking a football around the garden, that time when he'd accidentally smashed the glass panes of the greenhouse with a misaimed kick and his brother had taken the blame. He had blocked out his memories of Dimitri because when he'd been fourteen it had hurt too much to think about him. It still hurt twenty years later. And he was still angry. If his brother hadn't fallen in love with some stupid girl he would still be here, still laughing, still Alekos's best friend.

He hadn't spoken about Dimitri in all those years

and he did not understand why he had told Sara things that he'd buried deep inside him. He didn't want her compassion, he didn't want to want her so badly that he found himself thinking about her all the time. His crazy obsession with her would pass, he assured himself. Desire never lasted and the more often he had sex with her, the quicker he would become sated with her and then he could move on with his life and forget about her.

He walked back over to the pool and dived in, swimming length after length while he brought his emotions under control. Of course he did not need Sara. She was simply a pleasant diversion from his work problems.

She came to sit at the edge of the pool and he swam up to her. 'How about we have some lunch, followed by an afternoon siesta?'

'Hmm...' She appeared to consider his suggestion. 'Or we could forget lunch and just go for a lie-down.'

'Aren't you hungry?'

'I'm very hungry.' Her impish smile made his gut twist and he pulled her into the water, ignoring her yelp that the water was cold.

He felt angry with himself for his weakness and angry with her for making him weak. 'In that case I'd better satisfy your appetite, hadn't I,' he mocked as he untied the strings of her bikini top and pulled it off, cupping her breasts in his hands and playing with her nipples until she moaned softly.

He was completely in control, and he proved it when he carried her up to the bedroom and placed her face down onto the bed. He made love to her using all his considerable skill until she climaxed once, and when she came down he took her up again and only when she buried her face in the pillows to muffle her cries as she had a second orgasm did he finally let go, and felt the drenching pleasure of his own release.

By the middle of their second week in Greece the situation with GE started to look more hopeful, as increasing numbers of shareholders pledged their alliance to Alekos and refused to sell their shares in the company to Stelios Choutos. Alekos was still tense and Sara knew he would not be able to relax while GE and his position as chairman were still threatened. But, although she continued to be supportive, she had a niggling worry of her own that made her pop to the chemist during her lunch break. Of course, having bought a pregnancy test, she felt the symptoms that her period was about to start and, although the dull pain low in her stomach was annoying, she felt relieved that she wouldn't need to use the test.

The news came on Friday afternoon. Alekos strode into Sara's office, which adjoined his, and found her standing by the window, gazing up at the iconic Acropolis. She pulled her mind from her thoughts and her heart leapt when she saw the grin on his face.

'We won.' He swept her into his arms. 'Stelios's financial backers have pulled out and I've just had a call confirming he has withdrawn his takeover bid.'

'So it's over? The company is safe and you will continue to be chairman?' She blocked out the realisation that the end of the battle for GE meant that her affair with Alekos would also be over.

'I have the unanimous backing of the board, including Orestis Pagnotis.'

His victory made him almost boyish and he swung her round before claiming her lips in a fierce kiss that deepened to a slow and achingly sweet exploration of her mouth with his tongue. Sara was trembling when he finally released her and she moved away from him while she struggled to regain her composure.

'Congratulations. I never doubted you.'

'I know.' He no longer needed to wear the eye patch now that his injury was completely healed, and his eyes gleamed as he held her gaze. 'Your support was invaluable. We work well together as a team. We'll fly to back to London tomorrow and start focusing on what GE is renowned for, which is to make the best yachts in the world.'

Sara did not say anything then, but when the helicopter flew them to the island and they walked up to the house Alekos slipped his hand into hers. 'You're very quiet.'

'I was thinking that this is our last night on Eiríni— and our last night together. Today was the final day of my notice period,' she reminded him when he frowned. 'I've arranged for a temporary PA to fill my place while you hold interviews and appoint a permanent member of staff.'

He looked shocked, and that surprised her until she told herself he'd been too busy fighting for his company to have been aware that her notice period had finished. She followed him into the sitting room and looked through the glass doors that opened onto the garden where the swimming pool was a brilliant turquoise beneath a cloudless blue sky. She had fallen in love with Alekos's island and it would have a special place in her heart for ever.

Alekos crossed to the bar and poured them both a drink, as he did every evening: a crisp white wine for her and a single malt Scotch with ice for him. Usually they carried their drinks out to the terrace, but this evening he drained his glass in a couple of gulps and poured himself another whisky.

'You could stay on,' he said gruffly. 'Why do you want to leave? I know you enjoy your job.'

'I do enjoy it, but actually I never wanted to be a secretary. I only did it because I needed to help my mother pay the mortgage. Now I'm selling the house and I have plans to do something different with my life.'

'I see.' Alekos did not try to persuade her to stay, nor did he ask about her future plans, Sara noted. She ignored the pang her heart gave and reminded herself that it was time she took control of her life. 'We both know that our affair...or whatever it is we've been having for the past few weeks...was temporary. I think it will be better to end our professional and personal association once we are back in London.'

Once again a flicker of surprise crossed his sculpted features. She was possibly the only woman who had ended a relationship with Alekos before he was ready for it to finish, Sara thought wryly. It was only the thought of her mother's empty life that kept her strong when her treacherous heart and traitorous body both implored her to be his mistress for as long as he wanted her.

'In that case we had better make the most of tonight,' he said in a cool voice that forced her to acknowledge that she really did mean nothing to him other than as a good PA and a good lay. Knowing it helped her to harden her heart when he drew her into his arms and kissed her with such aching tenderness that she could almost believe he was trying to persuade her to change her mind.

It was just great sex, she reminded herself as he undid the buttons on her blouse and slid his hand into her bra to caress her breast. He stripped her right there in the sitting room and shrugged out of his clothes, taking a condom from his trouser pocket before he pushed her back against the sofa cushions. He hooked her legs over his shoulders so that she was splayed open to him and used his tongue to such great effect that she gasped his name when he reared over her and thrust into her so hard that she came instantly.

It was the beginning of a sensual feast that lasted long into the night and Alekos's passion and his dedication to giving her pleasure tested Sara's resolve to leave him to its limits. She wished the night could last for ever, but with the pale light of dawn came a reality that stunned her.

She woke to the sound of the shower from his bathroom and the horrible lurch her stomach gave sent her running into her own bathroom. There could be a number of explanations of why she had been sick, but although she still had an uncomfortable cramping pain in her stomach her period was now over a week late. The pregnancy test took mere minutes to perform and the wait for the result seemed to last a lifetime.

Alekos knocked on the door while she was still clinging to the edge of the basin because her legs had turned to jelly. 'I'll meet you downstairs for breakfast.'

'Sure.' She was amazed that her voice sounded normal. 'See you in a minute.' She almost threw up again at the thought of food, and the much worse prospect of telling Alekos her news. But not telling him was not an option. She wasn't going to make *every* mistake her mother had made, Sara thought grimly.

He found her on the beach, standing on the wet sand where the waves rippled over her bare toes. Alekos remembered how he had seen Sara walk into the sea the night they had arrived on the island, and his body tightened at the memory of how she had come apart in his arms. Sex with her was better than he'd known with any other woman but, *Theos*, he wasn't going to beg her to stay with him. The idea of him pleading with a mistress was laughable but he didn't feel in the mood to laugh, even though he had won the battle to keep GE. Curiously, he hadn't given a thought to the company since Sara had announced her intention to leave him when they went back to London.

'Don't you want something to eat?' he said as he walked up to her. 'The helicopter will be here to collect us in a few minutes.'

'I'm not hungry.'

She was pale and he frowned when he saw her mouth tremble before she firmed her lips. The breeze stirred her hair and Alekos smelled the evocative scent of vanilla. 'What…?' he began, unable to rationalise his sudden sense of foreboding.

'I'm pregnant.'

She said the words in a rush, as if they might have less impact. But they left him reeling. He stared at her slender figure, which of course showed no signs yet that a new life was developing inside her. Was it possible she was expecting his baby? He had never thought about fatherhood, apart from in a vague way as an event that he supposed would happen at some point in his future. His family impressed on him the need for him to provide an heir. But this was real. If Sara was telling him the truth, and he had no reason to doubt her, he was going to be a father and he couldn't begin to assimilate the emotions churning inside him. Crazy though it was, he felt a flicker of excitement at the idea of holding his child in his arms. *Theos*, he hoped he would be a good father.

In the years since his brother had died Alekos had become adept at hiding his feelings and his coolly logical brain took charge. 'You're sure?'

'I did a test this morning and it…it was positive. My period is a week late, but I thought…' she bit her lip '… I hoped there was another explanation. We've always been careful.'

Alekos went cold as he recalled that he had been careless that first time when they had been on *Artemis*. His hunger for Sara had been so acute that he'd made love to her a second time immediately after they'd had sex.

He stared out across the sea—flat and calm today, it looked like a huge mirror reflecting the blue sky above, but the idyllic scene did not soothe his tumultuous thoughts. His irresponsible behaviour had resulted in Sara conceiving his child and the implications were huge. He should have taken more care. He should have fought his weakness for Sara. Anger with himself made his voice clipped and cold.

'In that case a damage limitation strategy is necessary.'

She frowned. 'What do you mean by damage limitation?'

'How do you think GE's board members will react to the news that I have fathered an illegitimate child?'

he said grimly. 'Once the press get hold of the story—as they undoubtedly will—I'll be accused of being an irresponsible playboy and that kind of reputation will not go down well with the board or the shareholders, especially now, so soon after the hostile takeover bid. There is only one solution. We will have to get married.'

He looked at her stunned expression and ignored the inexplicable urge to enfold her in his arms and promise her that everything would be all right. Instead he drawled, 'Congratulations, Sara *mou*. You've done what many other women dream of and secured yourself a rich husband.'

She flinched as if he had struck her, but then her chin came up. 'Firstly, I have never been *yours*, and secondly I am not any other woman—I'm me, and I would never marry for money. Your arrogance is astounding. I'm certainly not going to marry you to save your reputation.'

Sara spun round and walked up the beach towards the house. She heard the helicopter overhead and felt glad that soon she would be on it and leaving Eiríni. She wished she could leave Alekos behind. She hadn't expected him to be pleased about her pregnancy. Pleased had not been *her* first reaction when she'd stared at the blue line on the pregnancy test that confirmed a positive result. She felt stunned and scared and very alone, and Alekos's implication that she was a gold-digger who had somehow engineered falling pregnant to snare him was so unfair that tears choked her.

'Would you deny the child its father then, Sara?'

She stopped walking and turned to find he was right behind her, so close that she breathed in his aftershave, mingled with an indefinable scent that was uniquely Alekos. 'You don't want a child,' she muttered.

'It doesn't matter what I want or don't want. The child is my heir and if we marry he or she will inherit not only GE but the Gionakis fortune. If you refuse to marry me I will financially support my child, but in the future I will take a wife and any legitimate children born within the marriage will bear my name and be entitled to inherit my legacy.'

Alekos trapped her gaze with his eyes that were as black and hard as pieces of jet. 'Will you deny your child its birthright the way you were denied yours, Sara? You told me you wish you'd grown up knowing your father. Can you really deprive your child of the chance to grow up with both its parents?'

CHAPTER TEN

ALEKOS HAD HIT her with an emotional body blow. He had aimed his argument straight at her heart, aware that she would do anything to give her baby a father—even if it meant she had to marry him.

She had tried to dissuade him. During the helicopter flight from the island and when they'd boarded his private jet bound for London, she had offered various suggestions of how they could both have a role in their child's life. But his response had been unequivocal. They must marry before the baby was born so that it was legitimate.

She looked across the plane to where he was sitting in one of the plush leather armchairs and her heart predictably gave a jolt when she found him watching her. He was casually dressed in grey trousers and a white shirt open at the throat, showing his tanned skin that had turned a darker shade of olive-gold from two weeks in the hot Greek sun. His hair was longer, and the black stubble on his jaw reminded her of the faint abrasion marks on her breasts where his cheek had scraped her skin when he'd made love to her numerous times the previous night.

Their last night together, she had believed. Now she

wondered if he intended their marriage to include sex, and if—or perhaps that should be when—he tired of her would he have discreet affairs that did not attract the attention of the press or the board members?

'I will make a press statement on Monday announcing our engagement and forthcoming marriage.'

Sara's stomach lurched. 'Why so soon? We should at least wait until I've seen my doctor to confirm my pregnancy. The test showed that I am about five weeks, and I believe a first scan to determine when the baby is due is at around eight to ten weeks.'

'I can't risk the media finding out you are pregnant before I've put an engagement ring on your finger. The board members are jittery after the takeover bid. The news that I am going to marry my sensible secretary and leave my playboy days behind will bolster their confidence in me. For that reason I've made an appointment for us at a jewellers so that you can choose a ring.'

Everything was happening too fast, she thought frantically. Yesterday she'd believed she would never see Alekos again after they had returned to England, but now she was expecting his child and he was bulldozing her into marriage.

'I don't believe a loveless marriage will be good for anyone, including the baby.' She imagined a future where Alekos had mistresses and she became bitter like her mother, and said rather desperately, 'It can't possibly work.'

'My parents did not marry for love and had a very successful marriage.' Alekos opened his laptop, signalling that the conversation was over. It was convenient for him to marry her to keep GE's board members happy, Sara thought. And by becoming his wife she would be doing the best thing for the baby. But what about what was best for her? How could she marry Alekos when she loved him but he would never love her? But how could she deny her baby the Gionakis name? The stark answer was that she couldn't.

The jewellers was in Bond Street and the price tags on the engagement rings made Sara catch her breath. 'Choose whichever ring you want,' Alekos told her. 'I don't care how much it costs.'

But diamond solitaires the size of a rock were not her style, and she finally chose an oval-shaped emerald surrounded by white diamonds because Alekos commented that the emerald matched the colour of her eyes.

'I thought you were taking me home,' she said when the limousine drew up outside his apartment block.

'This will be your home from now on. I'll have your clothes and other belongings packed up and sent over from your house. But I want you here, where I can keep an eye on you.'

She looked at him suspiciously. 'You make it sound like I'm your prisoner. Are you worried I'll leak the story to the press that I am expecting the chairman of GE's baby?'

'*No.* You proved your loyalty to me and to the company when you helped me fight off the hostile takeover.' Alekos raked his hair off his brow and she was surprised to see colour flare on his cheekbones. 'I want you to stay with me because you are pregnant and you need looking after.'

'Of course I don't.' She tried to ignore the tug on her heart at the idea of him taking care of her as if she were a fragile creature instead of a healthy, independent woman.

'You're pale, and you fell asleep on the plane and in the car just now,' he persisted.

'I'm tired because I didn't get much sleep last night.' She blushed as memories of the many inventive ways he had made love to her for hours the previous night flooded her mind. The gleam in his eyes told her he was remembering their wild passion too. 'Alekos…?'

'Yes, it will be a real marriage in every way,' he drawled.

Her face burned. 'How did you know I was going to ask that?'

'Your eyes are very expressive and they reveal your secrets.'

Sara prayed they didn't, but she carefully did not look at him when he showed her to a guest room in his penthouse because she didn't want him to guess she was disappointed that she would not be sharing his bed until they were married.

The following week passed in a blur. News of their engagement was mentioned in most of the newspapers and Sara was glad to hide away in the penthouse to avoid the paparazzi, who were desperate to interview the woman who had tamed the notorious Greek play-boy Alekos Gionakis.

Her father phoned to offer his congratulations, but when she asked him if he would attend her wedding with her half-siblings Lionel hesitated for so long that Sara's heart sank.

'Why don't you tell Charlotte and Freddie Kingsley you are their sister?' Alekos asked when he discovered her in tears. He had come home from the office unexpectedly in the afternoon and found her lying on the sofa.

She shook her head. 'I can't betray my father to his children. Perhaps it will be better if he never tells them about me and they won't know that he was once unfaithful to their mother.'

Alekos sat down on the edge of the sofa and studied her face intently. 'You're as white as a sheet. How many times have you been sick today?'

'Three or four.' She tried to shrug off his concern. 'Nausea and tiredness are normal in early pregnancy and I'll probably feel better soon.'

But she didn't. Over the next few days the sickness became more frequent and the dull ache on the right side of her abdomen that she'd had on and off for weeks turned into a stabbing pain. Sara had read that a miscarriage was fairly common in the first three months of pregnancy and nothing could be done to prevent nature taking its course.

For the first time since the shock of finding out that she was pregnant her baby became real in her mind. She pictured a little boy with black hair and dark eyes like his daddy and she felt an overwhelming sense of protectiveness for the new life inside her. 'Hang on, little one,' she whispered when she went to bed early that night, praying that if she rested her baby would make it through the crucial early weeks of her pregnancy.

The pain woke her some hours later. A sensation like a red-hot poker scourging her insides was so agonising that she struggled to breathe. Sadness swept through her as she realised that she was probably going to lose the baby and when she fumbled to switch on the bedside light the sight of blood on the sheets confirmed the worst. But the amount of blood shocked her and the pain in her stomach was excruciating. She felt faint, and her instincts told her something was seriously wrong.

'Alekos…' Dear God, what if he couldn't hear her and she bled to death, alone and terrified? She called on every last bit of her fading strength. '*Alekos*…help me…'

'Sara?' She heard the bedroom door open and the overhead light suddenly illuminated the room. She heard Alekos swear and she heard fear in his voice. 'I'm calling an ambulance.' His hand felt cool on her feverish brow. She tried to speak but she felt so weak. His face swam in front of her eyes as he leaned over her. 'Hang on, Sara *mou*,' he said hoarsely, repeating the plea she had made to her baby. But pain was tearing her apart and she slipped into blackness.

Someone, at some time—Alekos did not know who or when—had come up with the gem of wisdom, *You don't know what you've got till it's gone*. The quote had been painfully apt while he had paced up and down the waiting room while Sara had undergone emergency surgery to stop serious internal bleeding resulting from an ectopic pregnancy.

'An ectopic is when a fertilised egg implants in a fallopian tube instead of in the womb,' the obstetrician at the hospital where Sara had been rushed to by ambulance had explained to Alekos. 'The pregnancy cannot continue but the condition is not life-threatening unless the tube ruptures, which unfortunately occurred in Miss Lovejoy's case.'

An hour-long operation and two blood transfusions later, Sara was transferred to the intensive care ward and a nurse told Alekos she had been lucky to survive.

He'd known that, even without much medical knowledge. The sight of her lying pale and lifeless on the blood-soaked sheets was something he would never forget.

It had been much later, when he'd sat by her bed in ITU, steadfastly refusing the nurse's suggestion to go home and get some sleep, when he'd allowed himself to think about the baby they had lost, and the fact that he had very nearly lost Sara. He had spent his life since he was fourteen building a fortress around his heart so that nothing could hurt him like Dimitri's death had. So why were his eyes wet, and why did it feel as if a boulder had lodged in his throat making swallowing painful?

Five days later, he stepped into her room in the private wing of the hospital where she had been moved to after she was well enough to leave ITU and a ghost of a smile curved his lips when he found her dressed and sitting in a chair. He was relieved to see a faint tinge of colour on her cheeks, but she still looked as fragile as spun glass and his stomach twisted.

'You look better.' It was a lie but he suddenly didn't know what to say to her. The little scrap of life that neither he nor Sara had planned for her to conceive was gone. He did not know how she felt about the loss of their child, and he didn't want to face his own feelings. So he forced himself to smile as he picked up her holdall. 'Are you ready to come home?'

She avoided looking directly at him, and that was a bad sign. 'I'm not going to the penthouse with you.'

'I realise it holds bad memories. We can go somewhere else. I'll check with the doctor that you are okay to fly and we'll go to Eiríni.'

'No.' At last she did look at him and wiped away a

tear as it slid down her cheek. 'It's not the penthouse. I'm sad that I lost the baby, but we only knew I was pregnant for two weeks. I was just getting used to the idea of being a mother but now…that's not going to happen.' She took something out of her handbag and held out her hand to him. 'I need to give you this.'

He stared at her engagement ring sparkling in his palm and a nerve jumped in his cheek.

'Now there is no baby there is no reason for us to marry,' she said quietly.

Something roared inside Alekos. He felt unbalanced, as if the world had tilted on its axis and he was falling into a dark place. All he had thought about for the past days was Sara and the baby they had lost. *This* scenario had not occurred to him and he didn't know what to say or think or feel.

'There is no need for either of us to make hasty decisions. You've been through hell and need time to recuperate before we think about the future.'

She shook her head. '*We* don't have a future together. Your only reason for deciding to marry me was because I was pregnant with your child.'

'That's not strictly true. There were other reasons that are still valid even though there is no baby.'

'What reasons?' She stared at him and Alekos saw the sudden tension in her body and the faint betraying tremble of her lower lip. For a moment he almost gave in to the urge to put his arms around her and smell the vanilla scent of her hair. He was almost tempted to listen to the roaring inside him. But then he thought of Dimitri walking into the sea, throwing away his life for love, and the fortress walls closed around Alekos's heart.

'My position as chairman of GE will be strengthened

if I marry. The board members like and respect you—
as I do. I value you, Sara. We are a good team and I am
confident that if you were my wife you would run my
home as efficiently as you ran my office.'

To his own ears his words sounded pompous and
Sara gave an odd laugh. 'You make marriage sound like
I would be your PA with a few extra perks.'

'Excellent perks,' he said drily. A lot of women would
jump at the chance to live the wealthy lifestyle he was
offering. 'You would not have to work and could study
art or do whatever you want to do. And let's not forget
sex.' He watched her pale cheeks flood with colour and
was amazed she could blush when he knew her body as
well as his own and had kissed every centimetre of her
creamy skin. 'The sexual chemistry between us shows
no sign of burning out.'

'And you resent it,' she said slowly. 'The marriage
you described is not enough for me. I don't care about
your money,' she said quickly before he could speak,
'and I agree the sex is great. But you would tire of me
eventually. I was your PA for two years and I know the
short lifespan of your interest in women.'

'What do you want, then?' he demanded, furious
with her for reading him too well.

'The saddest thing is that you have to ask.' She stood
up and gathered up her handbag. 'My friend Ruth is
coming to pick me up and she's invited me to stay with
her because my mother's house has now been sold.'

It hit Alekos then that she actually meant it and
something akin to panic cramped in his gut. 'Sara, we
can talk.'

'Until we're blue in the face,' she said flatly, 'but it
won't change anything. I understand why you won't

allow anyone too close. I know you feel guilty because you think you should have done more to help your brother. But you can't live in the past for ever, Alekos. Love isn't an enemy you have to fight and I don't believe Dimitri would have wanted you to live your life without love.'

'Even though loving someone cost him his life?' Alekos said savagely.

'You don't know for sure that he did mean to end his life. You told me you never talked about Dimitri's death with the rest of your family. Maybe you should. Because a life without love will make you as bitter and unhappy as my mother was, and how I would become if I married you.'

Her words stung him. 'I don't remember you being unhappy when we were on Eiríni.' He pulled her into his arms and sought her mouth. 'I made you happy,' he muttered against her lips. 'Do you think you'll find this passion with anyone else?'

He kissed her hard and his body jerked when he felt her respond. She was a golden light in his life, and he realised that almost from the first day she had started working for him he had looked forward to her cheerful smile every morning and he'd felt comfortable with her in a way he had never felt with other women. They had been friends before they were lovers but she was prepared to walk away from what they had because he refused to put a label on what he felt for her.

He knew how to seduce her. He knew how to kiss her with a deepening hunger so that she flattened out her bunched fists on his chest and slid her arms up around his neck. Her body melted into him and triumph surged through him, spiking his already heated blood. She couldn't deny *this*.

He couldn't believe it when she wrenched her mouth from beneath his and pushed against his chest. He was unprepared for her rejection and dropped his arms to his sides as she stepped away from him. 'You want me,' he said harshly. 'We're good together, Sara, but I won't beg. If I walk away I won't come back. Ever.'

He held his breath as she stood on tiptoe and brushed her lips gently on his cheek. 'I hope that one day you will find the happiness you deserve. And I hope I will too. I can't settle for second best, Alekos.'

He froze. *Second best*. Was that what she thought of him? The same as his father had thought. *Theos*, she might as well have stabbed him through his heart. The pain in his chest felt as if she had.

Sara watched Alekos stride out of her hospital room and nearly ran after him. She sank down onto the bed as the enormity of what she had done drained the little strength she had in her legs after her ordeal of the ectopic pregnancy. The sense of loss that swept over her was almost unbearable.

When she'd regained consciousness and discovered she was lying in a hospital bed she had known immediately that her baby hadn't survived. The grief she felt was greater than anything she'd experienced. It was true she had only known for a few weeks that she was pregnant but there was a hollow space inside her and she felt as though her hopes for her future as a mother had been ripped from her as savagely as her child had been ripped from her body.

Now she had lost Alekos too. She would never see

him again, never feel his strong arms around her or feel him move inside her in the timeless dance of love. Because it wasn't love, she reminded herself. What she'd had with Alekos was wonderful sex that for him had been meaningless.

Much as she hated to acknowledge it, she had been just another mistress. The only difference between her and all the other countless women he'd had affairs with was that the board members of GE approved of her, which was why he had wanted to marry her despite her no longer being pregnant.

She knew she had done the right thing to turn him down. Her close brush with death when her tube had ruptured had shown her that life was too precious to waste a moment of it. There had been a moment when she'd thought Alekos was going to admit that he cared for her and she'd held her breath and hoped with all her heart, only to hear him say that he valued her in the same way that he might have said he valued a priceless painting or one of the flash superyachts his company was famous for building.

Once she would have been grateful for any crumb he offered her. She had been so lacking in self-confidence that she would have married him because she had adored him and didn't believe that a handsome, charismatic and sophisticated man such as Alekos could fall in love with his plain, frumpy secretary.

Meeting her father had made her feel like a whole person. Casting her mind back over the past months, she could see that she had taken more interest in her appearance because she felt more worthwhile, and maybe it was her new confidence that had attracted Alekos as much as her new, sexier clothes and hairstyle. But crucially she had forgotten that he'd once said love was simply a word used by poets and romantics to describe lust.

The sound of a deep male voice outside the door made her heart leap into her throat. But when she stepped into the corridor it was not Alekos standing in front of the nurses' station, arguing with a nurse and drawing attention from a crowd of curious onlookers.

'I don't care if my name is not on the visitor list,' Lionel Kingsley said loudly. 'Sara Lovejoy is my daughter and I have come to visit her.' He glanced round and his expression became concerned when he saw her. 'Sara, my dear, you should be resting.' He spoke briefly on his mobile phone as he walked over to her and Sara hurriedly pulled him into her room and shut the door.

'What are you doing here? There must be a dozen people who heard you say that I am your daughter.' She bit her lip. 'It's probably already on social media and once the press get hold of the story it will be headline news, especially as there is speculation that you will be the new Home Secretary in the Cabinet reshuffle.'

'None of that is important.' Lionel swept her into a bear hug. 'What matters is that you are safe and as well as can be expected after you nearly lost your life. Alekos phoned and told me what had happened, and how you lost your baby.' He squeezed her so hard that she felt breathless. 'I'm so sorry, Sara. For your loss, and also for my behaviour. Alekos used some very colourful language when he pointed out that I had failed you as a father twice. The first time by not being around when you were a child, and the second by not publicly acknowledging you as my daughter.'

'He told you that?' she said faintly.

'And a lot more. He reminded me I was lucky to have a beautiful, compassionate and loyal daughter. When he told me how you had almost died I realised how stupid and selfish I had been. I should have welcomed you unreservedly, and I'm sorry I didn't before now.'

'But what about Charlotte and Freddie?' Sara was reeling from hearing how Alekos had stood up for her to her father. 'How do you think they will take the news that I am their sister?'

'Why don't you ask them? Or one of them, at least,' Charlotte Kingsley said as she walked into the room. 'Freddie is in America, but he said to tell you that he knows who you remind him of now.' She smiled at Sara's startled expression. 'You and I do look remarkably alike and not only because we both have green eyes. All three of dad's offspring take after his side of the family, and Freddie agrees with me that we can't think of a nicer person to have as our sister.'

'I thought you would hate me,' Sara said unsteadily.

Charlotte clasped her hand. 'Why would we hate you? Nothing that happened in the past is your fault. I'm sad that I didn't know about you for twenty-five years, but now I hope you will be part of our family for ever…if you want to be.'

Sara glanced at her father. 'Aren't you worried that the scandal will affect your political career?'

Lionel shrugged. 'These things often blow over. I behaved badly towards your mother and my wife many years ago and the person who suffered most was you. Far more important than my career is my determination to try and make amends and be the father I should have been to you when you were growing up. And I'd like to start by taking you to my home in Berkshire so that you can recuperate, but of course I'll understand if you want to go home with Alekos.'

Her father looked puzzled. 'Actually, I assumed Alekos would be here. I know he refused to leave your bedside while you were in intensive care. And when he came to see me yesterday to tell me what he thought of me for treating you badly, he looked like he'd been to hell and back. But it's not surprising after he lost his child and could have lost you too. It's obvious how much he cares for you.'

Sara sat down heavily on the chair and buried her face in her hands. She felt as if she was on an emotional roller coaster from her intense sadness at losing her baby and the shock of realising how close she had come to losing her own life. She had rejected Alekos without considering his feelings about the loss of their child. Although her pregnancy had been in the early stages, it was likely that the trauma had reminded him of losing his brother when he was a teenager.

A sob escaped her and she felt a hand patting her shoulder. Charlotte—her sister—she thought emotively, pushed some tissues into her hand. 'Cry it out, Sara. You've been through a terrible experience and you need time to grieve for the baby.'

As Alekos did. But she knew he would bottle up his feelings like he had when Dimitri died. 'I think I've made a terrible mistake,' she choked. Alekos needed her but she had sent him away and her tears were for the baby, for her, but mainly for the man she would always love.

CHAPTER ELEVEN

ALEKOS HAD SPENT his childhood at his parents' house just outside Athens. As a boy he had spent hours playing on the private beach but after Dimitri died he had stopped going there.

He moved away from the window, where he had been watching huge waves crash onto the shore. The recent storm had made the sea angry and the heavy sky echoed his mood. He picked up his brother's death certificate from the desk in his father's study and read it once more before he looked at his mother.

'Why didn't you tell me Dimitri suffered a heart attack when he went swimming and that was why he drowned?'

'You never wanted to talk about him. If his name was mentioned by anyone you would leave the room. Your father and I were advised not to push you to discuss the accident but to wait for you to bring up the subject.'

She sighed. 'Dimitri was born with a small hole in his heart but later tests showed that the defect had healed by itself and it was not expected to cause problems as he grew up. Your brother was such a strong, athletic boy and your father and I more or less forgot that there had been the early problem. When we learned that Dimitri had suffered heart failure we felt guilty that we should have persuaded him to have more health checks. The reason why Dimitri drowned was something we could not bear to discuss with you and your sisters. Why does your brother's cause of death matter now, so many years later?'

Alekos swallowed hard. 'I believed for all those years that Dimitri took his own life. He was heartbroken when he found out his girlfriend had cheated on him and he told me he did not want to live without Nia.'

His mother frowned. 'I remember he was upset over a girl. Your father had arranged for him to go and work in the Miami office for a few months to help him get over her. You were not at home on that last evening and so you did not see how excited Dimitri was about the trip to America.' She looked intently at her youngest son. 'I'm quite certain your brother knew he had everything to live for. He often went swimming at night and told me I worried too much when I asked him not to go into the sea alone.'

'I blamed myself for not getting help for Dimitri after he told me he felt depressed,' Alekos said gruffly. 'I felt guilty that I hadn't saved him. I missed him so much but I didn't want to cry in front of anyone because I was fourteen, not a baby. The only way I could cope was by not talking about him.'

'Dimitri's death was fate,' his mother said gently. 'I wish I had known how you felt, but I'm afraid you take after your father in the respect of not discussing your feelings. Kostas believed he must be strong for the rest of the family, but losing Dimitri made him withdraw emotionally. I think he found it hard to show how much he loved you because he was afraid of losing another child and suffering the same pain and grief he'd felt when Dimitri died.' She wiped away a tear. 'Your father was very proud of you, you know. He admired your drive and determination to take GE forward.'

'I wish I had known that Bampás approved of my ideas. I regret I didn't talk about Dimitri with him. It might have helped both of us.'

His mother nodded. 'Honesty and openness are important in a relationship and you should remember that when you marry Sara.'

Alekos's jaw clenched. 'Sara ended our engagement because I can't give her what she wants.'

'Sara does not strike me as someone who craves material possessions.'

'She says she will only marry for love.'

'Well, what other reason is there for marriage?'

He frowned. 'I thought that you and Bampás had an arranged marriage?'

His mother laughed. 'Our parents thought so too. But Kostas and I had met secretly and fallen in love, and we engineered our so-called arranged marriage. Love is the only reason to marry. Why is it a problem? You love Sara, don't you?'

Alekos could not reply to his mother's question, although he suspected the answer was somewhere in the mess of emotions that had replaced the cool logic which had served him perfectly well for two decades.

'I understand why my father was scared to love after he lost a son,' he said. His voice sounded as if it had scraped over rusty metal. He had a flashback to when he had been in the hospital waiting room, praying harder than he'd prayed in his life that Sara's life would be saved. 'Love can hurt,' he said roughly.

'But it can also bring the greatest joy,' his mother said softly. 'I am glad I was blessed with Dimitri and it was better to have him for twenty-one years than not to have known him and loved him. The pain I felt when he died was terrible, but the happiness he gave me in his short life was far greater.'

It was a wonderful party, and she was absolutely having a brilliant time, Sara told herself firmly. She looked around the ballroom of the five-star hotel in Mayfair and recognised numerous celebrities who, like her, had been invited to the birthday celebrations of a famous music producer.

Since the news that she was the daughter of Lionel Kingsley, MP, had made the headlines a month ago, she had been on the guest list at many top social events with her half-brother and half-sister. She loved being part of a family and while she was staying at her father's beautiful house in Berkshire she'd grown close to Lionel, Charlotte and Freddie. They and her father had encouraged her to follow a different career path after she'd resigned from her position as Alekos's PA. She had started an art foundation course at college and her plan to go to university to study for an art degree helped to take her mind off the trauma of the ectopic pregnancy.

Long walks in the countryside and the companionship of family mealtimes had gradually enabled her to come to terms with the loss of her baby, although there would always be a little ache in her heart for the child she would never know. Getting over Alekos had so far proved more difficult, especially when she had told her father and siblings that she had broken off her relationship with him and they had asked if she was sure she had done the right thing.

Well, she was sure now, she thought dismally. Photos of Alekos at a film premiere with a busty blonde wrapped around him had featured on the front pages of all the tabloids. She was furious with herself that she'd wasted time worrying about him. Why, she'd even phoned him to check if he was okay because it had been his baby too. He hadn't answered her call or replied to the message she'd left him, and seeing the picture of him with his latest bimbo had forced her to accept that he had moved on with his life and she should do the same.

She was jolted from her thoughts by a sharp pain in her foot. 'Sorry—again,' the man she was dancing with said ruefully when she winced. 'That must be the third time I've trodden on your toes.'

'Fourth, actually.'

She hid her irritation with a smile. He had introduced himself as Daniel, 'I'm doing a bit of modelling but I really want to be an actor,' and he was very good-looking, although it was lucky he wasn't hoping for a career as a dancer, she mused. Unfortunately, his good looks were wasted on her. She wished her heart did skip a beat when he pulled her closer, but she felt nothing. Although she managed to put on a cheerful front, she missed Alekos terribly and couldn't stop thinking about him.

'Is there a reason why the tall guy over there is staring at me as if he's planning to murder me?' Daniel murmured. 'He's coming this way and I get the feeling it's time I made myself scarce.'

'Which guy…?' Sara felt her heart slam into her ribs when Alekos materialised at her side.

'I advise you to find another woman to dance with,' he growled to Daniel, who immediately dropped his hands from Sara as if she were highly contagious. But her attention wasn't on Daniel. Alekos swamped all of her senses and he was the only man in the ballroom.

He looked utterly gorgeous dressed in slim black trousers and a black shirt open at the throat to reveal a sprinkling of curling chest hairs. His hair was ruffled as if he'd been running his fingers through it—or someone else had, Sara thought darkly, remembering the photos of him with the blonde who'd been stuck to him with superglue. Temper rescued her from the ignominy of drooling over him.

'How dare you barge in and spoil my evening?' she snapped.

'I dare, Sara *mou*, because if I hadn't persuaded your pretty boy dance partner to back off I would have throttled him with my bare hands.' His dark eyes burned like hot embers and the tight grip of his hands on her waist warned her that he was furious. Well, that made two of them, she thought, glaring at him when she tried to pull away and he jerked her against his body. The feel of his hard thighs pressed close to hers was almost enough to make her melt.

'I am definitely not *your* Sara. Will you let go of me? You're making an exhibition of us.'

'I haven't even started,' he warned. 'You can walk out of the ballroom with me or I'll carry you out.'

She snapped her teeth together as if she would like to bite him, but to safeguard her dignity she allowed him to steer her out of the ballroom and across the hotel foyer to the lifts. 'Won't your girlfriend mind? Don't pretend you don't know who I mean. You must have seen the picture on the front page of this morning's papers of you and Miss Breast Implants.'

His puzzled expression cleared. 'Oh, you mean Charlene.'

'I don't read gossip columns so I don't know her name.'

'Charlene McCuskey is the wife of Warren McCuskey, who I'm sure you recall is buying *Artemis*. They are in London so that Warren can finalise the purchase, but he has come down with a virus and so he asked me to escort Charlene to a film premiere, which I dutifully did before I took her back to their hotel. Unsurprisingly, she is devoted to her billionaire husband,' he said sardonically.

'Oh, I see,' Sara muttered. Without fully realising what she was doing she'd followed Alekos into a lift, and as the doors closed and she was alone with him in the small space she had a horrible feeling that he saw way too much of her thoughts. 'Where are you taking me?'

'I'm staying at the hotel and we are going to my suite.'

'I don't want…'

'We need to talk.' Something in his expression made her heart give another painful jolt. The lift had mirrored walls, and her reflection showed her breasts rising and falling jerkily beneath her scarlet silk dress that she'd worn thinking the bright colour might lift her spirits. 'You look beautiful,' Alekos told her brusquely.

Her eyes flew to his face and after weeks of feeling nothing every nerve ending on her body was suddenly fiercely alive. The lift stopped, and as she followed him along the corridor and into his suite she wondered why she was putting herself through this. Seeing him again was going to make it so much harder to get over him.

'Would you like a drink?'

It would give her something to do with her hands. When she nodded he walked over to the bar, poured a measure of cassis into two tall glasses and topped them up with champagne. Sara remembered they had drunk Kir Royale the night they had become lovers on the yacht in Monaco. It seemed a lifetime ago.

'How are you?'

'Good,' she said huskily. It wasn't true, but she was working on it. 'It's been great getting to know Charlotte and Freddie. I feel very lucky that they and my father are part of my life.'

'I'm sure they feel lucky to have found you.' There was an odd note in his voice and, like in the lift, the indefinable expression in his eyes stirred feelings inside her that she told herself she must not feel.

'How about you?' She hesitated. 'I phoned you…but you didn't call back.'

'I was in Greece. I visited my mother and we talked about my brother.' He indicated for Sara to sit down on a sofa but she felt too edgy to sit, and he remained standing too. 'Dimitri died of a heart attack while he was swimming,' he told her abruptly. 'I finally read the coroner's report. My parents had their reasons for not talking about the cause of his death and I never spoke about Dimitri because I tried to block out my grief.'

'I'm glad you found out the truth at last and can stop blaming yourself,' she said softly. 'I hope you can put the past behind you and move on with your life.'

'Do you include yourself in my past and hope I will forget about you?'

She swallowed. Alekos had moved without her being aware of him doing so and he was standing so close that she could see the tiny lines around his eyes that suggested he hadn't been sleeping well. There were deeper grooves on either side of his mouth and she sensed he was as tense as she felt.

'I guess we both need to move forwards,' she said, aiming for a light tone. 'Make a fresh start.'

'What if I asked you to come back to me?'

Her heart missed a beat, but she shook her head. 'I couldn't be your PA now that we…' she coloured '…now that we have had a personal association.'

'A *personal association*?' he said savagely. '*Theos*, Sara, we created a child together.'

'*A child you didn't want*. Any more than you wanted to marry me.' She spun away from him, determined not to break down in front of him.

'That's not true on both counts. I did want to marry you. I didn't respond to your phone call because when you went to stay with your father after you left hospital, I agreed with Lionel to give you some space. You needed to recover from the ectopic and spend time with your new family.'

Sara shrugged to show she didn't care, even though she did desperately. Alekos frowned but continued, 'I also did what every bridegroom is expected to do and asked your father if he would allow me to marry you.'

Sara choked on her mouthful of champagne. '*You did what?*' She was so angry she wanted to hit him and for about twenty seconds she forgot that she wanted to kiss him. 'There is no way I would agree to marry you to keep the board members of GE happy.'

'Good, because that's a terrible reason for us to

marry,' he said calmly, although his eyes blazed with a fierce heat that melded Sara to the floor and stopped her rushing towards the door.

'I'm being serious.' She put her hands flat on his chest to stop him coming closer but he clasped her wrists and pulled her arms down, at the same time as he tugged her against him with a force that expelled the air from her lungs.

'So am I.' He stared at her intently and his jaw clenched when he saw the tears she was struggling to hold back. 'Why were you jealous when you saw the photo of me with Charlene?'

She flushed. 'I wasn't jealous.'

'Did you feel like I did tonight when I saw you dancing with that guy and I wanted to tear his head off?'

'Definitely not.' She didn't know what game of refined torture Alekos was playing but it had to stop before the intoxicating warmth of his body pressed up against hers and ruined her for ever.

'Liar,' he taunted. 'Were you jealous because you love me?'

She could deny it but what would be the point? She couldn't fight him or herself any more, and Sara knew she would be his mistress if he asked her because she'd learned that life was too short to turn down the chance to be with him, even though he would break her heart when he ended their affair.

But she still had her pride and her eyes flashed with green fire. '*Yes*, I love you. I've loved you for ever, even though you are the most arrogant man I've ever known.'

'But I am the only man you have ever known intimately, arrogant or not,' he said softly, his mouth curving in a crooked smile that tugged on Sara's heart. He sounded strange, as if his throat was constricted, and her eyes widened in disbelief when she saw that his lashes were wet.

'Alekos?' she whispered.

'Sara *mou*...' He held her so tight that she felt the thunder of his heart. '*S'agapo*. I love you so much.' He framed her face with his hands that were shaking. 'When I watched your life ebbing away in the ambulance on the way to hospital I was terrified I would lose you. And I realised then that I had tried hard *not* to fall in love with you because of fear. I associated love with the loss and pain that I felt after Dimitri died.'

'That's not surprising,' she said shakily. 'You were at an impressionable age when he died, and your brother was your best friend.'

'We became friends when you worked for me, didn't we, Sara? I liked you and I respected you when you put me in my place. I felt closer to you than I'd ever felt with any of my mistresses. But one day I walked into my office and I was blown away by a gorgeous sexy brunette. You can imagine my shock when I discovered it was you.'

She flushed. 'Before that day you didn't notice your frumpy PA.'

'I did notice you. Often I would find myself thinking about a funny remark you'd made, and I appreciated your fierce intelligence and your advice on how to handle work issues. I almost resented you when you made me desire you too. I knew I was in danger of falling in love with you and I told myself that once we were lovers my interest in you would fade. Instead, it grew stronger every day and night that we were together. When you told me you were pregnant I seized the excuse to marry you without having to admit how I felt about you.'

How he felt about her. Sara bit her lip and told herself it was too good to be true. 'You said love is a word that poets use to describe lust. Are you sure you haven't got the two mixed up?'

'I don't blame you for doubting me, *kardia mou*. That means my heart, and I love you with all my heart.'

Sara's head advised caution but her heart was desperate to believe that, incredible as it seemed, Alekos was looking at her with adoration in his eyes. She caught her breath when he stroked his finger gently down her cheek.

'Will you marry me, my Sara, for no other reason than you are the love of my life?'

That was the moment she knew she should have listened to the warning that it was all too good to be true. Carefully she eased out of his arms and closed her eyes to blot out the sudden haggard look on his face. 'I can't.'

'*Theos*, Sara, I will do whatever it takes to prove to you that I love you.' His voice cracked. 'Please believe me.'

'I do. And I love you. But you need an heir to one day run GE, and there is a strong chance I won't be able to give you a child because I lost one tube and there is a higher risk I could have another ectopic pregnancy.'

He caught her to him and buried his face in her hair. 'Then we won't have children. There's no way I will risk your life. I need *you*,' he told her fiercely. 'Nothing else is important. Whatever the future holds, I want us to share it together, the ups and the downs, for the rest of our lives.'

He tightened his arms around her so that she was

aware of his hard thigh muscles pressed against her. 'My body knew the truth before I was ready to accept it,' he said roughly. 'When we made love it was so much more than great sex.'

Joy fizzed inside Sara like champagne bubbles exploding. Hearing Alekos say he loved her wiped away the pain and misery of the past weeks and the future shimmered on the horizon like a golden sun. 'Mmm, but it was great sex, wasn't it?' Her smile was wicked and adoring. 'I think you should remind me.'

His laughter rumbled through her and the unguarded expression in his eyes stole her breath even before his mouth did the same as he claimed her lips and kissed her so thoroughly, so *lovingly*, that she was trembling when he finally lifted his head.

'I'd better warn you that this is the honeymoon suite and the staff have really gone to town,' he murmured. 'There are rose petals everywhere in the bedroom.'

Alekos had been right about the rose petals, Sara discovered when he carried her into the bedroom and laid her on the bed, adorned with fragrant red petals. He undressed her slowly, kissing each part of her body that he revealed, and when he removed her knickers and pressed his mouth to her feminine heat she told him she loved him, loved him. She repeated the words when he thrust into her so deeply that he filled her and he made love to her with all the love in his heart.

It was as wonderful as she remembered and more beautiful than she could ever have dreamed because this time Alekos didn't just show her he loved her; he told her in a mixture of English and Greek.

'Will you let me love you for ever, and will you love

me?' he murmured as he drew her close and they relaxed in the sweet aftermath of loving.

'I will,' Sara promised him and she meant the words with her heart and soul.

They were married three months later on Christmas Eve, in a church decorated with holly and ivy and fragrant red roses, and filled with their families and friends. Sara wore a white satin and lace gown and carried a bouquet of white lilies. Alekos looked stunning in a dark grey suit, but it was the look in his eyes as he watched his bride walk down the aisle towards him that made his mother and sisters wipe away tears. Sara's father walked proudly beside her to meet her husband-to-be, and her half-sister was her maid of honour.

After the reception at Lionel Kingsley's home in Berkshire, the happy couple flew to South Africa for their honeymoon. 'Somewhere hot where you can wear less clothes,' Alekos had stated when Sara had asked him where he wanted to go.

As it turned out, neither of them got dressed very often during the three weeks they stayed in a private bungalow at a luxury beach resort, a fact that Sara later accounted for her pregnancy that was confirmed a month after they returned to London. It was an anxious time until an early scan showed that her pregnancy was normal and they watched the tiny beating heart of their baby with hope in their hearts.

Theodore Dimitri Gionakis, to be known as Theo, arrived in the world two weeks early with a minimum of fuss and instantly became the centre of his parents' world.

'Love changes everything,' Alekos said one evening

as he held his son in the crook of one arm and slid his other arm around his wife's waist. 'You changed me, Sara *mou*. You showed me how to let love into my heart and now it's there to stay for ever.'

'For ever sounds wonderful,' she told him, and then she kissed him and no further words were necessary.

* * * * *

If you enjoyed this story, here are some more great reads from Chantelle Shaw for you to try!

TRAPPED BY VIALLI'S VOWS
MASTER OF HER INNOCENCE
MISTRESS OF HIS REVENGE
A BRIDE WORTH MILLIONS
SHEIKH'S FORBIDDEN CONQUEST

Available now!

MILLS & BOON®

MODERN™

POWER, PASSION AND IRRESISTIBLE TEMPTATION

Just can't wait?
Buy our books online before they hit the shops!
www.millsandboon.co.uk

Also available as eBooks.

0217/19

MILLS & BOON®

EXCLUSIVE EXTRACT

Raul Di Savo desires more than Lydia Hayward's
body—his seduction will stop his rival buying her!
Raul's expert touch awakens Lydia to irresistible
pleasure, but his game of revenge forces
Lydia to leave… until an unexpected
consequence binds them forever!

Read on for a sneak preview of
THE INNOCENT'S SECRET BABY

Somehow Lydia was back against the wall with Raul's
hands either side of her head.

She put her hands up to his chest and felt him solid
beneath her palms and she just felt him there a moment
and then looked up to his eyes.

His mouth moved in close and as it did she stared
right into his eyes.

She could feel heat hover between their mouths in a
slow tease before they first met.

Then they met.

And all that had been missing was suddenly there.

Yet, the gentle pressure his mouth exerted, though
blissful, caused a mire of sensations until the gentleness
of his kiss was no longer enough.

A slight inhale, a hitch in her breath and her lips
parted, just a little, and he slipped his tongue in.

The moan she made went straight to his groin.

At first taste she was his and he knew it for her hands

moved to the back of his head and he kissed her as hard back as her fingers demanded.

More so even.

His tongue was wicked and her fingers tightened in his thick hair and she could feel the wall cold and hard against her shoulders.

It was the middle of Rome just after six and even down a side street there was no real hiding from the crowds.

Lydia didn't care.

He slid one arm around her waist to move her body away from the wall and closer into his, so that her head could fall backwards.

If there was a bed, she would be on it.

If there was a room they would close the door.

Yet there wasn't and so he halted them, but only their lips.

Their bodies were heated and close and he looked her right in the eye. His mouth was wet from hers and his hair a little messed from her fingers.

Don't miss
THE INNOCENT'S SECRET BABY,
By Carol Marinelli

Available March 2017
www.millsandboon.co.uk

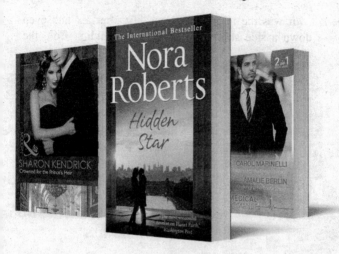